Erkin

Heirs to the Great
Sinner Sheikh San'on

Translated from Uzbek by A'zam Abidov

HERTFORDSHIRE PRESS

HERTFORDSHIRE PRESS

Published in United Kingdom
Hertfordshire Press Ltd © 2016

9 Cherry Bank, Chapel Street
Hemel Hempstead, Herts.
HP2 5DE, United Kingdom

e-mail: publisher@hertfordshirepress.com
www.hertfordshirepress.com

Heirs to the Great Sinner Sheikh San'on
by Erkin A'zam ©

English

Translated from Uzbek by A'zam Abidov
Editors: Carol Ermakova, Rano Xavier & Alan Cox
Design & typeset: Aleksandra Vlasova & Allwell Solutions

British Library Catalogue in Publication Data
A catalogue record for this book is available from the British Library
Library of Congress in Publication Data
A catalogue record for this book has been requested

ISBN: 978-1-910886-32-8

Contents

Introduction

Erkin A'zam is first and foremost an Uzbek writer, but an Uzbek writer of his time. The collection of stories published here, set between the 1950's and beginning of the twenty-first century, provide the reader with a rare window into the mores and customs of Uzbekistan during a period of great social upheaval as the Soviet Union tightened its grip on the country, only to collapse a few decades later.

A writer, playwright and screenwriter himself, A'zam's tales often reflect his own experiences. The longest story in this collection, *The Din*, traces the career of a young Uzbek author, a career which takes him beyond his hometown to 'that distant city,' Moscow. Here we see the juxtaposition of the national versus the Soviet, the changing role of national identity in art, and the direct effect Soviet policy had on the film industry, most notably by alternately promoting or negating 'national heroes.' Language is highly significant here – like the author himself, the screenwriter in *The Din* is acclaimed for his films in Uzbek. On a more personal level, A'zam conveys the subtle but far-reaching interplay of languages through the Russification of his Uzbek characters' names: Farhod becomes Farkhad, Ramazon becomes Ramazonov, various suffixes are added, such as -*ochka* (a common endearment in Russian) or -*jon* (an Uzbek suffix showing respect or endearment). There is, then, a kind of double-speak, two veils through which the social and political reality is perceived, with the protagonists sometimes favouring one over the other. It is this sense of national identity which creates the need to seek out and associate with 'fellow countrymen,' a trait sometimes bordering on obsessive nepotism. The common sense of isolation which drives A'zam's characters to stick together is poignantly conveyed by the epithets used for Russia and Moscow: 'the endless country;' 'the big Union;' 'the distant city.'

Tinged with this sense of nostalgia, the charm of traditional Uzbek life comes through very clearly, especially in *The Writer's Garden* and *A dog bit the Incomer's Daughter.* A'zam fondly describes the contrasting landscapes of his native land, with its tree-clad mountains, fragrant orchards and delightful gardens. The reader feels s/he is sitting with the characters in the *chaikhana*-teahouse, so vital to Central Asian communities. As the stories unfold, we learn of the mores and customs enshrined in Uzbek family life, the role played by women, and the respect given to elders. Despite the tumultuous political events which triggered far-reaching changes in the rich social fabric of Uzbekistan, many of these fundamental values remain unshaken.

The ongoing discussion on Internationalism which runs through *The Din* and other stories here is perhaps very relevant today. To what extent should one hold onto national identity within a multinational collective, or is it preferable – as our 'internationalist grandpa' maintains – to blur all borders, merging and blending the various nations with their distinct cultures into an amorphous single identity? Opinions vary, but the discussion is a stimulating one.

Heirs to the Great Sinner Sheikh San'on, then, provides the reader with food for thought, but also with intimate insight into one of Central Asia's most ancient yet little-known nations, Uzbekistan.

Carol Ermakova, MA.

A Tender-hearted Dwarf

(one small man's experience of growing up)

I

The problem was that he saw himself in quite a different light. He considered himself to be quite an imposing person, or at the very least, a man aglow with the light of grandeur (in his heart, that is.) He walked not with the rolling waddle his squat body might seem to dictate, but with all of his weight thrust forwards, leaning into his long strides. And when he spoke, it was in a slow, clear whisper, as if he wanted to underline his words and hold his listeners' attention.

But still, it was all quite useless. He was, undeniably, a dwarf. His grand manner and proud gait amounted to naught: indeed, they just made him look comic and infantile, like a child mimicking a grown-up. He could speak any way he pleased, but it made no difference, his voice still sounded like a thin, half blown flute.

Ah, but his heart, now that was quite another matter! It was a world apart. The soul is a king. The soul is a great jewel. The soul is misfortune. The Merciful One does not apportion the soul based on a human being's appearance, height or wealth.

The Dwarf saw himself, his appearance and his manner, in the light of that wonderful world, the world of the soul, and this contrast made him despondent. After all, he could not show the world his soul. And even if he could, any admirer of that soul would still see his external appearance first.

His soul, however, was especially fond of beauty. It was loving and caring, too. His soul's diary was full of tall tales. To lay that diary aside, to simply ignore it without leafing through the pages, would be to belittle our Dwarf (let's simply call him 'The Dwarf') even further. Without those stories his life would be paltry and he would become merely one of the millions of short people the world over, instead of being The Dwarf.

The Dwarf fell in love with every girl he met. And those whom he fell in love with were beautiful girls, but they were all either older or taller than he. Being a painter, he would come home and at once set about drawing a picture of his beloved, a portrait yet more beautiful than her actual appearance. And when he gave these picture to the girls they were always astonished by his talent, they would smile and thank him for his gift. But the next time they met him they would simply turn away as if they didn't know him. Or the Dwarf would see them with other men. It was always like that. Ignorance is bliss, knowledge brings torment as the saying goes. The Dwarf would suffered wretchedly then because of his fickle girls – until he fell in love with the next beauty.

Would there be an end to his sufferings? A limit? If so, then even our Dwarf himself could not foresee the exact extent or number.

As a boy, he had drooled over film stars. He would cut photos of the most beautiful ones out of Cinema magazine and festoon his bedroom walls with them. He even painted a picture of one of them, one who really touched his heart. He took that picture to Tashkent hoping he could present it to his muse in person. But he got sidetracked by other darlings along the way, and the picture of the actress, the most important lady in his life, was left behind in some flat he had rented. Funnily enough, the Dwarf now works in the same theatre as that actress, and when he runs into her his past feelings, his sufferings and regrets, all surface anew.

One day many moons ago his father had gone into his son's 'exhibition room' and, seeing all his pictures, had said to the Dwarf's mother, "We should marry that son of yours as soon as possible." The Dwarf squirmed. In fact, it was not until quite a lot later that he married, when he was about thirty, and, in keeping with our Dwarf's story, it was of course an unusual wedding. I hope I'll be able to tell you about it one day.

2

It was during his college days, when the students had gone to the cotton fields for their compulsory community service, that he heard it for the first time. From the lips of Aziza. That he was a dwarf and as such was considered unworthy. Aziza was studying in the Department of Theatrical Studies and she was a very beautiful girl. They said her father was a rich man. Every day a white Volga car would roll up at the cotton fields with dainty delicacies for her.

She was a nice girl. Even though she was the daughter of a rich man she could still tell one soul from another. Turning her back on the many future actors and directors who vied for her attention, it was our Dwarf with his fine manner to whom Aziza was drawn. Her other suitors envied the Dwarf as he recited love poems to her while they sat for hours around the campfire.

Once, after one such amicable evening, the girl let the Dwarf kiss her in a secluded spot and said:

"I would keep you all for myself if you were just a little taller, brother Dwarf. I would marry you no matter where you came from, town or country, and whoever you were, rich or poor."

In fact, the girl was quite tall, whereas the young lad nuzzling her bosom like a little kitten was indeed rather short. People might take them for a sister with her younger brother.

But to the Dwarf, those words were like a huge wall looming up between them.

After they split up, he suffered terribly, consumed, as usual, but he paid no attention to Aziza's words – he didn't regret being a dwarf. Until now he had never thought much about whether he was tall or short; on the contrary, he used to make fun of how stupid some tall people were, taking pride in his own wit and capability. In short, he believed that appearance was secondary, it was the inner world which really counted. But now he suddenly discovered that all this was just empty words, an unfounded notion, while in fact the world was for tall, beautiful people. The rest counted for nothing, no matter how valiant one's soul might be. Wit and common sense were overlooked. With beauty and grace you were half way to happiness, already on the stairway to fortune, all you had to do was use your wit and beauty as stepping stones. People with some physical disability often become unkind. Unkind people will never find happiness or good fortune.

And so he was snubbed time and time again. Now the Dwarf tried to ignore taller girls. But the majority of the girls he liked were tall… So when he ran into them he would speak to them from a distance, or standing on a staircase, trying to make himself look taller. He also developed his own peculiar habit of measuring his height when he stood next someone: do I reach his elbow? Her shoulder? Even in public places he would always glance around, measuring his own height. Oh my, everyone was taller than him! Had he been cursed by Allah?

Later the Dwarf learnt a little trick: when he met a taller man or woman he would take a step back and tilt his head as he spoke to them; that way the height difference between himself and others seemed less.

It was strange that even though he was short, he felt drawn to tall people and often tried to make friends with them. He was annoyed by dwarfs like himself, believing them to be cunning swindlers. His former classmate from the Arts College, famous Obid Asom,[1] was the exception to this rule. Firstly, Obid Asom was shorter than our Dwarf. And secondly, he was a very talented person, acclaimed and liked by all.

As our prophet has said: "All tall men are fools, except Omar; all short men is are schemers, except Ali."

3

Since his small stature was a source of troubles, the Dwarf began pondering what might have caused his dwarfishness. Anyone shorter than average is deemed a dwarf. People treat them as though they were just a half person, somehow incomplete, so they say things like: "Even though he's small…" "He's a bit on the short side, but…" "He looks really short, but…" and so on. In short, a dwarf is not considered a complete, whole person in his or her own right. Well, so what if they are short? A dwarf is a human being, too. It's just that his legs and arms are shorter, that's all. He, too, has a heart (and it may be

---

1 A famous Uzbek satirist and performer.

nobler than yours). He, too, has a mind (and it may be sharper and wiser than yours). Do you think these organs of his should be smaller, too? So many famous people the world over were short. Take Napoleon, for example, or Nero, Pushkin, Gandhi, Lenin, Stalin... right up to our very own Obid Asom. And then there's Peter the Great and Gulliver. If you put all you energy into growing tall, well, you could end up with a tall body but a stunted mind.

But there's a tricky point here: Did those great people become famous because they were dwarfs? Or did their height become a point of interest once they had become famous? It's a riddle.

Coming back to our own Dwarf, his forefathers were of average height, as were his parents. His younger brothers and sisters are all quite tall. His three daughters are also beautiful, tall girls. Only the Dwarf is short. "Ah, how did you end up like this?" his mother used to grieve over him. "Perhaps because you carried your easel all the time as a boy you became ... like this." (She can't bring herself to call him 'dwarf.')

Well, one of the Dwarf's ancestors must have been short. Sometimes he would start scolding his forefathers, just as one of his own descendants would no doubt scold him one day. The Dwarf already felt sorry for that hapless grandchild or great-grandchild of his. Or maybe this shortcoming began with him.

4

They say that there is a cure for every disease under the sun except death. Well then, how can you grow taller? Is there any way? Yes! Someone told him that if you eat one kilo of red carrots every day you will grow tall. So, the Dwarf decided to follow that rule. Every week he went to the bazaar, bought a sack of good carrots and ate them neat. But after two months he was in such a state that he couldn't even bear the sight of carrots. He stopped going to the bazaar. His height remained the same: 154cm. No change whatsoever. It turned out the carrot-eating method was a ruse. Or perhaps it didn't work because he was already an adult. He didn't pay any attention to what was written in old medical books: "Add red halila (myrobalan) to yellow balila (chickpeas), stir in some corn and the blood of a tortoise. Add a dash of cinnamon, a sprinkling of watermelon seeds, boil it all up in ten-year-old narcissus water, and eat it on the night of Laylat-ul-qadr."

Later he started using tried and tested methods. He changed his light clothes for dark colours, since dark colours make people look slimmer, but taller.

But this trick didn't bring the desired result, either. So he bought shoes with high heels and took to wearing them whenever he went out. But the extra height the heels gave him also made him feel sick. What's more, his feet suffered, too. But what's a fellow to do? Just grin and bear it. "Business before pleasure" as they say.

But this method soon became useless. It was funny to see him prancing about on his high heels when everybody else was already wearing the latest fashion: flatties. The girls made fun of him, pointing at his high heels saying: "It would be better to die rather than wear those shoes, dwarf!"

Farewell, O oppressive high heels!

Despite his best efforts, no-one treated him like a complete person. He was discriminated against not only in his love affairs, but also in other situations as well. Those who met him on the street treated him like a little lad, and he was like an errand-boy to his colleagues. Thinking about all this gave him the impression that his arms and legs had shrunk and he was somehow even more stunted than before. And so he decided to grow a moustache. Actually, it grew very well. The Dwarf was so happy: finally he, too, looked like a normal person! He grew a beard to go with it. Everyone who saw him was astonished: "My, a young lad with a moustache and beard!" Well, so what if he did have a moustache and beard? He was an artist, after all. Try telling a painter or a filmmaker what they should do! They can do whatever they like!

The Dwarf's happiness, however, did not last long. What comes around goes around. Nature has her law of equilibrium, and if it is broken, it will throw the rest out of balance, someone is bound to get hurt.

The Dwarf was unaware of what was waiting for him just around the corner.

5

By the way, he completed his military service after graduating from Art College. Or as he described it: "He was exiled in Astrabad for two years." When he returned, at first he couldn't settle, he felt restless for a while, but then much later he married, and his wife gave birth to three daughters, one after another. Yet the Dwarf never stopped investigating.

Straight after his military service he was sent to the theatre of a remote region as a stage painter. Although he did go there, he didn't paint anything; on the contrary, he just used to sit around drinking vodka. He didn't see any plays there worth painting for. When they needed a stage set they would just use some old set so as not to waste money.

The Dwarf gradually forgot his painting skills there and had a complete career change. The theatre team would often go out to the fields to give concerts and the Dwarf, an unwilling team member, would sometimes take the role of master of ceremonies, or sometimes that of administrator. He enjoyed life, turning the stage set workshop into his home. From time to time, some kolkhoz or other would commission some painting, and this earned him good money, but he quickly drank his earnings away with vodka and friends, most of whom were unlucky and untalented, yet still considered themselves as famous as Shukur Burkhon.[2]

Back then, if he had not bumped into his old classmate Khayrulla Hoshimov, director of a theatre which came to the region to play for field workers, he would never have returned to Tashkent but would have stayed out there in "the back of beyond" for a long time. Back in college, the Dwarf had played the role of a child in one of Khayrulla's first plays, and they had been friends ever since. While they were sitting sharing a bottle of vodka one evening out in the sticks, the Dwarf mentioned he was thinking of moving to the capital. Khayrulla was delighted: "Well, you should come to our theatre! I'll talk to our director-in-chief, Bahodir, myself."

Khayrulla was true to his word. The Dwarf once again became a resident of Tashkent. He began working at a reputable theatre in the capital. Though it was a decent place to work, it could not provide accommodation for the Dwarf or the other talented young professionals in its employ. [3]

---

2 A famous Soviet theatre and cinema star.
3 It was normal for the workplace to provide an apartment for its employees in Soviet times.

And so the Dwarf's vagrant life began again. His vigor was in decline, the excesses of his student life – which had lasted for almost ten years – were finally taking their toll; in short, he was in need of a warm home and some TLC.

6

The story of our Dwarf's wedding is a tale in its own right. No, not a tale but a comedy, or to be more precise, a tragicomedy. That year he was sent to hospital because of the ache in his legs. Since all the main wards were full, he was given a place in a special ward for two. For the first three days he was alone there. On the fourth day, the real lord of the ward arrived. His name was Armenian Uncle Levon, a man of fifty, a strong fellow going thin on top. With his two bright red cheeks, fleshy nose and ugly eyelids, he looked like a bad man. He was born in Kokand[4] and knew Uzbek very well. He was also an experienced man of the world, and a joker. So they soon became friends. Uncle Levon's many acquaintances would visit him in strict rotation one after another, so the ward was always full of food and fruit. The Dwarf, who became a sort of errand-boy, couldn't keep up, barely managing to dish out all the goodies to the nurses. He had to take care of Uncle Levon, too. You see Uncle Levon felt well enough during the daytime, but at night he was plagued by back pain. They say he had salt in his spinal cord. He probably had salt in his neck, too, which is why he couldn't turn his head properly. He would wear a scarf even in warm weather.

---

4   A city in Eastern Uzbekistan.

Feeling sorry for him, the Dwarf would massage his back and neck at night. And in these moments of relaxation the sick man would think about how to repay his new friend.

"Well, my little brother, it's high time you got married. How long are you going to live alone? Let me do something about it, let me find you a beautiful Armenian girl. I'm sure you've heard, Armenian girls make very good wives. They're hardworking, good cooks and very capable. She'll be your shield all year long as they say. If you marry one, you'll never regret it."

"Do you think that a beautiful Armenian girl would marry me?" asked the Dwarf hesitatingly.

"We'll persuade her, my lad, we'll persuade her! I know you Uzbeks usually don't fancy marrying other nationals, so maybe you'd prefer an Uzbek lass?"

"If I get married, I'll need a place to live. Besides, I have my theatre…"

"Put your theatre aside. And we'll solve your housing problem, don't you worry."

And so the Dwarf set about massaging this sack of meat with special care, setting his hopes high; well, the man did look like a businessman, after all.

"Of course, I would marry, but I still haven't found the right girl," he said, the flame of hope flickering in his heart.

"What do you mean, the city is full of girls?!" said Uncle Levon a bit angrily, and began talking about nurses by way of example: "Look how many girls we have here! Salima, Ra'no, Gauhar, Arofat… they're all fine. I'll speak to one of them for you, you just pick one out!"

The bridegroom-to-be, or more precisely, the man who wanted to get a bride, was lost for words. It was as though his generous roommate were bringing him to a beauty contest and saying: choose whoever you want! For a moment, Uncle Levon seemed like a magician, like Father Hizr.[5]

"Well, I hear Ra'no is already engaged," said Father Hizr turning into Uncle Levon. "Gauhar isn't bad, either but... well.... she wouldn't suit you, she's tall."

"They're all nice enough, but none of them is the one my heart longs for."

"Ah, well, now I see. Of course, you're an artist, you need poetry, fantasy!" Uncle Levon thought to himself, and all of a sudden said out loud:

"Let's do this: you will marry one of them, read 'nikah'[6] and then..."

"Nikah?"

"A fake "nikah."

"A fake "nikah?!"

"Don't flip! If you marry someone on a fake 'nikah,' a 'nikah' of convenience so to speak, then we'll register you somewhere and get a place for you to live. You'll just need to live together for a couple of months or so. Don't worry. It'll be just a formal 'nikah.' You don't even need to see the girl, but you will need her passport. It's easy enough to get a new passport for five or ten soms.[7] We can make this work! Then afterwards you can get a divorce. But you'll already have your own home. So after that you can marry anyone you like! Since you'll have your own home it won't be difficult to find a girl. Otherwise, you'll never have a place of your own. I don't think your theatre will be able to buy a place for you. You could get a hostel from them

---

5 A prophet who appears to a person four times in their life, a miracle worker who goes unrecognized.

6 Muslim marriage ceremony.

7 The equivalent of three lunches.

as an interim solution, maybe, but that wouldn't be enough for you. You seem like a decent man. I like your manners. And you do seem to have healing hands. (Actually, although he wasn't a handsome man, our Dwarf had good, strong hands; they were tempered by the hard work of painting.) I'd really like to help you. How do you like our plan?"

"Well, it's not bad, but is it doable? I can't really believe it'll work," said the Dwarf regretfully.

"Don't worry. Nothing is easy, but it's not impossible. First we need to soften a girl up with presents to get her permission. Alright, leave that to me. Which one do you like most? Arofat? She's hardworking, modest, well-mannered. But think carefully… Just say the word and I'll get to work."

But the Dwarf didn't say anything, as if he were suddenly struck dumb. He did not realize that Fate was bringing them together here, this very moment, building their future life.

The Dwarf, an artist, was making friends with all the nurses. He drew portraits of some of the doctors and all of the nurses. Everyone appreciated it. But for some reason he didn't paint Arofat's picture. And she didn't ask him to, either. Actually, the Dwarf had no intention of painting a picture of this girl who always busied herself with her job and walked with her head bent.

We can only surmise how Uncle Levon got her permission, but just two days later, when nobody was in the ward, Arofat came in and placed her passport on the Dwarf's pillow.

The next day, Uncle Levon's friend drove the new couple to a mullah to read 'nikah.' When they got back to the hospital, their kind "father and father-in-law", Uncle Levon, was preparing a bouquet of tulips and a bottle of champagne… Everything went smoothly, as if in a dream.

As soon as the "father and son" recovered and were discharged, the Dwarf went to see Arofat and get the other documents ready. Then he brought them to Uncle Levon who, as it turned out, was head of the municipal housing department. Within a week, the "bride and groom" were officially registered in the flat of a 95-year-old woman who usually lived with her daughter in another house. The newly-weds' flat consisted of one room and a veranda right in the city centre, in one of the shady houses near Revolution Square. Only old people lived in the small old houses around them. Water ran down the long pipe day and night making it look like a fountain in reverse. But no-one paid any attention to anyone. What more does a bachelor need?

Even though he was a dwarf, the people here were respectful, treating him like a man. And he got used to them, too. It's true that old men and women are harmless. From time to time, he would help them carry their shopping, change their light bulbs, or mend some household equipment. And so they considered him a very good man, and called him Pasha, good Pasha. What more did he need?

The Dwarf didn't know how to thank generous Uncle Levon. Then one day he asked him for a small photograph and in just two weeks he painted his friend's portrait on a large, framed canvas. He deliberately painted him like a young man, taking the curly hair from his temples and putting it on the top of his bald head. When he presented the portrait to Uncle Levon, tears came to his eyes. "Thank you, my dear friend, thank you so much!" said he, planting a kiss on the Dwarf's forehead. "It's perfect, you got it just right! I was really like this in my youth, I had curly hair. Your Aunt Maria will be so happy to see this!"

Later, the Dwarf and Uncle Levon became even closer, like father and son. They would often visit each other. When Uncle Levon's back played up, he would fetch the Dwarf, saying: "Ah, you have such healing hands!" And later still, he would bring him a bottle of cognac and presents for his wife Arofat and his daughters who lived elsewhere. It was none other than Uncle Levon who helped the Dwarf register the flat in his own name when the old woman passed away, and when the house was demolished and a bathhouse built in its place, it was Uncle Levon who once again helped him get a new flat in the desirable new Yunusabad district.

7

In the early days, Arofat would come to "her house" from time to time as a step-sister or an acquaintance. She never mentioned anything, she never hinted she might want something in return for her help; on the contrary, she cooked for the Dwarf and washed his clothes. Eventually, the Dwarf learnt a little about her. Arofat was a half orphan, and she and her sister had been brought up by her step-mother. The Dwarf imagined the step-mother like a witch in the old folktales, but Arofat said that actually her step-mother was not a bad woman. "She's a good woman, but she sometimes scolded us because she wanted us to be good girls, too." From the way she spoke, the Dwarf sensed that, as the elder daughter, Arofat had been rather a headache for her step-mother, since several match-makers had come to ask for her younger sister's hand, not hers. The younger one must have been prettier. The Dwarf didn't press the point, but he felt sorry for this poor, hesitant girl. He wanted to help her, but how? Had she wanted, this girl could have put him behind bars in a jiffy. May Allah be merciful! May Allah preserve him from evil and may his dreams come true! If he had really wanted to wed her, he would have known what to do with her now. And she was not indifferent towards him, she would come and go as she pleased, making herself at home. No, no. He may be bald, but his heart was too sensitive. As a girl, Arofat was rather squashed, sort of flat, her legs were short and rather crooked, and her cheeks were puffed up. No, no, the Dwarf could not do anything with her. Yet whenever she raised her head, something sorrowful could be seen in her sad eyes. Perhaps that's why they often spoke to each other without looking into one another's eyes.

According to their agreement, the time for "divorce" was fast approaching, but the girl didn't say a word. The Dwarf didn't dare mention it, either. But her silence vexed him. What kind of girl is she, anyway? Who would so quickly agree to the schemes of some sly Armenian? Well, so much for being reserved! She was too simple-minded, even naïve. No-one would believe you could find a girl like that in this city! Well, you may say she was simple-minded, yet her behaviour was impeccable and she knew what she was doing. What's more, she was caring and neat, and a real hard worker. She was a good cook, too. She could cook fantastic 'somsa' and had treated the Dwarf to it on more than one occasion. Ah, it was so delicious! In short, she could be a good housewife. But... The Dwarf's heart was not longing for such a girl.

Nevertheless, he got used to her. If she didn't appear for a few days, the Dwarf would wait for her impatiently. Once she quarreled with her step-mother, so she came to see the Dwarf and stayed with him. They slept separately of course. The Dwarf didn't even entertain anything untoward. He was no fool.

But a human being is not always so steady. One night when the Dwarf came home drunk after a banquet with his colleagues, he found Arofat there. She was ironing his trousers. She seemed so beautiful then. He chided himself for being ungrateful. His heart was on fire: what am I doing? Why didn't I appreciate such a caring girl?

He lifted her by her waist and jumped with her onto the bed.

They made love. But it turned out she was a virgin. Ah, you will be killed now, Dwarf!

He crouched down by the bed and cried:

"Please forgive me, Arofat!"

Weeping, Arofat replied:

"I wish we could be happy together now…"

The Dwarf's eyes opened wide: What? Are you talking about us living happily ever after?

But it was too late to undo his sin.

Nevertheless, the girl's words were honest and sincere.

In the morning, the Dwarf felt an utter wretch. And the girl washing up felt the same. He should learn to be more restrained. If only he could smash himself into little pieces! How he wished he could just get rid of everything, of this girl and of himself. Or, at least, he wished they had not lain together last night. He would willingly sacrifice half his life for that… But what could he do now, poor fellow?

After that, Arofat didn't appear for two weeks. One day when the Dwarf was reading a book in the evening, she came in, her head bent. She had a bundle in her hand. She had brought food.

Looking at her, the Dwarf's heart skipped a beat once again. He felt he wanted to see her, to be with her. He wanted to spend a night with her, but without getting drunk this time. So he did, and he certainly enjoyed it!

And so it happened several times. And they both seemed satisfied, since neither said anything.

Once the Dwarf came home from the theatre in a bad mood and saw Arofat there again. Suddenly he flew into a rage and told her to get out, yelling insults at her: "Get the hell out of here, and don't bother to come back!"

She picked up her bag and left the house without a word. Oh my, what kind of a girl is she? Why didn't she say anything? Why didn't she say, for example: "Where am I supposed to go? I have a right to live in this house, too, you know! It's my house, too. Leave it yourself if you don't want to share it with me! You tricked me with your fake marriage, you dragged me into bed, how dare you throw me out now, dwarf?!"

But, no, she didn't say a word, nor did she raise her head. As if she had known this would happen one day. So she just left the house like a sinner.

The Dwarf had dared to throw her out, but he soon regretted it. His conscience plagued him. But he soon justified his actions to himself again: I was right. After all, how long could it have lasted anyway?"

Arofat didn't come back after that. Three months passed. One evening the Dwarf was on his way home from the theatre. He was feeling down again because he'd been speaking on the phone that afternoon when all of a sudden he heard two girls chatting to each other on the other line: "What's Dilfuz going to do with a dwarf like that anyway? Jahongir is a tall, handsome guy with lovely curly hair…"

As our Dwarf was going down into Pakhtakor metro station, he caught sight of a familiar face and walked over to her. It was Arofat. She looked down and greeted him slowly.

"How are you, Arofat? Why don't you come to our house? I haven't seen you for a long time."

The girl raised her head and shot him a glance:

"I would have come but I was afraid you'd throw me out again."

The Dwarf melted at her words and, taking her by the arm, he asked:

"Where are you going now?

"To the hostel."

"Hostel? What are you doing there?"

"I'm staying in my acquaintance's room for a while."

"Look at me, tell me what happened?"

The Dwarf took her by her chin and made her look at him. She was weeping. The Dwarf looked her up and down more thoroughly. She was in a bad way. Something had happened to her. Her cheeks were puffed up even more than usual, her nose was red. The front part of her atlas dress was sticking out. It was obvious: she was pregnant.

It turned out that her family had found out and banished her from their house. It was as simple as that.

"Why didn't you come to my house?" asked the Dwarf at a loss.

"You told me not to come again."

Well-dressed girls were passing by, catching the Dwarf's eye; perhaps Arofat was the least attractive now.

Whatever she was, the Dwarf was still a good person. Suddenly he felt sorry for her, and his heart was filled with warmth, crowding out his egoism.

"My ugly lady," he said and hugged her slowly. "Let's go home."

Arofat followed him silently.

After that there was a small, stupid row, as a result of which two weddings were held: one in the city and one in the village. Later their first daughter was born. She was a very sweet baby. Then one more girl was born and then again, one more daughter. In short, as Arofat had predicted some years ago: "I wish we could be happy together now..."

Was the Dwarf happy now? It's true he had a house, children. But he was not satisfied with his wife. He did not want to see her. It pained him to think about her. May the Merciful One forgive him, but he had "created" his daughters after getting drunk, each time. It was strange: all three of his daughters were perceptive and good. Whatever people say about making love while being drunk was nothing but old wives' tales. Many a time the Dwarf had made up his mind to get a divorce, but how could he leave such sweet daughters, a wife and a good household? They say that whoever has a daughter will have a soft heart...

8

Times have changed. Now it's the girls who choose their men. And usually they want a tall man. In fact, their ideal would be a tall man with curly hair.

"Our Dear Viewer." The Dwarf subscribed to a tabloid which also published a weekly schedule of TV programmes. As soon as the paper arrived, the first thing our Dwarf did was to look at the "Matchmaker" column. And every time he read it he saw that beautiful, modern, intelligent, attractive, sweet and plump ladies were looking for a husband or a lover. The husband's had to be 180-190 cm tall, but not less than 170 cm. If he was a businessman or a wealthy man heading to America or a rich Arab country, well, that would be perfect. But the most important requirement was his height and appearance. Anyone shorter than 170 cm would never even get a look-in. So long as he's tall, it doesn't matter if he's ignorant and ill-mannered, or if he gets drunk every day, gets rowdy and beats her, she doesn't mind. Just imagine!

Of course, the Dwarf could always simply cancel his newspaper subscription, not look at those disgraceful pages. Yes, he could do that, but he was hopeful that someday, somewhere among all those ads he would find someone asking for any man, regardless of height, tall or short. But, alas! Everyone wanted a tall man...

No, no, even if he did find a woman was looking for just anyone, he wouldn't rush off to meet her straightaway. He was hoping for something else... But it would be enough for him simply to know there was such a woman out there. That would be a great consolation for him.

We know that the Dwarf's heart craves kindness, tenderness. We are also aware that he does not love his wife. So, the only solution is to find a lover. Far from fading, his old hope of finding love grew stronger year by year. But not every dream comes true. The key to our dreams cannot be found in this world. Beautiful women usually have handsome husbands. Or they might not be handsome, but they are definitely tall. Those who are not tall have such skills that any tall man will bow to them. And just because of that, beautiful women choose them. If they turn out to be unfaithful, well, a woman can find someone else in the blink of an eye. There are plenty of other fish in the sea. It's a market open for bargaining.

The Dwarf was no stranger to the wares and buyers at that market; he had seen them many times.

A long time ago, a young scholar from his hometown had taken him to a banquet. The house where it was held was like a castle, the banquet was splendid and impeccably organised. We shall not go into details, but, in short, the mansion belonged to a professor who was head of the admissions committee at a prestigious university in the capital city, a university to which not just anyone could get a place. So the banquet was a pompous affair with scores of postgraduate students happy to serve there. In fact, there were more hosts than invited guests!

The long table was set out between the flowerbed and the fountain. There were about ten people seated round it, mostly married couples. All of them looked intelligent, well-bred. They had studied together, and were all from the same village. The Dwarf envied this friendly team that had come from some far-flung village and settled in Tashkent.

There were two 'stars' at the banquet.

First of all, everyone was fawning over the man sitting at the head of the table in the seat of honour. Although he was seated like a religious official, he was in fact head of a large, profitable company. Apparently, the banquet had been organised in honour of his visit to the capital. It was strange that important scholars were sitting there attentively listening to him, munching kebab. Well, what can you do? Such is life.

This important person's attention was directed to another 'star', the cherry on the cake, a stunning woman by the name of Zubayda-khon. Basically, this man spoke to no one but her, merely acknowledging everyone else's remarks with a quick comment or a brief nod of approval.

After sitting for a while, the Dwarf soon realized that his task in that circle was to draw the "revered guest's" portrait as a keepsake. It seems this was what his the cunning friend had had in mind when he invited him.

And so our Dwarf unwillingly drew up a chair, took a sheet of paper from the bag he carried with him at all times, and set about sketching the portrait. The portrait was soon finished; it was easy for the Dwarf to dash off a plain, meaningless face.

The "revered guest" examined his likeness thoroughly, then praised it, saying: "Ah, this shows real talent!" Then he let the people around see it. He called the Dwarf over, shook him by the hand, and, slipping something into his pocket, whispered, "Now draw Zubayda-khon's portrait, too."

The first portrait had come easily, but this second one was much more of a challenge.

While he was drawing, the Dwarf pondered a puzzling riddle.

As he had gleaned from the introductions, this charming lady worked as a department head at a hospital for government officials, and the puny little man sitting next to her was her husband. The Dwarf was staggered. It beggared belief that this aristocratic-looking lady, who was able to enliven such high level dos in the capital with her mere presence, was actually a villager! What's more, how could she be married to that ugly man? How could she choose him when she had other, better, classmates, such as the powerful man at the head of the table...?

The history behind this confusing problem was very simple. Some years ago, back at school, this puny little man, the lady's husband, had been a star pupil. (In those days, the influential man now sitting in the seat of honour had been rather a dunce, he didn't know so much as his times tables, saying that "five times five" must be fifty-five since there are two fives standing next to each other.) It's only natural for girls to be drawn to boys at the top of the class. In short, Zubayda was green back then, like a bud. So it turned out that our lovers, now such an unlikely couple, had gone to school together, as lovers so often do. After they married, their life far from their home village, mundane household matters and other everyday difficulties gradually made this man smaller. But the lady, beautiful from the beginning, became more charming year by year, especially after giving birth to several children, a trait which ran through her whole family. Moreover, thanks to her high profile job and prestigious working conditions, she became used to mingling aristocratic circles as a fellow member; indeed, not only a member – more often than not she was the cherry on the cake. Seeing all these changes, the poor husband fretted, tormented by jealousy, and his sufferings made him smaller still. It was too late to change anything now. Even if he were a candidate of science or a great scholar, or even if he shunned all these pretentious, pompous circles and withdrew to his village to live out his days in vast fields full of blossoms, he would still be just "Zubaydakhon's husband."

... And so, deep in thought, the artist finally finished the portrait of the lady. He sighed.

Being a painter is indeed a good job. It brings its own pleasures.

But being a dwarf is dreadful; ah, the pain of being short!

9

This is a world of hopes. The Dwarf was still hopeful a miracle would happen one day and he would be tall. But soon he faced another problem.

Everything has its appointed time, but the hair on your head will not fall out overnight. Our Dwarf was always preoccupied about how to be taller. He would

trim his beard and moustache neatly, too, but he overlooked one other vital matter. As he was combing his hair one day he discovered to his dismay that this hair of his, which had been thick and curly some time ago, had grown so thin it could no longer be combed properly! He wanted to caress his poor head, but hair came out in handfuls leaving a gaping bald patch in one place. The mirror seemed to be mocking him, saying: "This is life, brother, and it's like a game of hide-and-seek. It's always playing tricks on you. Look, your youth has passed..." Am I getting old? How? When? What have I seen in this world so far?

His last hope was dashed – his hair was falling out! Once, long ago when he was preoccupied with trying to make himself taller, he had woken from a dream, weeping, for in his dreams he had seen he was bald. Now this nightmare had become a bitter reality.

Soon the rest of his hair fell out, too. Ah, so that's why his beard and moustache grew so well! After all, it seems only natural that hair should grow thick in one place and fall out in another. What comes around goes around. It is a law of nature, Dwarf, my little friend!

So now he began to worry about both his hair and his height. It turned out there are many "wise" people in this matter, too. One of them advised him to shave his hair using a razor, another recommended washing his hair with the water from soaked rice and salt water (the salt must be natural). A third person's advice was to rub garlic onto his head and a fourth said he should rub it with the lust gland of a young bull and yogurt made from the milk of a black ewe. One person even told him to wash his hair with kerosene. He still remembers how he did them all, stinking for days.

The Dwarf also enlisted his wife's help in this matter. Unaware of her Dwarf's real intention, she would bring him various herbal remedies and potions: the hard-to-come by "Banfi" from abroad, or "Dzintars" from Latvia.

In short, he did everything he was told. But everything seemed in vain. Once a special programme was aired on TV. An American chap let a cow lick his head and after that his hair grew lush and curly. The Dwarf saw it with his own eyes: a bald man was lying there and a cow was licking his head! The Dwarf shared this good news with a colleague who was suffering from even more dramatic hair loss, but he didn't so much as react: "I don't believe it! If that were true, Gorbachev would have had a head of curly thick hair long ago!"

After that the Dwarf began to use another tried and tested method. Like all experienced bald people, he began combing his hair in a particular way, skillfully smoothing hair from the sides of his head to his forehead. But as time passed he dropped this habit; after all, he couldn't always walk around with a comb in his hand, especially in windy weather.

And so he became both a dwarf and bald. And people didn't only call out to him: "Hey, Dwarf," but: "Hey, Baldie," too. Strange how Allah singles out one person and slaps him repeatedly.

In fact, neither his height nor his hair was the real issue. Provided you are strong enough, it doesn't matter whether you are tall or short, bald or curly-haired. But if you are weak, you just find any excuse. In short, it all boils down to whether fortune smiles on you. And to your heart, to how content your heart is. May fortune smile on us all! A fortunate person is not preoccupied with his appearance. He doesn't fret about some physical shortcomings or blemishes; that's just natural, after all. If he worries about his appearance and fixes on it, his luck will evaporate. And it's not easy to catch it again. If you are plagued by misfortune, a thick head of hair or a very tall figure are all to no avail. Allah creates everyone how he wants, and the hair on your head will surely fall out one day, so there's no point in losing sleep over it.

By the way, there is beauty in baldness, too; it's just another style of haircut. Baldness really suits some people. Everyone knows famous people look good even if they are stunted or bald. Even these 'defects' seem pleasant and attractive, even endearing. A human being is an unrepeatable miracle, and neither Jesus nor Moses can recreate him. Take this Obid-jon for instance. Can you imagine who he would turn into were he tall or average?

Once upon a time, the Dwarf had his share of good fortune, too (he wasn't bald yet.)

Before graduating from Art College, the Dwarf painted a large portrait entitled "Dream" as his diploma piece. Executed with flare and passion, it was a sensitive conglomerate of the most attractive aspects of all the beauties the Dwarf had ever painted since the day he first put pen to paper. It depicted a beautiful lady with long, luscious locks, gazing into the distance, a comb in her hand. It was published on the cover of San'at (Art) magazine. Soon after that, every other full colour magazine and journal was reprinting that picture under various titles such as "Dawn," "Attractive," "Apprehension," "Hyacinth," and "Virgin." It was also published in Art magazine in Moscow. And so soon the walls of hostels and shops, the windows of trams and buses, were full of nothing but "Dawn," "Attractive," "Apprehension," "Hyacinth," and "Virgin."

Articles appeared in various media outlets discussing the portrait in lively terms. It was widely acknowledged that it had been created with passion and talent, but some critics were struck by another aspect of the work, too. It was obvious that it somehow captured the morning time, but how should one interpret the rays of the full moon filtering through the window and the stars beyond? Was there some symbolic meaning here?

To be honest, not even the Dwarf himself could answer that question satisfactorily. He had simply wanted to paint it that way, that's all there was to it. There is no room for discussion.

He later found out that the portrait's strange quality and his "mistake" had made it famous.

Ordinary people found some "mistakes" in his work, too. For instance, they wanted to know why they could only see one side of the lady's face? Why wasn't she looking straight ahead? Could they see her whole face, please? Ah, but good things come in small doses, my friend!

Fame has wings, as they say. Though there was in fact only one portrait, since people called it whatever they wanted, it seemed as though there were in fact several similar portraits. As a result, our Dwarf became the author of not one but many famous portraits!

Yes, it's true, fame has wings. In those days, the Dwarf was caught up in a whirlwind larger than himself, so much so that while taking a stroll one day he even felt as though he were suddenly taller, as though he were soaring skywards. Wherever he went he heard people whispering, "Look, look, that's the famous young painter! He painted "Dream." Yes, that's right, "Virgin." They say he'll soon be the new Chingiz Ahmarov[8]..." In those days no one called him a dwarf, no one paid any attention to his appearance. Obid-jon, now so famous, was just a nobody back then. He was a graphic designer for the magazine Yoshlik (Youth) and could often be seen munching a pie from

8 Famous Soviet portraitist from Tartarstan who spent most of his life in Uzbekistan where he is recognised as national artist.

the Beshyoghoch bazaar, lugging a bag twice his size. But now he is a very famous person. Ah, the tricks of the world!

Of course, the Dwarf didn't let his fame go to his head, but he did rest on his laurels for a while, basking in the light of his work. That light was so dazzling that his next few pieces were reruns of his first work, "Dream." And so he turned into an average, run-of-the-mill painter. Apparently, he was not a talented artist, it was a mere fluke that "Dream" had been painted well. Yesterday's promising young artist paled into an ordinary illustrator, or just the Dwarf. So his present grievances, distress and malcontent all stemmed from the desire to get back to those famous years. Plus the fact that he had a rather different view of himself.

In college he studied at the Department of Theatrical Art. Requirements were different there. He gradually forgot how to paint colour pictures and portraits. Moreover, as we already know, they sent him to work out in the sticks. The situation was different there, he was drawn into an easier way of earning money. And so the years passed. But now he regrets his past. Yes, for ten years he had studied and learnt something, but what about the rest of his life? Had it all been in vain? What else could he accomplish?

He dreamt of doing something extraordinary, he wanted to prove he was no ordinary dwarf, he wanted to be famous again, too. Then, at least, he hoped, no-one would pay any attention to the fact that he was short.

But what could he do? Luck was turning away from him. To bring it back, he must be determined and passionate, he must give up the fruits and pleasures of this earthly life. And that demanded zeal and vigor, contentment and inspiration. There was no-one around him who could inspire him, so he needed a little luck again. After all, unlucky people are usually just ignored.

In short, everything was connected to everything else. He was still stuck in a vicious circle.

As time passed he disliked himself more and more. He was like a half man or not even a man at all. He had no stature, no hair and no luck. It would be better for him to leave this world, hapless Dwarf!

But he became more sure of himself after the chief playwright's next banquet.

10

The chief playwright was a generous and hospitable person. He used to bring his useless scripts to the theatre, where everyone would just ignore them. But later the theatre was bombarded with phone calls from some officials putting in a good word for the chief playwright, so much so that one of the directors took his script and, with the help of some actors, almost completely rewrote the whole thing, berating the author as he did so. And all the while the playwright would come and meddle in their work, asking them not to cut this, not to change that. He would often bring pilaf cooked in olive oil and fat to the rehearsals, and organised banquets both before and after the play, first for a smaller group and then for quite a large crowd.

This time the banquet was for an even wider circle and was being held at the Bahor Restaurant. Both invited and uninvited guests showed up, including some well-dressed ladies and gentlemen who were nothing to do with the theatre and who had not been seen at the performance the day before, either. The banquet was as sumptuous as a wedding breakfast. In fact, it was a wedding, the chief playwright's wedding, the solemn celebration of his victory over the theatre. So the guests all came to celebrate his success. The Dwarf had seen the majority of them at similar free banquets on earlier occasions.

As usual, the tables were laden with all manner of fruits, foods and drinks.

The Dwarf had also played his part in putting on the performance, as assistant to the chief stage artist Tolik-jon. Actually, the talented chief stage artist wasn't at all keen to work on that play, so in fact it was he, the Dwarf, who had done most of the work. Nevertheless, there he was, sitting at the foot of the table, as if no one cared whether he was there or not, while all the other actors and workers were having a whale of a time.

The banquet was opened by the director-in-chief. In his speech, he skilfully avoided any mention of the author's play, and, having asked the rest of his team's permission, he left the banquet with his poet friend. Apparently, he had another banquet somewhere else. So now the others round the table were free to have a good time. Those who just yesterday had been criticising the author harshly now started to praise him. They predicted that if he worked on the play a little, it would become better than "The Riot of Brides."[9] The author sat in the seat of honour, bathed in glory.

When people spoke about the stage sets and scenery, all praise went to Tolik-jon. Well, sweets are for the boss, as they say.

Soon lively music and dance started up, the guests all forgot about the playwright and his play, where they were and the reason for the banquet. Everyone let their hair down. Actors upset by some quarrels at the theatre soon began to enjoy themselves.

---

9 A very famous comedy by Said Ahmad.

Our Dwarf's attention was drawn to a girl dancing in this happy throng. He thought he knew her, but where had he met her before? Was she one of the guests? She was so beautiful, and was dancing so gracefully, every move she made was so pleasing and becoming.

It is usually like that: a beautiful woman always looks familiar. But unfortunately it usually turns out she doesn't know you at all.

Impressed by her dancing, the Dwarf was gazing at her when she suddenly spun around and smiled at him. Yes, there really was something very familiar about her! Otherwise... But at that moment another man, whose name was Nurali, blocked the girl's way, leaving the Dwarf alone with his unfulfilled desire.

Ah, one more trick of the world!

But who was that girl?

The Dwarf, a bit drunk by now, gazed at the dancing ladies and suddenly felt humiliated.

Outside, thunderclaps resounded, shaking the whole world and warning people of ignorance. It was spring. One more spring! Inside, everyone was happy. Life is passing. No one cares about the Dwarf. He was forgotten. O Merciful One, what injustice is this!

All of a sudden, he felt he was the odd one out in that circle, humiliated like a dog, needy and poor. Deeply disappointed, he put his head in his hands.

"Hey, everyone's gone, except you and me. Let's go."

Raising his head, he saw Qamara standing in front of him, pressing her bag to her breasts like an eighteen-year-old girl. As usual, her face was covered in makeup, and the scent of her perfume made his head spin.

Actors usually speak to each other directly and frankly. Because she used too much of makeup and her eyes were always on the move, this woman was openly called a prostitute. She never felt ashamed by that; in fact, she didn't even mind.

"I have a headache, sister Qamara. Please ask someone to take me home," the Dwarf asked slowly.

"Oh, why do you have a headache? Stand up. There's no one left, my dear," said sister Qamara tugging at his hands. "I'll take you home myself."

The Dwarf looked around but he could only see two servants. Where are the other guests? What's Qamara doing here?

Qamara was a woman who had never given birth to a child. She had divorced a long time ago and lived alone in a one-room flat behind the theatre.

So she brought the Dwarf to her apartment and spent a good night with him there. In the morning she said:

"When will you come again, my dear? I rarely see a man like you …"

The old bitch! So you don't have anyone these days, then? You would never have come near me a few years ago, but now just listen to you! There was a reason why they called her a prostitute and now here she is admitting she sees many men…

The Dwarf regretted spending a night with her. Was she really sister Qamara? The famous actress Qamara Rahimova? Wasn't she the lady our Dwarf had loved in his youth, but would never dare to approach? Where is that lady now?

The Dwarf couldn't recognise the woman in front of him; nor, for that matter, did he understand himself, either. Ah, such a terrible state of affairs!

"What would you do with me, Qamara?" asked the Dwarf, not taking her seriously. "Can't you see what I look like?"

"Well!.." said the woman shaking her head. "Don't worry, honey, everything will be fine…"

That day the Dwarf went home thinking he had become an evil person, as if he were somehow covered in dirt.

Enough! He would never go down that road again. His wild youth was already over. It was time to put a stop to lusts and desires. What happened happened. He would not do such things any more. His daughters were growing up, it was his duty to take care of them now.

11

But our Dwarf didn't know that his heart was still young. He didn't yet know that he would fall in love again. He didn't know he would suffer dreadfully like the best of lovers, Majnun.[10] But worst of all, he didn't know that just as his dream was finally about to come true, it would turn into an yet another unfulfilled desire.

One day, when the Dwarf was heading to meet with his director friend Khayrulla Hoshimov, he ran into a girl backstage. She was wearing a white dress, had lovely long hair, and was very attractive. Our Dwarf happened to be in a good mood, so he embraced her on the spur of the moment. (This sort of behaviour is generally nothing to be ashamed of in the world of theatre.)

"Oh, who are you?" exclaimed the girl.

The Dwarf did not release his "prey" go but led her by the hands to a lighter spot.

"Oh, it's you?" asked the girl, breathing deeply. "You frightened me."

---

10 Figure from eastern poetry Majnun and Layla.

"Surely it can't be you?" asked the astonished Dwarf remembering the banquet he had attended that spring.

"And is it really you?" the girl asked again.

"Do you know me?"

"Why not? You're a painter, right?"

"How do you know that? And who are you?"

"What do you mean?!! You see me every day! Are you kidding? I've been working here for more than a year. I'm Safsar, brother painter, Safsar Nishonova. Don't you remember, I played the role of the younger bride in "The Riot of Brides?" And you painted everyone's portrait except mine, since you didn't know me."

The Dwarf didn't know what to say: was it a dream or was it real?

You see, the girl standing in front of him really looked like the lady in "Dream."

Where have you been for the past year, Dwarf? You may be a dwarf but you're still a human being, a man, with a heart full of hopes, but what were you looking at all that time, my dear fellow?

Do you think a man who dislikes himself will pay attention to what's happening around him? Besides, it's not easy to pick out a pearl.

"Sorry, I thought you were sister Qamara..."

"Oh, do you wish I were?" asked Safsar playfully. "Do you think I'm worse than sister Qamara?"

Does that mean the Dwarf was belittling himself?

Does that mean he would not have embraced her if he'd known she was Safsar?

Or does that mean he should be grateful that the girl is putting up with his advances?

Does that mean that the jeweller who cannot differentiate between a pearl and a piece of glass is not a jeweller?

Does that mean that even a hermit walks with his eyes open? Or does that mean that she wanted to tell him he was a fool? Take your pick, brother, whatever is true!

"When, when do you want me to paint your portrait?" asked the Dwarf, not wanting to leave. "I'll start right away, just tell me."

"Well, next time, thank you. I'll come to your workshop myself. Now I have an appointment with brother Nurali. So we'll meet again, agreed? Let's shake on it!"

The Dwarf stood there motionless.

12

"Are you real or are you a dream – ah, I know not..."[11]

Our Dwarf set about gathering information about this wonderful angel right away.

It turned out that Safsar had married a fellow student when she graduated from art college and had gone to work for a theatre in Samarkand. She lived with her husband for two or three years, after which, apparently, they couldn't live together any more, and divorced. Her husband was later jailed for some crime. She had a daughter. And it was true that she had been working at this theatre for a long time.

Her ex-husband had got a place at that institute because he would make a very good Farhod or Tohir.[12] While Allah could withhold some things from some people (from wretches like the Dwarf, for instance) this man was given everything. He was

---

11 From a poem by Asqad Mukhtor.
12 Heroes from Uzbek epics.

a tall, dashing young man, just like Farhod or Tohir from the famous epic poems. However, he paid little heed to his studies and was not a good student. He fell in with a bad crowd from the Behyagach area and learnt to smoke marijuana. Once he and his mates spent the night with some girl from the north, a jaunt which almost landed them all in jail. This hooligan could have been expelled from the institute, but the professors, including the Principal, valued him very much, and since the Principal could do as he pleased, the lad stayed. He was popular with the ladies, too, many of whom wished they'd married this handsome lad instead of their own husbands. Yes, they knew he wasn't a good person, but they still simply lost control whenever they saw him. He may be a scoundrel, but, well, he was a good scoundrel.

The Dwarf wondered how Safsar had ended up marrying him.

Yes, Safsar was one of the beautiful people, too, but how come she had married this guy?

For the Dwarf there was something special about her which set her apart from other women.

How could he have overlooked her before? How come he hadn't run into her at the theatre earlier?

Perhaps he had seen her, but perhaps he just wasn't interested in women. Actually, original pieces are not always appreciated at first glance. Besides, there were many other women working at the theatre. The Dwarf had been disappointed by them, so now he treated them all with equal indifference. Sometimes if a woman dresses differently she can turn herself into a new person, so maybe our Dwarf met Safsar now when she was all dressed up nicely?

Are you real or are you a dream – I don't know..."

And so our painter prepared his tools and a piece of Chinese card. It was good for him to start painting portraits again. In order to devote more time to the portrait, he decided to make a sketch first and then use colours. He waited for the sitting eagerly.

But sometimes Safsar's daughter was sick, sometimes she had to go to a rehearsal or some other place. She often spent time with Nurali. She always found some excuse, saying she would make the time and come to the Dwarf's workshop soon.

"Are you real or are you a dream – ah, I know not..."

Back in his workshop, the Dwarf waited for her anxiously, rearranging his tools. "But you are busy entertaining others."[13] Since the Dwarf loved reading poetry, he passed the time reciting poems he had learnt by heart many years ago. He would go out into the long corridor, stand guard by Nurali's room and pine away.

"Ah, why do others love you so, my dear?
Yet you love them not, you come not near.
Strange, they do not suffer or pine,
Ah, they are not men, they are a horse herd."[14]

Our love-struck Dwarf learnt another pastime. He folded a sheet of paper into the form of a flute and began blowing it. He would play wistful melodies with his paper flute. Those who saw him thought he was daft, that he was like the lover Majnun. People laughed at him and mocked him. But his flute continued to play its mournful melodies.

The Dwarf thought about Safsar day and night.

"Whenever I remember you, I lick my lips,
You are a joy; in its light, your lover weeps."

---

13 By Alisher Navoi.
14 By Uljas Sulaymon.

At night, the Dwarf would speak with her in his thoughts, holding her, kissing her...

In short, he fell hopelessly in love with Safsar just as though he were an eighteen-old-year lad.

But he knew his worth. He also knew he was bald, he was a dwarf and he had his own wife and children. While she, Safsar, was a beautiful young lady. So they were as far apart as heaven and earth.

So what did his unfathomable heart want?

He wanted to lay his bald head on the lady's breast just once, he wanted her to caress his unlucky head, and then he wanted to weep together with her because of such happiness...

This was his only dream, nothing more. If this came to pass, he would no longer have any unfulfilled desires in this world.

"Would I ask you for wealth, my dear?
But you are busy entertaining others."[15]

13

The Dwarf openly envied Nurali, who was rarely seen at the theatre. He worked there part-time, but no one knew exactly what he did there. The Dwarf remembers he – Nurali - had designed several posters in the past. He had worked at a broker's firm somewhere. Then he had made friends with Tolik-jon, who gave him his office while he himself moved to

---

15 From Asqad Mukhtor.

the chief director's office. These two talented and selfless men, with their full-grown beards, had worked tirelessly until morning, planning a new genial play, chewing on nothing but dry bread.

Tolik-jon was an interesting person, too. Though he was the head painter, he didn't care about the colleagues he supervised. His companion, this director-in-chief, was enough for him. He didn't worry about Nurali or Erali, about what they did. He was a strange man. If you asked him something in Uzbek he would reply in Russian. His real name was Tolib-jon, but people used to call him Tolik or Tolya. He was first called "To'lik-jon" by the theatre's previous director, who had previously worked at the ministry of agriculture and who used to wear a Chust[16]-style skullcap on his bald head.

As for Nurali, well, he was living it up in that free, artistic environment. The Dwarf had good reason to envy him. Nurali was tall; our Dwarf didn't even come up to his chest. But he was thin and when he walked his unkempt hair flew here and there. He had an ugly face, but his sparse beard and moustache made him look like a tough man. He had slanted eyes. He wore odd clothes that not everyone would want to wear. In other words, this good-for-nothing wanted to be different. Nevertheless, he was a very polite and communicative person. With his European education, he was always at pains to look like an Uzbek man, but he often overdid it. When he greeted someone, he would bend his tall figure, put his hand on his chest, and keep saying: "thank you very much" all the time, as if he thought no one else ever thanked anyone. Just say: "thanks," that'll do, mate!

---

16 A town in Uzbekistan.

There was something else about this jerk which attracted women like bees to a honeypot. Beautiful ladies would come to his office from time to time and wait their turn. The Dwarf always saw him sitting with women, smoking and drinking coffee.

But this dear, sweet man, so rumour had it, cared nothing for his wife and children. His wife had brought their twins to the theatre and complained about her husband director several times. Nurali's wife, a young and attractive lady, told the director that "her husband had not spent nights with her for two months." She was bitterly disappointed. But if she divorced him, she would be left without anything, since Nurali's father was some judge or prosecutor or other; in short, a rich man. Where could she and the twins go, leaving that mansion to him? If she would just be patient... But this creep has not been sleeping with her, and maybe never would again... So the director consoled her, saying: "He thinks he's still young, don't worry, sister, I'll speak to him." But Nurali just smiled hypocritically and said, "Oh, shut up, Dilya, you know I love you!"

Nurali also had his own headquarters somewhere. The Dwarf didn't know what he did there. It irked him that Safsar used to spend her time with this bastard.

"Do not be tricked by cheaters, oh, sweetheart,
Do not wander in a faithless land, beloved,
Ah, they would but kiss thee then go free –
For none of them can love thee quite like me."[17]

14

---

17 From Muhammad Yusuf.

This sudden love changed our Dwarf's appearance, too. Before, like many other painters, he would often just throw his clothes on carelessly, or go unshaven for weeks, but now he began to dress smartly, to shave and comb his beard and moustache every day. Arofat, unaware of what was going on, kindly brought home a copy of Zdorovye (Health) magazine one day. It had some good tips on how to make yourself taller. One man who followed those instructions grew a whole hand-span. Ah, how happy our Dwarf would be if he could grow a little!

So the Dwarf picked the most suitable trick: a stretching exercise. There was no need for him to go out every morning and do exercises in the children's playground. No, there was an easier way. Tucked away in a neglected spot at the back of the house, the Dwarf found a long, shiny clothes rail that had once been lying around in the theatre. He measured it up to fit to the width of his balcony and cut off the surplus. He measured the middle of the bar and drilled a hole there, then he fixed it to the ceiling, at a height convenient for him, and hey presto! He had a perfect horizontal bar for himself! From now on he could hang and do exercises there any time he wanted. And he could simply take it down when guests came.

And so he began to do exercises every morning using the bar, gradually progressing to other exercises. He could feel his energy levels rising day by day. Now he was no longer slack and indifferent, his body was firm, sure of itself, and he spoke without hesitation. He felt more alive, too, and love burned strongly in his heart.

Well, let his heart grow, if not his height.

15

Finally, she came. "The faithful angel who kept her promise."[18] Thinking that his work would be called "Hope," the Dwarf picked up his pencil.

Safsar came to his workshop three or four times, and each time she sat for one hour. She had to pick her daughter up from kindergarten, plus she had a play in the evenings. When she left, the Dwarf felt exhausted and sat down in the snug basket-like chair Safsar had just vacated. This happened again and again. Although his work was not hard, he felt both agitated and tired.

She was a strange woman. It's true that first impressions can be deceptive. For a while she would sit gladly, talking about anything and everything, but soon she would become sad and gaze off into the distance. The Dwarf did not know what to add. There is a wall, agitation, awkwardness between them. Hope, hope! Patience, patience!

The Dwarf was unable to glean anything more about Safsar from these brief encounters which lasted but a few hours. Whenever you asked her something, she would look into your eyes, astonished, but say nothing in reply. But then later, as if coming to her senses, she would smile pityingly, saying simply "yes" or "no."

However, as he worked, staring intently at her face, our Dwarf realized that he had fallen in love with her for no reason. Once when his brush suddenly slipped from his hand, Safsar turned her face in such a grandiose way...

Every time she came there was something different about both her appearance and her mood, as if she were a different person each time. "She was new and new, totally different." And although her face pleased the Dwarf each time, oddly enough after she had left he could never recall the countenance he had

---

18 By Usmon Nosir.

just been staring at for hours. Yet he could easily call to mind the faces of his acquaintances and even some other people he had met just once or twice on the street. But hers eluded him.

Apparently, what the eyes see and what the heart feels can be two different things, especially when the beloved is settled deeply in your heart.

One thing troubled and upset the Dwarf: Safsar never wanted to see her own portrait. She explained simply that it would not be interesting to look at it when it was finished. "Art should be secretive," she added. But the Dwarf remembered she had once asked him: "Paint me like a bird, as if I'm flying high."

In general, the portrait was painted quite easily. Since Safsar's looks were familiar to the Dwarf from his youth, imprinted in his mind, where she grew more lovely as the years passed, and especially since he had already painted her – albeit differently – in his previous work "Dream," so it was not so difficult for him to prepare this portrait. Now she was to be reborn as "Hope," a perfect image.

While he was working, Qamara would wait for him by his door. It was clear what she wanted.

"Don't you see, sister Qamara, I'm busy," the Dwarf told her angrily. "Don't bother us."

Later he was taken aback by his own words. With two curt phrases he could explain his attitude to both of them. "I'm busy! You are bothering us, Safsar and me. As you see, we both are busy. But you are deliberately bothering us, sister Qamara! And Safsar, you see that sister Qamara is going to hinder our work."

The plan was shattered just as the portrait was almost ready to go on show: the theatre team was sent to Namangan! As usual, Safsar couldn't find the time to come to the Dwarf's workshop.

So the portrait and the rest remained half finished. Well, what could he do?

When the theatre team left, the Dwarf stayed behind alone, and deeply regretted not joining them. There was nothing to do but wait. "Are you real or are you a dream – ah, I know not…"

16

The rest of the Dwarf's adventures are full of strange coincidences. Neither we nor he invented them. Not at all. In fact, this is all quite natural, even though it seems like the events of a strange fairytale

The day after the theatre returned from the trip, the Dwarf went away on sick leave; he had to go to Chortoq Resort to treat his sore foot. And his leave started the very day after his colleagues came back. Coincidence?

Returning home by bus at the end of his last working day, guess who our Dwarf caught sight of among the passengers?

None other than Safsar, with a big bundle in her arms, on her way to visit her sister in Yunusabad. Coincidence?

The Dwarf helped her with her bundle and asked how their trip had been.

Safsar was sad for some reason. So she answered his questions unwillingly. The Dwarf assumed she was just tired. After all, everyone knows how draining travelling can be. Especially trips like that one, they are always so chaotic.

Even though their conversation was not going well, the Dwarf walked her to her sister's house when they got off the bus. When they say good-bye to each other, the Dwarf remarked that he should finish the portrait when he got back from his leave, in autumn.

"It would be better not to finish it," said Safsar jokingly. "I don't like finished things. After all, when something is ready, that means it's finished, it's over, doesn't it? When something's not yet finished, it's always on your mind. And is there anything perfect in this world, anyway? Oh, I almost forgot! I brought you a present from Namangan. You'll know what it is when you see it. Can you guess what it is?"

The Dwarf's heart brightened up. Gazing at the girl, hope filling his heart, he bade her farewell.

That night the Dwarf dreamt the perfect farewell scene. The two of them were walking through a grove of trees in the evening quiet. They were both happy. The Dwarf saw that he was not dwarf at all, he was even taller than Safsar. All of a sudden, a young couple sauntered by, arm in arm. It was the Dwarf's daughter. When they were several steps ahead, she turned and yelled: "You're a dwarf, Dad, why are you walking with a lady taller than yourself? Don't you see she's crippled? She's limping, she's... And you're a dwarf! Dwarf, dwarf, dwarf..."

He woke with a start, worried. While he had been walking with Safsar yesterday, a tall couple really had sauntered past them. But they were not arm in arm. They were just talking to each other. And someone had shouted something at them from behind. But the Dwarf had been deaf to all but Safsar. But he did remember the girl was dressed in black. There was a picture of a dragon on her T-shirt...

According to Arofat, their elder daughter Hilola was becoming friendly with one of her classmates. "Don't think twice about it, it's nothing. And don't go getting the wrong idea or getting upset. The boy seems tall and strong, he's the son of the man with bushy eyebrows who teaches the village folk

53

how to grow cotton. He keeps an eye Hilola, sticks up for her against the bad guys. It's good for Hilola, but of course she's still young..." Seeing the Dwarf didn't like the idea of this, Arofat chided him gently, saying: "Don't worry, she's still a baby, she doesn't understand anything, but she's a smart girl, and careful, so don't worry, please."

The Dwarf realized Hilola often dressed in black, too. Black clothes are all the rage now. But he didn't remember whether Hilola's T-shirt had a dragon on it or not. If he called and asked her about it he would reveal his secret. Isn't it shameful? Isn't it disgraceful? Hilola wouldn't admit to it anyway, she'd just say: "Look, everyone's wearing T-shirts with dragons now!"

But it was true she did see her father: there was no other dwarf around those parts. And what about her? What was she herself doing?

That was a secret that no one would dare reveal. Otherwise, it would sound like a person with no trousers mocking a person with torn trousers.[19]

Pondering this again and again, the Dwarf came to a conclusion: so what if they had seen each other? His daughter should be proud of seeing her ugly dwarf of a father with such a beautiful lady! She couldn't tell her mum, anyway. But even if she could, the Dwarf wouldn't care, since he didn't feel embarrassed about it. Let everyone know he'd fallen in love with Safsar and really loves her very much, with all his heart!

17

---

19 An Uzbek saying.

"Are you real or are you a dream – ah, I know not…"

When the Dwarf returned from his vacation, bad news was waiting for him.

His work called "Hope" had been placed on the marble stand in the theatre's lobby. The portrait was encircled with a black border, and a bunch of flowers stood beside it…

The Dwarf did not know how long he stood there, motionless. Someone approached him, led him away. It was Tolik-jon.

"Yes, old man, it's so sad. What a pity, she was such a beautiful woman!"

Then they sat somewhere and drank tea. Or maybe it was coffee.

According to Tolik-jon, Safsar committed suicide by hanging herself. It happened about ten days ago. One morning she closed her room and did not go out for a long time. When they opened the door, she was already dead. It was unbelievable. Such a young and beautiful girl! People had different opinions about her terrible death. Some said an enemy had given her poison. Apparently, her family was hiding something. Some people said that she was sick, nervous. They say that one or two days ago her ex-husband had come to see her. But no one knew what he wanted. A stranger's life always seems like a bottomless well. It's a pity, the team had been planning the role of Ofelia for her. She was such a talented girl. And sensitive like Turgenev's heroines. But what's to be done? Such is life. On that black day, they had not been able to find a better photo, so they fetched the Dwarf's portrait and stood it there. "Hope you don't mind. I put the black border round it myself, so you can take it off later. Your portrait seemed better than a lifeless photo. It's vivid, original. Eh, such bad news we have, brother… What about you? How was your vacation?" asked Tolik-jon.

"Are you real or are you a dream – ah, I know not…"

A month or so passed before the Dwarf could come to his senses. He did not believe Safsar was dead. He kept thinking she must be alive, she'd just gone to Samarkand with her drug addict husband. Yes, she was alive! If only it were true!

The Dwarf took the portrait down, cut off the black border and hung it on the wall of his workshop. The work now carried some perfect meaning. The Dwarf used to gaze at this creation of his for a long time. Again and again he relived those moments he and Safsar had spent together. Then he thought about her last days and felt sorry. He hoped she might have thought about him at least once. But he disliked himself for even thinking along those lines. And he so started again from the beginning...

Tears came to his eyes. "Paint me like a bird, flying high," she was asking him. So, she had flown away now. Ah, what happened to you, Safsar, my angel? I found you late and so quickly lost you. I never wanted anything from you, Safsar, I had no right to that. I just wished you might live in this world peacefully. That was enough for me, Safsar. But what happened to you? Did you hurt someone in this world, Safsar? I knew we weren't suited to each other, but what could I do? Ah, but my heart matched yours. My heart belonged to you, Safsar, can you hear me? You were telling me you had brought me a present from Namangan. What was it, Safsar? Was that really dedicated to me? Now I will never know what it was. The only thing that remains of you, my only keepsake, is this portrait, "Hope." The portrait that I dedicated to your bright days was used for your black day, Safsar. You left this world knowing that there was a poor man like me who loved you. You gazed upon me, Safsar, so I have already been reflected in the very pupil of your eye... That's enough for me, Safsar. And you will remain in my heart forever. Perhaps everyone – your friends, your parents, your daughter – will forgot you, but you will stay in my heart forever.

Even if I die, you will be in my soul, my Safsar! "Were you real or were you a dream – ah, I know not..." I will never know, my angel! Ah, but it was true that "I was in this world because you, too, were here."

One month later, life doled our Dwarf one more blow. "Hope" was lost! Someone took it from his workshop. The Dwarf was at his wits' end. He questioned everyone, but no one knew who had taken it.

Who needed it, and why? It was a mystery. There are many more questions than answers in this world, and this was just one more.

Having lost his only keepsake of Safsar, "Hope," the Dwarf fell seriously ill. He spent several days in hospital. Later, he tried to restore "Hope" in his mind.

But time heals everything. And so his sufferings finally came to an end, leaving one more scar on his heart.

"Were you real or were you a dream – ah, I know not..."

18

One day as the Dwarf was on his way to an art shop to buy some tools for his painting, he ran into Nurali. He was with two girls. Nurali saw the girls off, and invited our Dwarf to his "headquarters." Even though they were not such close friends, the Dwarf agreed to go with him (Nurali was somehow connected with Safsar, too). The Dwarf crossed the street and bought some snacks from the shop opposite before they went in. When they reached the door on the ninth floor, Nurali gave him a meaningful look, saying: "One moment, please, let me tidy my flat a little." But when he went inside the flat, the Dwarf was surprised to see there was nothing there to tidy! There was a round table with a broken leg, two chairs, a large easel, and a bed in one corner. There were some pictures by other painters on the wall. They were signed, and the Dwarf recognized many of the signatures.

It was not a painter's workshop, but the empty room of a miser.

"Where's your own work?" the Dwarf asked him, seeing that his companion did not use this place as a workspace.

"I took my own work to my house," said Nurali smiling indifferently. "Some pieces are in exhibitions. In Moscow. Haven't you seen them?"

The Dwarf was taken aback; he had never seen Nurali's work in Moscow. Indeed, he didn't even know if his companion had any good pieces to speak of. He was wondering who had given him this flat right in the city centre. What had he done to get it?

"Let's not talk about creative work, let's drink," said Nurali impatiently opening a bottle of vodka.

They drank.

"I hope you know that the time lag between the first and second glasses shouldn't be more than five minutes."

They drank again. And again. They spoke about everything under the sun, and finished a bottle. They wanted more. The Dwarf took all his money from his pocket and gave it to Nurali:

"Hang on," said Nurali, putting on his jacket. "The janitor doesn't know you, so I'll nip out and fetch some vodka myself. You might want to take a rest on that bed."

As he moved over to the bed, the Dwarf caught sight of a canvas behind the easel. It looked familiar. He reached over to it.

That was the one! The portrait he had painted! In one corner, over the original signature, there was a crude new signature: "Nur." So Nurali had swiped it and shown it in his exhibition! Bastard!

Having put the portrait gently back its place, the Dwarf tottered over to the table and poured a cup of tea to steady himself. Then, as if he had not seen anything, he sat down on his chair again.

Nurali brought vodka. They drank one glass each.

"Did Safsar come here?" asked Dwarf, suddenly fierce as a lion.

"Safsar? Which Safsar?" said Nurali. "You mean that Safsar Nishonova? Stupid girl. She used to come here every day asking for medicine. She knew my brother worked at a chemist's. Her heart was sick. Life cheated her and her husband was unfaithful. Just imagine! She used to say no one was to be trusted in this world. A stupid woman. But she was so beautiful... I tried to spend a night with her, but she never came. She was so nervous. If I only could have brought her here... Such a shame..."

"Hey, aren't you talking about a dead woman?" said the Dwarf, shivering.

"Forget it! "Dead woman" you say? Yeah, so what if she died? She was alive before, right? And she was a real beauty!"

"Nurali! What are you saying? What's happened to you? Are you drunk?"

"Nothing. No reason. Forget it!"

Nurali was just standing there, his face devoid of any meaningful expression, arms folded across his chest, smiling coldly. No reason. Just for nothing. O Allah!

At that moment the Dwarf realized who this man really was. This jerk, with a blunt knife in his hand, lived without sufferings, just for fun. He never thought about the consequences. He just puts his knife to your throat, saying: "No reason, just for fun." He's brazen and bad. Curious, do women really like such people? Well, maybe only women who are after a bit of a lark, like him, might do. Yes, such people are different, totally different.

The Dwarf didn't know what to say. What could he say? Help!

"You're a piece of shit, Nurali! A real bastard!!"

"What?"

Unexpectedly, Nurali grabbed the Dwarf by the scruff of his neck and, swinging him round like a puppy, threw him out. "Get out of my sight! Dwarf! Midget!" And he slammed the door

Lying where he landed, the Dwarf kicked at the door. It opened.

"Give me Safsar!"

"What are you on about? Have you gone mad?"

"Give me the portrait!"

"Which portrait are you talking about?"

"Give it to me! Otherwise..."

The door closed, and opened again a moment later. Four scraps of cardboard landed beside him. The Dwarf angrily gathered them up and stomped down the stairs...

Back out on the street, he remembered he had no money for a taxi. He stopped an approaching trolleybus. For some reason, it was running without its trolley poles or contact 'shoes'. The trolleybus rumbled to a stop. There was not a single passenger on it. It was too late.

"Dear friend, please take me to Yunusabad," the Dwarf started to ask the driver as he got on.

"The trolleybus will go to the park," said the tall driver without looking at him.

All of a sudden, the Dwarf noticed a picture on the front window. O Merciful One, is that his "Dream?" Did they print it without letting him know? Where had they found it again?

"Brother, stop your trolleybus."

"Already in Yunusabad, are you? Ok, get off."

But instead the Dwarf asked the driver to turn on the light, and stared at the picture. It had been printed by some entrepreneur, with a calendar for the Year of the Snake. The artist took the pen from his pocket, crossed out the title "Dream," writing "Unfulfilled Desire" instead.

"Hey, what are you doing? Get out, you drunk!"

"Whatever I do is my business, since I created this picture myself!"

"What are you saying? Get out, dwarf!"

"Don't believe me?" – the Dwarf took the four pieces of cardboard and laid them out in front of the driver. "Look, it's the same, isn't it?"

"Well, it does look like this one," said the driver looking from his to the Dwarf's picture and back. "It really looks like Sevara! How do you know her?"

"What did you say?"

"Sevara. We went to school together She married another man because I didn't go to college. I loved her. I still love her even now... Shall we have a drink together? I've got a bottle. I was going to take it home. I was thinking about her just now..."

"Well, if you loved her and are still thinking about her, I suppose you must be a decent sort of chap. Let me introduce myself. My name is Dwarf."

"I can see you're a dwarf, what's your real name?"

"My name is written there. I can tell you my name but you'll still just think of me as the Dwarf..."

The trolleybus was hurtling along at breakneck speed.

"Where are we going, my friend?"

"To Yunusabad, to your house."

"The trolleybus doesn't go to my house; it'll stop half way."

"Don't worry, we'll make it go! This trolleybus goes wherever it fancies!"

19

The 'barefoot' trolleybus really did choose where it went. It stopped in the middle of a field.

Though it was night, the sky was bright, blue, with cotton wool clouds. It was autumn, but it looked like spring; the meadow was full of blossoms and flowers. The sound of running water came from somewhere. Here, water usually only flows like that in autumn and spring. Young grasses and tender shoots were whispering with each other, sharing their secrets like humans. This is what they do in spring. But in autumn they weep, like parted loved ones; they wither and die. This is what the poets say. We say that if one heart fits another heart, especially if they are drawn to each other, then blossoms or dry grass, rain or shine, autumn or spring – it's all the same to them.

The two companions lay down in the meadow.

They took the vodka with them.

They are not just chance companions. They sense an affinity to each other. They share their secrets. As if they have been close friends for a thousand years. Their hearts are in harmony. One of them is a dwarf and one of them is tall (look, girls leave such tall men, too!).

"There is no love in this world."

"There are so many fickle people in this world."

The two men wailed loudly into the night, where nobody sees them in the darkness.

They finished the vodka. Their sorrow was coming to an end, too. And anyway, they were lying on the grass, it was getting damp..

The Dwarf started to tell his companion about his old sorrow.

"Don't worry, my friend, there is a cure for everything except death." The tall man began to describe the cure, while the Dwarf listened to him attentively. "Let me take you there. You'll see for yourself. You'll be taller than me before long."

"No, it's useless," the Dwarf told him, not convinced. But hope flickered in his heart. "I'm without Safsar now..."

"Let's swap our height: you'll become tall and I'll become a dwarf. I don't care about my height now, either. It's all the same to me now. Sevara is not with me... Let me see that portrait again..."

The Dwarf took the portrait from his bosom and created "Unfulfilled Desire" from the pieces.

The two men stared at the portrait in the moonlight.

"Unfaithful Sevara..."

"Poor Safsar..."

Leaving the grief and suffering of this world behind, the 'barefoot' trolleybus returned to the city.

It was odd that the Dwarf did not know there was such a pleasant spot in the city centre.

You've probably seen the tram lines near Independence Square. Just nearby, in an open place above the old library, is a secret enclave enclosed by high walls. It looked like an aristocrat's palace. The walls are quite old (by the way, the street name is still hanging there: "Stalin Street"). Though the walls seem ancient, when you enter the courtyard, you'll be struck by the grandeur of the place. Even though it was late autumn when the driver took our Dwarf there, flowers were everywhere. It was a peaceful place, too. It reminded the Dwarf of a

communal courtyard where he had once lived, only this courtyard was prosperous and wide with shady trees.

The Dwarf's companion took him to a smallish house at the
foot of the garden, hidden among flower beds and various trees.

The owner of the house was waiting for them on the doorstep. Seeing the Dwarf's new friend, he bowed low as a sign of
deep respect. They shook hands and embraced.

The owner was an old, small, balding Korean man. His thin
hair hung down from his temples to his shoulders, and he was
wearing ridiculous shoes, like a child.

"Shang shung san khuva chu!" said the old man to his distinguished guest, putting his hands to his guest's belly button,
bowing down, and for some reason tweaking his nose.

"Chu khuva san shung shang," said the guest in reply, and
then introduced the Dwarf to him, explaining something.

What was he saying? Was he saying that the old man should
make the Dwarf taller? Strange, how could a trolleybus driver
learn such a difficult language?

The old man turned to the Dwarf and greeted him like an
Indian, joining his palms at his chest.

According to our "interpreter" the driver, this person who
used a mix of Korean and Indian greetings was a cousin of Kim
Ir Sen, and had in the past healed Chan Kayshi, Mao Tzedun,
and even Stalin. He had intended to heal Hitler, but had been
unable to get hold of a plane ticket. He was a good healer who
considered himself a student of Avicenna. He did not acknowledge Tibetan medical procedures and disliked the Dalai Lama.
He was looking for manuscripts by the famous eastern healer
Abu Bakr ar-Rozi. His only shortcoming was that he did not
speak a single foreign language.

So, when our "interpreter" interpreted something, the
cousin of Kim Ir Sen just shook his head, meaning "that's true."

Then they turned to the practical part of their visit.

On the orders of the healer who had personally healed Comrade Stalin (curious, which part of his body did he heal: his paralyzed hand? his pitted face? his stuntedness? or his unhealed mind?) our Dwarf, a new patient, suddenly found himself stark naked right in the very entrance hall.

The student of Avicenna led him to a darkened room.

With difficulty, the Dwarf clambered onto the shiny bed equipped with a strange device and lay on his back. The healer who healed only great leaders (except Chingiz Khan and Napoleon; unfortunately they had passed away earlier, other-wise he would have healed them, too) put the Dwarf's feet together, and, pulling them with a belt, fixed them tightly to the device at the edge of the bed. Then he wrapped a similar belt under his patient's arm, round his back, and fixed it to the device at the head of the bed. After that all hell was let loose.

The former candidate to become Hitler's healer took a seat at the head of the bed and gradually started to rotate a rack that looked like a machine meant to draw water from a well, or the handle of a meat-cutter. Every time he turned it, the healer kept asking the Dwarf the only Uzbek words he knew: "Yakhshi, yok? – Is it good or not?" Apparently, he wanted to know if it was painful or not.

First, the Dwarf's figure straightened, stretched, tightened, then some cracking sounds came out – bones, joints, knuck-les, knees...; then lightning flashed in his eyes, and finally he wished he'd never been born to experience such searing pain. At last, willing to remain forever as he was now, dwarf and even midget, he yelled:

"Yok, yok, yok! No, no, no!."

"Good, good," uttered the butcher-healer indifferently. Then a candle appeared in his hand. In the candlelight, he took long needles from under his tongue and pricked them into our Dwarf's body, anywhere he could: is it good or not? Is it good or not...?As if pricking weren't bad enough, the butcher-healer twisted the needles, evidently having a whale of a time.

Finally, the Dwarf's whole body was full of needles; he could neither move nor breathe properly. He was crucified like Jesus, who had been so harshly punished for his faith. But what had the Dwarf done to be punished like this? It's shameful! He felt as if electricity were coursing through his whole body.

After that the healer moved onto the last procedure, which seemed simple enough. He took balls of some unknown substance from his pocket, put them onto the needles and lit them with the candle in his hand. Sparks started flying out from all over the Dwarf's body.

The Dwarf wondered why he couldn't do all this with the light on. But the oppressor-healer was doing things just the way he wanted. After all, he was the cousin of Kim Ir Sen, the same famous healer who had healed Chan Kayshi, Mao Tzedun, and Stalin! And he was an admirer of Avicenna and a future student of Rozi to boot!

The semi-darkened room was full of smoke from isiriq, a plant used for incense. After all that torture, the Dwarf was almost enjoying himself now. He became drowsy.

When he opened his eyes, the room was very bright, his hands and legs were still bound, his body was free of needles and despite some pains, he was feeling light as a bird. The miracle worker, the healer, was standing on a chair in the centre of the room, his hands on his belly button, bowing: Good or not, good or not, good or not?

All's well that ends well, as they say. Well, maybe that's true, maybe it's not. But putting up with all that pain and humiliation was quite another matter. Well, what could he do? It's not easy to become perfect in this world. He who can bear pain achieves his goals.

What else could he do? He couldn't be born from the beginning again, could he? If you don't suffer, how can you gain your beloved?

During the course of this treatment, the Dwarf came across so many famous people in the courtyard. All the lovely ladies he saw in Tashkent turned out to be "citizens" here, too. In fact, only the high and mighty dwelt in the courtyard. From internationalist statesmen striving to unite the Uzbek people with the Soviets to poets who sang loudly: "the Motherland is flourishing, the people are free!" at a time when the people had barely come through repression – all lived here. The Dwarf thought the majority of them had already passed away, but, curiously enough, here they were, living in this apparent paradise. The Dwarf knew them all, but they didn't know him.

There was one particular incident. As he was passing a large house he caught sight of the infamous Zamira-khonim at the window. He was amazed she was still alive! May Allah forgive him, but even while she was alive, he had mistakenly believed she was already dead. He had heard she had once had a home and a performance house in the Darkhon area, but thought she had passed away a long time ago. True enough, she would disappear, let people forget about her for some time, and then later unexpectedly rise to fame again out of the blue, letting people know she was still alive and well, organising pompous jubilees, performing on TV shows, and being aired on the radio. Every time she made a public appearance, she looked younger and younger. So her secret was here, with the healer! It was strange how the old woman could bear this torture. And why not? She needed that fame, so she had to put up with all the sufferings, too. She was a strong woman. Otherwise she would have already turned into dust. Even now she was sitting at the window painting her eyebrows with osma. And the Dwarf had seen her doing exercises, too, shaking her head towards him.

Well, had all those sufferings born fruit? The answer is "yes." However...

At first our Dwarf (actually, he was not a dwarf anymore) used to walk slightly stooped, unfamiliar with his new tall stature. A thin man before, the new tall version of himself now became even thinner, making it all but impossible for him to keep his balance when he walked. In short, it was clear what would happen to a tall man should he be stretched. Moreover, every time he went outside he got bruises on his forehead, since he didn't know how to walk like a tall man. The ugliest thing was that one of his arms became longer than the other, trailing down almost to his knees. It was impossible to cut it or hide it under his shirt. It turned out that, since our former Dwarf was neither a leader nor a commander, the accursed Yakshi Yok healer had simply made a mistake in his procedures. The tall man, our former Dwarf, developed the habit of hiding his anger and walking around with the hand of his long arm thrust into his pocket. Unaware of the secrets of tall people, our hero would often topple over. As everyone knows, when we take a tumble, our hands usually come to our aid, but since one of the tall man's hands was thrust in his pocket, just imagine how many bruises he got! One on top of another...

Now let's turn to his head. At first his bald head became stubbly, then later grew a crop of curly hair. It looked like the hair of a black man, and was most unruly: he could neither comb it nor wash it properly, either.

Well, all that was bearable. The real tragedy lay elsewhere: he could no longer recognise himself. His thoughts were not his own. He disliked his own actions, his own words. When he spoke, he felt as if it were some other person speaking; when he heard something, he felt as though it were coming through someone else's ears; when he ate, he felt he as though he were using someone else's mouth. Even when he lay with his wife at night, it was another person there instead of him...

In short, he turned into a person he had never wanted to look like. He forgot that he was a painter, as if he had never held a brush in his hand.

Other people's attitude towards him changed, too. Those who knew him mocked him. His wife and daughters looked at him differently, as if he were a stranger. And his daughters looked like witches to him, while his wife — who had looked like an old hag before — became very dear to him. But when he wanted to make love to her, it was the same situation: it was another person instead of him...

Finally, our tall man was fed up with all the changes in his body. Being this other person irked him. Now he dreamt of becoming Dwarf again. So one day, he made up his mind and went to the mysterious courtyard once again.

But when he entered the garden, he saw a funeral ceremony in progress. Someone had died. Judging from the number of government cars outside, it must have been a famous person. A lot of people were standing near the house of the deceased, heads bowed. There were many famous faces and government officials among them.

The tall man walked through the place of mourning, not standing tall, just pretending to be a modest person, but then he was faced with another calamity. There was an ambulance further on, and two nurses were carrying a heavy stretcher covered with white cloth... O Merciful One! What had happened to this apparent paradise, this small corner of eternity?

Distressed by the scene, our tall man strode over to the edge of the garden and gradually came to his senses. Allah be praised, there was also joy there. On her lawn bright with flowers, our ever young sister Zamira-khonim (though she was actually as old as our grandmother) was dancing delightfully, far from the sufferings of the world. When she saw our hero she playfully raised one eyebrow.

Apparently, a wonderful event in the history of the Uzbek arts was soon to be held. This almost forgotten artist would become younger, famous once again. A great jubilee was to be held in Navoi theatre, and our dear sister was to sing and dance. The celebration would continue.

The patient, our Dwarf, entered the familiar room, an ache in his heart.

The healing room was dark and full of smoke. He turned on the light and … guess what he saw?

Someone lay on his back on the bed like a long gut. His body, full of needles, was blackened and burnt.

The Dwarf approached the bed and fear overwhelmed him: it was Kim Ir Sen's cousin, the miraculous healer Yakshi Yok!

The horrified Dwarf saw that this man who had healed so many famous people was in fact short, even shorter than the Dwarf himself!

So this meant he himself wanted to raise his stature, even at this old age. Well, that's not a bad thing in itself, but who helped him turn that device? It was a mystery, just like the healer himself.

The room smelled really bad. The Dwarf opened the windows and breathed in the fresh air for some time as the smoke in the room slowly wafted out. All of a sudden the Dwarf turned, and fear washed over him again.

Someone, apparently the healer, was speaking:

"A soul hurts from fear. The frightened soul is worse than everything, even worse than being a dwarf."

Who was that? Who was speaking? The healer didn't know Uzbek, did he? Wasn't he dead? Was he here? If not, who is that?

The sound was coming from himself, from his own body...

The Dwarf ran out of the room like a madman and bumped into someone on the doorstep. None other than Aziza! - That giggling girl who had so mercilessly sentenced our Dwarf in his youth.

By the way, she was not a young girl now but looked like a beautiful aristocratic lady clad in a most expensive dress. She also lived here in this place, the residence of aristocrats. Her father was a rich man, so she in turn became the wife of a rich man.

"Hello, Aziza-khon! I'm Dwarf. You remember, we studied together? Do you remember what you told me in the cotton fields so long ago? Look at me now..."

The aristocratic lady paused for a moment, looking at him closely. But she didn't recognise him.

"No, you are not the Dwarf, you must be crazy. If you were the Dwarf I knew then I would not let anyone else have you. I wouldn't care if you were a townsman or a villager, I would marry you right away!"

"Just a second, Aziza-khon, it's me..."

But she quickly turned into Qamara and gave the Dwarf an angry look. "Stupid!" she said, then added, "Crazy!" And, leaving the Dwarf behind, she went some distance away before turning back again. The Dwarf recognised her this time: it was Safsar! Safsar!..

"Safsar! Safsar!.."

All of a sudden, Safsar ran round the garden and vanished, entering the room the Dwarf had just left.

The Dwarf stepped out and onto the street, and finally came to his senses. Glancing back, there was no courtyard full of secrets; there were only cold iron fences instead.

Suddenly the 'barefoot' trolleybus stopped near him. The door opened and the unlucky lover, Sevara's admirer, appeared. He approached the Dwarf with arms wide open ...

Where the devil had he been, this fellow who had got the Dwarf into so much trouble?

20

The next day, Sunday, the Dwarf opened his eyes, numb. His whole body ached. His heart was in trouble. Scenes from yesterday's adventures were replaying in his mind. He could not remember exactly where he had gone, whom he had met, or what had happened.

The room smelled bad. Was that the healing plant, isiriq? Who was burning it? Was that Yakshi Yok? The Dwarf felt the familiar pain in his body again.

He went out onto the balcony to exercise on the horizontal bar he had fixed. He jumped up, but could not reach the bar and fell down in the corner, blood pouring from his temple.

His daughter Hilola flew over to him, saying: "O Merciful One!" and hurled the bar out of the window.

"To hell with it!... Who was that with you yesterday?"

"What?"

"I've never seen such a face. He kept on smirking but didn't say a word."

The Dwarf raised his head to look at his daughter, but jumped back, frightened: a dragon, she was a dragon! Mouth wide open, she came closer... to eat... But then in a moment, the dragon shrank smaller and smaller, and turned to a harmless picture. Hilola's anxious and astonished face appeared in its place. Staring at that face, the man lying in the corner recognised himself... It was his fate, what else could he do?

The Dwarf went into the bathroom, rubbing his temple, and came face to face with the mirror on the wall. A man with bloody cheeks, a dishevelled beard and moustache, red eyes, and a dirty face was looking back at him from the mirror.

He was a dwarf, and bald. He was ugly. He was untalented and unlucky. He was an oppressed person... Well, there you have it...

The mirror was broken into pieces, like on old man's wrinkles. The Dwarf quickly closed the door with his shoulder, thinking that troubled Hilola might walk in. He peered into the mirror again, and the blood running through his veins woke his dozy cells.

All of a sudden, the broken mirror began to show a perfect picture. A small "Hope" appeared in the bottom corner. That unfortunate woman was shedding bitter tears. Safsar was weeping... (Who else should weep if not her?) The tears gradually filled up the scene. Amid the tears – right in the centre – was the suffering Dwarf. "That Very Offended Person."

A long-forgotten, unfathomable shiver overwhelmed the painter.

Gooli-gooli

Until recently, wherever I went,

I would be the youngest amongst those present.

Today, I noticed that the majority of people are always younger than me…

I wonder when and why this happened.

…briskly walking and hopping from stone to stone, he makes his way down the slope from his secluded spot deep in the ravine.

Here, the mountain-spring water flows inexplicably through all the nooks and crannies, gathering into a small lake at the bottom of the ravine. The water, just enough of it to make a water-mill run, flows down, trickling over the rocks.

Silently, he looks down for a moment, and then deliberately unties his pants and begins to pee into the water. In the meanwhile, he gazes at the countryside that lies further beneath him.

When he finishes peeing, he kneels down by the lake and drinks handfuls of water...

* * *

"It's been a thousand years since the Monkey has left for the next world, so there is no reason for us to visit him," said Mahmud as we left Salom's funeral.

"It's only right for us to visit him, bro," I said. He'd know what I was thinking about ever since I had heard of the Monkey's death on the previous day, wouldn't he?

My accomplice unwillingly turns his car into a narrow cobbled street with orchards on either side, and drives towards the mountain.

"Why do they say it's not good to badmouth the deceased? Is it really not OK to call a bad person bad?"

"He's a human being, bro, just a human being," I said, lost in deep thought. "For one, it's true to say that they cannot come back and defend themselves..."

"You could say he's a man who became a monkey!"

At that moment, I wasn't hearing anything he was saying.

* * *

The Monkey always sat at the back of our classroom. He would have obscured the blackboard had he been sitting at the front: not only was he tall, but also big-boned and humongous. It would have been nice for him to have sat there quietly, but no. Sometimes he would tease Mastura, sitting near him, by pulling her hair. Other times he would steal an apple or a quince from someone sitting in front. If the teacher noticed and reprimanded him, he would just smirk and say hoarsely: "Eh, eh, what have I done?"

He was four or five years older than all of us, and he had even been a classmate to the majority of our brothers and sisters. "Why don't you ask your parents? He might have studied together with your ma or pa," laughed Mahmud. "He must be thirsty for knowledge and never grow tired of studying." The Monkey paid no attention to such jibes and just smirked, but whenever someone teased him too harshly he would just say, "You punk!" That's it. Either he didn't understand what people around him were saying, or God did not give him the understanding of what self-esteem was, in general. He was a bit of a fool and a bit of a lump. He was a monkey. Otherwise, he could have blown away pupils like Mahmud with one breath!

He only came to school occasionally. Otherwise, he worked delivering dried animal dung and straw to his aunt's house, on his donkey. He would carry a torn textbook in his pants, and a folded notebook stuffed into his shirt. He would snatch pens and pencils from his schoolmates. But he wrote or read nothing. It seemed like he didn't know how to read and write. He was too unskilled and stupid (at least, according to Mahmud).

The Monkey would sometimes speak Russian. In particular, he could swear and curse with perfection. He had learned this at the hospital. When we stared at him speaking Russian, he would say, "Eh, eh, if aunty Katya squeezed you between her legs, you would even start speaking Chinese!"

The Monkey sat next to Rahima. No one had actually seen the lice on Rahima's head, but since she wore a ragged old headscarf and a dirty tattered dress, one would presume that she also had lice in her hair. She lived together with her blind grandmother in a big, remote orchard, without walls or a gate. Nobody knew if she had parents, or where they were for that matter. So the others knew of the existence of only Rahima and her blind grandma.

A little odd, this girl was also one who had studied together with our brothers and sisters. As Mahmud would describe it, she was a pupil of the "Yo" class.

Sometimes in the middle of a lesson, Rahima would run out of the classroom, burying her face in her hands and crying. When the teacher shouted "Tojiqulov!" – his surname - at the Monkey, he would smirk as always and say, "Eh, eh, what have I done? It was her who put her legs on mine!"

After incidents like that, Rahima began to appear at school only very occasionally. Eventually she never returned and we all completelyforgot her... Is she alive now? If so, where even is that poor unfortunate classmate of mine?

The Monkey lived at his aunt's house. He also was an all-round orphan: he had neither a father nor a mother. One night many years ago, his father had knifed his mother, and then handed himself in to the police, with the bloodied blade in his hand. The court proceedings were held in the central orchard, from where his father was then taken to prison. I had not witnessed the court proceedings myself, but many bad rumors of that day still resound in my ears. Some people have said that he was going to be shot; according to other rumors, he would be sentenced to twenty-five years in prison. Some said he had been sent to Siberia, and that whilst he was on the plane he threw down a letter out of the window, and the letter landed right in the pan on which grandma Mayram (his mother) was baking a flat bread. In the letter, he had allegedly sworn that he would return one day to kill all his wife'sremaining relatives or else he would marry his own mother. Some people argued that, clearly, he had been executed a long time ago, when summer was at its hottest. There were many other rumors going around as well.

As a child, I would overhear these rumors from people's conversations held on the veranda of the mosque-shop, the place where many people gathered, always full of interesting gossip.

All one could say was that our Monkey was a creature who had arrived into the world as a descendant of that killer. By the way, following a mobile zoo coming to the village he truly became the Monkey. Before, he was known simply as Mumin or Mumin-the-tall; the son-of-a- bitch, or wait, no-no, Mumin-the-bald!

In fact, he was not even bald, as there wasn't a single bald spot on his head, and in fact his hair was curly as hell. Last year, when we went down to the Qo'shdaryo cotton fields, he, with his great lumbering figure, had only picked four kilos of "white gold" in the whole day. Back then, the staff would hold an evening meeting, and the PE teacher Orziqulov took him to a separate room. Inexorably, his teacher kicked him in the stomach with his boots, while firmly grabbing onto his curly hair. Nevertheless, the Monkey had not cried at all, nor had a single hair gone missing from his head.

For a long time after that, that 'brute of a teacher' (as the schoolchildren referred to him), Orziqulov, kept talking about it: "Although I beat him harshly, he said nothing ... he just stayed silent. It was as if he had a heart of stone. And his hair was as strong as a belt; I grabbed it, pulled at it, but no hair could be pulled out, just imagine!...I was a bit drunk at the time..."

However, the Monkey's interpretation was a little different. "Fuck him! It was actually me who beat him up! Didn't you see him walking strangely? I kicked him between his legs!"

* * *

Whether shiny bald, rugged bald or dimpled bald – all of them were suddenly under threat. A campaign was launched targeting all bald people and baldness in general, which was considered to be a vestige of past. The one who was going to build a communist society had to be completely perfect, healthy, and, if possible, curly-haired. (By the way, the king of the "great country" who introduced this idea was a shiny bald person himself. But no one would dare to challenge him and his head, or attempt to cure his lack of hair. In fact, that was impossible. Firstly, the king was too old. The baldness on his head was too and therefore cureless. Moreover, where would you find the equivalent of aunty Katya, who would put that aforementioned head between her legs and de-lice it? Even if you had found such a person, he or she would be sent to hell bald themselves.

Right in the middle of the lesson, either three or four doctors would enter a classroom, headed up by either the school principal or a medical official. No one would be able to run away, since a trap has been laid, with all four corners of the classroom covered. The doctors would walk through row by row, and check everyone's head one by one, seeing whether anyone has a scar, and if it is infectious. Whether anyone is bald. The doctors' assistant would write down everyone's family name. Finally, an ominous judgment would be pronounced. Those who are blacklisted would start weeping; some of them would try to run away while either the school principal or a medical official chased after them. Some would try to remain seated in their places, saying: "I am not going anywhere", while others pulled them out. In short, this scene would look like absolute Armageddon.

Five schoolchildren from our class had the illness. Even Rahima became bald. Poor girl, what would her blind grandma do all alone in that big orchard? Where did these lice infecting this girl's head come from? They may well have come from Mumin, her desk-mate. "Eh, eh, she is not bald, her head just looks like a field that's been reaped with a sickle," he giggled.

Those sentenced to the verdict of baldness were all taken to the hospital in a special vehicle without a single window. It's true that three or four days later, one of the bald schoolchildren, Sodiq, returned from the hospital. It turned out he was not bald; the scars on his head were not found to be infectious, so his head was greased with ointment and he was released.

Yet, we did not get to see the rest of our bald classmates in school for another two months. They were sent to the infectious diseases unit of the district hospital. It was impossible to approach that place, as it really smelt bad. If someone happened to as much as pass by that unit, a bad smell would accompany them for several days.

Fearing that the bald children would escape, while in the unit, they were always lined up according to their height and marched in a line. Anyone seeing them like that would have surely run away terrified. They could in theory pose a danger, as at times some of them would step out of the line, approach a passer-by and attempt to rub their head on the passerby's body, saying: "I'll infect you as well!"

The formerly bald children later informed us that they had their heads shaved with a blade, before being passed on to aunty Katya one by one. After a week or so, aunty Katya, a butch nurse with a giant behind, would rub a remedy on the kids' heads, plucking any infected hairs out with a special device, one at a time. Surely it must have been painful! So the process went something like this: firstly, aunty Katya would squeeze your head between her strong knees. Is that under the hem of her dress? Wow, isn't that cool? Could you see anything? Yet you would not be able to see anything, as you would be busy fearing for your life. Your legs would start twitching in agony; as your hair was being pulled out: very painful stuff indeed. You would start speaking Russian, yelling: "Enough, enough! I can't bear it anymore!"

"Bear with it a little longer, dear," aunty Katya would console you. Some kids would yell: "That's enough! Fuck off! Fuck you Aunty Katya, you and your big arse!" At some point you would notice a wet patch beneath your feet. What? Who did that? Was that aunty Katya? Whoever or whatever did it, you had to face the fact was that it was wet beneath your feet.

They say that bastard Mumin would try to put his hand up a certain place. Aunty Katya would then strike his head with her fist, saying: "Ugh, you asshole, take your hand away!" Mumin, the bloody rascal, would giggle: "It's too interesting, I can't help it."

The process of removing the infected hairs would have to take place two or three times, and then another balm would be rubbed all over the kids' heads, before they were bound up with cheesecloth. The end result would resemble a German soldier's cap. Once that cap dried out, new healthy hair would grow. In most cases, that hair would become curly.

Mumin left the hospital with curly hair, nevertheless, he remained, as he was called before, Mumin-the-bald!

* * *

It wasn't only Mumin: it was true that the rest of the kids who had passed 'through aunty Katya's legs' also grew thick and curly hair. By the way, in two months, out of those who could not speak Russian well at school, they all began to speak Russian very well. It was as if aunty Katya wasn't a nurse treating bald kids, but rather a Russian teacher. However, the nickname "baldy" remained with all of them regardless of their thick hair.

Thus, the campaign to eradicate baldness among schoolchildren was successfully completed. It had finished, yet that bad smell lingered forever, as if it had absorbed not only into the scalp, but also into the brain, from time to time emitting bad odor.

Moreover, the majority of formerly bald kids became somewhat characterless and merciless.

Thank God that the heads of the elderly remained untouched. Perhaps it was because they wanted to keep their hair as a mangy keepsake; or maybe they considered poor aunty Katya, who would not be able to handle taking care of everyone, despite her strength. Or maybe they were afraid that the summer productivity would go down, and the speed of building a bright future would fall; or maybe they wanted them to serve as a reminder of the peculiarities of the former times. It was true that the younger generation responsible for the future of communism (including Mumin-the-bald) had to be healthy, yet the elderly were the generation of days past, and they weren't going to be around for long. Therefore, using aunty Katya's smelly but potent remedy on the elderly was considered to be a waste.

However, according to some rumors, only Vahshiy Orziqulov, among the grown-ups, had used aunty Katya's services; an intensive procedure he undertook in his house, as he lived alone. Wearing sports clothing all year long, with his eyes bulging, constantly threatening to whack everyone around him with his fist: ever since, this PE teacher has become even more brutal and atrocious, which was clear evidence that he had really used aunty Katya's services.

It's true that the hair on his head was not as curly as Mumin's, but it was plain, smooth, always shiny and strong enough to make it impossible to pull a hair out of his head, even with pliers. That being said, there was no one who would dare to grab his hair and kick him in his stomach.

* * *

A mobile zoo came to our district after the district was dissolved and before Mumin-the-bald became the Monkey. People in the mosques and shops, and everywhere in general, thought that the zoo had been brought here as an inspiration or consolation.

The country needed cotton and plenty of it, or as they called it, "the white gold!" No one knew what was the main reason for this. Either the hard-working bald king of the country had nothing to do, or the country's treasury had run dry. In short, the king began to merge and unite districts and regions. Throughout this process, profitability was taken into account: a district or a region was deemed either 'with prospects' or 'without prospects', and naturally the ones without prospects, i.e. the ones which were state-dependent and sponging off the government were merged with the more profitable ones. The history or the origin of the dissolved areas, together with the people living within them, were just ignored regardless of whether they were with or without prospects. It was an approach that only considered profit, and nothing else. Let it be a billy-goat, as long as it gives milk. We needed milk!

And so, Jiydali District, the famous Jiydali that knew nothing about cotton and did not even want to learn anything new; the district full of chatter-boxes, and talented art-lovers who preferred to rest in teahouses and discuss political and social issues, was found to be sponging off and 'without prospects'. Therefore, it was merged with the avant-garde Qo'shdaryo District, founded in the vast wilderness ten or fifteen years ago, which delivered an abundance of caravans of white gold to the motherland's storehouses and was flourishing year after year.

Naturally, the administrative and management centers tended to spring up in such profitable places. A modern communist town called Dashtobod was chosen as the regional Center. The great trasfer to the Center had begun. All enterprises and organizations, big or small, began moving from Jiydali to Dashtobod. Great or small managers went after their respective managerial positions, and those who became redundant also moved there, or to other cotton-producing and profitable places.

Aunty Katya and her relatives, who had settled in this place long time ago, due to it being one of the most sought-after destinations, following the liquidation of the district also left Dashtobod and other affluent sites of residence for the regional center, as if they had been deprived of their food, sausages and butter.

Before they left, they played naughty European music and danced past midnight in her garden. This continued, until the quarrels at the cinema hall and all night promenades ceased, leaving the lively district as quiet as a graveyard.

In what had previously been a prosperous and crowded Jiydali, now only the elderly men and women and young children remained. There were several offices, yet only two government representatives in place: Avaz-the-police-officer and Sobir. They were relatives: an uncle and a nephew. All day long, the uncle would wait for the phone to ring in his office, whilst the nephew walked around the teahouse waiting for a quarrel, with the gun case dangling on his side stuffed full of cotton, instead of a pistol. That was it.

Only by late autumn, did the men who had left in search of harvest, return with some money tucked behind their belts. During that time, Jiydali would be revived again, with many people on the streets day and night, reminded of the past joyful and delightful times. When the winter passed, people would again leave for the cotton fields, and the village would be once more left in desolation, like a house where somebody had passed away.

The naturally proud residents of Jiydali could not bear such an injustice, and therefore kept writing complaints to Tashkent, Moscow and beyond. They were particularly active on the days following the announcement that districts would be merged. Both young and old were out in the streets day and night. Everyone was discontent and even furious. It looked like a picket line or a mourning procession. People could not bear the thought that a beautiful place like Jiydali has become dependent on the lowly Qo'shdaryo.

(More than forty years have passed since this story took place. As you may have noticed, I am referring back to that period in our history).

* * *

Our mosque-shop was one of the trendiest places to get together. The mosque was built in the center of a merchant neighborhood near a pond encircled by willow trees, and was consequently turned into a shop that sold various household goods. So people gave it this name: the mosque-shop. One could not call it just a 'mosque,' since it did not look like a mosque or a sacred place, but had a wide terrace with ancient engraved columns. One also was afraid to call it just a 'shop,' since Koranic verses had been recited there in the past and at one timeit was a sacred place. So the easiest and safest solution was to simply refer to it as the 'mosque-shop.'

The terrace that opened up into the street was always full of people. There, from early spring till the days grew cold, you would find the local neighborhood elders: Soli-the-screamer, Ahad-the-Sufi, Ismoil-the-shoemaker, Rajab-the-dark and the rest of them, all wearing long robes; all of them perpetually sitting down on either the lumpy pressed cotton, the hump-backed scales, the colorless crates or the tea-boxes, debating and discussing complicated issues. The destiny of Jiydali, along with the rest of the world, was decided in those debates.

Of course, the debaters and negotiators all spoke with each other rather philosophically. There was only one preachy character there, who had never sat down, and who would never ever sit down, and who was always pacing up and down the terrace. Yes, he was no ordinary human being, but a real character. Whenever he spoke about something, he usually referred to himself by saying "my persona" or "with regards to my persona." He resembled a fairytale forest dweller. Actually, his name was Urmon-the-dwarf. Although everyone reproached him, nicknaming him "writer-provocateur," Urmon-the-dwarfwas a sharp-witted and disagreeable former correspondent of the district newspaper. Unfortunately, when the two districts were merged, the newspapers' editorial board was moved to the home of his opponents – Dashtobod – and this energized correspondent became jobless. As he would later explain it himself, he "decided never to leave Jiydali, since he was a true patriot."

It was known that a jobless person's job was to fight for justice until they have given their every last drop of blood to the cause, that is, until death. So, Urmon-the-dwarfwas one of those who diligently followed that particular principle.

"What a pity that such a wonderful and beautiful place, which was once praised in folk songs, has become a home for nobody but owls! I simply cannot tolerate this! I cannot bear it as a human being! And neither as an individual!" announced Urmon solemnly.

He was indeed a very interesting person. He was incredibly short, but possessed great zeal. When he walked, he raised his head up high, marching like a soldier with his arms swaying by his side, and ever advancing with an aura of greatness, as though he were a general. Although he had never been aunty Katya's client, the hair on his head was a little curly. He always had four fountain-pens lined up in his chest pocket, wandering around as if he was ready to write down anything at any moment with the fifth pen that he held in his hand.

Those who did not know him would most likely think he was stupid. I also felt that maybe he was a little absent-minded and knew him to be occasionally drunk. You would never see him depressed. If you scolded him openly, he would just smile. Do you really think a healthy man would behave like that?

"Keep your words in check, correspondent!" Soli shouted at him loudly, with his owl-like eyes and deep voice. "What do you mean by owls? Why do you call it abandoned? What owl? Where is this owl; show me, where?"

"Ah, you red-skinned commoners! You are so simple-hearted, Soli-boy!" giggled Urmon-the-dwarf. "Don't you know what an exaggeration is? It's a metaphor," he explains.

"You, put your scholastic words into your pocket! Whom are you calling red? Whom do you mean?!" looking at what he was writing, the yellow-skinned Soli-the-screamer continued, turning completely red.

"Actually, it was all you, Urmon-boy, who kept writing anonymous letters and destroying our Jiydali," Ahad-mahsum butted in, coming drunk out of the shop after gulping down a bottle of wine.

* * *

An ordinary thief would target one house at a time and burglar one place after another, right? But that particular night the cries were heard coming from all four corners of Jiydali:

"Stop him!"

"Get him!"

"Don't let him get away, quickly, run!"

From now on, this would take place every night. Everywhere you looked, there was panic; suddenly everyone was talking about it and since the thief had also paid a visit to our house, I got to glimpse him with my own two eyes. Normally, our neighbourhood is fairly peaceful, but after the thief had combed through yet another nearby village, we heard that he mainly targeted houses that didn't have any men present. Alright, we thought, let him come then, but what did he take? Nothing. He just came by to frighten us and make fun of us, that's all. Thieves are rather interesting people, aren't they?

Now, these thieves were very strange indeed. Actually, one couldn't really call them thieves. Even if you wanted to call them thieves, they were too harmless and positive to contend for that title. What they did was very curious indeed: they would turn over the lids on the pots or shake down all the apples from a tree and gather them in all one place, or they would even cut open a watermelon, yet not touch a single slice. They would wake a person up by pulling off their blanket only to cover another person with it. Once even, they stood up on the roof and urinated over a villager's garden, yet in the morning people discovered the garden had been ploughed with a hand hoe.

So now, every morning, in place of their usual greetings, the villagers would exchange their stories with one another:

"Yesterday, in our house…"

"Two days ago, in our neighbour's house…"

"This morning, I discovered…"

What else could they do? All the able-bodied men of Jiydali had left to make a living someplace else and only the old and disabled men and women and children had stayed back in the village. So what could they do?

Moreover, these mischievous thieves were most definitely interested in visiting houses where only the women remained. As darkness fell, people would anxiously make their way home. Even when everyone retreated to their beds for the night, they would grab a long stick to take with them and fall asleep while holding on to it with both hands for protection; while others chose to keep a pitchfork by their bedside. Still others resorted to having a rest in the daytime and just like watchmen did not go to sleep at night. Mothers frightened their children into obedience by saying: "Look, the thief is coming!"

In short, these thieves had brought a sense of danger to daily life in Jiydali. But the two local officials were minding their own business. Uncle Policeman would go to bed early in the evening, resting his head on his loaded revolver. Whereas the nephew policeman would tap on the revolver case on his hip to check if it was still there, and then run home, for he had a young family to attend to.

One night everyone heard Soli-the-Screamer's victorious shout:

"Ugh, you thieving rascal, I got you!"

Well done, Uncle Soli, well done!

The latter was the fittest and the strongest person in our entire neighbourhood. Truly a giant; all muscle and a rough man indeed. So, we naturally expected that he would definitely dispatch of the thief right away. Jiydali was all set to celebrate this momentous occasion! However, only a moment later the village once again grew quiet. It was only the following day that we discovered the details of the encounter during the discussion that took place in the area next to the mosque-shop.

"I grabbed him by his clothes, but he managed to get away," Soli-the-Screamer raised his voice: "He looked like a spook or an old hag and he was way hairy!"

"Yes, yes!" someone pitched in. "He looked like a monkey, just like the monkeys that came here once with the travelling zoo!"

"Is it possible that some of them were left behind?" someone enquired.

"It was only four monkeys that ever came here, Hamro-boy!"

"Anyway, I fought him, but wasn't able to hold on to him in the end," the hero of the discussion proceeded impatiently. "So he jumped over the wall and ran away. And what a high wall it was! It took Egam-the-builder, nearly one month to build that wall. My God! The thief had something on his feet, I heard it squeak, like springs or something. Otherwise, it would be completely impossible for him to jump over that wall! Ugh, you rascal, if only I could lay hands on you again!.."

"It can be done," said Ismoil-the-hat-maker, who spent even more time hanging out at places to do with the war since the war has ended. "It's possible that the Secret Service has been conducting some sort of special training." People suddenly felt alarmed by this news.

"The Secret Service?!" said Rajab-the-dark, completely at a loss. "How could they do their training and get us all into a state of panic like this? Why haven't they informed us in advance?"

The hat-maker smiled. "Why would they inform you? They would no longer be a Secret Service, if they informed people!"

"That's so weird, why would they choose Jiydali of all places for such training? Do they think we're a training ground? Why they did not go to Qo'shdaryo for that?"

"They may have considered this a suitable place, since it's all the way up in the mountains."

"Let's just call it what it is: it's a godforsaken place, along with all of its residents!" said Urmon-the-dwarf appearing from out of nowhere all of sudden. "So, we will write about it!"

No one else commented. Grave silence fell upon the crowd.

After sometime, a man in robes, called Ismat, enquired:

"Soli-boy, did he say anything while you were strangling him?"

"Hmmm, I can only remember hearing his shoes squeak, I can't recall anything else."

"Well, that's interesting, because when he came to our house, I heard him say: 'Gooli-gooli.' I don't know what it means."

"You could've misheard it, Ismat-boy."

"No, I clearly heard him saying that: 'Gooli-gooli!'"

"Forgive me please, if I am mistaken, but could it have been the name of one of the women in your house, perhaps?"

"Firstly, we do not have any "Gul-pul," we only have Halima and Salima in my house!" Ismat-boy replied angrily, taking offence. "Also, it wasn't just me who's heard it. For example, Hamro-boy also heard him saying that at his house. Could you please confirm?"

"Yes, that's right," said Hamro-boy.

"'Gooli-gooli?' It sounds like an Uzbek word," said Ahmad-makhsum. "Would the Secret Service people be Uzbeks?"

A young man wearing a military uniform who has recently returned from his army service joined in the conversation:

"Maybe he used "h" instead of "g?" In Russian it means…"

"Yes, that's enough, young man, we know what that means. We too were once soldiers like you," replied Soli-the-Screamer.

Urmon-the-dwarf, who used his bag for a chair and was sat in the corner, busily writing something without interfering in the discussion, suddenly stood up and began to read out loud:

"Moscow. Kremlin. To the First Secretary of the Central Committee of the Communist Party, a close friend of Jiydali, dear comrade Nikita Ser..."

"We know the beginning by heart, Urmon-boy, read what you have written at the end," said Soli-the-Screamer impatiently.

The correspondent paid no attention to it and without any offense he read out the ending:

"... in addition to annexation, they also sent in thieves and spies to us..."

The sound of horse hoofs and neighing resounded from the cobbled road. It was our Daddy Shuro! He was going to stop by for a moment and then "return home victorious, having defeated the enemy".

Ever since that day Jiydali was filled with talk of 'Gooli-gooli'. People started saying 'Gooli-gooli' instead of greeting each other, and instead of saying good-bye. Everyone in the village, young and old, was equally involved in using it.

* * *

During those hot summer days, as the fairy-tale thief terrorised Jiydali, many surprising things happened one after another.

Starting with myself: bride-Olma became aware of the fact that I was afraid of cats; I captured the Monkey when he behaved like a monkey; then the poet and I were both deprived of our beloved; Musallam eloped with the newbie drummer and Egam-the-poor became Egam-the-rich in a blink of an eye.

Even I, myself, doubted that all those things took place that particular summer. They may all have happened somewhat earlier or later, but it was an undeniable fact that they had all taken place. The only joyful and positive thing among those was the fact that Egan-the-poor became Egam-the-rich.

Egam-the-poor was the poorest person in the village. According to the classification of our friend Mahmud, Egam found himself at the very bottom of the list. And so, this person had become a rich man overnight (later, he once again went to being poor, but that is another story). Egam-the-poor became Egam-boy (Egam-the-rich) not at night but during the day or to be even more precise, in the evening when he came back home exhausted after his workshift. He won an automobile "Volga" on a thirty-kopeck lottery ticket that cashier Zina forcefully handed to him, adding it to his pay in place of some change!

Everyone in the village knew each other, but only his few relatives and neighbors really knew Egam-the-poor. He was an ordinary builder working on a construction site. As a poor newcomer, he also was an outcast: since he only had a tiny room with a corridor to his name; outside which he stood his colt on a small piece of land with several apple-trees growing on it.

Oh, sorry, he also had one more apple in his house: Olma[20]-the-bride, a rosy cheeked, mischievous yet beautiful woman. (She actually had a different name; it's just that my grandmother used to call her by that name, hoping to one day have such a beautiful daughter-in- law). And there was one more apple – a young girl, Egam's daughter.

She featured in another story of how a beautiful lady became the wife of a twisted 'dwarf' of a person. It remains their secret and we don't want to know about it.

So in short, one day this man won a "Volga". In the village, there were only a few people who had ever seen such a car make. The famous Shepherd only had one vaguely similar to it.

However, this long-awaited "Volga" never reached the house of Egam-the-poor (since he had no gate that would allow the car to get through) and so it went directly to the house of Qodir-the-rat.

Qodir-the-rat was a warehouse overseer of the village administration. He had everything but the "Volga" in the warehouse. There were many rats in it. But Qodir-the-rat was the biggest one.

Prior to the car entering his house, the Rat and Egam-the-poor had to become like brothers. This is how it was done: first, the warehouseman invited the poor man as a guest to his house, culled a sheep and entertained him very well, even giving him a robe as a gift and as a sign of his goodwill. If anyone had wanted to investigate, everyone would somehow be found to be related

---

20 Olma - apple

to each other. However, despite all their best efforts it was impossible to find any common ground between Qodir-the-rat and Egam-the-poor, since one of them originally came from a mountainous area and the other one from the steppe. They also spoke different dialects. So, what could we do? Nothing! Egam became the younger brother and the Rat became the elder brother. They both wanted this, that's it! Does the elder brother have a right to give something as a gift to his younger brother? Yes, Of course. It's a personal issue indeed. No objections at all! If so, no wonder if the younger brother Egam-the-poor presented his "Volga" to the elder brother Qodir-the-rat, right?

Encountering such great respect being paid to him for the first time, poor Egam (now Egam-boy or Egam-the-rich) had drunk too much at that goodwill party. At midnight, when the Rat, disgusted with Egam-boy, asked him to leave to return to his own house, "the newborn younger brother" was pleased to say to his "elder brother": "How about I spend one night in my elder brother's house?" So they reluctantly let him sleep on the outdoor tea platform, the supa.

Having gained an elder brother, Egam-the-poor completely changed: he started wearing a beautiful skullcap and a suit and began looking as handsome as he could, strutting proudly down the street. Hence he became Egam-boy (Egam-the-rich), blessed by God!

Now, Olma-khon had also changed: she began resembling Musallam, the former daughter-in-law of Daddy Shuro. It was funny: she shook her head strangely as she walked, half turning her cheek at people, as if she was upset with everybody.

Living in such a small house was not befitting for this vainly stylish couple. Our close neighbors, they both felt ashamed of living here, so not long after they bought a big house at the end of the village, at the apple orchard. I was even more happy than them about it. Thank goodness, I will not have to see that arrogant rich person now. The matter was settled...

* * *

While messing up the life of the entire village, that jerk of a thief for some reason never came to our house. At nights my younger brother and I kept watch for him, taking turns; but he never turned up! With every subsequent day while all the children got "presents" from each other for telling their stories about the thief, we couldn't say anything and had to remain silent. This sometimes really got to us.

So one of those days, as I arrived and sat down exhausted on the terrace after bringing hay from the mountain having gone out there with my friends, my mom said to me:

"Sonny, how about you sleep tonight at bride Olma's? Her husband went down to Qo'shdaryo to build a wall. She is a young woman and might be afraid of staying alone at night."

Though we had been neighbors for three or four years now, I always hesitated to approach this woman because she stared at me every time I saw her.

"Oh, no, she has got a cat!" I tried to object.

"Come on, little brother, come on, don't be shy. I will put the cat in the barn!"

I saw bride-Olma smiling at me through the hole in the wall. So I could not fabricate another excuse. In the evening, I unwillingly went to her house.

She prepared an iron bed under the apple-tree for me. As for her, she was going to sleep on the supa platform, together with her daughters. I entered their house and went straight to bed. I was really tired, so pretty soon I fell fast asleep.

In the middle of the night I felt something plump brushing against my face and I immediately woke up. Was that a cat? Someone was breathing quickly. I caught a scent of fragrance.

"Don't tell anyone, sweetie, I love you."

"Eh, go away!" I replied, shivering.

I was going to get up and go home, but what would I say to my mom? Yet I was afraid that something bad would happen again if I stay. Too frightened by what had happened, I did not close my eyes until the dawn. The cat in the barn mewed until morning.

After that, every time without fail, upon seeing me, bride-Olma would give me a chilly stare, as if I were a freak. I also ran away from her as if she were a cat I was annoyed with for jumping me in the face.

By the way, that very night those infamous thieves finally broke into our house. My younger brother was asleep when they came. They shook the pear-tree at the end of our garden and gathered all the pears in one place. Also, all of the pears got bitten into. The following day, when I boasted, telling the children about them, Mahmud became aggravated:

"Nonsense! It's not the thief, it's the doings of the Monkey, our very own Monkey. Several days ago our neighbors panicked saying that he came to our house and made rustling sounds. Later, we found out that my aunty went out at night."

He may've been right. His aunty was blind, but she was able to freely move across the yard using the cable they hung up especially for her.

One night, as I returned from the cinema-hall having watched the Indian movie entitled The vagabond for the tenth or eleventh time, I saw a shadow sliding down our neighbor's wall. My heart stopped beating. The Thief! What should I do? Do I need to yell?

Before I raised my voice the shadow approached me and squeezed my throat:

"Gooli-gooli! If you tell someone about me I will kill you! I just wanted to eat an apple, since this neighbor of yours has a good apple-tree."

Oh My God! It was the Monkey! Our very own Monkey!

If I am not mistaken, the exact same thing happened on the same night when Egam-boy was left to sleep on the supa of his "elder brother's" house.

* * *

Who knows why, perhaps as a result of so many letters of complaint written by Urmon-the-dwarf, or maybe because some good person decided to entertain the people of Jiydali who have been spending their nights facing up to danger for such a long time, in any case, a famous singer from the Kitob District who played tor, a musical instrument, by propping it up against his shoulder, came to our village one day. He gave a big concert at the central club. The drummer accompanying the singer was also a funny kind of guy, playing his tambourine drum in a rather curious way: one moment putting it on its left side, the next moment moving it to the right and then holding and playing it in front the moment after. From time to time he threw the tambourine up to the sky or laid it down flat resting on his finger and spun the tambourine around as if it were a globe.

As he performed, it was not entirely clear how this disabled drummer managed to spot the rope-like braid of a local beauty watching the performance. Her hair was indeed rather long: it caught the drummer's attention while he was on stage, although it originated from somewhere in one of the front rows. The drummer simply hypnotised the people of Jiydali with his performance and must have captivated the beauty too. As a musician, he really was able to do that.

It was plain to see that he had fallen in love. In the meanwhile, he tried not to stare back at the beauty and her long hair, but he could not contain himself either. It was as if this pretty girl's very long plait had ensnared his heart. She was indeed such a beauty, that many people in Jiydali were in love with her. Following this encounter, Musallam-the-long-plait left for the Kitob District together with the crippled tambourine-player.

This daughter of Nurmat-the-newcomer was truly the most beautiful girl in our Bozorboshi neighborhood. When she passed by in the street having painted her eyebrows with "osma" and walking ever so elegantly, all the men sitting at the mosque-shop would stop their discussions for a moment and fall silent;

it seemed that everyone felt a similar emotion stir in their hearts. Oh, what a beauty she was! Her two side plaits cascading down her back were so long that they swept the floor; and the rest of the hair just followed in their stead. This was our Musallam-the-long-hair!

Swayed by the virtue of her hair, last year Daddy Shuro got his son Amalbek to marry Musallam. However, this young man neither valued her long hair nor could make it grow any longer and within a month Musallam-the-long-hair left him, returning to her father's house. Yet they did not get a divorce, since both of them hoped that they would reunite again.

Having heard the bad news about Musallam-the-long-hair, Daddy Shuro's old lady, his wife, cursed her son, who at the time was drinking vodka with his friend sat upstairs on the second floor:

"Shame on you! It would be better for you, if you had hanged yourself!"

Later, when she came back after visiting her neighbors, she was approached by a shaking, sobbing Amalbek emerging from the shed:

"The rope snapped in half, mum... Do you have another rope?"

So when our Daddy Shuro, who "returned home victorious, having defeated the enemy" entered the house, having tied his horse by the gate, he saw a group of women encircling his wife at a small pond under a tree. The women were trying to stop his aged wife, begging her:

"Please, dear, don't!"

The women then proceeded to pull Daddy Shuro's wife out of the pond, but she once again struggled free, set on drowning herself:

"No, leave me alone, leave me to drown! I was disgraced, neighbors! What if Dad hears about it?"

Daddy Shuro, who had heard about Musallam earlier while out on the street, watched them for a while and then let his wife to do what she wanted:

" Let her go for it, leave her alone and let's see what she's will do." The frightened and embarrassed old woman leapt into the water. The women screamed. In panic, the old woman tried to step back, raising her hands, as she got soaked, her face and clothes were wet though and through, she looked around and at a loss, stood up right in the middle of the pond. The water only came up to her waist. Feeling even more embarrassed by having witness this ridiculous scene, Daddy Shuro threw away his dignity and angrily shook his fist at her. As he raised his whip, he shouted: "Come out of the water, bitch! I heard that Musallam's stupid mother also got wet trying to go down into the water; do you want people to say the same about you?!" (In the lingo of people of Jiydali, 'getting wet' stood for the shameful act of adultery.)

At that time, spoiled Amalbek, who was playing cards with his friend, popped out his head from the second floor window and shouted:

"Hey, dad, what did you say? Whose wife got wet? Whose mom went into the water? Mum, hey, mum, be careful, there are bits of broken glass under your feet!"

A week later, Musallam-the-long-hair returned from Kitob District. According to the rumors, the tambourine player turned out to have a wife and four children. The-long-hair made an excuse saying that she "went to try to get into university, but could not become a student." No one asked her, "Did you really go to university in August, Musallamkhon?" However, it became clear to everyone: this newcomer's daughter with her beautiful figure and long hair, who used to be carefree, was fed up with the fresh air of Jiydali and would not stay here much longer; she would one day leave this village for good.

* * *

That day, the usual discussion at the mosque-shop started with a harsh critique of Musallam- the-long-hair's great grandma who also "got wet" and ended with Amalbek who "looked like a man." Then, they discussed all the reasons why the number of such women had increased in Jiydali village over the past years, although the place was originally was full of faithful people. In the end, they all concluded that "the water we are drinking now" was the reason for all these misfortunes.

"The water in the river becomes clean as it flows from rock to rock, but ours doesn't... This might also have an effect," said Ahad-mahsum.

"Maybe that is why the government had merged us with Qo'shdaryo without informing us," tried to guess Rajab-the-dark.

"True, the government never informs anyone. They just get on with their work without letting anyone know".

"Yes, their water is way better. It is because their water flows freely and does not make people sick from drinking it," suggested Safar-the-nos-maker whose daughter married a man in Qo'shdaryo.

Soli-the-Screamer   got angry with his words:

"Don't say that, Safarqul, your forefathers had all drank this water too. Or do you really think that it's only nowadays that this water has started making people crazy? Remember, yours is not spring water either, it is full of bits of tobacco and ashes!"

"Some strange people were seen at the beginning of Qo'rg'ondaryo river. They did not look like geologists searching for minerals," said one of the men wearing a robe. "It seems that they added something to our water."

"Who? Who was that, adding something?" Soli-the-Screamer angrily enquired again. At that moment he was ready to bring those strangers to account by stringing them up with a rope.

"Who else? Of course, it's them!"

"Who are they?"

"Don't you know them? You know them!"

In fact, everyone, including newborn babies in Jiydali knew who "they" really were.

"Yes, you are right! This is what they have done!" said Soli-the-Screamer, finally calming down.

This was the case every single time: the residents of Qo'shdaryo were always to blame for everything, even for a cloud untimely appearing in the sky. (Having listened in on the discussion I was now afraid of drinking water and restrained myself for several days, drinking cold tea only. I thought this would cause me less harm and I would not behave strangely as a result.)

"I am ready to go, it's time to pray now," said Ahad-mahsum as he stood up. "What time is it, Nabi-boy?"

Nabi-boy was not even able to check his watch, since Soli-the-Screamer got angry again:

"Hey, Ahad-mahsum, take a seat. How can you trust the clock in Jiydali? Don't believe it!"

That day, the minutes of the meeting were not announced, since the person who would normally write them down and then loudly read them out and who happened to disobey the officers – both the uncle and the nephew - was taken to Qo'shdaryo by a special group of policemen, who beat him up and demanded that he stops writing letters of complaint. Some people say he was put away in solitary confinement and was kept there without food and water.

"He would not stop writing while in there either. His only aim was to write a complaint about the Head of police."

"The Head of police must have taken revenge on him, that's why he was taken away and put in jail."

Rahmon Bolta stood up slowly, shook out the edge of his robe and concluded sharply:

"He was the only person in Jiydali who was alive!"

"So what will happen to all those letters that we have written to Kremlin?" murmured someone from the same group.

* * *

I am not aware of other things, but in our Jiydali, in those times, there was no such thing as "loving each other", someone "falling in love" with someone, or "getting married". It seemed, such notions were considered utterly fictional. Moreover, any adventures normally described in books could happen maybe somewhere else in some remote country but not in the orderly and honest Jiydali, for sure. In Jiydali, where only the simple-hearted people lived, if for example someone overheard that two people had feelings for each other, both the girl and the boy would turn red-faced, as if they had done something wrong. It was totally different when someone "gave their heart to the other person," or "a man liked a woman, and hence wanted to marry her" or vise versa – that was acceptable. Once they got married, they would live a long life together.

I remember well that the screen mechanic Sayfi-the-trendy was the first person in Jiydali who got involved in a "love story." Leaving his beautiful wife and his two children behind, he fell in love with the crimson-lipped Flyura, who lived in the "newcomers' house" on the central street. As the villagers got to know about it, they would wait for them to stroll down the village streets, in order to see what it means to "fall in love".

I too saw them with my own eyes: these lovers walked down the central street together hand in hand. They did not pay attention to anyone and arrogantly strolled on: Sayfi-the-trendy looking up the sky and Flyura, with her crimson lips. As if they wanted to say, "Look, villagers, we love each other very much!" I remember our neighbor Sattor-the-coppersmith saying: "My God, does he think someone would snatch away his lady? Does he think that it is not love unless you grab hold of each other's hand, oh my gosh!"

It is true that not long after, Sayfi-the-trendy returned back home into the bosom of his beautiful wife and two children, since the lady with crimson lips had fallen in love with another man, an auditor from the same region.

In our school, the schoolchild who popularized this fairy-tale feeling of love was our Poet friend! (Of course, at the time he was a young and rather green poet.) Obviously, even before him, schoolboys used to write secret love letters which included love poems and in return the schoolgirls used to embroider the first letter of their own name and the name of their loved one (for instance like this: "E" – "M") on the two opposite corners of a beautiful handkerchief, decorating it with beads. Later the girls would present the handkerchiefs to their loved ones. But our Poet acted frankly in this matter, he did not keep it secret that he loved. He was a real poet! He had no one, before whom he would feel embarrassed or no-one to be afraid of, since his father passed away when he was a very young child. So, who do you think he fell in love with? You wouldn't believe it – it was our Russian teacher, the charming Natalya Dmitrievna! To our Poet it seemed that she was Natasha Rostova[21]!

'Natasha Rostova' was an 18 or 19-year-old young lady, who, prior to her graduation from a teaching college, in the spirit of that time, was "banished" from faraway Poltava to a remote country on a mission to teach the mother-tongue of Pushkin and Tolstoy to the locals. As soon as she arrived at our school, both teachers and schoolboys fell hopelessly in love with her.

---

21) Translator's note: Natasha Rostova is a central fictional character in Leo Tolstoy's novel *War and Peace*.

It was clear that while all these lovers were keeping their secret hidden in their hearts, none of them would dare to openly speak about it. Only the Poet was like an open book and could reveal his secret. He was a true Poet indeed! Others did not write poems, or even if they had written any, they were not true poets. Coincidentally, Natasha Rostova loved reading poems very much. So the two poetry-lovers found each other very quickly.

As for us, the rest of the lovers, we were forced to desperately wait for Saturday to arrive. The Russian language and literature club used to take place in our school on Saturday evenings and go on till late night, making the most of the light emanating from the ceiling of cashier's office at the cinema. Drawing shut the tips of the raised collar of her red coat and turning her face towards the falling snow, bare-headed Natasha Rostova used to expressively recite poems by Sergey Yesenin for our benefit:

I do not regret, and I do not shed tears,
For all, like the haze of apple-trees, must pass.
Turning gold, I'm fading, it appears,
I will never be young again, alas.

As we all intently listened to her, we did not pay any attention to the poem or the melody, but instead allowed ourselves to be charmed by the voice of the girl reading the poem, her pretty mannerisms and her pure joy that resembled that of a little girl.

Oh, could we find those times now? No way!
Turning gold, I'm fading, it appears,
I will never be young again, alas.

And then...

* * *

Once we became second-year university students, we returned to the village for our winter holidays. One evening, as we were coming back from a party, all of a sudden, the Poet stopped in his tracks outside the white building on the central street, known as "the newcomers' house."

"Natasha is no longer here," he lamented, as he wept. "Natasha is no longer here; my friend, you know how much I loved her."

Both of us were drunk and we just stood there under the low canopy of the cashier's office at the cinema. Snow was falling from the sky indifferently, as if it had witnessed such tears and wailing many a time before. The white houses across the road looked washed out in the mist. There was no light in the windows of the room underneath the old mulberry-tree where Natasha Rostova had lived in the previous year.

Last winter, the fatherless and modest Poet came to Natasha Rostova's house armed with five volumes of books by Yesenin that he had bought using his savings from his student grant in order to present them to her and upon his arrival he discovered a half-naked Orziqulov, the sport teacher there. Natasha Rostova, as the hostess, attempted to behave with propriety but it was obvious that she was embarrassed. So she disappeared to the kitchen, in order to fry some fish, leaving the Poet and Orziqulov alone. Faced with such an awkward situation, the Poet drank mixed alcohol toasting to "the success of our students" and soon became drunk. He hardly remembers what happened after that. He did however remember well the scene at the doorstep: Natasha Rostova asking him to leave, saying good-bye and expressing her desire to meet again. When he came to his senses, the Poet found himself under the old mulberry tree, covered with snow. He could not remember who insulted whom or who beat whom up. What he did remember was that Orziqulov, a brutal man, threatened him by saying "What are you doing here, fuck off!"

This was a new turn of events for me. Being arrogant and fairly proud, our Poet has never spoke a word of his inner anguish to anyone. Even if he did share it, he would never admit his lost and pitiful state. But this time he would spill everything, without holding back.

A lover, drawing from his poetic core, he proceeded to openly share with me what was in his mourning heart.

But I, wondering about his story, couldn't even open my mouth about another secret I was afraid of telling anyone. I really did not want to add more suffering to his sorrow. Moreover, that was my own secret that I couldn't share with anyone else.

…At the end of the summer, on the eve preceding the new school term, the sixth-form students were called in to help with repairing our school. We whitewashed and painted the walls. However, the main purpose of the school visit for me was to see Natasha Rostova, who for some reason had arrived from her motherland earlier than planned. All of us had sorely missed her during the summer holidays.

After chatting with my friends at the pond, for some reason I wanted to go to our classroom. As I walked through the half-lit corridor and approached the classroom, I saw a woman with bulging eyes who opened the door as I walked past. She was holding a pail in one hand and a mop in the other. I still remember that as she passed by me she gave me a strange look.

As I opened the door, I was shocked to the core by what I saw. At first, I thought they were beating each other up... I was afraid of closing the door and quickly squeezed back behind it. I was shaking as I had seen something awkward and I didn't know how to react.

There was a mess in the classroom and a strange voice and whisper.

"Don't touch, please!"

"Will you give me an excellent mark, Natashka?"

"You're such a stupid guy, couldn't you find another time to talk about it?"

Natasha Rostova and our Monkey were there, in the classroom all by themselves!

For some reason I recalled people talking at the zoo:

"These monkeys do this thing in broad daylight, but human beings do it at night."

"Yes, that is why they are called monkeys."

"Well, human beings too can act like monkeys sometimes..."

That time the Monkey and Natasha Rostova were indeed acting like monkeys!

I don't remember how I found my way back to the pond. The children were still listening to Mahmud's story, who was enthusiastically telling them about the movie he had watched the day before: a man did this and a woman this. No one noticed my return, however.

Sometime later, the Monkey came out of the school, hopping along. He was in a good mood!

"Gooli-gooli!"

"Fuck you!" I exclaimed suddenly.

"Why? What have I done to you, man?"

I quickly rose to my feet and began hitting him. But the Monkey choked me and whacked me on my ear.

"Have it your way!"

Uh! O-o-o-o-oh! As I lay down at the very pond, all covered in dust, for the first time I realized that I've just witnessed one of the bitter truths of this world in action. The good grapes are usually the lot of a dog, aren't they? But why is this?

Eventually, a man will get used to the fact that good girls will not always become the destiny of good men. So now, whenever I see a beautiful girl, I recall that bitter truth and wonder: whose lot is she going to be? So here I was, lying down and wondering if any girl would ever look at me.

After that, whenever I saw Natasha Rostova, I felt uneasy and would try to run away, yet inside I still felt a longing to see her, in order to experience that bitter pain time and time again and find myself running away from her again and again.

I stopped attending the Russian literature club. Natasha Rostova then also began to teach other classes and not only us anymore. I heard from other schoolchildren that our "unfaithful" teacher had praised the Monkey saying "he was the strongest of them all!"

Unfortunately the children were not aware of the story I was aware of. I have never shared that story with anyone, not even with the Poet!

But whenever I recalled it, I always wondered: what was the cleaning lady doing there? Why did she look at me with her strange bulging eyes? Why did she pass by me without saying anything? That was another mystery altogether!

...Having calmed down a bit, the Poet began to recite a poem:

I stared at your photo in deep torment,

Remembering those times we had spent...

Oh, I realized at that moment:

Love can make one happy or unfortunate.

"Did you write this poem just now?" I asked him amazed. "This is so good! Do you have her photo with you?" That time I also wished to see her face.

"No, this is from my poem entitled "Where are you, my sixteen-year-old?" replied the Poet. You couldn't tell if he was boasting or being humble. We stared at her face on our group photo. She was pictured there with her head tilted to the side. Then, our Poet's old feelings resurfaced again and he asked if we can go and see the room where Natasha Rostova used to live. However, I firmly objected to him doing that and took him home instead.

... Later we had learned all the details from our schoolmate, "Patriot of Jiydali," who did not leave to study with us, choosing instead to stay in the village.

One day, the playful Gulbibi, whom Daddy Shuro cursed because she got together with Vahshiy (Brutal) Orziqulov, found out about her husband's unfaithfulness and came down to Natasha Rostova's house. Finding them in bed together, she smashed up all the doors and windows in poor Natasha's house.

Gulbibi, who had been brought up as a true Komsomol22 member, did not stop there.

To cut the long story short, the charming young lady, resembling a beautiful gazelle, who came to us all the way from a distant country to promote Yesenin's poetry, was finally blacklisted and banished from the district, carrying the sack with her belongings over her shoulder.

Where is she now, that beautiful teacher who had entertained us as teenagers? Though I had never proclaimed it like the Poet, I had also loved her with all of my heart!

... You would probably think, what a dishonourable ending to this first love story between these two lovers. Don't be too quick to jump to conclusions, because this love story has an even more sorrowful continuation to it. The Poet himself told it to me several years later with great enthusuasm. Indeed, he

---

22 Komsomol – a communist youth organisation

spoke about it with great excitement! Because by now the feelings of love that we had felt in our youth had departed and all the old pains had been healed.

In connection with a certain anniversary of Pushkin's epic poem entitled "Poltava", according to tradition, young poets from around the "boundless country", who recited their poems while beating their chests, were to gather in Poltava City for a literature festival. Our Poet, who was a little more known by that time, was also on the list of invitees. Upon hearing about Poltava City, his heart began to overflow with sweet anticipation. Before his departure to Poltava, he searched through his old notebooks and in one of them found a piece of paper. It was an address, handwritten by the "teacher in the red coat" during a poetry reading dedicated to Yesenin.

"This is my sister's address. When you become a great poet you can visit us." she told him. And so, his dream came true. When the Poet reached Poltava, instead of attending poetry readings dedicated to Pushkin, he looked for the teacher of his childhood, walking through the streets of that city. Finally, he reached an old-looking place on the outskirts of the city and walked up to the second floor of a two-storey building. An older woman opened the door and after greeting him and wiping her hands on her apron she said:

"Haven't you seen her? You've just missed her. Yes, us sisters, we live together. She did not marry. She works at the post office and no longer teaches. She has just gone out. If you run quickly you can still catch up with her."

But the Poet was not in a rush. Earlier he'd seen a woman pass him by. She gave him a strange look as she walked. So the Poet tried to leave this place as soon as possible. Perhaps, the poor lady whom destiny has turned into an ugly woman had also recognized him and since she did recognise him, she took her chance to run away? The Poet laughed out loud that time, saying: "There was no one there to ask me: 'What about yourself? Just look at your own face in the mirror!'"

You would probably wonder how a poem is usually written? Here is a new poem idea for you. It should be called "The poem about obsolete love."

* * *

The village suddenly fell silent: either the thieves have grown tired or the villagers have become exhausted from talking about them. Yet still, somewhere in the village, on some nights, rumours would emerge about the thieves, but they were not serious and proved to be just an echo of the old panic.

It seemed everyone in the village was bored, because everyone has gotten used to hearing about thieves on a regular basis. After all, the thieves were not harmful, they just sometimes frightened the people a little bit.

In the mosque-shop, people specifically discussed this issue: "Were they really thieves?" The villagers' opinions on this differed vastly.

"A real thief would have stolen something from our house, but he did not touch anything!" the old hat-maker said pitifully. "They must have been not thieves but Secret Service officers! So they must have just finished their training program and left."

"But, brother, there were cases when some thieves had also entered the bridal's chambers instead of the groom's," Ahad-mahsum said. "I heard that the Monkey has also entered some houses. He is the child of a cannibal!"

For some reason no one raised any objection to his words, neither did anyone approve of them. It looked like some other men in the group besides the Monkey would also gladly enter the brides' chambers to entertain themselves.

According to rough calculations, the biggest harm that was caused by the thieves came upon Sayfiddin Kulol who had become a paralytic. His son Hasan took him to the city to treat him.

"What about his safe? Did he also take his safe with him?" the man wearing a robe asked.

"You could check it for yourself at night, if you go there!" Soli-the-Screamer replied sarcastically.

* * *

We travelled down to the cotton fields at the beginning of the school year. We stayed in a remote field of Qo'shdaryo. We slept in the camel-house, going to sleep on rice straw. There was not too much cotton in the field. Savage Orziqulov was our curator in the field. He used to follow us as we worked in the fields, wielding his stick. He did not know who to beat since the Monkey did not come down to the cotton field that year. Upon leaving school, he became a disciple of Urin-the-driver.

"Until when should I feed this bull? It's time for him to work and earn his keep," his aunts' husband said. (In those times it was reputable to work as an apprentice like the Monkey, covered in black machine oil, and we all envied such apprentices.)

With wet aprons around our waists, we looked for unopened cotton balls from dawn to late evening. Schoolgirls, with lice crawling around their heads, sorely missed our abandoned and burglarized village and shed bitter tears, saying "Jiydali, oh Jiydali, when will we see you again?"

On one of those gloomy and cloudy days, teacher Orziqulov, who went somewhere in the morning, appeared in the cotton field, yelling:

"Stop picking cotton! The bald one has gone! There's no need to pick cotton now!"

He was way too drunk, hardly able to stay on his feet. As he approached us, scolding and using bad language in Russian, we became aware of the news.

The bald king has been removed from his post. He was replaced by another gravedigger – a hairy disciple with bushy eyebrows. Everything should be perfect from now on!

Teacher Orziqulov insulted the former king before the schoolchildren:

"Bald head, rascal! Fool! Fuck you!"

Later, my father told me: "the bald king also was praised when he was first brought to power."

* * *

In the spring of the following year, our martyr village was going to be rebuilt again. Finally, the truth has prevailed! It became known that the annexation of the district happened due to the bad policy of that time. Moreover, some scoundrels "from amongst us" had pursued such a policy in the hope of getting better positions.

Festivities and rejoicing reigned everywhere! The whole of Jiydali bore likeness of a place celebrating a big wedding! Saying: "It was me who rebuilt your district," with his hands tucked behind his back, Urmon-the-dwarf strode taking big steps up and down the central street five times a day. He considered himself the local hero!

Those who had left the village in search of some money for everyday life began to return. Jiydali became crowded and suddenly newly prosperous. Many people forgot all the funny stories about the thieves in the village; only some women who had been afraid of the thieves in those past days recalled those funny stories whenever they were upset with their husbands.

Not long after, we started working in the regional center, and therefore lived in the city for one or two years. Later, I came to Tashkent to study at the university. I was not aware of the latest news from Jiydali. The most interesting things I heard, when I went there, as I did from time to time, was that Musallam-the-long-hair, who used to change her lovers, this time got married to a ropewalker. They said that her kids were also ropewalkers. It looks like they walked on ropes using the long hair of their mother.

Also, this time as Daddy Shuro tried "to defeat the enemy" with all of his heart, he could not manage the "returning back to the motherland" bit: the old man who had lived through so many hardships passed away as he was on his way somewhere, falling from his horse. The spoiled Amalbek did not remarry after that. It looks like the-long-hair had made a scar with her mystical hair on the sensitive part of his body.

"Musallamkhon made the right decision to leave that time," said Mahmud. "She was the pearl of Jiydali. She could not find a person that would fit her from amongst us here. Unfortunately, we were all too young at that time!"

Some years ago, I met bride-Olma at a funeral ceremony. I learned that her husband Egam-the-rich returned to being Egam-the-poor and passed away a long time ago. I recognized her at once, as I saw her in a group of women coming out of the gates. Her eyes were lightless, but there was something in her that had not yet changed. She looked at me like I was a stranger. However, as she passed by me, she suddenly drew closer and asked, "Are you still afraid of cats, little brother?" I was shocked to hear these words from that old whore.

Anyone could go on living quietly, but not Urmon-the-dwarf. He was sentenced to a prison term after writing too many letters of complaint about the First Secretary of the district. Upon his release, he brought back with him a number of Georgians and made friends with them. He found a one-legged statue of Stalin somewhere, had the second leg added to it and placed the statue in the center of his yard. Then, he started to justify "the great and famous leader of the nations," saying that there was no discipline in the country. Yet, he could not manage to hold back and was sentenced again. Later he died of too many complaints. I do not know what happened to the statue. They say that his alcoholic son broke it into pieces, saying, "My father became the victim of your existence, you evil man!"

The Monkey was also sentenced after harassing his aunt's dumb daughter. Actually, the dumb girl was an excuse, since no one was really upset because of the harassment, since she was his aunt's daughter and even the brother-in-law was pleased with it, moreover, the girl was mute. In fact, the drunken evildoer Monkey had boasted in one place, "You do not know me, I am a Secret Service officer, and I was counted amongst the thieves in the past!"

Years later the Monkey returned back to the village having become a crazy, stupid person. He headed straight to the graveyard in Qurghondara and began living there. He became "the Sheikh." He used to live there all year round. By the way, we came across him several years later.

As we were looking for a suitable place to shoot a film entitled "The man," we found a small but very beautiful spot at the foot of the mountains. As we approached the slope beside the ravine, a wild-sounding cry spread across the place:

"Gooli-gooli, gooli-gooli!"

Someone hopping from stone to stone was fast approaching us. It was our Monkey! He was wearing an old coat and a pair of quality jeans and an old sombrero hat with holes on his head. His vintage clothes and general appearance made this jerk come across like a modern person. His jet black hair protruding from his hat and pompous sideburns suited him very much.

When he came closer, he saw me and stopped in his tracks. He did not look back at me after that. He did not even speak a single word to me. He only spoke a little with our film director, Yusufjon.

Yusufjon was completely charmed by this extraordinary person that we suddenly encountered on these empty mountain slopes. So he examined him from every side. His eyes lit up.

"Do you live here?" he asked.

"Gooli-gooli," the Monkey replied, extending his long arms to either side of him like wings.

Yusufjon turned back to us:

"What is that 'Gooli-gooli?'"

"Er, that is his secret word," said Mahmud.

"Wow, isn't it cool, 'Gooli-gooli?'" observed Yusufjon joyfully. "So this whole place belongs to you?"

"Gooli-gooli."

"Can we just walk around?"

"Gooli-gooli, gooli-gooli."

Walking briskly, the Monkey began to walk back up to his place. Glancing back at us, Yusufjon followed him.

At first, they both ascended to the only grave at the ravine. Then they walked through the ravine and came up to the old wagon without wheels left there by geologists, which served as the Monkey's shelter. They stood there for some time, receiving the same answer to everything: "Gooli-gooli" from the Monkey and then returned to where we were.

As we were about to leave the place, all of a sudden the Monkey grabbed me by my sleeves and asked me in a normal voice:

"Hey, leave me behind some money. I am keeping your water safe here, you villain!"

Mahmud who was walking in front turned back and interrupted the conversation:

"Go away. Go-go!" he said, treating the Monkey rather rudely.

It looked like Yusufjon overheard our dispute, so he took out some money from his pocket and put it under a rock on the side of the path. The Monkey rushed to get it from underneath the rock, snatched it and ran away.

"That was a waste, Yusufjon, he is not worth it," said Mahmud. Yet our film director was interested in the Monkey and began enquiring about his background.

I gave Mahmud a meaningful look.

"Eh, he is a crazy man," Mahmud said, diverting the conversation to another topic. Else Yusufjon would say that he would like to shoot a film about the Monkey. After we reached the lakeside, while Yusufjon was enjoying taking in the sights. Mahmud called me over:

"That evildoer used to come here every time he wanted to take a piss or do a number two..."

"Really? Who told you this?"

"Some people saw him, bro," he cut off.

Yesterday, Mahmud told me another story. Three months ago, a coffin went missing in Kutarma village graveyard. People only noticed it's gone missing on the day when an old baker from the same village had died. Everyone wondered about it. It was a strange case indeed. Out of necessity, the people in the neighborhood were forced to borrow a coffin from the neighboring graveyard of Qizilcha village.

By the end of the summer, the lost coffin was found. A shepherd herding his livestock in Qurghandara by some chance spotted the coffin near the ravine. The shepherd thought it was an empty coffin and tried to lift up its lid. (Coffins in Jiydali are usually the covered type.) He then saw that the coffin was tied with wire from inside. He could hardly pull the coffin open and once he did he saw a hairy creature lying in it with his clothes on.

"Did they hold a funeral for him, and read a prayer before burying him?"

"I did not attend, to be honest. I think they did. I don't know for sure."

* * *

We came across a derelict old house with many trees around it, left our car there and then began to climb up the slope.

"Do you know if he had a wife and kids, Mahmud? I asked.

"Eh, who would dare to marry him? But did have many kids! If you look, you can find his kid in every street. It is interesting that those kids are almost all of the same age, as if they had been all born in the same year. The Monkey's children!

"Oh, you should've been called Darwin!"

... "As you live and observe different destinies unfold, sometimes I think that Darwin could be right."

... Sleepy yet chatty, three or four people were sitting on the clay platform under the quince-tree. Look, our Soli-the-Screamer was also here. He had double-layered glasses over his eyes and his speech was slow. He did not recognize me. When Mahmud introduced me, he revived a bit and said:

"You have a good habit, my nephew. I remember how you, together with your dad, used to visit houses during your vacation, offering people your sincere condolences. Thank you. Indeed, this is your own people and visiting them is a kind of debt you owe them."

"Hey, brother, I heard that the thief scared you as well in the past, it was at night, right?" a middle-aged person wearing a new skullcap asked me. "He remembered this and laughed every time he saw you on TV. It was while he was still a healthy man."

"Who are you talking about, Mardonqul?" asked Soli-the-Screamer as he was hard of hearing now.

"We are talking about this man's friend, the Monkey, oh sorry, Mumin-the-deceased, May Allah bless him."

"We have to go visit some other places," said Mahmud, impatiently reading a prayer.

"...Mahmud, who was that old man singing up on the platform?" I asked when we reached the foot of the hill.

"The Monkey's father," said Mahmud without any enthusiasm. "The one with the skullcap was his aunt's son."

"Whose father? Did he have a father? I thought his father had been shot dead."

"Oh my God! You wouldn't have even recognized us, if you did not come here for three or four years in a row. You see, his father returned and got married. He had three or four kids. They all look like monkeys. One of them is a drug addict. The rest of them became rich men by working and earning big bucks either in Korea or Russia. You've probably noticed the multi-storey houses covered with darkened glass at the ravine. They all belong to them."

I wouldn't be surprised if someone told me that the Monkey, whose house we have just left after offering our condolences, was alive.

"Really?"

"If you believe that the Monkey is dead, this is not a lie either, my friend."

"The mysteries of those past years haven't been revealed, Mahmud, have they?" I ask, thinking about the past. "The times when thieves terrorised Jiydali…"

"Eh-he, that is an old story. The closed pot is still closed. Who would now ask about those times? More than forty years have passed since then."

"They say that all mysteries or secrets will one day come to light."

"It's only a saying. Some secrets will not be revealed, not even in forty years and will forever remain unexplained. It wouldn't surprise me if the saying you just told me was invented at the same time as this mystery was revealed, forty years down the line."

Despite spending all of his life in these mountains, my friend Mahmud was wise and he was right.

We slowly crawled downhill in our car. Jiydali lay right in front of us, my lovely Jiydali!

I was absorbed in deep thought. So many people drink water from one brook, it's unbelievable. But there are so many mysteries and secrets.

"Gooli-gooli," I said to myself. "Gooli-gooli…"

As the car turned to the lakeside, I lifted my hands and reached across to turn the car's front mirror towards me, then studied my own face, trying to read into it. Mahmud gave me one strange look and then quickly averted his eyes. We are driving down a narrow path that can only fit one car: if you do not take care, you might fall into abyss.

The Writer's Garden

Brother Shukur liked his garden, too... I dedicate this humble work of mine to the blessed memory of the deceased master of our storytelling, Shukur Kholmirzaev. May he be pleased with me. May Allah be merciful to him.

The author

He was a writer of average acclaim. According to "sages" like us, that is, who eagerly devoured every book available. He had definitely read some of the classics by famous authors such as Mark Twain, Daniel Defoe, Gianni Rodari or Mikhail Prishvin, and he had even heard of Harry Potter, who reigns supreme over the children's world today. However, he was an "ignoramus" who knew nothing about the brilliant flagship writers of our circle: Joyce, Proust or Dos Passos. Moreover, even though some of his writings were included in scholastic books, for some reason — perhaps because he never held an official post, or perhaps because he was too mild and withdrawn — he was not counted among the representatives of "great literature" and writers like us just disregarded him.

However, if the truth be known, he was closer to real literature than the majority of those well-known fathers and brothers; you could even say he was a loyal citizen of that literary world. Incidentally, he was not only a citizen but also a self-sacrificing worker, but more about that later. He did not know how to write lies, since he was unable to create fabricated words. In short, it was impossible to add falsehood to his writings and, actually, there was no need.

Unlike other formal writers, it had not been his childhood dream to become an author, nor did he start his creative work by writing a short poem, nor was his work published in one of the ubiquitous newspapers posted on a wall somewhere. He had neither a good curriculum vitae like that of some master poets, nor a grandmother who could tell his younger self enchanting folktales at bedtime. Do you think a poor orphan who did not even know his own mother could have a grandmother? His only dream was to become like his revered teacher of literature. In fact we can say that this teacher changed his whole life. Having read the boy's essay on nature, the teacher said to his young admirer: "You could become a good writer one day!" Yes, those were his very words: "a writer." The teacher's declaration rang in his ears as if it was his destiny. Otherwise, how could this unfortunate orphan, brought up by a crazy, strict old woman in a remote mountainous village, ever think of becoming a writer one day?

Many years later, in the days when everything depended on how much money you had,[23] it became apparent that if he was not going to be a writer, he could be a good gardener instead. Gardening is really a nice job: if you feel shy about selling your produce at the bazaar you can always find someone eager to

---

23 A reference to Perestroika and the times that followed.

make a quick buck who will buy your harvest wholesale and sell it on for a profit. You just turn around to do something and the speculator himself will leave the money for you. But he was ashamed of completely abandoning his creative writing and devoting himself to horticulture alone. Isn't it cowardice to abuse your sacred dream in the post-perestroika transition period when you have already become famous, writing for such a long time?

Actually, his gardening work was part of his love of literature, too, since he came to this garden, and to gardening in general, through literature. Nature was his main theme and inspiration. He made friends with nature and considered her a true miracle. Just imagine: you stick a twig into the soil and one day it will become a shoot, it will grow and sprout buds, then branches will emerge, it will turn into a tree and finally it will give you delicious fruits! And the fruit have great health benefits. In spring the trees will become so beautiful, dripping with blossom. In autumn, they will turn yellow making your heart grow wistful. In winter, they will become like a snowy queen. If that isn't a miracle, what is?

There was one more reason for him not to turn himself over to gardening completely: people in his neighbourhood, especially in his half-built horvan, called him "professor". Why "professor?" If he were a professor, he should know something besides pruning and grafting. Well, he did indeed know something else!

(Let us also call him "professor." No matter whether he is good or bad, if we call a writer "professor," we hope that real professors will not be offended. Actually, writers, too, are professors to some extent: they challenge us to love literature, to be a good person and refrain from doing evil deeds. If you call him something different, in this circle of intolerant and nit picky people you will be asked a lot of tricky questions, such as: "Who wrote that?" "Who is the target audience?" "What did he write?" So it is better if you just call him "professor," and that's it! But there are so many professors who preach like mullahs with turbans, or who preach without.)

In fact, it was the Chairman of the Writers' Association, the Writer-Chairman, who gave him this nickname.

Back then, our hero worked as an editor at a youth publishing house. The boss called him to his office one day and introduced him to a handsome giant of a man. He was a kolkhoz director in one of the horticultural districts near the capital. But even though he was an important director, this man had an incurable disease: writing. He could not live without writing. Hey, isn't it better for you to take care of your gardens, to think about fertility, to fulfill the annual plan and get awards and become a hero? If you still have some spare time left over, go to see how the laborers are doing and help the poor, man! But, no, his hands itch, he cannot live without writing!

The boss did not beat about the bush:

"Consideration of the manuscript of our kolkhoz director is in our plan!"

The editor wrinkled his forehead but could not remember such a proposal in the annual plan.

Are you a fool? If there is nothing about it in the annual plan, well, it should definitely be there when the boss says it is there!

The kolkhoz director's manuscript was weird. Not only had this "headache" been typed up on an obsolete typewriter, but to make matters worse, some local literature teacher who had studied in the capital had made some 'corrections', too. The manuscript looked like an "excellent" essay by an excellent pupil, who often used flowery turns of phrase and complex grammar. And the excellent pupil had been brought up reading books by those famous father and brother writers.

So, what to do next? The manuscript had been added to the publishing house's plan so published it must be! All the more so since the boss himself had given the decree. And the head of the department also repeated incessantly: "You should edit the manuscript and turn it into a good piece! That's all you should do!"

Something about the author-cum-kolkhoz director appealed to our young editor. For instance, when the publishing house boss charged the young editor with this mammoth task, this giant man, the avant-garde kolkhoz director, looked at him with eyes full of compassion.

The literature teacher who had 'corrected' the manuscript had really given it his all!. The editor of the publishing house approached the director and asked him for the original manuscript but since the kolkhoz director was run off his feet with the harvest, it was his driver, Olashovur, who brought it. (Our kolkhoz director was a master of nicknames: he called Olloshukur[24] Olashovur[25]. Our hero later became close friends with this Olashovur.)

The editor took two weeks of leave (he could just as easily have asked for two months) to devote himself to the manuscript, all but rewriting it, and finally transformed it into a good piece of literature.

Several days after the book was published, the author strode into our young editor's office. Gently pushing aside the editor's outstretched hand, the writer-giant hugged him instead:

"Thank you so much, professor!"

---

24 Grateful to Allah.
25 Energetic, busy.

The kolkhoz director was no skinflint. On Saturday, he invited the editor to the kolkhoz, sending Olashovur to pick him up. He arranged a fine banquet right in the middle of his beautiful garden. He presented the editor with a new robe. The scene was repeated the next day, too.

Once he was a bit lubricated, the poor editor – who had never had such respect lavished on him before – promised to make a 'mutual creative cooperation' with the kolkhoz director in the future.

It was not long before the local press began running reviews, one after another, praising "the kolkhoz director who wrote such a magnificent book in addition to his main duties in the kolkhoz." Our writer-editor's own books had never met with such acclaim, but he did not begrudge the author this glory; actually, he was even happier than the author himself, since this was his own work after all.

Later, our editor met the authors of those accolades at several harvest festival celebrations, and in particular, at the great garden of the kolkhoz director. They repeated their eulogies at those banquets, turning them into beautiful songs, exaggerating and effervescing like the champagne on the table. But the kolkhoz director, busy with hospitality, listened to them rather indifferently, absent-mindedly.

A year or so later, the publishing house received a new manuscript written on a thick shop-keeper's notebook in a slip-shod way. Thank goodness that this time the literature teacher had not made any 'corrections'! Perhaps he had been promoted to headmaster for his services last time... Be that as it may, it would take more than two weeks or even two months to turn this manuscript into a good book.

Where could that giant of a man, burdened with kolkhoz duties, find the time or the inclination to write anything? The secret was revealed by his driver, Olashovur, who had already become a close of friend of our editor. Every morning, the kolk-hoz director came to his office and wrote at least two pages, mopping the sweat off his brow and double chin with his hand-kerchief. To support the director in his moments of inspiration, Olashovur would ply him with tea. We, in our turn, should also praise such bravery: bravo, kolkhoz director, bravo!

Actually, it is not difficult to write something to amuse your-self: all you need is a little time and inclination – that's it. But writing a real book, a good book, well, that is quite another matter, and very difficult, oh, so very difficult! So do you think that a 'prestigious' author whose incomplete work is published as a book and whose ears ring with praise is able to compre-hend this reality?

But the kolkhoz director was also wise. He made an agree-ment with his director friend, negotiated two months' leave for his "professor," and whisked him away to his Great Garden.

The "professor" was given a light, comfortable room in which to live. As in the famous poem, an apricot tree grew by the window, although admittedly the tree was more humble now, its blossoms scattered on the ground below. Silence. Only the voice of the typewriter is heard, tick-tick, tick-tick, tick-tick. Food and drink appear whenever you want them. The old care-taker is at your service. He is also your personal cook. He is older than our editor but very nimble on his feet. You only have to call him, saying: "Hey, Eshon![26]" and he will appear before you in an instant. Sometimes, even though you don't ask him, he wipes the typewriter with his rough, dry hands. He doesn't talk much but is keen to be of assistance. He knows his place.

---

26 Meaning Man, Mullah, a term of respect.

Mischievous Olashovur talks enough for them both! He usually appears at night bursting with information and anecdotes. They sit outside and drink vodka together. Sometimes Olashovur brings a manlike woman taller than himself who always laughs at every little thing. He calls the cook, saying: "Hey, Eshon!" and silently holds a finger to his lips, crosswise. The cook, pleased with the name our editor gave him, nods: "understood," and hurries to the kitchen to prepare food for them. After the feast for three, Olashovur takes his girlfriend by her arm and heads for a room in the corner. On his way, he does not forget to mention: "She has a friend, by the way, if you like?" Though he is bored in this quiet place and wants to entertain himself, our editor does not show it, just putting his hand to his chest and saying: "Thanks, thanks a lot. Enjoy yourself." Laughter and giggles are heard from that room for a moment, then it soon becomes quiet, absorbed in the night's secrets.

This place springs to life once or twice a week. Distinguished guests arrive from the capital. The summer seating area will be bright and full of laughter until well after midnight. Then all of sudden a hush descends on the garden; the guests have all left, spirited back to the nearby city.

Sometimes, the ever-busy host – the author – approaches the editor.

"How are you doing?"

"Not bad, sir."

"Is everything OK?"

"OK."

The giant sweaty author embraces the puny editor. The editor, who never tires of cursing the author's hands and scolding his kin but who is in need of kindness, soaks it up in the kolkhoz director's wide bosom, as if he senses the scent of the brother or father he never knew. But the next day the same thing repeats again. Reading the weird sentences in the notebook, the editor is riled once more, ranting: "Huh, it would be better if your fingers were all broken than to write such nonsense! A curse on your father!" The editor wishes he were in a position to live a proper life and leave this kind of job; ah, then he could write what he wanted. If only he could! Curses! Damn it!

When he feels angry, he goes out for a walk. Exhausted, he never tires of strolling among the fruit trees. The orchard is his only comfort in this place. He stops near each tree and speaks to it, sharing secrets.

One day when the kolkhoz director came to give some special orders about an evening banquet he saw the editor as he was walking in the orchard.

"Our garden's great, isn't it?"

"It is."

"It is the Garden of Eram, the great garden! I planted all the trees and nurtured them myself," said the director proudly. "Are you a fan of trees like me, professor?"

"Yes, I love them."

The kolkhoz director looked at him silently, then left.

The next day, Olashovur came to him in the afternoon, saying: "Let's go, I'm going to take you to a particular place," and he drove the editor to a grove of trees near the city. He pointed it out to him and asked:

"Do you like this place? It's well-watered, a good place. I think it will be in great demand soon."

When they got back the editor asked Olashovur why he had shown him that lovely spot, but the driver did not want to let on, so he just said:

"Just following orders, professor, just following orders. The Boss asked me to take you there. If you want to know why, you'd better ask him."

One week later, the two of them went there again. The kolkhoz director was with them this time.

In one corner, where construction had already begun on several houses, a plot of land was cordoned off by a wire fence.

"Professor!" said the kolkhoz director. "Just close your eyes for a second, open them again, and this land is yours! May it serve you well! Amen!"

Dumbfounded, the editor did not know what to say. The kolkhoz director measured something out then ordered Olashovur:

"The house should be built from here. One big room and one small room. That's enough for a writer, isn't that right, professor? It should be built in two or three months. With electricity and water. Understand, Shovur-bek? Period!"

The editor could not sleep a wink, his heart was bursting with joy! Such great good fortune, oh Allah is merciful!

His wife had died a long time ago, his only son was married with two children, and the five of them lived in a three-room flat in Chilanzar. Now God had given them more space! His dream had come true!

The editor quickly went to the city and took the money he had saved over the years from his fees with the intention of giving it to the kolkhoz director when he came to see them on Sunday.

"Put it back in your pocket, professor!" said he, frowning. But as the editor insisted, he merely turned to his driver and said: "OK, take Shovur and buy furniture, a TV and other home appliances with it."

The house was built ahead of schedule and the proud owner moved in with his few possessions. Ah, how happy he was to have such a house! And with its own land! He set about turning one plot into an orchard. He began by sorting the trees. He brought saplings and flowers from the Great Garden. He grafted the trees and pruned their dry branches. By the following spring, he had turned his patch of land into a blossoming garden. It turns out our editor had green fingers, too. Consulting with others, he soon learned the secrets of gardening.

Soon afterwards, the kolkhoz director's second colourful book was published and another round of reviews, praises and banquets got underway at the Great Garden.

The distinguished author of two books now became a member of the Writers' Union.

However, his joy was short-lived this time. By the end of the summer, the kolkhoz director had fallen gravely ill. He was diagnosed with incurable cancer. The editor visited him every week. He would never forget what the kolkhoz director told him sorrowfully during one of his visits:

"I cannot fathom you poets. You created a poet out of me, well done! Money and riches can drive anyone mad. You may want to go on stage to perform, without feeling ashamed of your age or grey hair and beard. Strange, who forced me, a peasant, to become a poet? But the merit is yours. You worked hard on my works. Do you think I'm stupid? Why did I need all that? Look, everything will be left behind." He was so light-hearted that even in this situation he joked, saying: "What do you reckon, should I take one of my books with me? As a keepsake. I could put it under my head and lie on it in my grave. I could read it when they are through with questioning me Up There. They say there will be plenty of time in the other world. You won't be busy toiling in the fields or whatever. So, what do you reckon, professor?"

He passed away, but he left this garden as a legacy and a memory. May his grave be full of light! The editor thought that those past years working for the generous kolkhoz director were the greatest times in his life. But then the times changed so quickly, what used to take twenty years happens in a matter of months now. The publishing house where hundreds of people used to work turned into a small workshop almost overnight. The offices of its former employees were taken by some firms and enterprises. You can no longer stroll unhampered along the pavement, shops of every shape and size crowd right up to the curb. If you don't pay for using a toilet, an old woman sitting there will banish you. The children, who so recently brought food to the director, barely greet him today, saying: "Business! We are going to do business!" If you are not careful, these rascals might kick you out to boot.

The publishing house, unable to turn a profit from its publishing business, was kept afloat by the rent it charged those enterprises for office space. Naturally, in these circumstances, despite his experience and talent, there was no room for the editor with his old-fashioned ways, unable to adapt to the changing reality. Since he had come to this job from far away, he simply resigned.

But how could he live now? What was he to do? The new year showed him the way. He made his home – this garden – his job. This was the solution! No need to traipse to work every day, hanging around for a meagre salary. No need to kowtow to the boss any more. There was only one thing to do, such a simple, straightforward job. A very profitable business!

O Allah! There were so many people eager to become famous writers! But obviously, to become a famous writer you first have to get a book published, and to get a book published you first have to write it. And that was the tricky part. There were people who wanted to see their unwritten books in print. The kolkhoz director was an honest person – he at least wrote something by himself. But the editor's new clients were different — you had to write everything for them, right from the first page! It was a strange time: scholars were sidelined, overlooked, while those with no talents proclaimed themselves learned. Those with bulging pockets started to publish their books, regardless of whether they had any creative flair or not. The talented writers could simply gape at this; penniless, they could not come anywhere near a publishing house, so some of them just gave up their creative writing, focusing on how to earn their daily bread instead. The quick-witted, however, were on the up, even though their writing was mediocre at best. They began to write books to suit the current situation and market needs. Anyone able to write anything decent some-how left the country. Go ahead, the floor is yours now, O sly, quick-witted ones!

But, first of all, such "creative works" had to be edited. There was an answer to that problem: a man known as "the professor" living in a garden on the outskirts of the city, a man just waiting for you to write books for yourself!

Utterly fed up with the burden of writing on behalf of some-one else, of inhabiting another's mind and becoming their like-ness, he would jump with a shout: "It would be better if your fingers were all broken rather than write such nonsense! It would be better for you to cut out your tongue rather than call yourself a writer!"

But what could he do, since it is impossible to speak out? He remembers how on the eve of perestroika they published his story about his childhood, a story about how he wanted to run away from his aunt's house to his father's hometown, and with his royalties he could buy one pack of cigarettes. Then he smoked those special cigarettes one by one every morn-ing for twenty days before smoking his usual cheap "Saraton" cigarettes.

The professor's only comfort was this garden, these trees. By then, to save money and also because of his smokers' cough, he had given up smoking and started taking snuff instead; he grew a thin beard over his chin, the top of his head was bald and he had donned a skullcap. No one could believe he was a modern writer, some even thought he was one of the newly emerging mullahs.

Actually, his son was a religious man. This thin and pale lad who worked as a calligrapher came to see his father twice a month carrying a small bundle. Father and son would sit on the supa under the apricot tree for some time just looking at each other, and only when it was time for the son to leave would the father ask him:

"Are you still studying?"

"Yes, alhamdulillah, thanks to Allah."

"You can recite your prayers, but be careful, son!"

"Say 'astaghfirulloh,' may Allah forgive us, Father".

Although the professor repeated this word to himself, he did not understand its meaning.

One other person often came to see the professor, too: his old friend Olashovur. By the way, the deceased kolkhoz director took this nickname with him to the grave. Now Olashovur was not merely Olloshukur; formally, he was Ollohshukur.[27] He always quoted verses from the Koran or hadith, the words and deeds of Prophet Muhammad. The two old friends would sometimes sit on the supa and reminisce about the good old days, about their 'dear father' the kolkhoz director, or talk about trees and grafting saplings.

---

27 a *hoji,* i.e. someone who has fulfilled *hajj* in gratitude to Allah.

And each time, the professor felt an inexplicable urge to ask him about the woman he used to bring to the orchard, but he felt ashamed to ask, since he was a hoji now.

The professor's other – secret – comfort was a woman who brought him milk every day. Every morning something pleasant stirred in his soul when she appeared with the milk, and if she didn't come, he worried about her. They say her husband is paralyzed. But the professor never entertained any untoward thoughts about the woman. Never!

Sometimes she came with her two sons. Actually, she was a healthy, simple-hearted yet wise villager, but to the professor, who had not visited the city nor met a woman for months, she seemed like an angel. The professor himself, however, had not been so angelic in the past. After his wife passed away, he found a proofreader, a woman named 'Sahiy-khon'[28] but he later lost interest in women. It's true that nicknames are not given without cause.

Back in the days when Ollohshukur-hoji was Olashovur, he had become a clever, farsighted man under the kolkhoz director's protection. "You shall see, this place will soon be in demand," he had once said; well, now it was indeed in demand. In three or four years, villas had sprung up around his simple house, but the professor paid no attention to them; his small house and garden were home enough for him.

Over the past two years, however, the scene had become increasingly odd, and everyone who saw the dilapidated slum in the middle of those sumptuous villas thought that "he should be removed" from there. His neighbour was a famous rich man who took the two houses on the left to build himself a

---

28 Meaning gracious.

pompous new mansion then later began encroaching on the grove to the right.

In fact, it was Yormat who appeared there first. (His real name was something else, but when the head of the neighbourhood committee, Saidjalol, introduced him as "the manager of our brother the rich man," the professor remembered the office manager of the rich man in the novel The Sacred Blood and nicknamed him Yormat). He was slightly taller than Obid Asom[29] but his panic and policy were ten times greater. The rich man himself showed up two or three times, but all the work was overseen by this manager. He was always talking on his mobile phone, drove a Damas, and never took a moment's rest. He single-handedly managed the twenty to thirty laborers, masters and "MAZ" and "KRAZ" trucks needed to build the mansion. Everyone was amazed by his energy.

Actually, it was thanks to this rich man that the road was tarmacked, gas pipes were laid and electricity was available day and night. It was true that "there is something good in every misfortune."

One day, when the construction was all but complete, a young lady arrived in her Mercedes. (According to the all-knowing Saidjalol, she was one of the rich man's younger wives and the mansion was built for her.) Black sunglasses on her forehead, she skipped into the mansion like a young, playful girl, popping out again half an hour later. After a moment's thought, she walked right up to the professor's house. Greeting the professor as though they were old acquaintances, she perched herself on the edge of the supa, looking out over the garden.

"Oh, what a beautiful garden! It's so cool and shady here!"

---

29 A very short Uzbek comedian.

"Welcome, daughter," said the professor to his unexpected guest. "Come and walk through the garden. Pick some fruit, help yourself. Don't be shy, it's my own garden, I grew the trees myself."

"Honestly, I like this garden more than that one," said she, pointing to the neighbouring mansion towering above the wall.

"Thanks, daughter, thanks," said the professor. "This garden is yours, too. You can come here and relax whenever you wish."

"I was told you are a writer, right? My uncle is a poet. He wrote all the songs they play on the radio."

The professor picked several beautiful flowers and two peaches and handed them to the lady as he saw her off.

Several days later he met the rich man, too.

One evening when the professor went out onto the street, a man standing a little apart from the guests grouped round the line of fashionable cars came up to him. He was a handsome man of about forty-fifty years old, dressed all in black.

"Hello, professor? Yes, writer! Everyone says you have a lovely garden. Why don't you invite us over?" said he as he held his hand out to the professor.

"Welcome, sir," said the professor, somewhat abashed. "Please come in."

"Some other time. Please come to our house. Your colleagues, poets, are here. The greatest ones!"

That evening, the walls and supa of the great mansion were festooned with twinkling lights, and a banquet continued until well into the night. Apparently, the best singers and musicians had gathered there that evening, forsaking weddings and other celebrations in the city. A strong sound system had been set up in the mansion so all the neighbourhoods far and wide knew about the banquet, too.

The professor, however, did not go anywhere. On that summer's day, he closed his doors and windows and tried to do something inside.

These banquets became a weekly affair and lasted until dawn. On such evenings the professor would often close himself up inside his house, but because of the loud modern music he could neither read nor write, so he would just sit angrily in a stuffy room until early morning when he managed finally to get a little rest.

For about two years he knew no peace or quiet. When the building work began, he had been tormented by the noise of trucks, the yelling masters and laborers, the dust and all manner of other irritations, but now there is a new nuisance: the racket of parties.

In fact, the owners of the mansion did not live there permanently and only came there for banquets or at weekends to swim, but again it was noisy. According to Saidjalol, something about the new mansion was not to the younger wife's liking, and now one gardener, one janitor and one errand-boy live there.

Though he was a close neighbour, the professor had never been to this mansion. He had never seen its two-storey building, its well decorated, domed supas, or its marble pool lit by underwater lights at night. The professor suffered because of this mansion with its gaudy mod cons, but for some reason or superstition, he really did not want to pass through its gates.

On one side there was a banquet going on, on the other side some new construction was underway for the younger wife, replacing the grove. Again loud noises, sand and gravel, dust and grit rule the neighbourhood. What can you do? You should just be patient. If not, run away or die. Where could you go? Wherever you go you'll run into some disturbance. It's not your lot. You value your own life. So the only solution is to endure it all!

One of those days, when the professor was reading a book on the supa pretending not to hear the noise, Yormat came to his house. He was accompanied by Saidjalol, who was in the habit of barging into everyone's house without permission, tying the edge of his robe up round his waist. He used to take gossip from one house to another. No one knew if he was friend or foe. A very strange person he was.

"Listen to me, professor," said short Yormat gently hitting him on the chest. "Give the garden to us!"

"Which garden? Why? What's the matter?" asked the professor, flustered.

"We will build a good house for you," said Yormat pointing to the grove next door. "You think this is a house? The new one will be ten times better than this one. You shall have a modern house!"

"Yes, ten times better!" his companion chimed in.

Perhaps if someone asked the professor for his life he would offer it, but they were asking for his garden, the garden he had cultivated himself with the sweat of his brow and the toil of his hands.

"Yormat-jon, my little brother, I cannot believe my ears!"

The manager ignored the strange name the professor used; he was here to resolve this issue rather than to correct his name.

"Your garden will be annexed to the big garden, the Boss's orders!" said Yormat. "Otherwise, you'll be stuck in the middle and that won't do at all. Listen, professor, you'll win if you give your house to us!"

"It will be annexed! You will win, professor!" added Saidjalol enthusiastically, as if he, too, would win something.

"Think about it, it's a good option! By the way, the boss has another request for you – you will write a book for him about his life. You will be rich, professor. Do you agree?"

"But my little brother, I am an old man living alone, you see. Please, leave me in peace."

Yormat turned his back abruptly and left, saying:

"One day this garden will be ours!"

That night the professor woke with a start. Sweat was pouring from his body. He wanted to throw up, as if vomiting would make him feel=better. He tried but couldn't. Poisonous water came to his mouth instead. Something was burning inside his body, as if someone were yanking his bowels out...

He suffered terribly until dawn. He should go to see a doctor.

In the morning, he closed his door and windows, and, a bundle in his hand, he waited for someone to pass by in a car.

Suddenly a Damas appeared in the distance. It was Yormat! The professor tensed. The sensitive manager quickly grasped the situation. He asked the professor to get in, taking him by the arm. He took him to the nearest hospital, saying not a word all the way.

It turned out that the professor's old disease had flared up again. "We must cut your bowels," the doctors said. "Otherwise they will split open."

So they cut his bowels. The professor came to his senses only on the third day after the operation.

But alas, one misfortune always brings another. The very day after the professor began to walk again by himself, just as he was reaching for something on the bedside table, he was suddenly struck by a heart attack.

He was again moved to intensive care. His condition was serious. The doctors didn't know what to do: two bad diseases had captured the old man.

Ollohshukur visited the professor at the hospital every two days. His own son, the mullah, was also there from morning till night. Who else did he have? Where were his disciples, the ones whose books he had written?

Well, we cannot elude our fate. A sick man does not care about anything. But while he was in hospital, something was happening in his garden.

The energetic manager Yormat, together with his ever-ready companion Saidjalol, boldly entered the professor's garden and started to measure it step by step. Then they both sat themselves down on the supa, made a decision and drew up a plan. The only thing they were waiting for was bad news from the hospital!

But the expected message did not come. And so all the preparations were put on hold. The mansion was closed up. Silence ruled in the neighbourhood. Even Yormat was nowhere to be seen, as if he had vanished into thin air. Only Saidjalol still went about his business, spreading his gossip from house to house.

The professor stayed at the hospital for a long time but, gradually, he recovered. He felt well, his mood lightened. But he missed his garden.

The day after he was discharged, the woman who sold milk came to his house with her children. She apologized for not visiting him in hospital. Sitting on the supa, they spoke about their lives. The professor, his heart filled with joy, stood up to pick two buckets of fruit for the woman. By the time he returned, she had washed the dishes and cleaned the house. Then she picked up the two buckets with difficulty (her children did not want to leave this garden with its generous uncle), asking her children to carry them, saying in passing that she would be happy to wash the professor's clothes.

There was nothing to trouble a man in her speech or her actions for she was an honest woman. Ah, how good it is that there are such pure, loving women in the world!

Having survived such an arduous test, the professor decided to live differently. After all, he didn't know how long he had left, so he had better do something good. Indifferent to his surroundings, he busied himself with his soul. Autumn was at the door, the nights were cool now. Was it necessary to entertain guests, swim and arrange a banquet in this weather? he thought. In fact, the summer holidays were over, the majority of people had left the horvan for the city, and there was almost no one to speak to.

The writer began to write a book which had come to his mind as he lay ill in hospital. In this book, called The Eternal Trees, he would describe the life of a tree in comparison with that of a human being. And for this he need go no further than his own orchard, he need only mull over his own life and ponder about the trees in his garden. It's a pity that a human being will surely lose in this comparison! For example, our kolkhoz director has passed away, but the poplar near his office is still alive. One day you will die, but the house you built and the garden you cultivated will remain. A human being cannot even equal the tree he himself planted!

The air was fresh. As a poet once put it: "Now it does not burn, it only shines." Sitting on the supa all day long, the writer taps his book out on his typewriter, sipping the fresh air. The milk lady's younger child sits next to him. The boy came with his mother in the morning and stayed with the writer. From time to time he wanders into the garden, plays with birds and picks fruit. Then he, too, sits at the edge of the table and begins to write something. As the writer praises him, saying: "Ah, you might become a writer one day," he feels happy, and writes more and more.

"Uncle, which is better: a comma or a full stop?" asks the writer-to-be raising his head from the paper.

The writer who wrote and edited so many books is at a loss.

"A full stop could be better. A comma can be used several times in a sentence, but a full stop is used only once."

"But the comma has a longer tail, hasn't it?"

"A comma means the sentence should still continue, but when you put a full stop, that's it, the sentence is full, it's stopped."

"Isn't it better for the sentence to be continued rather than to stop too quickly?"

The writer looks at his disciple attentively: "It's better if it continues than if it finishes… What? That's strange."

Then he strokes the child's head, saying: "Ah, you will become a good writer!"

One of those lovely clear days, Saidjalol, a long-expected but unappealing chap, appears before the professor and sits on the edge of the supa. He spent his summer in the Chartak resort, he says, and just got back yesterday.

"Have you heard, professor? They arrested your neighbour while you were in hospital and threw him behind bars."

"No, I didn't know that. What happened?"

"Listen. He hung himself in the prison!"

"O Allah be merciful! Really? He was such a young man. Such a shame. I'm sorry to hear that."

"Well, as the wise saying goes: Don't do evil deeds, otherwise you will be punished."

"Do you know where our Yormat is?"

"Who knows – perhaps he is serving some other rich man now. Don't worry about him, professor, the likes of him will always be safe and sound. I saw him in the Alay bazaar before I went to Chartak. You'll never guess who was with him? You remember the boss's youngest wife, right? The lady who came here in her Mercedes? Well, believe it or not, Yormat was with her, arm in arm. I was shocked!"

"Let's change the subject," the writer says. "I feel sorry for the poor young man."

"Why do you feel sorry for him, professor? He got so rich, amused himself with parties and such like, enjoying himself his whole life – he had plenty of everything! Yet you feel…"

All of sudden, the writer shivers. He gazes at Saidjalol. He gazes at him again and says:

"We all die one day, Jalol-khon!"

It also was a reprimand for him: "Go, you are hindering my work!"

Just then, the young disciple still busy writing something carried away by his inspiration, raises his head and asks:

"Uncle, what is better: a question mark or an exclamation mark?"

A dog bit the Incomer's Daughter

We were playing cards at our local chaikhana[30] when we heard the news: the Boss's dog had bitten the outsider's daughter!

Gosh, when did it happen? How? Was the dog sick? Everyone was puzzled: that dog barks incessantly, how had it managed to bite someone at the same time?

Everyone was indignant, too.

"An outrage! It's an outrage!" shouted public correspondent E. Safar, jumping to his feet. "How it could happen to the child of an outsider? We should write about it! I shall most certainly write about it!"

"Sit down, please, my little brother," the aksakal-elder consoled him. "You can write about it later. By the way, you have tried to write about that dog before, haven't you? Before you write, we must consult. That's the rule."

He knows the rules and laws governing any undertaking, that is why he was a candidate for local leadership. For example, if you start a sentence, saying: "This brook..." he likes to give you

---

30 Traditional Uzbek teahouse.

a little lecture, adding: "True enough, it's a brook but water flows there."

"We have to get rid of that dog, brothers," said the migrant driver. "I'll kill it myself! I just need to get my hands on some poison!

"You drive through many cities, surely you could have already found some poison or arsenic somewhere ?" the Candidate of Science remarked pointedly.

The senior lecturer objected to his words.

"Oh my! You can find poison in Eskijuva bazaar. You can find anything you want there, from liquid mascara to a camel which has been through the eye of a needle! Why do you need poison when a tiny needle will do just as well? Just put a needle into a lump of dough or meat."

"Ah, but you have to get close to the dog first!" said the Candidate of Science, panicking at the mere thought.

"Don't be upset, brothers," said the ever-amiable elder. "First we have to consult with the Boss. That's the rule."

"What will you consult with him about?" asked the modest merchant, irritated by these words. It was not a good day for him; a plan he had been hatching for the past year had fallen through, and his documents were sent back from the planning department without even a second appraisal. Moreover, a public figure had offended him earlier that day, saying: "It's a big sin to name a small shop after Sultan Ulughbek of the Timurid dynasty! Let's reconsider it when you plan to open a big supermarket." They overlooked the fact that the merchant's younger son was called Ulughbek. But here, he also had his eye on the leadership and its honorary pay. Well, would you be able to ask him if you're about to kill his dog with poison or a needle?

"Think I'm such a dimwit, huh?" said the elder, gazing at his opponent. Then he shrugged, stepped down from the supa,[31] and wended his way home. leaving the 'members of the trade union' – or rather, that amicable group of neighbourhood households – where they sat.

The self-elected aksakal-elder's behaviour did not reassure the others sitting on the supa.

"He's spying for the Boss," said the merchant.

"Such an outrage!" moaned E. Safar. "Eh, poor child!"

"And the girl's an outsider!"

"You are right. The father takes a bundle to the bazaar, works from dawn until dusk, and has to work as janitor of a resort, too. Where can he get money?"

Who and how they earn was one of their favourite topics.

"Why is he an outsider? Where did he come from?" asked the migrant driver.

"Who knows. He probably came here hanging on a train and later stayed on as an outsider," said the assistant professor, who was also from elsewhere. "We are all outsiders if you dig for details, my friend." Then after a pause he added: "In this world."

Just then the outsider himself appeared from behind the wall, as if he had heard everything they had been saying. He was not aware of the misfortune that had befallen his daughter, and, as usual, was walking slowly and indifferently, shouldering his bundle.

Everyone sobered up at once. But no one dared say a word. What could they say? After all, they did not know any details... Maybe the dog had only frightened the girl, and if so, they would

---

31 A traditional platform found in teahouses or private houses for relaxing, chatting and drinking tea.

not want to break bad news to him. He will go home now and find everything out for himself.

Drawing level with the supa, the outsider put down his bundle, bowed, and slowly went on his way again.

He always did that: bowed a greeting, and went on his way. It has been more than a year since he came here, but he does not want to mingle with his neighbours. He couldn't even if he wanted to, since he is an outsider.

But he has a villa, nevertheless. They say that he came here to guard the secret house of his relative the prosecutor. This was not the only villa in this horvan:[32] strangers came and went, living in them temporarily. You could never find the real landlord.

The outsider was an ugly man but he had three very beautiful daughters. All the young men in the horvan had fallen in love with them. And now, the Boss's dog had gone and bitten the middle daughter.

Apparently, her father called the emergency line; an ambulance soon appeared at the horvan walls. It hurtled past the supa, turned to Garden Street, and was soon passing the supa again. But try as they might, it was impossible to tell who was inside; the white curtains were drawn.

Just as interest in the matter was at its peak around the supa, the tradesman's wife strutted by, all tarted up. Her husband went to scold her, and came back with more details.

It turned out that the Boss had asked the outsider to guard his villa and, of course, to feed his dog from time to time. So his daughter had taken some bones and gone to the villa to feed the dog, which was usually tied to a kennel by the gate. But the

---

32 This refers to a walled neighbourhood being reclaimed from the scrubland on the outskirts of a town.

dog managed to get free, and bit her. Where? There was some confusion, but the dog had bitten a most vital part of her body.

"O Allah!" cried the fiery E. Safar, jumping up again. This public correspondent, hot tempered even as a boy, had worked at the school before his retirement, so he was easily roused now. "We mustn't close our eyes to this incident, comrades! We must take appropriate measures! I will write about it! I don't care whether he is the Boss or not! Such an outrage!"

His zeal was infectious. No one felt like playing cards any more. The flame of rebellion burned in each one's heart, but no one knew quite what do to about it.

"If I don't find poison right away, you will never see me here again!" said the driver. "I have children, too, and I have to take care of them!"

"Yes, it's better to think about how to get rid of this dog rather than to quarrel over leadership," said the soft-hearted candidate of science. "Let's agree: whoever resolves the matter of this dog, he shall become our leader, and we shall elect him! Let it be so!"

Struck by these words, we all left the supa one by one.

* * *

"We" means us, according to E. Safar, "part of this nation." Our correspondent is right. Although we are a motley crew — the former trade union boss, our aksakal-leader; the freelance journalist for a tabloid with a tiny readership, E. Safar himself (it was his penname); the two candidates of science (one is assistant professor); the migrant driver who travels far and wide to earn money for his numerous children; and the modernist tradesman dreaming of opening a shop on every corner — we are all part of this one nation, aren't we?

We gather at this makeshift chaikhana at the weekend to play cards, sometimes from mid-morning to midday, sometimes in the cool of the evening. When the tradesman joins us, we sometimes play for money, too. The aksakal-leader, the oldest person in our neighbourhood, usually brings a large plate full of apples or grapes from his garden. The tea is often brought in turns from the house of the two scholars who live next to each other. As he drives by in his red Damas, the tradesman inquires after his various shops around the city and drops off one or two of bottles of vodka for us. Later he brings tomatoes and cucumbers and joins us. Though our makeshift chaikhana has never been registered formally, it is a good place to get together.

As the cards are dealt, we talk about everything under the sun. But our thoughts generally centre around how to register our horvan as a fully-fledged neighbourhood,[33] and how to build a good chaikhana and a separate room here. Fine, but who will do this job? Registering the neighbourhood could be delegated to our correspondent, since he is quick-witted and is good with his pen. Who could do the rest? Hey, look, what about our Boss? Though he does not play cards with us, he built walls around the horvan on his own initiative and fixed a strong gate, so he would probably be supportive if we asked him for more. In fact, he is the one who always solves any problems relating to the supply of electricity, gas or telephone services in the neighbourhood. He did not wait for the aksakal-leader but simply settled the bill out of his own pocket. Yes, he is a good and generous person! But: people are really fed up with his dog. The dog does not look like his owner. Well, you should put up with

---

33 By registering, the *horvan* would be eligible say, for electricity, sewage etc.

the fire since you've already eaten his pilaf, as the saying goes Sure, we should be patient, patient... And actually, we have all got used to its barking now. So much so that whenever it stops barking we are all upset, as though we have lost something. The dog was the neighbourhood's good luck charm. Let it bark the whole day long! Barking is its task. In fact, it's a good thing – strangers won't show up or lurk around with it carrying on like that. So let it bark! But...

Finally, we get around to the main issue. The neighbourhood's name is already agreed: 'Aralashqo'rg'on' or Motley. Hope the office that names neighbourhoods officially won't raise any objections. But who will be elected as our aksakal-leader? The group becomes divided. The game of cards peters out, and the oldest person in the neighbourhood, who always wants to lead something, will begin to argue openly or secretly with our neighbour, the tradesman. The first will cite his rich leadership experience, the second his wealth. We are all spectators. It's all the same to the rest of us, since we are just common folk.

The tradesman who fights against the aksakal uses advanced methods of intrigue and from time to time he gazes at the beautiful supa, stroking the paint of its wooden slats.

The supa is wide and strong, carved with an ancient and royal design. Seven or eight people carried it here from the nearby recreation centre when it closed down. In all honesty, we simply helped ourselves to it, carried it off over the wall. Well, it was just lying unused in a forgotten corner of the recreation centre, one leg broken. The driver had noticed it some time ago, it was he who gave us the nod. He used to take a nap on it when he was tired of driving. But it was the aksakal, the former head of the trade union, who suggested giving it to the people of the horvan. The tradesman was responsible for bringing it to a proper place and repairing it, bringing it to life again with two coats of green paint. And so an old, useless supa became a gracious meeting point. "The main craftsman" shamelessly claimed he used half a cubic metre of timber and six kilogrammes of German paint on it. And what did you do, miserly aksakal?

According to our assistant professor, a long time ago, the famous statesman – who was a peasant by birth and who hit his forehead against the doorframe every time he went in or out of his office – liked to sit on this supa and sip tea, propped up on his elbow. Ah, how pleasant it was to lie there when weary of trade union issues, drinking royal green tea and watching the leaves of the tree above you, dreaming about your bright future. But today it is we – the representatives of the time our grandfather dreamt of – who sit on this supa sipping tea. Playing cards are scattered in the middle of the circle, and everyone's only wish is to trick another player. Put the ace in its place! Well done! Did you throw the Jack and the ace? You should take it all! I've pressed your Queen recently! Didn't you see? Don't cheat, comrade! No! I said no! It was my turn! Well then we'll have to deal again! Hey, I'll do it, stop!

Where did this motley circle appear from?

A long time ago, our block of flats in the city was knocked down, a new roundabout was built in its place, and we were given land here. Since it is some distance from the centre, those who were able to build a house here built one, while others just gave their plot to someone else, sold or exchanged it. And so an interesting community gradually emerged here. But the land is well watered and fertile. The official who handed this beautiful place over to people like us with one single scrawl of his signature was, apparently, too lazy to come and see the spot for himself, or just dashed off his signature hurriedly to get quarrelsome people like E. Safar off his back as soon as possible. If he had had so much as an inkling that this place would turn into a fruitful venue three or four years hence, well, the likes of us would not be here at all! (The assistant professor, fond of his yarns, claimed that a hundred years ago this land belonged to Mirzakarm-boy and that his servant Yulchi[34] toiled on this very spot. Who knows, maybe it's true, maybe it's not. Were the author Oybek alive today we would certainly ask him, but now we simply want to believe it.) One side of the horvan bordered onto a famous convalescence home, the other side bordered the recreation centre. Lower down was a row of new houses. People gossiped that a motley crew lived there, and that is how it got the name "Aralashqurghon," which means a mixed hor-van. And it was true; this place is home to a range of people from a migrant driver to former minister and prosecutor.

* * *

If the dog had not bitten the outsider's daughter, we would not move until midday, since it was Saturday, a day off; we would all just sit around playing cards and relaxing.

As we sit there, a silver Lacetti would draw up at the horvan gate. The Boss! All of a sudden everyone would sit up straight, saluting the Boss, hands to the chest.

The Boss would be sitting on the back seat in his black sunglasses. He would turn in our direction and give an unwilling wave of the hand: are you still sitting here? Well, carry on then.

Some would gaze after him with jealousy, some with envy, enjoyment and hope. Sometimes we gossip about him, too, but without coarse criticism, since we all suspect that there may be a spy among us.

---

34 Characters from the work of Oybek, a Soviet Uzbek poet and author who wrote about life in Uzbekistan (1904-1968).

But today, the supa is empty and no one notices the Boss's arrival. Perhaps he is surprised, too, seeing the empty supa; he doesn't know what happened today.

The Boss was a slim man, not too big, not too small. But his policy was great! They say he had been a minister until recently. Now he was the director of a famous enterprise, far better than the ministry! When he met someone, he would tilt his head to one side and look at him querulously, but harmlessly. On such occasions no one would dare question him. You had the feeling that if you began speaking to him, something bad would happen. The Boss merely greeted people, then kept silent. He was well-balanced and modest. In short, he was a mysterious person; maybe that is why he is the boss!

The Boss usually came in the evening, after sunset, and, donning a fashionable cap like those worn by the young folk, as well as shorts, he would spend his time with his dog. Sometimes he would go for a walk with his dog like a gentleman, rattling its chain. Occasionally he would play with the dog, bounding about together. Sometimes he would sit in a folding chair and stare at the dog, deep in thought. Yes, he was a great dog-lover.

Take the ceremony of walking his dog, for instance. First, the Boss's driver, who greets people too often, asks neighbours to clear the way as if warning of some danger. Once everyone has moved aside and the path is clear, the dog in its leather collar will pass by, owner in tow, looking here and there and barking proudly.

Every day before noon, the silver Lacetti appears at the high gate – it's the old driver, who greets every person he meets by touching his hands to his chest. He's bringing food for Sinbad (that's the dog's nickname). That's the only time the dog stops barking: when it is eating. And all of a sudden a strange anxiety settles over the people of the neighbourhood ... what's the matter? Is everything OK?

Well, the matter is that Sinbad stopped barking two times a day, having some temporary break: when its owner or the driver comes, and when everyone in the horvan goes to sleep. By the way, even then the dog does not rest, since the sleepers might be scared by this dog in their dreams, even though they do not hear any barking.

Everyone started to call it "The Boss's Dog" after E. Safar wrote a critical but unsuccessful article (it was not factual). In fact, it was not a small puppy but a huge tiger-like beast and its bark echoed round all the houses in the horvan, bouncing off the walls until you felt you were surrounded by mad dogs.

The Boss himself does not live here permanently. Actually, he never even spends a night here, so the villa is generally empty but for a group of modern youngsters in skimpy clothes, who usually come here at the weekends to swim.

This house was built at the lower end of the horvan and looks like a fortress within a fort. Actually, it originally belonged to a famous rich man who was arrested two years ago and who later hung himself in prison. Now it seems the villa had been bought just for the dog – the dog didn't guard the villa; on the contrary, the villa sheltered the dog.

The Boss was not an arrogant person, but he did not sit with people in the neighbourhood, since he was too busy with his work and had no time for empty chitchat or playing cards. So he only came to his villa to play with his dog. Once, on the eve of Navruz, the eastern New Year, we invited him to make pilaf together. But as usual, he did not want to join us, handing over a wodge of cash instead. But when the essence of the event was explained to him, he thought it was an official gathering. The aksakal later informed us in a whisper that he had allegedly asked if he should deliver a speech and wear business attire. "Oh no! I'm afraid he'll show up in shorts and bring his giant dog!" someone retorted. But neither he nor his dog came. And so we gradually got used to his ways.

To be fair, the Boss never did anything bad to anyone. Quite the opposite, the aksakal could speak to him on behalf of the community and ask for help in the slightest of matters. He really was a generous person. He helped everyone in the hor-van as much as he could. Someone asked him for his cement, someone asked for his timber, someone has taken a fancy to his decorative bricks while someone else has their eye on the trendy leftover tiles in his shed. He gave out whatever he had, as if he were in debt to everyone in the neighbourhood. Such a generous man he was!

The first person to recognize his generosity was our aksakal.

* * *

When the aksakal finished reciting his namaz (he had recently learned how to recite a prayer), his three granddaughters (who had come to help their grandparents during the summer holidays) passed the telephone receiver to him.

"The assistant professor is asking for you."

"Hello, what's up?" asked the aksakal. When he heard what was up, he asked again: "Who is behind all this?"

"You won't believe it: it's my neighbour!" said the assistant professor.

"That's odd. What does he want? Or does he have some agreement with the tradesman?"

"If I only knew, aksakal, but he's obviously angry because he hasn't been accepted for the position of assistant professor.

He's making excuses, saying he's not published enough, but the truth is he's simply been cold-shouldered."

"Do you know what that profiteer is going to do?"

"Well, I saw him heading off somewhere in his Damas not long ago. Something must have happened in one of his shops."

"Serves him right!"

"Now it's your turn, aksakal," the informant encouraged him. "Hurry up! You should find a solution! You know I'm always on your side. I hope the matter of our wall will be settled, too."

"We'll see," said the aksakal getting angry as he hung up. "Everyone's just out for themselves! How long will you be quarrelling over a tiny piece of land? May you perish, fake scholars!"

The aksakal went out into the yard and, seeing his wife, sitting at a corner of the veranda salting tomatoes, he asked her:

"Where is that younger son of yours? Is he writing poems again, hiding away somewhere?"

He had not seen his son since he came back from the supa. His son was on vacation, but whenever you saw him he was standing in front of the mirror on the veranda combing his hair. In the mornings, his father would ask him to tidy up the messy tools and other stuff in the garden, but they still lay there, untouched.

"I saw him going down into the cellar, it's cool down there. He said he had a headache. He came before you got back. He looked pale.

"Call him."

The lad appeared at the top of the stairs, and the sight of his tousled hair angered the aksakal:

"What were you doing, poet?"

"What should I do?" said the sleepy son. "Don't make fun of me."

"I didn't see you combing hair today."

"You scold me when I do that."

"Look at this feeble young man."

"What do you want me to do?" asked the son, unexpectedly starting to weep. "You call me a poet, but do I look like a bad guy?"

The aksakal calmed down but scolded his son again:

"You shouldn't always sleep like that! You are a young man now! How can you be called a man if you are always skulking away somewhere?"

(Later he regretted his harsh words; he had only wanted to lick his son into shape a bit.)

The aksakal's mind was frozen and he didn't know what to do. "Whoever resolves the matter of this dog, he shall become our leader, and we shall elect him!" That's what that reticent with eyeglasses had said, and those words rang in his ears. Ah, I'm appalled by voters like you!

If the truth be known, the aksakal didn't have much time for officials. As head of the trade union, he had always quarrelled with the plant managers, protecting the interests of common laborers. Unfortunately, he had to go along with them, otherwise, those common people would turn against him and not support him during elections.

But what is the situation today? Can he approach the Boss now and directly say to him: "Listen to me, brother. You have to get rid of your dog. The people living in this neighbourhood demand it."

Actually, this was a good opportunity. If he cannot solve this issue he will lose respect in Aralashqurghon, and lose his leadership of the horvan. This was his chance to prove himself.

In his clean clothes, the aksakal sat on the dusty spot where his grandchildren had played earlier.

Having spent all his savings on this house, last year the aksakal was penniless and at a loss. His younger child had managed to get a place at university, but he could barely pay the fees. And to make matters worse, the person who had brokered the deal between them and the university was asking for a hefty hand-out, though it was not clear whether he had in fact helped the admission process or not. The aksakal's two brothers in the city could not support him, or even if they could, their wives would not allow them to help. There was nothing else for it, the aksakal had to go to the villa and address the Boss.

As usual, the owner of the villa was playing with his dog. When the aksakal told him about the "contract payment" for his son's education, the Boss lumbered out of his large folding chair and pulled a wodge of dollars from the pocket of his shorts to give to the aksakal. In a panic, he refused to take the cash, but a week later the Boss transferred the necessary money directly to the university electronically. "I'm in your debt," the aksakal had to him then, but the Boss just shrugged, saying: "Don't mention it, please. We're neighbours, aren't we?" He helped many people in the neighbourhood in many ways, no strings attached.

So which Muslim could go again to him and ask for something more? Besides, the question of leadership in the horvan cannot be solved without the Boss. Everything will go wrong if he raises an objection.

Coming out with a plate of windfall apricots, the aksakal's wife was surprised to see her husband sitting there in the dust:

"What are you doing sitting here like this? What's up?"

Just then the aksakal's grandchild called his Grandpa:

"Grandpa, Grandpa! That correspondent is asking for you on the phone!"

* * *

There was only one person in Aralashqurghon who was not in debt and who did not take anything from the Boss: E. Safar!

The public correspondent went home that day and racked his brains about how to get rid of the Boss's dog. He thought he suffered more than anyone else because of that dog; since his house was right opposite the Boss's villa, the barking was as loud as if the dog were in his own backyard. How long can you just be patient? Naturally rather hot-tempered, sometimes he could bear it no longer and yelled: "Shut up! Shut up, as Allah is my witness!" But the dog didn't understand why the man was shouting and paid no attention whatsoever. Its owner – who could understand perfectly well – would show up from time to time, but the correspondent knew when he would come and on those occasions, he simply bit his tongue.

But one day his patience ran out. He wrote a critical article entitled "The Boss's Dog" and took it to his tabloid. The editor of the tabloid read the article and handed it back, saying: "This article will offend the Boss. Instead of writing this, you'd better feed the dog some dough or meat with a needle inside. No need to use the paper for this, E. Safar!" But the editor calmed down later and came up with another suggestion: "OK, I would agree to publish it if you spread this valuable paper under the dog in the evening."

"Do you really think it would let me?" E. Safar retorted angrily. The editor shrugged his shoulders, meaning: "It's your business, do whatever you want." Apparently, the Boss had another villa in the editor's neighbourhood and the "singing dog" there might be even better.

Offended, the correspondent stopped bringing articles to the paper for quite a while.

Finally, under the relentless rain of the dog's barking, E. Safar found a solution: they should write an open letter to the Boss on behalf of all the people living in the horvan. Since no one dared approach him individually to complain, this was the only way to resolve the issue.

The correspondent drafted a letter, using his best writing skills. The letter included a little praise, a little request and a little requirement. In one place he even added something like: "It's a pity that the dog bothers public correspondent E. Safar, too."

He signed this request-requirement first. Then he started ringing his neighbours, without waiting for the evening get-together at the supa.

The tradesman's wife told him her husband was in the city on shop business. This greedy man is planning to open a small shop by the supa. Perhaps he is hoping for the Boss's support – after all, he has to fill the shop with some goods from somewhere, otherwise who would go in to buy something?! By the way, he doesn't care about anything, just so long as no tax officer or policeman turns up to inspect his shop. He wants to develop his chain of shops and can think of nothing else.

The migrant driver was not at home, either. Maybe he's gone to find poison?

The candidate of science who so bravely laid down the gauntlet at the supa the other day did not want to sign the letter at all, because the Boss had helped him fix a telephone line in his house. He was afraid that if he signed it the Boss would simply cut the line. And he could not live without a phone, since his mother was elderly and ailing in the city.

The assistant professor put it briefly:

"Well, correspondent, please do not add my name to it! It's childish, and I don't like signing anything."

E. Safar replied sarcastically:

"Be frank, my friend. Weren't you the one who acted all snobby, saying the Boss was a close friend of your director?"

When the candidate for the leadership, the aksakal, heard about the letter, he thought a little and said:

"Isn't it a bit foolish, my correspondent friend? In any case, he is an official!"

"If so, he should control his dog! Can't he even manage a dog?"

"Well, don't be angry, please," the aksakal tried to soothe him. "What if you send your letter without signatures, Safar-boy?"

The correspondent was not offended by this suggestion, but the aksakal was being overly naïve:

"Don't you know that an unsigned letter is considered nothing but a blank piece of paper?"

"Let them consider it whatever they want, but the fact is that this letter will go to the right address."

"Well, who will pass this letter to him then?"

"Who? Surely no one has to give this letter to him in person? What if we just toss it into his villa through the slats in the gate?"

"Who would do that?"

The aksakal didn't say anything.

"You!"

"Me?!"

"Who is a candidate for leadership, you or me?"

The receiver was hung up.

E. Safar tore the letter into pieces, went out into the yard and began yelling at the top of his voice:

"Stop barking! Stop it! Shut up, as Allah is my witness! Even pop music is a hundred times better than this!"

* * *

Everyone except E. Safar was present at the evening get-together. E. Safar had high blood pressure so he couldn't join them. Serves him right! Trouble-maker!

We all sat there on the supa like good friends and neighbours, as if nothing had happened. The same game, the same scene. The driver told us a new director had been appointed to the recreation centre which had been scheduled for demolition. They say the new director was really cool.

However, just as we were cutting into a watermelon brought by the tradesman, a most extraordinary thing happened: the Boss's dog that "charmed" the tranquility of the horvan stopped barking! Silence reigned! It was most odd: everyone looked at each other as if we had all lost something very dear. Everyone had to know as quickly as possible: is everything OK?

Just then a girl's voice floated up from the lane:

"Grandpa, Grandpa! Grandma is asking for you. Come quickly! Quickly!"

"Oh, that's my granddaughter!" said the aksakal, getting up with difficulty. "Why are you yelling? What's up?"

In a moment everything became clear. Unbelievable! The aksakal's younger son had shot the Boss!

Everyone jumped up, leaving the sliced watermelon scattered on the supa amid aces, Jacks, Queens, and Kings.

That was a very bad day.

Half an hour later, two ambulances raced by. There was no doubt that something terrible had happened.

Everyone who heard about the incident was anxious to find out all the details. Everyone rushed over to the scene, but no one dared come too close. After all, it was the Boss who had been shot...

The details crystalized that evening when we all gathered as usual at our supa.

It was true. the aksakal's younger son had indeed shot the Boss. But he had not meant to kill him. He just went there to shoot the dog. As it happened, just as he approached the villa and took aim at the dog, which was still barking incessantly behind the high iron fence, the Boss himself came out with some food in his hand. Someone said that a bullet struck his hand, someone else said it struck his mouth (may Allah be merciful!). E. Safar's wife said that through a gap in the fence she saw blood pouring from the Boss's nose and mouth. Maybe it's true, maybe it's not.

Actually, there are always only two witnesses of such incidents: those who committed them, and Allah himself. There will be thousands of assumptions, though.

What about the gun? Where had the boy got the gun from? It soon became clear that the aksakal's son found it in the cellar. It was covered with rust so the boy cleaned it, greased it, and had even used it once or twice to shoot a sparrow. After that... The gun had been presented to the aksakal many years ago when he went to Irkutsk for a training program. How he could bring a cold weapon all the way back home? Maybe the gift-giver had also handed him a special paper allowing him to transport it?

Where is the boy now? They say he's run away, but no one knows for sure where the scoundrel has gone. Because of him, the aksakal cannot go out, he has to sit at home taking medicines. "I'm to blame, I'm to blame!" he keeps repeating. For some reason, no one informed the police about the incident.

Well, why did the boy want to kill the Boss's dog? In revenge! He had fallen in love with the outsider's daughter, you see. He even dedicated poems to her. Oh my, it's true that love drives men mad!

As we all were sitting at the supa the next day, several people drove up and took the guilty culprit, the giant dog, away in their closed car. The neighbourhood kids ran alongside the car, barking, right up to the main road.

One or two days later, a strange panic spread throughout the neighbourhood: have you heard? the Boss has gone mad! He caught some disease from the dog. (There were some who were gladdened by these woeful tidings.) The doctors will be here soon to take blood tests from everyone in the horvan, they say. The outsider's daughter went mad, too. She needs forty injections in her belly.

These strange events threw up many baffling, enigmatic questions. And that is true of real life, too, isn't it?

We never saw the Boss in the horvan again. They say that his villa is up for sale. One day someone said it had been sold, but that was never confirmed, since the villa was very expensive. Though the Boss was a generous and tolerant person, his villa did not serve anybody else.

Some people mourned the Boss's absence – how could they ever see their dreams come true without his generous help? But others were glad – how could the Boss ever ask for his money back now? And some, of course, genuinely felt sorry for him.

Our aksakal still could not go out to the supa. He worried that the police might show up on his doorstep, that's why he took so many medicines. He stopped thinking about leadership. His son hid himself somewhere. Some say he is in Kazakhstan, some say he is in Russia. In short, no one knows his whereabouts.

After two months, the outsider's younger daughter married the son of her aunt living in the village of her father. The villagers were not aware that the dog had bitten her, so she could hide her story there.

One day, the cool director of the recreation centre came with his four assistants and took back the supa, which had witnessed all these historical events. The tradesman argued with them, demanding they repay him what he had spent on paint. E. Safar wanted to write a critical article about it, but one evening he was dropped off at home, drunk, by the cool director's car. After that he stopped meddling in the matter.

And so it was that the neighbourhood where barking had once reigned supreme turned into a peaceful place.

THE DIN

Distant city, distant pasts

1. Good news and a mysterious namesake

Two pieces of news came hot on the heels of each other from a distant city and left Farhod Ramazon in quite a quandary. In fact, they threw him into utter chaos, causing him to relive an event of several years ago, as a result of which his present, everyday life was reduced to confused pandemonium. True enough, those events are all behind him now, for better or worse; who knows, life might have proceeded gradually, but, like unexpected thunder, everything was suddenly turned upside down.

The first news came in the shape of an email from Ravshan Akobirov. Farhod could have perhaps, at a pinch, expected a letter from someone else in this world, but he never thought he would ever receive a message — especially not such good news — from this fellow.

"Farhod-jon, I congratulate you from the depths of my heart!" the sincere message began. "Forgive me for not informing you earlier. Maybe you have heard that I have been negotiating with Hollywood film companies for a long time? I feel I have quite a good relationship with them, although they only bore fruit yesterday. By chance, someone gave me an old copy of The Star of the East magazine published in Tashkent in which I read your novel The Insurgency of Love. As if sensing good news in advance, I had the novel translated into English (by the way, the translation was made by our own *Farhod*, he has already mastered this job) and sent it overseas. So, unexpectedly I received good news. Once again: congratulations, brother! In short, we are about to become very lucky. As per their proposal, I must start preparations by the end of this year. If permission is granted, the film may be shot in Uzbekistan. What do you think? But we need to come to a mutual agreement about some aspects of the script as soon as possible. You know that certain reasons prevent me from coming to Tashkent. Are you planning to travel to our part of the world? It would be wonderful if you could come. I have some other things to tell you, things which concern you ..."

For some reason "our own Farhod" was written in Italics. Was he boasting? And why Farhod? Who is he?

All the words that followed in the P.S. were particularly surprising: "Are you still upset with me, your brother? Don't worry. Please, forget that, it is all in the past now..."

Farhod was completely flustered when he received the next letter about a month later.

"Dear Farhod! Thank you very much for... forgetting your old friends! What else can I say? I hope you have already received Ravshan's letter. Accept my sincere congrats, honey! If you only knew how proud I am of you! Hollywood, I hear! Well, that's not an easy thing to say, Mr. Romazanov! (It was written exactly like that — "Romazanov"). Aren't you planning to visit us? I heard that your film is in the run-up for the forth-coming film festival. It has a strange name, hasn't it? Something like "The Girls' Guardian?" Who is that 'guardian'? Not you, I hope! Remember?... Hmm, don't say that's what you mean by 'guardian'! Okay, don't be angry, I'm just kidding. Oh, I almost forgot: how is your ear? Let it buzz, don't worry, let it buzz. Don't listen to it. Who needs a sound ear to write a story that can attract even Hollywood?! It would be better if you follow great Beethoven, my dear friend. With your "Guardian" moving forward, why don't you come here? The "Girls" are ready over here! But frankly speaking, we are facing some problems these days. It would be great if you and I could meet and talk. Your namesake Farhod is about to finish school. He is going to study in London. He needs to obtain a passport. This man is going to be an Uzbek, huh! I need your advice. Talk to you more when you come. I hope you did not forget me. A kiss for your famous potato-shaped nose!

Your own Vika.

P.S. I have got news for you. I was in Moscow recently and met with your old friend Sur'at Nabiev there. He said he's got married. You won't believe it: he's married his Lida again! It seems she returned from Algeria. Isn't it cool? Now let me kiss your nose once again. Let me... Okay, here we go!"

Today, Farhod Ramazon realized he had not visited that distant city, Moscow, for almost 17 years! Seventeen! Vika and Ravshan Akobirov, who had once hurt him so badly, had gradually faded into something akin to a forgotten nightmare.

Why hadn't he visited them for such a long time? Well, he could have tried to go. Or maybe he did not want to visit them? But why?

There was reason enough for that. But, in fact, he was afraid. He really was worried...

2. In the sky

"Farkhad Mirzaevich, wouldn't you like a drink?.." asked Bakhtiyor.

When travelling abroad, Farhod Ramazon generally slept in the plane. But he could not sleep this time. His thoughts were an unruly jumble. He could not concentrate, could not recall those past events one by one to identify where he had been callow and slipped up. In fact, he was not even sure it had been a mistake or if he would behave differently if he could turn back the clock. Only Allah knew that, only Allah!

Farhod Ramazon, the head of the delegation, had intentionally moved to an empty seat at the back of the plane to hide from his colleagues, but all of a sudden, this man of culture and arts was troubled. He wanted to smoke. In the plane! Three or four years ago he had, with great difficulty, managed to rid himself of this evil habit. Ah, too bad he could not refuse this young actor's offer of a drink. The actor's father is an old friend of his and holds the prestigious title of People's Artist. Extremely fond of company, he is an excellent cook. In the chaikhana teahouse, donning his apron, he fries liver so well that after eating that fried liver no one has the will to taste his pilaf, even though it is even more delicious than the liver. And so he always ends up parceling the pilaf up on a platter and taking to it one of his lady loves. One of them turned out to be a pilaf-lover, so many a long year ago he married her, leaving his first wife, a school teacher, as well as one daughter and this boy Bakhtiyor. Who knows, they say that the daughter of the People's Artist put a red mark on her forehead and converted to another religion. Yes, it's amazing how easily fatherless children can renounce their faith.

Several years ago, Farhod Ramazon had somehow grown apart from the People's Artist for no particular reason. Now he has no time for social gatherings in tea-houses. In fact, he tries to avoid them, only attending official meetings and ceremonies. But Bakhtiyor is the son of his old companion after all, so he cannot say no to his offer of a drink. And this young actor is a very pleasant lad, too. His face and eyes are always smiling, he is handsome and well-mannered. Whenever anyone sees him, they immediately cheer up despite themselves, griped by an urge to be young again. As soon as the plane took off, Bakhtiyor began chatting with the passengers in his row, drawing other passengers' attention. Then he took off his pullover, slung it over his shoulder and began strolling around between the rows. Sometimes he leant over someone's seat and spoke about something, sometimes he stopped unhurriedly and questioned the polite flight attendants as they went about their duties, tray in hand, their scarves neatly folded into flying swallows. But no one wondered at his behaviour and no one got angry with him, either. All the women in the cabin had their eye on him. He was the famous young actor, Bakhtiyor Azizov! Everyone in Uzbekistan knew him and liked him. He was seen on television every hour —sometimes he advertised a brand of beer; sometimes he advertised the bright side of life, a healthy life; sometimes he was the star attraction of a TV-show; sometimes he was the main hero in a long, boring series, or in another, he played out the bitter fate of a young drug addict. He is also the "guardian" of girls, the star of the film to be premiered at the film festival tomorrow. At first, scriptwriter Farhod Ramazon did not want this well-groomed yes-man in his film, but after watching the video auditions, he agreed that this troublemaker could play the main hero: he changed and became exactly what the scriptwriter wanted. Now he is on his way to the film festival with the rest of the winners. What can you say here other than to wish him good luck?

Bakhtiyor was relaxed and carefree at all times and in all circumstances. With a simple letter or phone call he could swiftly solve his friends' problems, even those which some influential officials couldn't settle. And so he was loved and cherished by all.

Now he is young and hot, the world is his oyster, beautiful young ladies fall at his feet – do you think he will calm down? No, he will turn out like his father, for sure.

How about us? How did we spend our time?..

"Farkhad Mirzaevich, wouldn't you like a drink?" the young actor repeated in Russian, breaking his reverie.

Deep in thought, Farhod Ramazon started, and turned to the young actor.

Bakhtiyor was kneeling in the aisle, a flat dish in his hand, smiling that very becoming smile of his which melted even the coldest of hearts.

"I don't drink," the disgruntled head replied with a frown.

So many years have passed since the Uzbek language was widely used in Uzbekistan, but these people still want to speak their "second mother tongue". When playing a role in a film they always speak good Uzbek but whenever they speak to each other, they use this other language.

"Please, teacher, take this," the young actor beseeched him, in Russian again, but then, as though something suddenly dawned on him, he quickly spoke in Uzbek: "Please, just one!"

"Well alright then, pour, pour, but only one" replied Farhod Ramazon loosening up a little.

Bakhtiyor filled a plastic cup with a liquid which shimmered like black tea and joyfully handed it to Ramazon. Satisfied, the lad took a piece of chocolate from his side pocket and gave it to the writer.

Perhaps because of that or perhaps for some other reason, but the writer suddenly craved a cigarette.

Farhod Ramazon beckoned a passing flight attendant and asked for water. It's a tried and tested method: if you drink too much water and have a little patience, the urge will pass.

Remembering Vika's letter again, he began to think about his "old friend" Sur'at. He was vaguely aware of the events mentioned in the P.S.. Sur'at had mentioned it when he came to his mother's funeral a long time ago.

Farhod Ramazon remembered how he and Sur'at had gone to that distant city together. Together they had studied at the institute, too, worked at the television company for several years, and attended a scriptwriters' training program. But Sur'at was always unlucky, even though he grew up in a rich, influential family in Tashkent; in those days his father was the director of the only lemonade plant in the city. Farhod had visited their family several times, he knew his parents as well as his brothers and sisters. Sur'at studied well everywhere, you could not tell that, actually, he was none too bright. He was a master at coming up with an interesting story line. For example, a young actress frequents various circles to research people and in real life she becomes a skillful actor. Or an old man gives some medicine to his old wife and she becomes young again. So Sur'at had mastered the requirements of the film industry, he surprised many with his wonderful ideas, but when it came to writing them down on paper, well, he always failed. As a result, he had no work of his own, only joint projects created by several authors.

What about you, Farhod Ramazon? Aren't you a bit like your meek and unlucky companion, too?! For a long time you have been sitting in one place as a nursing your career and have not written anything of value. Now all you can do is give advice to others, teach them, while writing or scripts are as insignificant as a fly to you, something quite useless. You traded everything in for this art of leadership, renouncing everything for the luxurious trifles which go with it. Yes, you really could call it a trade-off, albeit with some hesitations and emotional pain. It is always cushier to lead the company rather than to do the job yourself. Ah yes, it is such a sweet, tasty marshmallow cream – one lick and you're hooked, writing flies right out of the window.

In fact, many stories remained in his heart without ever appearing on paper. He thinks about it at night sometimes, it worries him. There's a stabbing pain in his heart like a splinter, making him want to leap right out of bed and write it all down, but then either fright or lack of courage or just the wearisome grind of everyday life holds him back. And the next day, ensconced in his routine work, the feelings of the night before seem trivial and insignificant. This pattern is replayed over and over, until gradually even this one will be forgotten and you will find pretexts to justify yourself, and even to be proud of your actions.

And so he never wrote "The Death of the Father" or "The Deputy." They remained stories in his head for years, but now they sit heavily in his heart like stones, while his heart itself has become an immovable stone. After receiving Ravshan Akobirov's letter, he rummaged through his old papers, found Insurgency of Love and reread it. Thanks perhaps to the unexpected acclaim this book was now enjoying abroad, after reading it he was truly amazed: is this really my work? Did I really write this book myself? Where is that pencil I wrote with? Can I at least find some broken stub? He wrote that script in the depths of anxiety, yet at times he was as free as a bird.

Locking the door of a solitary room at the back of his house, he downed almost a whole bottle of vodka, lay down on the sofa and, despite his age and high rank, shed the bitter tears of a hurt child.

Sometimes, heartily sick of all the red tape and requirements from on high, he wants to jack it all in. He dreams of sitting at home, pouring his heart out onto paper. But would he have time now? Would he find the strength to do this? Allah only knows. And this is not his only burden, he has other troubles too...

Last time Sur'at came to Tashkent (poor man, he had lost so much weight, gone bald; in short, he was in a very sorry state) he sat in Ramazon's solitary corner sipping whisky at the table laden with bountiful food and said some strange things.

"When will you go to the capital?" he had asked then.

"Did I leave something in your capital?" - the devoted citizen of an independent country and a responsible leader who could never travel abroad without proper permission replied.

"Don't you want to see your son? He must have grown into a handsome boy by now."

"My son? What are you talking about?"

"Didn't you have a child by Vika, Lagutina's daughter?"

Though the owner of the solitary room was trying to be a good host and not show his inner feelings, he really wanted to get rid of this old friend who was filling his plush room with unluckiness and grievances, so he did not pay enough attention to his words, taking them as friendly banter. But, even though he was tipsy, too, he soon sobered up at the name which fell from his guest's lips. Suddenly soft rays shone like the mellow autumn sun as his heart filled with feelings grown dull with dust over the past year.

"How is she? What has she been doing?" he asked, trying to not reveal his secret.

"Who? Vika? I haven't seen her for years. They say an influential Chechen businessman married her. Later I heard she was with your teacher, Ravshan Akobirov, remember him? Maybe you saw her in several TV series a while back. You may have heard, her mother, Gulya, is doing well. She's become "a good film grandmother" as you would say. There's not a cinema magazines published without one of her articles, believe it or not. She holds the Moscow cinema scene in her palm now. But she is a very nice woman, a good person. She always tries to take good care of me whenever we meet. Anyway, she's definitely one of us, not an outsider"

Numbed by this news, the host was too embarrassed to ask for more detail. But he couldn't take in anything else. Apparently Sur'at was now talking about his own wife. His Lida had come back to him (from the bosom of an Arab producer?) … they have been living in the same old house since then… The host must have been gawping, open-mouthed, since Sur'at sat in silence for a while then said: "What else can I do? There's a child between us. Though we live together in one house, we both have our own ways."

Understood. It means they live together but 'entertain themselves' with another.

Farhod took a strong dislike to Sur'at after hearing this. "Weren't you planning to move to Tashkent? We could find you a woman here: who cares if she's blind or deaf. Besides, there are so many girls in the villages. Didn't you use to dream about those country girls?"

All those years ago when they finished their training program, Sur'at married Lida and stayed on in Moscow. He worked at the Filmmakers Association as an editor on national scripts, but when his work was not going well and his family life was ruined, he had come to Tashkent and told his friend about his misfortunes, about his plans to marry a Muslim woman and live in a remote Uzbek village.

"But now I think it's too late for that," said Sur'at, already tipsy. "I can't leave my child, he depends on me. Who else do I have? So it's too late, too late."

"What about me? It's late for me, too…" thought Farhod to himself.

* *

Farhod Ramazon glanced around the plane and gestured to Bakhtiyor who was leaning over talking with a girl sitting near him.

"Yes, Farkhad Mirzevich."

"Do you still have that drink?"

"One second," replied Bakhtiyor with a flourish, and rushed to bring that drink.

This time Farhod Ramazon finished the liquid in the plastic cup. Let it be like that, let it make him sleep!

When Bakhtiyot moved away, Farhod Ramazon spread his body out on his seat, gently fiddling with a screw in his glasses. There was nothing to be heard, as if there were silence everywhere.

Actually, the noise of the flying plane with its bustling cabin was gradually receding; all the din of the world was moving into his own ear, into his own mind.

Farhod Ramazon slowly closed his eyes. The scene around him began to fade, other scenes took its place.

Vika, Vika, Viktoria… Dildoria…

* *

3. The guest bedbugs:
Farhod-Fidel-Fedya-Castro-Comandante

This was young scriptwriter Farhod Ramazonov's first real visit to this resort reserved for filmmakers of the "Great Land." It was tucked away deep in the forest. True, as a student on the advanced training course, he had made the journey here with Sur'at to see their famous fellow countrymen: the great Master of the Uzbek film industry and two other teachers, Sobit Yahyoyev and Tal'at Rafiullin. Back then, as students, they had taken with them a small sack of red carrots, two kilos of frozen meat for pilaf and two bottles of vodka. They wanted to get to know those great masters a little, and, frankly speaking, to let the masters get to know them, so that they would look favourably on them back in Tashkent. However, when the great Master met the two young men with uncertain futures, he merely declared: "I have backache and my bladder hurts" then quickly disappeared back into his room. The others started drinking, striking up some endless discussion with Ivan Ivanovich; no one paid any attention to the pilaf products brought by their young disciples, except for Rafiullin who simply said: "Later, guys, later."

In short, two friends who had come there in high hopes ended up forgotten in a corner, pouring too much alcohol into their empty stomachs and returning to the city like drunkards, without having heard anything worthwhile or making any connections.

So all in all it is better to say that Farhod was seeing this place for the first time.

From the airport he went directly to the Filmmakers Association, picked up his permit there, briefly looked in on Sur'at, and came straight here, choosing to decline his friend's offer of going to his remote single flat and listening to his never-ending tales of woe. By the way, Sur'at phoned him regularly in Tashkent so there was very little left to talk about.

The resort was spacious and well-built. On one side there was an old style three-storey brick construction, with a higher modern building in front, not far from the courtyard. There was a cinema hall alongside it, a mirrored kitchen encircled by trees and a row of small wooden chalets set among the pines, allegedly intended for single or other separated people.

Farhod went to the old building; the administration office was on the ground floor.

Now, seated in an old armchair, he is waiting for Valentina Grigorevna Samokhina's reply. According to the notice typewritten on a piece of cardboard hung on the wall, she is the duty administrator. At the big desk behind the brown wooden screen, Ms. Samokhina was giving Farhod's passport and permit a thorough examination before registering him. She was a young, mischievous lady.

"Oooh, sunny Uzbekistan again!" she greeted him cheerily. "Lots of friends of yours are here."

Farhod did not ask who those friends were; it was all the same to him.

"Ramazonov Fidel Mirzaevich," the lady said, not looking in the passport. "Where is "Castro"?

This question was the bane of Farhod's life, it even weighed on his soul. Wherever he goes he faces the same question and never knows how to reply. What should he say? That it was his father who had given him this name, so they should go and ask him?

So he just stood up and walked over to the counter. A large cat eyed him from the far corner of the desk; seeing Farhod, it began to meow. Where the devil had this evil spirit emerged from? It hadn't been there before! Seeing the ubiquitous cat always put Farhod in a bad mood.

"You know, Valentina Grigorevna..." he addressed the lady, quickly glancing at her name on the wall.

"What if we do not know, Fidel Mirzaevich?" said the woman tilting her head to one side. "What should I know here?"

"You see, Valentina Grig..."

"Valya! Just call me Valya!" she interrupted him quickly, raising her voice. "You can call me Valya, Commandante, You have my permission. I quite understand. Ah, the sixties, a romantic period, the island of Liberty, "Viva Cuba!", "Cuba is my love!" Am I right?"

Exactly! How does an ordinary concierge know all that history?

Right you are, Valya! The fiery revolutionary had visited Uzbekistan, too. All the newspapers carried his photos posing alongside those famous "creators of white gold.[35]" Mirzo Ramazon, a simple, romantic Komsomol, named his first child after that bearded man, hoping he would become someone great. He never thought that his son would be teased. That was a time of Fidels, Angelas and Robertinos,[36] Valya-khon! Today, one of them is known as dictator. Another, whom the whole Soviet Union supported with cries of "Free Angela Davis!" turned out not to be a real woman, since she married a black woman with curly hair similar to hers and anyhow, she now fights against Communist ideology. The true gender of the third, the "Italian nightingale," whom the whole world followed

---

35 i.e. cotton pickers.
36 A reference to naming children after famous heroes: Fidel Castro, Angela Davies, Robertino Loretti.

when he sang "Jama-aica!", is up for discussion: rumour has it he 'went pink,' became gay and married a man. His husband, they say, is so young he hasn't even heard of the famous song "Jamaica"...

This is it, my dear Valya-khon! Then the father wanted to match his son's name with his school, but, unable to find a Spanish school, he sent his son to a Russian school instead. His late grandfather Ramazon-boy was enraged and cursed the revolutionary: "I'll rip that Castro's beard off! Haven't you got any local names? What's that Pidel-midel anyway? Why don't you call him Farhod or Fayzulla?" His grandfather was furious when he heard that his grandchild would go to a Russian school, too: "A Muslim child should receive a Muslim education! What did I raise you for, Mirzo?! To become a pagan?!"

And after that, Farhod became Farhod! He never introduced himself as Fidel; on the contrary, he was always embarrassed by his own name and tried to hide it.

Admittedly, there were some who envied him when they found out his real name, but he himself was always embarrassed by it. In those days, changing your name was fraught with difficulty; even now it is no easy task - you have to jump over thousands of hurdles!

At university, he was known as "Fedya" until one day someone accidentally called him "Castro" after which he was called "Commandante". It was common to have two or three names in those days. Ravshan was Roma, for instance, Gulsum - Gulya, Sobir - Sashka, Zuhra - Zoya, and so on

Once when he was introduced to a Cuban student living in a neighbouring hostel, he made fun of Farhod saying: "If you're Fidel, where's your beard then?"

"Alright, macho, follow me. I'll show you to your room," Valya said, taking a key from the wooden keyboard and heading for the stairs.

As he followed her to the second floor, Farhod caught sight of a beautiful woman ahead of them and his head started to spin.

Why do women look so lovely when you are on a trip? Ah, and the women here are especially beautiful, as Farhod knew only too well, having assured himself of this on more than once occasion while attending special courses here. (A few days later, he would learn that even this woman who looked so serious now would be willing to let her hair down with anyone, not that he could benefit from it now - he was already dizzy.)

Entering a room at the end of the corridor Valya plumped up the two pillows on the bed and, opening her arms wide, said as if she were about to take a nap, too:

"Come on in! Now you can have a good rest, Fidel Mirzaevich! Please call me if you need anything. At your service twenty-four hours a day! The room's not bad, is it?"

"It's all the same to me, thanks."

As soon as the concierge left, Farhod put his luggage in the wardrobe and flopped onto the bed: he was exhausted.

He was asleep in a minute. His whole body was relaxed and balmy, as if he were floating in warm water... Wow, is that Valya? Yes, she has leapt into my arms! Ah, such an embrace! Her body is so hot! Is she tickling me? Good heavens! No, she is scratching me with her long fingernails again and again. Oh, no, it's the cat, that black-and-white moggy I saw downstairs!

Farhod jumped out of the bed. He checked his neck and limbs: he was breaking out in a horrendous rash. Something was biting him! Is that a bedbug? O Merciful One, what's that doing here?

Standing aghast in the middle of his room, he scratched frantically for a while before rushing to the concierge, leaving the door open.

Valya's face reddened abruptly at his complaint. Glancing round, she quickly murmured:

"I beg your pardon, Fidel Mirzaevich, please forgive me." Stroking Farhod's hand with her soft fingers she added, "Please don't tell anyone about it. The last guest in that room was messy man, I suppose he left the bugs there. I wonder how he could be a producer, such a creep! Nothing but a miserable bug-feeder! Don't be offended, dear, I'll give you another room, a lux! With windows opening onto the green forest! You will enjoy living there, no doubt about it!"

"Thanks, thank you so much," said Farhod as he scratched his body obliviously.

"If you see even so much as an ant biting you in that room, you may call me and I will soothe your rash myself," said the lady, taking another key from the keyboard and fluttering her eyelashes playfully. "By the way, someone was looking for you."

"Who?" asked Farhod, surprised.

"Oh, the name escapes me. The most famous one, you should know..."

Farhod thought for a moment: "Who can it be? Surely not the Master? He's over seventy years old, he couldn't possibly be here. So who can that famous person be?"

4. Master. Mirzo Bobur's blue-eyed mother - film bride

Before the start of any discussion about any scenario at the so-called Artistic Council, the chairman, a former lighting technician and undisputed coward, will definitely ask the following question: "Has this scenario already been checked by the Master?" If not, whatever you try will be useless and you will need to show the scenario to the Master first.

The Master is a 70-year-old man, head of our film makers, who also led this organization for many years, and who has two or three internationally acclaimed films under his belt, thanks to which he enjoys worldwide renown. I call him "our film grandpa". Film-grandpa!

Generally speaking, if you add the word "film" to any other word you will immediately have a new word such as film-grandpa, film-grandma, film-legend, film-master (chairman), film-richman (film producer), film-slave (assistants, decorators), film-sweetheart, film-companion, film-loneliness. I frankly call myself "film-hapless-one". If I were not hapless would I write a scenario or would I study how to do it? I liken a scriptwriter to poor parents who have just played out their daughter's wedding. They bring up a girl with so many hopes and expectations, but an admirer comes along and takes her away, promising to give the parents a horse or a camel. After the suitor takes her, he will do whatever he wants with her. After all, you can't meddle, can you?

Writing a scenario is like that, too. I have lived through that. There are many examples in my life, and I'll tell you about them all in good time.

See, I took the floor and almost got sidetracked!

So coming back to our film-grandpa:

No one has seen him around here for the past five to ten years as he lives in his summer house on the outskirts of the city. He lives there all year long. Alone. His wife passed away some time ago. By the way, why do I say alone – what about those ever-present "Sabo"? Alright, I'll tell you about that later.

I went to see him at his residence several times, too. Before setting off this time I pondered whether I really needed to go all that way to see him. Would this foul old man understand anything? His time has already been and gone; today there are so many new film methods, new forms and acts. How would that moldy film-legend living so far away know anything about them? But they say that a beggar's anger hurts him more, so my proud head was bowed down.

It's not a good idea to go to see the Master empty handed. You should know that. If you are generous you can buy something special, but at the very least you should take a bottle of "White Stork" cognac with you. That's the only one our Master drinks, but it's not easy to come by.

Suppose you went there. The sleepy old man will definitely be sitting in the shade of a tree. He will barely open his eyes. "Read," he will order. You will sit in front of him and start reading what you have brought, sweating profusely and feeling shy. The Master closes his eyes, sniffs from time to time. He seems to be snoring. Don't pay attention to that, just go on reading, otherwise you will lose. The cunning old dog intentionally becomes gullible. All of a sudden he might open his eyes and ask a tricky question. His question seems to be very simple, even primitive. But don't be fooled — it will not be easy to answer that question. The Master will formulate a question touching on the very crux of your script. For instance, he might ask the following: "Why did you only write this? Go ahead, please!" Or "Why is that character of yours such a chatterbox? Does he ever shut up at all?" If you don't know what to say but just bow your head, the old man will do the same. Woe to this condition! If you raise an objection, or if you just mumble something general, not to worry — he will continue himself. The knowledge you gained from the advanced courses will vanish and you will face a totally different world. A strange bouquet will appear before you instead of forty to forty-five pages of script.

In short, you will arrive with a scrawny goat and leave with a staggering ram.[37] Our film-grandpa is such a wise, sharp-witted person!

One more thing I should point out is that our Master always wears a net-like jersey. Nowadays you will never be able to find another jersey like his. You would be lucky to find one in cinematography warehouses that keep very old props. The old man must have bought a whole sack of those jerseys with the state awards he received all those years ago.

As the script reading reaches its climax, the Master moves towards his none-too-large two-storey house and quietly calls: "Sabo!"

This will not be the same Sabo that you saw last time; this one will be different. They are all called Sabo. That was the name of the Master's late wife.

So never be surprised if you see these various Sabos in a film one day. And don't be surprised if you never see them again on the screen. They are all so-called one-time "stars". If any of them manages to become the Master's favourite, well, "bravo," otherwise they are doomed to fail. The Master is not to blame, she has already served her purpose. And now, you should get out of his sight!

At once a beautiful lady will appear near the house bearing a tray laden with fruits and sweetmeats and the "White Stork" you brought. This is the future film-sweetheart! Dainty, she trips along, puts the tray on a table, fills a glass with cognac and passes it to the Master. The Master gazes at the shimmering scarlet liquid for a moment then downs it in one. After tasting a

---

37 An Uzbek saying.

piece of watermelon and salad he sits down in the rocking-chair and closes his eyes. It means he is enjoying himself. Hey, Sabo, why are you just looking at him? Why aren't you contributing to his pleasure? Don't teach her: she knows what to do. She gradually starts rocking the chair like a cradle. But it's you she is looking at. Should you stop reading the script, she flashes you a comely smile. And that's when you should be really careful. Don't rush, don't think something sweet, otherwise you may regret it. Now, in a minute or so, the Master will open his eyes and look up. As if on cue, Sabo, leaning forward quietly, embraces his neck and kisses his temples. Then she starts to massage his shoulders and hairy chest or gently scratches his thick white hair with her delicate fingers.

These divine fingers are moving for us! This charade is for us! All of this is dedicated to us! Ah, my young lad, stop gazing at her! Avert your eyes! Don't be a fool! Just try to get "good luck" for the script in your hands!

In fact, if you are patient during such examinations and if you answer the Master's questions courageously, you may consider yourself lucky. "Give me a pen! Do you have a pen?" he will ask. Then he will take a pen along with the script from you and will scribble his verdict right there on the text, not on a blank margin: "Read. Acceptable." Then he will pass the pen to his Sabo: "Sign." The lady, trembling here and there, signs on the margin: "Sabohat".

Now we can congratulate you on your success, comrade author! From now on you can boldly take your script to the above-mentioned chairman or even to a higher level boss. I bet no one will dare reject it!

I will never forget how I visited the Master with my own work called "One Single Glance".

I noticed that the old man was not sitting in the same place. So I put the "White Stork" aside and slowly made my way to the garden. I sat down and waited for him under the apricot tree. Suddenly I felt light spray coming from the marble pool by the house. It was him, the Master! Oh my, the old man! He was swimming so well! Doing the butterfly!

I kept silent and did not approach. But time was passing and our swimmer showed no intention of stopping. I felt a bit embarrassed. What's more, I was afraid he would see me and say: "Let's start here, I will continue swimming and you will read!"..

Thank goodness!

"Sabo-o!" climbing the stairs, the old man emerged from the pool, shivering.

At once Sabo (another one) hurried towards him with a flannel towel.

Good heavens, the Master was stark naked! But he did not worry about it.

Sabo approached him, wrapped him in the towel, and, with her arms around his waist, took him into the house.

Now, both the Master and the student are sitting under the same apricot tree. The whole story will be played out once again. "Start reading". Snoring (when sound of the water makes him drowsy). Risky questions. A short discussion. "Sabo!" "White Stork", relaxing on the rocking-chair, kisses, massage, and so on and so forth.

Before he orders "Give me a pen!" the Master will express his main objection:

"No, the girl... I mean the bride, she should not die! You should not kill her. Let her live. Otherwise, where is the humanistic approach? Well, so what if that driver did look at her once? So what if he was jealous, lustful, and wanted to have himself a

good time with her because she is on her own? Or the girl…
I mean the bride… is a weak creature, too; she also wants to
have some fun since her husband is faraway. But nothing happened between them. Just imagine! See what I mean?"- he says,
slipping into film jargon again; just add several terms to those
exclamations and you will get the film jargon! – It is called life,
my dear, it is life!

That time I did not like such rebukes, since I thought they
were too rough and could rock the whole foundation of the
work, shatter the essence of the script. However, the Master
was right. Later I thought about it once more and came to the
conclusion that my script would be better, more natural, more
realistic and more meaningful if I took the Master's advice. After
all, he's right: there would not be enough women in the world
if every woman who looks at a man flirtatiously or is looked at
flirtatiously suddenly ups and hangs herself, drowns or jumps
off a cliff. Where is the humanistic approach here?! So what if
their eyes meet once? Is it a tragedy? Just imagine!

* *

They say that when you speak about a wolf its head will appear;
if you speak about a fox its paw will appear; and if you speak
about a hare, its ear will appear.

Both the ear and the paw appeared.[38]

* *

In the room whose windows "open onto the green forest"
Farhod grew anxious. He was afraid to just relax and switch off,

---

38 Uzbek sayings.

thinking about pleasant things as Valya had suggested: what if this room were full of mice or rats?!

Bored, he strolled down to the grounds and sat on a bench at the end of the courtyard. As he took a cigarette out of his pocket, he remembered the panic of a tall doctor: "We do our best to improve oxygen in your veins with various medicines and injections, but you destroy them all with smoking!" Involuntarily he put the cigarette to his lips and lit a match: "Here, oxygen is everywhere!"

Just then a man and a woman came out of the grove of trees. They were having a lovely conversation with each other.

"No, you listen to me," the woman was speaking in a shrill voice. "Let me tell you what I didn't like about it! There is neither plot development nor a denouement – only empty scenes from start to finish! Fair enough, some of the shots are good and skillfully edited, but…"

"That's what I'm talking about, too, my dear," the man said, trying to chime in with her. "Those scenes will set the mood. Think about the symbology! Do you remember the part where the girl is wandering, lost, in the forest and sees her father's hat hanging on the branch of a tree? That is a wonderful detail, isn't it?

"No, no, don't go overboard, please. Those are old-fashioned methods, nothing compared with Bergman's work!"

"Alright, my darling, let's just stick to our own opinions. Can you at least agree to disagree?" the man rounded the discussion off, and led his companion to the next bench.

Farhod recognized this talkative woman at once. Her name is Elmira Kamolova, a film critic and blue-eyed beauty of mixed descent. She is the amazing daughter-in-law of our wonderful Master. Film-bride. I didn't know she was here, too. "There are many friends of you're here."

The man speaking to her was a handsome man of about 40 to 45. His blond curly hair, although slightly thinning above his forehead, hung down to his shoulders. His poignant blue eyes held a kind, gentle look, and a yellowish leather jacket was slung over his shoulder.

This rather arrogant, coquettish lady, who would give people the cold shoulder even in Tashkent, suddenly caught sight of Farhod in the courtyard. With a cheery wave, she led her companion over to him.

Farhod tossed his cigarette into the large ashtray by the bench and stood up.

"One of our talented scriptwriters," Ms. Kamolova introduced him to her

companion. "A real talent! He's finished the advanced classes. His first film directed by Ravshan Akobirov was very well received by our audience, especially since it was the first film produced in Uzbek. What was its name, Farhod-jon? Something like "The Early Return of the Storks?""

"Actually it was called "When will you return, Swallows?"" Farhod corrected her, thinking to himself: Huh, you call me talented, say how my film was the first produced in Uzbek, that it was famous, that you know all about it, so how come you forget the title? Some film critic!?

Then he added: "Brother Ravshan wanted to shorten it, he called it simply "Swallows"".

Ms. Kamolova paid no heed to Farhod's comments, she quickly began to introduce her companion:

"This is the well-known Armenian producer Chaldratyan![39] Arthur Chaldratyan! I hope you've seen his films. You know

---

39 A reference to Vigen Chaldranyan.

"The Mansion on the Mountains" and "The Secret of the Old Castle", right, Farhod-jon?"

Farhod had heard about Chaldratyan, but he had never watched his films, so he dodged the question and just said, "Yes, of course, that's good."

"Arthur Artyomovich is a great fan of Bergman, and you? I am…"

"Elimra-jon, my dear friend," the director exclaimed. "Bergman and Chaldratyan are totally different! Don't offend me, please."

"Come now, you are not allowed to get offended!" replied Ms. Kamolova, and, as if they were close, she very lightly clipped his ear, after which she asked Farhod: "When did you arrive?" But without bothering to wait for a reply she hastened to add: "Many of our mutual friends are here, you must have seen them already."

"Our Master is also here, isn't he, sister Elmira-khon?" Farhod asked

Kamolova, who was five or six years older than he.

"The Master you say? Why? How? He can hardly move at all now, how on earth could he come here?"

At that very moment an eight- or nine-year-old boy playing with other

children on the far side of the courtyard ran up to Ms. Kamolova, calling "Mummy, Mummy!" His mother bent down, holding her face to the child's for a moment. Not wanting to be left out of this tender scene, the soft-hearted Mr. Chaldratyan stroked the child's head.

"Babyor, Babyor!" the children called from across the courtyard.

"Now, go and play with your friends," said Kamolova gently pushing her son forward. Then she turned to Farhod. "Well, talk to you more soon," she said.

The couple strolled through the grove to discuss the ins and outs of Bergman and Chaldratyan.

And therein lies the essence of this lady's job. She spends her time at various festivals and resorts, clad in her bright khan-atlas[40] dress and traditional embroidered robe to give her an "ethnic" look (as a matter of fact, Farhod had seen her like that at the Riga film festival). The beloved only daughter of a greater leader, doors swing open for her. But to give her credit, she is a beautiful lady, her Russian is excellent and she is very eloquent. So why shouldn't she attend festivals and enjoy herself? She is considered "an expected guest" wherever she goes, both at home and abroad. But what is there for her to do at home, anyway? Take care of her drunken husband? May Allah be merciful! Her husband should be grateful to her for giving him some money for his vodka. Not "White Stork" - "Chasma-spring" is good enough for him. Given the choice, she would never have married this incurable alcoholic. Their fathers, both state officials, had wanted to become in-laws so the marriage was arranged. But no mater what happens you should not forget your past. They say that you will be blessed according to your merits. So the Master helped his daughter-in-law with her studies, guided her into this field and brought her here as his film-bride. Thanks to the Master, she became "the best film critic" and now lives very well. Her husband is available when she needs him, if not, he is not available at all, he simply vanishes. What more could this film-lady want?

That smiling Armenian chap seemed to be a good person. But we are sure that our film-sister can easily string along many

---

40 Very bright traditional Uzbek dresses.

a Chaldratyan. (Later that same day, at lunchtime, sitting at one table with Ms. Kamolova, Mr. Chaldratyan waved Farhod hello from afar with the same smile on his face. It seems as though he had become one of our temporary brothers-in-law, too.)

Farhod sat on his bench a while longer and smoked one more cigarette before getting up and going back into the building.

He bumped into Ms. Kamolova's son by the stairs.

"What's your name, lad?" he asked in Uzbek, but since the boy did not understand, he repeated his question in Russian.

"Babur," the boy said indifferently.

He looks like his grandfather – the Master gave this name to him.

"Mirzo Bobur! Do you know who he was?"

The boy answered directly, as he knows:

"That's me."

"If you are our Mirzo Bobur then Allah alone knows what will become of the others," Farhod said to himself.

The boy glared at this odd, gloomy uncle in astonishment and ran off to play with his friends who called him "Babyor".

Alright, now we know that Bobur was Babyor, but who was "our most famous and best?"

5. "Our most famous and best". A magic bell

"May I join you?" a stranger approached him.

Farhod, who did not want to enjoy the view from the room with "windows opening onto the green forest" had fallen asleep at midday and was now so ravenous that he was tucking into food he would never normally even nibble. With a mouth full of food he looked at the stranger, not recognizing at first. A good-looking, silvery-haired man, who looked like a Hindu, was standing smiling nearby. Farhod never expected to run into him here!

"Hey, brother Ravshan! Is it really you? Salam aleikum!" he said, getting up to greet him, the spoon still in his hand.

"Well, put your spoon down first," Ravshan Akobirov said ironically.

When two people who do not like each other or who have fallen out meet in a foreign land they will forget everything and greet one another warmly. It was the same this time, too.

"When did you arrive?" asked Mr. Akobirov after sitting himself down opposite Farhod; according to his old habit, he sometimes addressed Farhod with respect and sometimes without.

The dinner table by the window was meant for three, but the original occupants had left the day before, so the old kitchen-lady had asked Farhod to sit there.

Mr. Akobirov said he had taken a week's holiday. He had come here to attend a workshop for filmmakers of "The Great Motherland" due to take place in the next few days. He mentioned he had some other things to do here as well.

Mr. Akobirov didn't like the food the kitchen-lady brought. He pushed it around his plate a bit with his fork then turned to the waitress angrily, addressing this lady as old as his mother with the tone he usually used with his wife:

"Nina-khon, do I have to tell you again and again: I don't like this stuff! Take it away!"

The poor woman felt guilty and, putting her hands to her heart, she said:

"Sorry, Ravshan Usmonovich, please forgive me, may Allah be merciful! I forgot. I

didn't know you were moving to this table. I will bring you something else, just a second, please."

She brought Mr. Akobirov's food at once.

A famous filmmaker whom Farhod had met once backstage passed their table:

"Greetings, Ravshan Usmonovich!" he called warmly.

"Greetings, greetings," replied Mr. Akobirov indifferently.

And this was repeated many times. In response to the greetings and respect shown by many others present at the dining-hall, Akobirov merely waved nonchalantly, letting Farhod know how influential he was over here.

Apparently, everyone here knows him very well. Well-known in the "endless country", he was the famous filmmaker Ravshan Akobirov, the mind behind a new trend in Uzbek filmmaking! Farhod had almost forgotten he was "our best and most famous". In fact, he never expected to run into him here. By the way, the reign of the Master is over; only people of his age could know him personally, and people of our time might only hear his name.

Like film-tourist Elmira Kamolova, Mr. Akobirov also spends most of his life in this part of the world. Though he used to be an assistant to the lighting technician in Uzbekistan, here, in the film industry of the "endless country" he is an influential person, member of the board and secretariat! That's why he considers those around him beneath him and can shout at people like Nina-khon.

Actually, this man was the one who had brought Farhod into the film industry in the first place and supported him. It was he who had bought Farhod's first script "When will you return, Swallows?" right after he graduated from the courses when the young writer could not sell anything to anyone. The cowardly chairman gave his consent and did not even send it to the Master for consideration, since Mr. Akobirov was a man of the Capital. "If Ravshanbek Usmonovich buys it, what can we say, we can only wish him good luck!" he crooned obsequiously.

The script carried a keen meaning for the wise, but today it is considered a weak, shabby work. Nevertheless, it became famous once it was filmed. Everyone but Farhod liked it very much, it was even nominated for the Youth award that year. It was a cheerful and harmless performance that would not "touch" anyone or anything. Later Farhod realized this is just the kind of film which appeals to the masses.

After "Swallows" Mr. Akobirov and Farhod fell out and became estranged. This was the first time they had sat down together after so many years. Until today, they had only greeted each other from a distance if they happened to meet.

Farhod's new film was to be shot in Parkent, as it was close to Tashkent. As the scriptwriter, Farhod was on hand with his writing tools; if any changes were to be made, if anything needed to be added or removed, he would be there to fit them to the rest of the script.

The first day didn't go so well.

According to tradition, to allay any possible misfortune, a few plates were smashed and a few corks were popped. In short, the day was greeted with celebrations. But as the day wore on, Farhod felt that it was not his script they were following but something rather different. Surprised, he approached the producer, but Mr. Akobirov pushed him aside, saying: "Go and sit over there, don't interrupt us." When Farhod asked about the script he scolded him: "What are you talking about? I've got it all up here, in my head! I don't forget!" This reprimand made everyone in the courtyard laugh, including the ladies lazily sunning their white bodies, their faces covered with straw hats. Farhod felt ashamed. But he didn't give up, so finally, exasperated, Mr. Akobirov, who was lounging on a deck chair with a bottle of mineral water chatting to his buxom white-bodied ladies, asked his assistant to fetch the script. It turned out there was in fact no script to be fetched. It had been left in the hotel. At this, Farhod simply turned away and left, sulking like a small child. He hitched a ride back to the city in a passing car. On the way back he was secretly hoping someone would come after him, but no one did. In fact, no one came to see him all that day, nor the next, nor the days to follow. When he told his tale to some colleagues, they all said: "Don't worry. If the script is with Ravshan Akobirov, he'll make a fine job of it, you'll see."

In general, when your film is being shot, it is better not to show up at the set, otherwise the producer might fly into a rage if he catches a glimpse of you there. You might also look like a foolish nephew lolling at his uncle's feet. Farhod had already found himself in such a weird situation several times, he knows all about it. When everything is fine with the filming and an episode has been shot very well, everyone starts to hug each other, and some will congratulate you, too. If everything is going badly, everyone will glower at you, since you are the one who brought all these problems down on them. And in that case, it is better if you leave at once. Let these ungrateful, unpleasant chaps stew in their own juice!

Preparing the film is particularly perilous. Something is sure to bother you, something will get lost or something will go missing. The situation on set is tense, the loud-mouthed producer is too angry. Everyone is anxious, everyone feels tormented. And worst of all, no one is calling for lunch. As if someone has just died or is writhing on their deathbed. Over there, to one side, a dozy cameraman sitting on a folding chair covering his face with his umbrella-shaped hat is complaining that "The sun is rising from a different angle and his film could burn". To the other side, a spoiled actress fusses that she cannot possibly be filmed in this dress, and the whole process grinds to a halt. Or a mosquito bites (close-up) an actress right in the eye as she impatiently waits near the spring for "Roll!" The actress's eyelid turns red and swells up at once. She rubs her eyes with her little finger, but glowers at you with her other, healthy eye and shouts: "This is all thanks to you! Couldn't you think of anything else instead of this damn spring?!"

Another time, camera rolling, an actor says whatever comes into his head, anything but his lines. Just try to point out he's ruined your words! The producer starts to hiss: "What's the difference? Hey, you, go and sit over there, do not interrupt!" But when it is time for the sound check, you will be obliged to recreate sentences for the actor, rebuilding word structures from what he has uttered, swapping a's for b's to accommodate his speech defect. Look, what's happened, poor unfortunate man, Asrorqul!

Sometimes the famous People's Artist signs his autograph for those admirers hovering at the edge of the set, upsetting the apple cart. The impatient cameraman stares at the producer, but the producer dare not say anything to the People's Artist (it was only with great difficulty, in exchange for one camel, that he could be persuaded to act), so he vents his frustration by shouting at someone else instead. Once he has calmed down, he eventually asks his assistant to call the People's Artist. Refusing to be rushed, the People's Artist is happily chatting with one of his admirers, so he turns to the cameraman and says: "Tell the producer he can pick up filming tomorrow, we will still have time tomorrow."

Another black cloud covers the sky above the set.

The scriptwriter cowering in a corner starts feeling ashamed: "Did I mean to waste so many people's time with this script?"

In short, once the script has been approved and work begins, everyone wishes the author would vanish, or better still, wither and die! A writer whose books had been made into films once gave Farhod some good advice: "Sign the agreement, get your money and never let them clap eyes on you again, my young brother!"

Or vice versa: just stand there and patiently bear those humiliations!

One night about three months later, Mr. Akobirov phoned Farhod at home. As if nothing had happened, he greeted him warmly and said: "We will be working on the sound check tomorrow, so please come to the studio at about 10 o'clock." Having said that, he hung up: there was nothing more to say! Relieved but curious, Farhod headed to the UzbekFilm studios the next day. As a result, within a week he had rewritten all the dialogues and got rid of them. What else he could do, he had already taken part of his fees and spent them?

Later, during a grand ceremony attended by everyone who worked on the film, Mr. Akobirov pushed Farhod towards the microphone and introduced him to the audience, hugging him: "Please meet this young and talented playwright!" and so on and so forth.

But Farhod still does not know if this man is his friend or enemy. He is a real chameleon: a friend one day, an enemy the next.

He is arrogant, that is why he is disliked by many, but everyone acknowledges his films and admires him.

After lunch, as they were filing one after another down the long mirrored corridor to the dining hall, so many people greeted Mr. Akobirov warmly, even bowing their heads, but he did not reciprocate nor speak to anybody – as usual, he just nodded his head or flapped his hand at them, nothing more.

When they reached the door, Mr. Chaldratyan approached them quickly and held his hands out to Mr. Akobirov, who shook the extended hands and signalled to him that he should leave them alone. But when he caught sight of Ms. Kamolova as she tried to slip away, he said in Uzbek:

"Hey, Elmira, didn't you recognize us?"

Ms. Kamolova did not say anything, merely gave a nod and left the dining hall.

"I hope you know this woman," said Akobirov, fixing Farhod with a strange look. "She 'serves' everyone even here, the slut."

Though Farhod was not close to Ms. Kamolova, that word made him uneasy.

"Let's get a breath of fresh air now!" said Mr. Akobirov when they reached the courtyard, and he led Farhod to the grove of trees dimly lit by ground lights.

The two of them walked for a long time along half-dark paths.

Mr. Akobirov had given up smoking so he was always chomping chewing gum. It is a week now since he arrived but he wanted to know all the news from Tashkent in great detail, and what filmmakers were talking about there.

"Did you come here to get some rest or are you going to write something here?" he asked.

Farhod told him about his own illness, that he has some hearing trouble,

that his ear squeaks all day long and he cannot get treatment in Tashkent, so he came here to see more professional doctors.

"Let your ear squeak all the time, so long as it does not hurt," Mr. Akobirov joked.

"I'm fed up with this noise in my ear, brother Ravshan! Otherwise I wouldn't have come here. They say it's not easy to treat. I read in the paper that Chinese doctors know how to cure it. I heard a medical centre called "Qi Gong" opened here, too, so two or three months ago I sent a request for permit to the big Union. I received a message two weeks ago that the permit is ready and I should get my visa. I already had one since I visited Hungary last year for a festival.

Mr. Akobirov stopped chewing, lost in thought for a moment:

"Was the permit ready? Yes? Look, what do you need that Chinese mumbo-jumbo for? Why don't you just buy a hearing aid instead?!"

Farhod did not like this advice. He wanted to protest: "I'm a young man, I'm only thirty!" But he bit his lip; after all, how can anyone feel the pain in someone else's body?

So they chatted about work and scripts. Farhod complained that his pain stopped him from concentrating on work. Mr. Akobirov said it was a long time since he'd set eyes on a good script, he's out of a job for now. And then he mentioned he was going to work on a bigger project.

Mr. Akobirov was living in the new building opposite. As they were saying good night, he let slip that he had a bottle of very good cognac, why not drink it together? And he invited Farhod up to his room, but Farhod excused himself and went to his own room over in the old building.

They became closer again.

"Mr. Ramazonov, someone called for you," shouted Valya as he was passing the reception desk.

"Who was it?" he asked.

"A woman! She had a very beautiful voice," said Valya pointedly. "I wrote down her phone number."

Surprised, Farhod could not think of anyone who would ring him here. Several women he had studied with in the advanced classes were so-called "part-time dancers." Maybe it was Tamara? Tarona Samed-qizi Qurbonova, a great admirer of Mevlana Fuzuli. But she must be an old woman by now, she was several years older than him.

When he saw the piece of paper he was even more puzzled: an unfamiliar number, an unfamiliar name: Gulya Lagutina. Hang on, hadn't he heard of her somewhere some time? But who she was? How did she know he was there? Only two people know: brother Ravshan and Elmira Kamolova. And Sur'at... OK, why so what does this Gulya Lagutina want from me?

Farhod looked first at his watch and then at the clock on the wall: it was late. Better call her tomorrow, he decided.

"So, Fidel Mirzaevich, are you satisfied now?" Valya teased him. "If she's a beautiful lady, why don't you call her? Give her a ring, let the bedbugs bite her, too! By the way, are there bedbugs in your new room as well?"

"Not yet," Farhod answered. "I'm afraid they might attack at night."

"Don't you know, those bedbugs are afraid of the dark. But if you need someone who's not afraid, feel free to call, Fidel..."

"Farhod!"

"Farhod?!" wondered Valya shrugged her shoulders. "Who's Farhod?"

But the crafty Farhod just shrugged his shoulders: "I don't know," he said.

"So, her voice is very beautiful." Absorbed in pleasant thoughts, it was a long time before Farhod managed to fall asleep. Besides, he was jetlagged and there was a three-hour time difference.

When he did finally drift off, he dreamt he and Mr. Akobirov were going to work on a joint film. Gulya Lagutina was meant to play the leading lady.

But who was she?

6. One more Uzbek – "Uzbek woman". Vika's room

"Really, you didn't know I'm an Uzbek?" asked Gulya as she was preparing coffee, rattling the cups. "Though not one hundred percent, I am Uzbek. Didn't Elmira tell you? Or Sur'at?"

"No," Farhod confessed openly. "Your name rang a bell but now I think I just read it in papers and I do not know you. Neither Sur'at nor Elmira said a word about you."

"Elmira rang yesterday and told me you were here, otherwise how

could find you? She's a friend of mine, she is a little older than me but we studied together at the All-Union State Institute of Cinematography, VGIK."

They had bumped into each other several times over the last few days but this was the first time they were sitting together chatting leisurely.

"Well, if you don't know, listen," his hostess began as she moved a cup of

coffee over to Farhod's side and poured a cup of tea for herself. "As I mentioned, I'm half Uzbek. Do you want me to show you my passport? My ancestors are from Tashkent itself. I myself grew up in Tashkent and finished school there. My mother is Polish; her parents came from Ukraine during the war. My Mum and Dad don't live together any more, they're divorced. Our family is an international family like that! Do you want to know my real name? It's Gulgun! My Grandma named me. She used to call me Gulgunoy. So when Gulgunoy Mansurova got married, she became Gulya Lagutina as you see her now! That was how it was back then, you know. But I wasn't so lucky in my own marriage, either. I got married when I was a student, but we were divorced a year later. He was from a military family, a test pilot. I later heard he was accepted as an astronaut but he couldn't fly. He was an astronaut that never saw space! This is my short biography. There's nothing praiseworthy there. I know about you, Farhod, I'm aware of your films. I've been wanting to meet you for a long time. It was impossible when I went to Tashkent. That's why yesterday when I heard you were here I rang you. Well, I promised "Soviet Culture" that I would prepare an interview with a young Uzbek filmmaker. Whether you like it or not, I'm here as a representative of Uzbekistan. But you, you don't even know your representative, shame on you!"

Farhod was listening to this open and somewhat confused woman with surprise. In a minute, she had told him everything.

"Oh my, this one is a real mix, too," he said to himself. "People like this have mushroomed recently. A hybrid will later find another hybrid. Gradually their bloods will mix. "A production of mixture film!"

Troubled, Farhod looked out of the window: it was already dark and he was wondering how he would reach the hotel.

As if sensing his thoughts, Gulya said nonchalantly:

"Don't worry, you can stay here. You can't take a taxi from here, my friend. Anyway, I have enough space. Vika's room is empty."

Farhod, thinking like a man, sipping the Armenian cognac he had brought (his hostess did not drink at all), was frightened by this offer and immediately thought the worst. Then he looked at Gulya, who was clearing the dining table, preparing her pen and paper for the interview, and felt ashamed of his thoughts. Gulya was about 40 years old. She had probably once been a real beauty but later stopped paying attention to her figure and looks, forgetting everything but film and the film industry. She would support your point of view no matter what you said, and no matter who you talked about, she would always find something good in him or her and praised them all. She was both optimistic and compassionate, wasn't she? No, women are really better than us men, a thousand times better!

Back at the hotel, Farhod rang her after breakfast, but for some reason he did not want Mr. Akobirov to find out. Gulya Lagutina answered quickly and said she would be more than happy to see him at the Film-makers' Union – in Sur'at's room. The offer was acceptable enough and Farhod liked that.

First he went to the clinic that belonged to the Union: he had to get a permit to see a doctor. The otolaryngology specialist, an old lady who had grown up in Tashkent, took good care of him. As she was checking his ear using a variety of methods, she regaled him with many stories from her childhood. Then she informed him she had a good friend who worked at a clinic on Salom Odil Street and wrote a note for him. Farhod wondered: did she say Salom Odil? Yes, there was indeed a street called Salom Odil, and the clinic was there. But who was Salom Odil? The old lady did not know, she just said it was the name of the street and explained how to get there. Farhod had not heard this name before, either. Maybe he is a Tartar or Bashkirdi scientist or poet? Or maybe a doctor? Be that as it may, the clinic named after him was situated in a remote corner of the city. So remote in fact that Farhod could barely find it. Unfortunately, the great specialist recommended by his fellow countrywoman was off that day so he had to see another doctor instead. As a result, he received the same diagnosis, very similar to the one he had received in Tashkent: cochlear neuritis, in other words, his sound receiving ligaments had become numb and started to dry up, and it is very difficult or almost impossible to regenerate them. The only way is to undergo is treatment from time to time and put up with those buzzes or hisses patiently. That is all!

When he presented the consultant with a book by Omar Khayyam published in Tashkent in Russian as a token of gratitude, the ugly doctor just handed it back to him saying she had plenty like that at home. Ashamed, Farhod wished he had given her some money instead, and left the clinic. He checked the time; it was almost noon, so he hurried to the Union.

On entering Sur'at's office, he saw a woman who looked like a gypsy. She was wearing a voluminous, floaty dress, with tinkling copper bells dangling round her ears and neck. (The room's true occupant was apparently out.) The 'gypsy' stood up when she saw him coming in. "Are you Farhod Ramazonov?" the hand she held out to him was bedecked with jangling bangles. "I expected you to be older, or bigger."

That was Gulya Lagutina! For some reason Farhod was disappointed. But this gypsy-like woman made a strong impression on him. So they chatted about various things for a while, and then she took him on a tour of different offices.

Each time they entered, she introduced him as "a talented playwright and a young founder of Uzbek filmmaking." People like Farhod were evidently two a penny here, since the women sitting in their offices (Lagutina's friends?) did not pay much attention to her words, just said: "Fine that's nice!"

Finally they came to the editorial boardroom of the Film-Almanac journal. Actually, 'the boardroom' was two rooms. Last year Farhod had sent one of his scenarios here, the one that was rejected by the Artistic Council on the pretext that 'its national-exotic colour was too rich' and that the Centre would not approve it.

Calling from the second room, Gulya Lagutina greeted them warmly but then began chatting with another woman who looked Armenian or Azeri. This second woman, unaware of the author's presence (Farhod was standing in the first room and the door was ajar), was speaking in a loud voice: "The scenario was given to a specialist, and he returned it with the criticism that it doesn't reflect national lifestyle well enough." Then the two ladies could be heard whispering to each other: "Is he here?" asked the first. "Yes!" came the reply. Several minutes later, Lagutina appeared; her joviality had evaporated. "Look, they haven't read your work yet. I talked to them, don't worry, I'll write a review of your scenario. Rest assured, everything will be fine," she tried to pacify Farhod. But even with his poorly ear, Farhod had already caught the gist of the conversation. He thought his colleague Su'rat, a mean, unlucky man, must be behind this.

He wanted to get out of this place as soon as possible. He did not want to see Sur'at. At least not today.

As if reading his mind, Lagutina said, "I have to prepare the text of our interview in two days, let's go to my place." Farhod hesitated, but how could he turn down this kind stranger's offer?

On the way out, despite Lagutina's protests, he popped into a small shop nearby to buy a bottle of cognac, some salami and cheese to take to her flat in Medvedkovo.

They chatted in Gulya's roomy kitchen for an hour and a half or so. The guest, behaving like a stiff stranger at first, was now at ease, reassured by his hostess's caring sincerity, and emboldened by the cognac. He began answering her questions more light-heartedly. He felt as if he had been here before, as if he had already spent time in this kitchen. And Gulya herself seemed to be an old and trusted friend.

The four or five page interview was ready surprisingly fast. True, they did not "invent the wheel;" the questions were all general, ranging from tasks faced by the Uzbek national film industry, attention to young people's work, to some personal questions, future plans, etc.

Since the interview focused on filmmaking in the native language, they gave it the title: "Film: language is the expression of a nation's soul."

Gulya said she would find a photograph of Farhod in the Union's archives.

They chatted about other things, too.

And so Farhod decided to tell this lady who became so close in just a day all about his own health problems. Gulya listened closely, as if she were his elder sister:

"No, no! It's not true!" she said suddenly. "Don't believe what the doctors say, Farhod! There is a cure for every illness. It's just that we don't know about them, we can't find them. You should definitely see Zuzi, the famous psychic healer! Haven't you heard? He's healed so many people. I'll give Plato Sokratovich a ring straightaway, he lives next door to Zuzi. He can have a word with him, believe me. Otherwise it's hard to see Zuzi without an introduction."

"Did you say Plato Sokratovich?" Farhod asked in surprise. "Is that his real name?"

"Yes, do you remember Knyazev? That famous film critic with a bushy heard? Such a brilliant person! Well, now he's not in cinematography any more, he's very much into democracy. But if I tell him, I hope he'll agree to see you."

All a flurry, Gulya was already about to call.

"It's too late to ring now," said Farhod, feeling somewhat embarrassed.

"Oh, don't worry, he doesn't sleep at night, he stays up thinking about democracy," Gulya laughed. But she glanced at the clock above the door and calmed down: "OK, I'll get him tomorrow. Rest assured, Farhod. There is no disease without a cure. You don't have to suffer! You are still very young, aren't you? It's you talking yet I feel as though something were howling in inside me. I feel it as a great burden myself!

Eventually they started to talk about Sur'at.

"Poor man!" said Gulya; she felt sorry for him. "He was left all alone, poor chap. Maybe he told you, his Lida fell in love with an Algerian producer and left him. She left her two children with her mother. She must have a heart of stone, may she perish! I really feel sorry for poor Sur'at. After all, he's from Tashkent, too."

Farhod was surprised. When Sur'at had visited him last autumn he had said they divorced because they could no longer get along together. Maybe he was too ashamed to tell the truth.

Nevertheless, Farhod was surprised Gulya was so compassionate and kept feeling sorry for Sur'at; after all, he had seen for himself earlier that day what kind of a person Sur'at really was. Perhaps she'd known him before – Sur'at was not born into this world today, was he?

"I heard Ravshan Akobirov is with you, too," Gulya said. "I haven't seen him at the Union. I was going to interview him for The Art of Filmmaking magazine. What a talented person! We really should be proud of him!"

"Actually. I think he's looking for me now to take a stroll together, so I'd better be off," said Farhod getting ready to leave. But it was already very late, well turned midnight.

So Gulya set about putting clean sheets on the bed in the small room.

"Alright, it's ready. You can sleep in Vika's room. She's at summer camp now." And so saying, she went back to the kitchen.

The click clack of the typewriter was heard from there for a long time.

He was in Vika's room. She was studying at VGIK like her mother had,

But, according to Gulya, she had chosen not to become a filmmaker but an actress. So this was the Vika-room. It looks like her.

It was quite comfortable. Three walls were covered in funny photos of famous actors. Books were piled on the table in the corner and on the windowsill, too. There was a tape recorder, "Vesna," near the table and lots of cassettes. Playing cards were scattered on the floor in the far corner. Who does she play them with? Her Mum?

A large light brown fur skin was spread out on the floor in the middle of the room. It had once belonged to a snow leopard. Gulya explained that a Caucasian friend had given it to her.

Farhod closed the door, took his trousers off at a leisurely pace and looked at the photos. So which one is our actress-to-be, then? Hard to tell. All the women in the photos are beautiful and attractive. And Vika could be one of them. Yes, here it is: a small framed photo of her hugging her Mum. Gulya is prettier and plumper in the photo, too, but her daughter is an ordinary adolescent, very young. Heaven knows what is she like now.

Farhod stretched out on the ample bed, breathing in the sweet smell of fresh linen washed with fragrant detergent.

He had not yet adjusted to the local time so the sound of the kitchen clock kept him awake for a while.

Finally he drifted off. In his dreams he saw a strange man... no, not a stranger but a very familiar old man, who approached and choked him. Farhod woke in a sweat. For a brief moment he could not remember where he was. Taking his watch from under the pillow, he realized that in Tashkent he would be having his breakfast now. He got up, got dressed and went out into the corridor. Through the slightly open door he saw Gulya sleeping, her head on the typewriter, her hair dishevelled.

Without knowing quite why, he felt somehow ashamed of lying longer in his bed. Or perhaps he did not want to see Gulya in the morning. Either way, he washed his face in the bathroom and crept silently out onto the street.

The sun was already up; apparently, the day would be stuffy.

Farhod's task was to find the Chinese "Qi Gong" medical centre that day!

7. Snowed in. The internationalist grandpa. The dancer who forgot her knickers

… Someone starts to choke me very tightly. I try to open my eyes but can't, my hands and legs won't move. Someone's holding me down, strangling me. I wheeze, I croak. His paws are like iron! Finally I manage to free myself. Finally I slowly open my eyes. Through my eyelashes I glimpse my oppressor: the Internationalist old man! We are ideological opponents. Not only ideological, but on other issues, too. For instance, on our stomach's needs. We have become secret rivals over that girl, too. So what else could he do but choke or murder me?! Well, we have been quarrelling, arguing sharply many a time. I insulted this man who was the same age as my grandpa, disgraced him, and even openly mocked him. He endures whatever you do to him – he is too patient and forgiving. But, like an impudent fledgling, I always attacked his most sacred beliefs, his most precious ideals. I was inexorable! Ah, but the crafty old man was biding his time, waiting for the right moment. And now, seeing I am asleep, he pounces.

"Farhod-jon, wake up! You are delirious!" – That Internationalist old man really was standing over me, trying gently to wake me. "Wake up, Farhod-jon. You're lying on your back. Do you want me bring you some water? You didn't not eat properly and now you're delirious. Tut, that's no good at all."

His nodding and fussing irritates me. I silently turn away.

This man was full of stories, and, maybe in an attempt to cheer me up, he began reminiscing about the good old days. In particular, he deliberately started talking about "our subject" in our dialect:

"It was back in the days when I was heading the Komsomol in the Kushdaryo region. I received a letter of complaint from a remote mountainous village, addressed to me. A girl was being forced to marry an old man, so she was asking for help. I knew those mountains like he back of my hand, I'd roamed all over on horseback. So I knew Besthtol or Burgutdara, Majnunarcha or Echkibulogh – I'd been everywhere. Because of the letter, I decided to go to Zarang to inspect the work of the Komsomol committee in that village, too. The next day I took one of the local activists and headed into the mountains. The girl knew nothing about politics, she was a shy thing, so we spoke with her stubborn father and resolved the problem. Then my companion decided to stay in his village for a couple of days, so I had to go back alone. Actually, that was what I'd planned all along; I fancied roaming the mountains on my own for a bit. But that wasn't to be. Suddenly another travelling companion appeared before me! It was already dark and I was heading down through a forest of fir trees. At a fork in the track I heard a rustling noise coming from somewhere in front of me, and someone called out: "Brother, stop, please!" A second later, a girl or a woman in a headscarf darted through the fir trees clutching a small bundle and appeared just in front of my horse. "Brother, please take me with you! I'm going to study and become a Komsomol!" she said. She looked like the girl who had written the letter, although I had not seen her face during our discussion earlier on, she'd been cowering with her head bowed. She explained her father had banished her from their house. "Go wherever you want, just get out of my sight!" her father had told her. Well, what was I to do? I didn't worry about what might come of it, I just pulled the girl up onto my horse and we rode together. There's a spring near Tulkidara, under the oak tree. Maybe you know it. It's a hot spring. Anyhow, we stopped there for a while to rest in the meadow. The girl took a bunch of grapes and some other fruits from her bundle and we ate them. From time to time I glanced at her. O Allah, I'd never seen such a beauty before! Her face and eyes were as clear as that spring, so pure! I must have been about your age, Farhod-jon. Right in my prime! To be honest, I entertained some juicy ideas, but I behaved myself well. I was a party member after all, head of the regional Komsomol branch. If I couldn't control myself that day I would destroy my own future. May Allah be praised, He kept me from evil, my will and determination got me through. Ah, but a person's soul is a strange thing, Farhod-jon. Sometimes you remember your past and regret things you didn't do. Well, we all see what is written in our fate. So I settled the girl in a boarding school in the local district. She studied there and became a member of the Komsomol. When she finished school she worked at the district branch of the Komsomol Committee for three or four years. She truly was an active and talented person. And I told you before how stunning she was. Well, perhaps her beauty helped, but anyway, she was sent to Tashkent to the Party High School. Later she headed the regional Women's Committee, worked as Deputy to the Chairman of the Executive Office and held many other high level offices, too. Her name was Barfina Akobirova! When we met at various regional meetings, she would always say, "How are you, comrade Mansurov!" I was the First Secretary in your district, Zarang, back then. I would always joke, saying, "I've eaten many a grapes, but I can never find the taste of those grapes we ate together! I've eaten many an apple but I can never find one to compare with the one we ate together." She would smile and say, "Forget about that, comrade Mansurov! Forget about those apples and grapes!" Later she married a Russian, a widower who worked at the Party Inspection Office. His name was Khudyakov Leonid. Everyone called him "Latif-aka." Khudyakov is Khudoyakov, which means 'Allah is alone'. He spoke Uzbek very well. Those two communists, though they believed in Allah, didn't have any children. Soon after that I was called to Tashkent for another job and I don't know what happened after that. And I don't know where Barfina Akobirova is now. Maybe you know, Farhod-jon?"

As a boy I remember hearing my father saying things like: "Ms. Akobirova came" or "Barfina-opa said such-and-such", but I had never set eyes on her, nor did I know whether she is alive or dead.

So I merely replied indifferently: "I don't know her."

The old man's long story was making me sluggish, my thoughts were drifting far way. His words floated over me like a lullaby. Drowsy, I finally fell asleep. In my dream I was right at the Tulkidara gorge. Evergreen pine trees carpeted the slopes all around. There was a lone tree with a spring under it. A young man and a girl were sitting at the spring, apples and grapes spread on the grass beside them. The man was picking grapes from one bunch and popping them into the girl's mouth. All of a sudden the scene changed, he was on top of her, molesting her. As I looked at them, I suddenly realized the girl was my sister, Halovat! Rushing over, I hurled myself on top of the aggressor. All of a sudden he turned into the Internationalist old man. I myself was a child. So the young man jumped up and began beating and choking me, calling me "scamp" or "rascal." I could neither move nor speak. Someone was running around. She was waving her arms around and laughing. I was in a poor state, half choked and beaten up, but I did manage to glance at the girl waltzing around. It was Munira, the lovely dancer who forgot her knickers!

"That's too bad," the old man repeats again, as if he felt sorry for me. "This is all because you didn't eat. You've not eaten anything since yesterday, you know."

He was standing right in front of me but could not make me speak, so he slowly left the room. He himself was full, he'd eaten four helpings of pork at lunchtime. His eyes were not watering; he was not feeling sick, his head did not ache. But he was bored. It was really boring to sit with this stubborn man in one room. He'd better go to see his deal little Munir-ochka. This old man and that sweet lady get on well together. They could sit and chat away in Russian all day long. When the old man joked she could not stop giggling. Sometimes they spent hours on end together. She never even so much as looked at me. "Sobir-jon Mansurovich, are you here?" she would say as she entered the room, and, with a quick hello to me, she would pull up a chair for herself, sit down beside him and hold her face out for him to kiss. "My dear Munir-ochka," the old man would say, kissing her cheek and hastily taking some sweets from the suitcase under his bed. The girl immediately pops a sweetie into her rosebud mouth and starts sucking it, puffing out her cheeks. "Sobir-jon Mansurovich," she says, ah, such a naughty girl! Can't she say "Grandpa" in Uzbek or Russian as a sign of respect, or is she too ill-mannered for that? Sobir-jon Mansurovich, just imagine! Or are you that Komsomol girl, Barfina Akobirova?

Perhaps she already knows I like her, and that's why she ignores me, conniving to meet with the old man as if she wanted me to be more and more jealous! Anyway, that's how I feel. Otherwise, even if there were no young man around, what would she do with this stinky old man if he had no sweets? You could expect everything from a young, energetic lad, but an old man is already old, he is harmless and incapable. One other thing united them, too: they were both "Internationalists" – one of them is a half-blood and the other is pro half-bloods. But to be honest, I sometimes wish I were either a half-blood or pro them, just to catch this girl's attention!

So her spoilt cheekiness serves a purpose. She was the charm and pearl of the "Shodiyona" dance troupe, a group consisting of seven dancers. One day before the first snow fell outside our hostel we went to a rally in a remote place. "Shodiyona" were due to dance after the Internationalist old man's usual solemn remarks and my own speech. All of a sudden there was a racket backstage. "Where are my knickers?" Munira (or as her friends called her, Ira or Irka) was shouting at her fellow dancers. "No, I will not go on stage without my knickers!" Ah, she was shouting for all to hear, the flirt!

It turned out that, thanks to sister Ma'mura, head of the troupe, darling Irka's knickers had been left behind at the hostel. But all seven dancers had to go on stage to perform the famous dances such as "Suzana" and "Haft Paykar". The very heart and harmony of those dances is spoilt if one dancer is missing, or if there are eight dancers instead of seven.

They decided to perform without one dancer, after all, "everything happens as it should", but sister Ma'mura, ashamed in front of the organizer Anatoliy Vasyuk, changed her mind. Fellow dancers offered Ira-Irka their own knickers: "Take mine, please," but Munira-Ira-Irka replied with a flirty smile: "I want my own, I don't need anyone else's!"

Finally it was decided that the empty bus would trundle back through the snowy streets and bring the knickers. Until it returned, the concert was postponed and the veteran of war and labor, old Bolshevik Sobir-jon Mansurov, had to take the floor once again to talk about glorious days gone by to keep the audience busy.

After that evening, many people should have lost interest in Munira. I don't know about the others, but we, the two rivals — the Internationalist old man and myself — were kinder on her. Actually, everyone was struck by how wonderfully "the girl who forgot her knickers" danced that evening!

"She's a very nice girl, isn't she, Farhod-jon?" the Internationalist grandpa said saucily one day as she left their room. "Why don't you give it a go?"

Though this suggestion really appealed to me and the same thought had often crossed my mind, the mere fact that this old man had suggested it irritated me, so I glowered at him, disgruntled. The old heathen, just give him half a chance and the old devil would be willing to probe himself! What if the girl is disappointed and clocks him one on the head?

A moment later the old fox started to justify himself:

"Only kidding. I meant you are a young man, I just wanted to test you." A bit later still he confessed: "Sorry, Farhod-jon, when you get old you become a useless ruin like me."

That was the truth. Thank goodness he had admitted what he was really thinking about.

Interestingly enough, it turns out the old man went to see her again. He was so bored, and I was poor company. He would bring her here later. If the girl saw me like this she would definitely comfort herself with the old man! Although he was over seventy, he was still strong and healthy. His still looked immaculate, like a true statesman, with his hair smoothly combed, his face clean. He only had to dye his hair to become a young man again! He dressed very well, too (he wore a jacket and tie even when he was just in our room) and sprayed himself with cologne five times a day. So in that case, what's the difference, young or old?

Well, just take a look at the young man! Sick for two days, bedridden! His eyes are glassy; he feels like vomiting and has a pounding headache. When his blood pressure was taken with some instrument found somewhere by the only person who loved him, Tolya Vasyuk, it was so low he might even die! Hearing that bad news, Vasyuk whistled: "Is your heart still beating?" Then he promised to bring cognac from the city the next day. But even that was only a temporary cure, since the old man kept harping on about how it was all down to not eating. But there was nothing to eat, or to be more precise, there was plenty of food, but it wasn't for the lad, though it was fine for the Internationalist grandpa!

He's never fussy about the food in the dining hall, he just eats whatever they give him, two or three portions of it. Maybe that's the secret of fine physique and robust health.

I, on the other hand, was both finicky and whiney from the beginning. Were I to list all the kinds of food I have not eaten until now you would be surprised I have eaten anything at all, barely enough to stand upright. I suffered a lot while studying abroad, especially in the advanced classes. But what can I do, it became a habit. By the way, can you imagine, I can't even drink milk!

All I have eaten since yesterday are two eggs, some bread and then more bread. How can you survive this cold winter and the snowy world on such a diet?

I don't even know what brought me here to these cursed places.

"Swept by the Ghost" was my scanty award after the film "The Swallows". With this award the Komsomol Central

Committee claimed me for its own. It gives me no rest, day or night, calling at any time it fancies. Suddenly I was in hot demand, I was overloaded with requests-cum-orders, inter-viewed on radio and TV, sent on various useless business trips, lots of Agitpoezd[41] which seems so pompous but are actually so frivolous!

Later this same Central Committee would also ask me to write something about those events. So I became a master of reporting: you know ours is a creative process, so if we do not write something today we will definitely write something tomorrow, and so on and so forth. Even if you carry out all their orders to the letter, they call upon you all the same, because you already belong to them since they presented you with an award!

On New Year's Eve I was again called by the Committee. It outlined a very responsible task. It was necessary to cre-ate a film that should praise the unselfish activity of our young countrymen working tirelessly in the fields in the vast northern part of the "boundless country." But first I had to join the par-ticipants of an Agitpoezd initiated by the Central Office and familiarize myself with the lives and conditions of those living in remote areas, and, if possible, prepare a draft scenario. So, here we are, thanks to that initiative. For more than a week we have been working feverishly. Every day we take a bus and head out to some remote villages to ask how our valiant young people are doing and to learn more about their work. The most important thing we do is inspire them to work better, to break new records. The Internationalist grandpa tells a story from his Komsomol years, the "Shodiyona" dance troupe performs their

---

41 Literally: agitation trains, i.e. propaganda wagons on the move.

best dances, and I write something about the event or speak to the audience.

But an unexpected snowfall has kept us from this pressing activity. It has been three days now since we moved anywhere, just sitting in our bedroom. Everyone and everything has ground to a halt. Everything, that is, but the snow. Everything around our hostel on the shores of Lake Ilmen is covered by a blanket of white snow! Not a single tiny black dot anywhere! White reigns supreme! White, white, white. It is freezing outside. Anyone going out will soon regret it. Well done, poor Vasyuk, who, braving the subzero temperatures, goes out to fetch food for us on his sledge. But we sit in the warm rooms, eating and drinking with pleasure. The "Shodiyona" dance troupe rehearses several times a day, shaking the whole building. The old Internationalist and I discuss something for hours on end.

I was the only one who did not eat or drink like others and got sick.

Furthermore, I became a roommate and even a fellow countryman with this old Bolshevik, can you imagine?

It's true that we had been friends at first. Now I think that a wise man could learn so many things from him. But in those days I was neither sensible nor clever. I insisted on answering questions right away. I always tried to show off, assuming I was cleverer, more truthful and more intellectual than whoever I was talking to. Ah, I was so young and callow then!

The relationship between this interesting old man and myself went that way, too. Poor fellow, whenever he opened his mouth to say something I made a face and prepared to attack. He was always ready to offer the olive branch,, while I was always on the attack and won every time, being as I was a representative of Glasnost, the time of openness and trust.

Even though I am a Muslim, I almost forgot there are qualities such as etiquette, shame and mercy in the world. Is he to blame for being born earlier, for growing up in that period or for his thoughts moulded by the times he lived through?

The first day when I introduced myself to him and told him where I hailed from originally, the old man's eyes glistened and he almost stood up:

"Oh, we are countrymen! Give me your hand, my younger brother! I worked there for exactly eleven years. I was head of Komsomol for seven years, then later I became the First Secretary of the Zarang District Party Committee, a post I held for for four years. My elder son Ilhom-jon was born there, so he is an out and out fellow countryman with you! There is no place in that oasis that your brother Sobir-jon did not visit. You are young so you might not know me, but I think the old people will remember me. Yes, the elderly people all know me. I spent eleven years of my life there, so they should. Well, what about you, who are your parents?" When I told him about my family the old man shouted as he clapped his hands. "O Merciful One, why didn't you tell me earlier? Your father Mirza-jon is one of my brothers! He was also a member of the Komsomol. He was a strong man. How is he now? What has he been doing? Send my regards to him when you go back. How could I not know you were from Zarang? That is a splendid place by the mountains! Ah, such a wonderful spot!"

I remembered that my father used to say his name with great respect, "Brother Sobir-jon, brother Sobir-jon." And now I see the very man himself. In those days when people said his name – "Mansurov, Mansurov" – that name seemed so powerful and frightening to us children. Now see where we run into each other!

I remember that he was an expected guest at my circumcision celebration, but he did not come. I was told that he attended the circumcision ritual itself, but I was in no condition to look around or recognize people...

The same day the old man and I became like dear friends, even like father and son.

The next day when we went to the first event together I listened to his speech and understood him completely. A Russian man, perhaps, would not be able to speak beautiful, pure Russian as eloquently as he did. Each word he spoke was to the point, meaningful, and essential, and he spoke them at such an easy pace, nicely and clearly as if reading from a book. Admittedly, his speech was full of the slick, official jargon familiar to all, but when you listen to him you will surely be surprised. His Uzbek was so beautiful, too! He never used dialect, slang or pidgin but the pure, clear Uzbek as spoken in Ferghana (by the way, he was the First Secretary there, too). No doubt, everyone would say: "Bravo!"

However, two days later I was disappointed; the first distress covered my soul.

At that meeting our grandpa, the old man, delivered the same speech, without skipping a single word, without a mistake and with the same melodious tune, like a nightingale! That meant he had learnt one speech off pat to deliver everywhere! Perhaps he had rehearsed in front of the mirror again and again. So that was his only talent, his only art!

After that, whenever he launched into his memorized speech, I would always mutter to myself, "Sing, my nightingale, sing!"

Once a book exhibition was organized in the same hall after one event and both the old man and I were checking some books there, when all of a sudden he yelled passionately:

"Vladimir Il'ich! O Allah be praised, these are the very three volumes I don't have! I lost them somewhere moving around with my career!"

"Eh, teacher, do you really want to take them with you? You can probably find them in Tashkent, too." But the old man bought them eagerly.

He also brought a bunch of books by "new great and famous leaders" from some event I was unable to attend. I saw him stashing them all under his bed, without showing them to me.

"Why are you collecting all those books, they are all written in riddles?" I said one day without keeping myself in check.

The old man's eyes bulged, but he didn't say anything.

"Never tell anyone else what you told me earlier, Farhod-jon," he advised me politely that evening before we went to bed. "I beg of you!"

According to a light-hearted drummer, Abdusamad, the old man maintained I was not a bad person in and of myself, but my ideology was bad. I was amazed that this man does not know the times he is living in! He seems very cowardly.

The way he pretended to be a healthy, energetic young man irritated me. Perhaps his little Munir-ochka makes him behave like that. He shaves twice a day and sprays his "Shipr" cologne around, filling the room with its pungent smell. It always makes me think of my late grandfather, Ramazon-boy, who passed away when he was younger than this old man, and who was both a well-balanced and prudent person. Why did you have a long white beard, Grandpa? Why didn't I ever see you using cologne? Was sixty-seven the right age to die, my dear Grandpa?

I was fed up with this old man's overly kind concern, fed up of him trying to force me to eat something. After one of our usual discussions about something or other, I popped out into the hallway to smoke, and when I came back in, I saw him sitting there like an ordinary old person, bent over and burdened. I felt sorry for him then and chided myself: you are a despot! But the old man ruined everything straightaway: "You haven't eaten a thing today, Farhod-jon!" The old man's burdens vanished in a second.

When I harangued him, he was always initially perplexed and momentarily embarrassed, but after delivering his notorious speech he regained his strength. No matter what you talk about, he relentlessly tries to link it to his good old days and starts harping on about the then-leaders in glowing terms: "They were real Leninist-Communists!"

"Whoever they were, Leninist or Communist, in the end they were all covered in a shroud![42]" I chime it sullenly. He stares at me for a moment, sighs deeply and repents: "Though we do not read namaz or pray, we are also Muslims, Farhod-boy!"

Thus, as time passed, our relationship deteriorated, until we became open rivals.

The two latest discussions were especially tough. The old man's Internationalism triggered the first while the Uzbek Pavel Korchagin was behind the second quarrel.

After Munir-ochka's next appearance, the old man proudly started talking about his forefathers and his mixed descendants:

"Ours is an international family, Farhod-jon. My wife is Ukrainian, one of my sons married a Polish woman, and the other married a Russian. My elder daughter married a Jew, the younger daughter lives in Yerevan. She studied with an Armenian chap at the Moscow Conservatoire and married him. My grandchildren are like that, too. One of them married a

---

42 A reference to Muslim funerary practices, in other words: 'they all went to the grave.'

general's son in Moscow. So one of my in-laws is a general, and my grandson-in-law is a pilot!

"Gracious me! That's a really mixed bag!" I exclaimed huffily, as if I were somehow implicated in that mix. "So not one of them married an Uzbek man or woman, right?"

The old man did not understand my caustic comment or mistook it for encouragement so he went on delightedly:

"Yes, yes, that's correct! Isn't it good that wherever you go you see your own relatives?! This is what our times demand! Is it a bad thing if all peoples become a single nation? That is called Internationalism!"

"What about Uzbeks? What is their bloods mix, teacher?!"

"Uzbek, you say?" the old man was a little flustered. He had never thought about it from this angle. There were no answers to such questions in his infamous speech. Nevertheless, he found something to say, devil that he was: "Well, isn't it better if the bloods mix? That way the blood is regenerated, people look younger, so the nation as a whole would be more comely and more talented, too. That's right, isn't it?

"No, it's not! It's not good!" I said angrily. "I don't need that kind of nationality or hand-me-down looks and talent! That's not a nationality! If everything were as you say, would there be any nationality left in the world at all?!"

"Well, alright, don't fret, please," the crafty old man tried to pacify me. "Come on, let's go. It's lunchtime."

"You can go by yourself! You know I can't stand the food from the Internationalist's pot!"

The old man stared at me in surprise for a while, then nodded his head and left.

That evening we did not discuss anything. The old man seemed somehow pensive, even sad.

Quite frankly, it was all the same to me what kind of family this crazy old man had; he'd eaten his own brains along with the pork! I didn't care if his children had international marriages or were of mixed blood. Let them turn into the devil incarnate and wed an alien descended from a UFO! What disappointed me was the fact that this darned old man was boasting about it all, as if he were shouting: "Behold and envy me! We are the example to follow!"

In my student days, when I was back home in Zarang during my vacation, my Grandma would call me and ask:

"Don't you want to marry your aunt's daughter? Or have you found someone there? Your aunt's daughter is so beautiful. Well, she will have someone, too. Is the girl you found nice? Is she Uzbek? Is she a Muslim girl? Mark my words carefully, my lad. Wherever or whenever you marry, make sure you marry someone from our own kin and nationality! See what I mean? If you don't, you will trouble me in my grave. I will never be at peace! There is wisdom in these words, my child!" Then (may Allah be merciful to her) she would pick up her sewing again for a while, her needle flashing in silence until she began again:

"Well, who knows, in fact you will never be able to run from your own destiny. When I was a little girl, one of our neighbours had a daughter called Zaynab, a real beauty. But she ran away with a stranger the same age as her father. Her brothers went to Samarkand to look for her and bring her back, but she told them: "I love this man, so go and tell that to our father! I don't care if he curses me, that's up to him!" Ah, such a crazy girl! After that people used to say: "Heart – Zaynab's heart". It means you should not believe your heart all the time. You should also consult your mind. I know you are clever, my child…" Then she would fall silent for a while, then smile and say: "My son, even your own people are not trustworthy.

Nations are also different, they do not stand alone, and there are thousands of them. Each of them has its own particular dream, intention, taste, and so on. I don't understand those who say: "Let those lovebirds enjoy their life." Are they talking about enjoyment? Don't worry, my son, don't pay attention to the words of your old Grandma. Live and learn. Actually, be it a Muslim or a Christian, they are all slaves of Allah. They all have their own hopes. But do not forget the advice I gave you earlier, my son."

What was the old woman trying to say with her admonitions back then? Or was she also an internationalist like this old man? Who knows. Anyway, you cannot go to her grave and ask her.

The last argument between the internationalist grandpa and myself happened one day before the snow storm, while we were in a very remote village to meet a hero of our time, the avant-garde machine-operator Toshpulat Kurbonov.

"He is a very nice guy, isn't he, Farhod-jon? He looks just like Pavel Korchagin!" the old man said with delight. "I hope you'll write a good piece about him."

"What the fuck for?!" I yelled making an obscene gesture. Later, of course, I regretted it. But I couldn't say anything else, I was too angry. "What are they doing? Shit! What do they need? Did they say it from the depths of their soul? Fuck it!"

The old man did not argue with me; he just jumped off his bed and left me alone in the room.

We didn't exchange a good word until we got back to Tashkent.

Toshpulat was the same age as me. But he was a strong, handsome, muscular young man. He was also well-mannered and very polite; whenever you ask him anything, he answers with a pleasant smile. You warm to him immediately.

A group of young Komsomol members, headed by Toshpulat, was camped right in the middle of a large field; in fact, they were "assaulting" the field. The camp consisted of several mobile wagons and tents covered with tarpaulin, as well as various tractors, long trenches and sand hills beyond. The ground was frozen and it was bitterly cold.

In this freezing weather, the members of the brigade gathered in an open place between the tents to watch our performance. Even though the majority were our own Uzbek young men, as usual, the old man spoke to them in his "second mother tongue". Being stubborn, I spoke my stories in our native Uzbek language. Suddenly I felt Toshpulat, who was standing beside me, slightly shake my arm. I had also taken a liking to this man when we first met.

When the poor "Shodiyona" dancers, freezing and shaking in their atlas dresses, began their performance, the audience cheered them on with warm applause.

After the event, Toshpulat invited us to the central tent for some food and tea. We all hurried inside. They had set up a dining table using long wooden boards supported by bricks. There was no tea on the table but it was laden with other products such as vodka, salami, salted cucumbers and herring.

My concern that they would freeze in this cold vanished. The tent was quite warm. There were two bonfires at either end, and the branches piled onto the concrete burned red hot. We learned that they sleep in sleeping bags at night. "Those who still feel cold even in their sleeping bags live in those wagons. The married couples stay there, too," Toshpulat explained.

I asked him various questions as we ate, jotting his answers down in my notebook. He said that the Central Komsomol Committee had promised to award him with a diploma if he came to work here.

"Well, suppose you get that diploma, what will you do then?"

"I don't know, Allah alone knows what will happen," he shrugged. He was a very simple-minded person!

His fellow companions were also from remote villages of Uzbekistan. Many of them didn't know what to do after they returned from military service. There were no good jobs or comforts in the villages. Some of them were unable to get married – their parents were quite old, it was better to help them rather than to hold a wedding. And just then, the Komsomol hired them all with pompous slogans about patriotism, self-sacrifice and devotion.

"Tosha-a! Where are you?" called a woman in rubber boots, flashing her gold teeth. "Again?"

"My wife," Toshpulat said slowly, feeling a little ashamed. "Come in. What do you want?"

His wife looked a bit uncomfortable at the sight of the guests, too, but she quickly spoke her mind:

"Well, lads, don't you want to offer me some food and vodka?"

She downed a glass of vodka on the spot, munched a piece of salami, thanked them, and went out after joking with her husband and showing her fists.

Our hero had emptied several bottles of vodka since the dinner started. He was good at this, too, no doubt he would receive many other "awards" as well Does this young man think about his future? Well, how could he think about the unknown? He is happy today. A day has passed, but his wife, that old witch, what would she do with this simple, quiet chap at night? They are both drunk now. Something might happen. What do you care? Leave them alone. One day he will go back to his village from this foreign place and leave a swarthy girl or boy with his wife. And our Internationalist grandpa supports them, if you please!

As we said good-bye to each other, I asked Toshpulat for his photo. He hurried to fetch a beautiful photograph of himself in an army overcoat taken during his military service. Feeling sorry for him, I hugged him: 'bye, poor hapless fellow, Pavka Korchagin!

Now, this naïve lad will be over the moon for days: "They'll write an article about me and publish it in a newspaper with my photo! All my villagers, including my parents and Halima, will see it," he might think.

But that's a vain dream, my friend!

Whenever I think about that evening, all I see is Toshpulat's old witch-wife, dressed up like a man, with her false teeth, a glass of vodka in her hand, and poor Toshpulat feeling ashamed, glancing sideways.

Where could that strapping young lad be now, the one in the photo (which, incidentally, I ripped up in a rage)? I would run in the opposite direction if we met again. But he was a good lad. Perhaps his love, Halima, had waited and waited for him but then married another, who knows.

It's only in fairytales that a good husband will have a good wife…

The last time we fellow travelers who had insulted and hurt each other during that unforgettable snowfall at Lake Ilmen met was when we both went to present our reports to the Central Office of the Komsomol. The old man was so glad to see me again, as if he had met up with his own son. He did not want to say farewell: "Here is my address. Please come to our house, be our guest, Farhod-jon. Come with your wife. I will introduce you to my wife and children. We will make friends again and visit each other. Please come, I'll be waiting for you. When can you come? The cherries in my garden are almost ripe, you can pick them and have yourself a feast."

The cherries finished, whoever wanted to eat them had already done so, but I didn't go. What was I supposed to do with that fickle old man? I was afraid of finding myself face to face with him again. So I kept my distance.

It was, however, impossible to get rid of him completely. Actually, that last time we met was not our final farewell. I could leave the rest of my travelling companions, but this old man would hound me all my life.

But I did not know that then.

Years passed, several heads were replaced after the "master of light" chairman, and finally Farhod Ramazon would take the chair as the real man of film championing the Uzbek cause.

One day his secretary would inform him that a woman was asking for him. But the head, ruffled, would say: "Who is she? Don't I have anything better to do than chat with women?"

"She is not an ordinary woman, she is an actress," the frightened secretary would reply.

"I've seen so many actresses, what's so special about this one?"

"She knows you personally."

"Do you think the rest of them don't 'know me personally'?" he would say. But he would let the woman in. "Well, call her."

An unfamiliar woman entered the office. She was beautiful, rich looking and rather arrogant. Yet there was something vaguely familiar about her. She held out her hand and lent her face towards Farhod Ramazon as he stood up to greet her. But seeing his hesitation, she quickly tried to introduce herself: Lake Ilmen, heavy snowfall, brother Sobir-jon, "Shodiyona" dance troupe... Farhod Ramazon made a face as if he were trying to recall a late relative. Yes, Munira-Ira-Irka! The girl who forgot her knickers! For the sake of days gone by, he offered her a seat.

The purpose of the lady's visit was her audition for the part of main heroine in a new film called "The Echo of Love". She hoped her old acquaintance and brother, Farhod, would help her. He would not ask her if she is planning to change her career in dance for one in film; he would not be surprised by her decision. Today, not only dancers but even those who have never even set foot on stage try their hand at acting. But brother Farhod is very busy these days, and, by the way, his position has changed, so he can nonchalantly say that it is not his job to decide, and that it is up to the artistic board to make a decision. "But aren't you the head of the artistic board, brother Farhod-jon?" she asked.

Farhod Ramazon was surprised not by her blunt request, as though she had done something for him at Lake Ilmen, but by the fact that she was speaking in pure Marghilan dialect! And this happened at the time when everyone was trying to learn Uzbek, despite internationalism or the crave for mixed blood.

"You can do as you please with me, even hurt me, but please, help me, brother Farhod-jon," beseeched the lady. "I don't wear others' hand-me-downs," he would say to himself.

They find themselves back at Lake Ilmen again, in the snow storm, with the kind-hearted grandpa, brother Sobir-jon. "I sensed you really liked me then." Again they relive the funny story about forgotten knickers, yes, knickers! "Where are my knickers?" she kept shouting back then.

But all of this is in vain. Useless!

Finally the lady jumps up and shouts at the chairman in her native language: "We'll see, we'll see!"

And the chairman replies significantly: "Find another patron!"

So, did the chairman want to take revenge on this lady whom he had once loved? No, no, not at all! On the contrary, it irked him she was putting those good memories up for sale. That's all.

As a result, she would play the heroine in "The Echo of Love" not with Farhod Ramazon's help but with the help of other influential people. "We'll see!" But the film never made it to the big screen, it was found lacking. But the chairman had no hand in this.

A few months later, Farhod Ramazon received a phone call: "Such and such, a lady you know well, is going to play the lead in a film. But the film director is stubborn, he does not want her to star. Please tell him... We would be at your service, brother!"

"Thanks, many thanks. But forgive me please, brother. If you are such a rich man, you could start your own studio, produce your own films, and this lady could star in all of them, you could even play the leading man alongside her! But my job is different. I don't deal with street art, sorry," he would say, and hang up..

Two or three days later, "the brother" comes to pay a visit in person. He is that same brother who is always present at weddings and every other ceremony, who knows everyone and is known to all!

"I just wanted to see you, brother."

"Welcome, brother."

He came, saw, spoke, and tried to use all his usual wiles, but, alas, it was all in vain. So he slowly stood up and left.

Farhod went out with him to see him off (well, to tell the truth, to relax a little). He was surprised to see several women at the reception tucking into a delicious-looking cake. Perhaps those janitors at the door were smoking Marlboro cigarettes outside just then...

Following Farhod Ramazon's advice, "the brother" would later found a group of female singers called "Semurgh". "Se murgh" means 'three hens', not three chicks. Gradually the number of chicks would increase, the group would turn to "Simurgh", thirty chicks. A "Simurgh" cinema company would emerge, too. All members of the ensemble, dancers and singers, are lovely young chicks. Later they would all migrate to the film industry to become actresses. "Simurgh" productions would be shown on all TV channels. Farhod Ramazon, who heads other branches, would snidely call them "Brother Film Productions." And indeed, "our brother", who is so far from the arts and quite inexperienced, would indeed become a producer!

Once, on the eve of a state holiday, Farhod Ramazon was invited to a celebration at a restaurant. And whom should he see there but the "Simurgh" troupe warming up for a performance. The "brother" – who by that time had already ingratiated himself with Farhod Ramazon – called him over to the group of dancers and singers. As if showing off, "the brother" circled among them, touching and kissing his "chicks". Weren't they embarrassed or jealous? "You can take anyone you like," 'the generous brother' said to him as he felt a certain swelling in his companion's groin.

Unfortunately Munira-khon was not among them. She had probably already become a hen and was 'entertaining' in some other place, seeing Lake Ilmen in her dreams!

8. "Qi Gong". A man who shrank.
   ## Beat the nationalist!

When did he first think of going to China?

In Nedelya weekly Farhod read a lengthy article entitled "The Wonders of Qi Gong." "Qi Gong" meant physical culture or motion in general. The article claimed that one could cure oneself of many diseases by using this method, including the din in the ear.

Well, is there any way to go to China? He thought about it and finally hit upon an idea. Thinking not only about political sensitivity but also about that great country's geographic location, Farhod sent a request to the Central Filmmakers' Union stating that he was planning to study the life of the democrat-poet Furkat in Yorkent and write a scenario called "It was written in his destiny." And for this he, Farhod, would need to take a trip to Uyghuristan. In his letter he also mentioned that the first film about the poet, "Furkat", was released the very year he was born (who would bother to check?) and that he had always had a great interest in the poet's creative work, especially in his complicated fate.

Who cares whether the scenario is ever written or not, his purpose is to go to China!

When he read in another issue of Nedelya that a Qi Gong medical centre had opened in the capital of the "boundless country," he could not wait even a moment; he made up his mind there and then to go and see the senior doctors.

* *

He thought that this place of miracles would enjoy a prime location right in the city centre, but in fact it was tucked away in the basement of a high rise residential building on a street worse than that Salom Odil Street which even many of the locals had never heard of. There were not many patients waiting their turn. Farhod tried to strike up a conversation with one of the noise-plagued patients but he turned out to be deaf. He could not understand anything, only hissed and gurgled, murmuring something which sounded like "bath, bath" as if he was trying to say that the noise in his ear sounded like water gushing in the bathroom. He was well on in years. Farhod would have to live quite a while longer to reach his ripe old age. Actually, he, Farhod, would not care if he were stone deaf at that age, but not now!

A female doctor, short and completely round, of an indeterminable age, ushered him into a treatment room. She invited him to take a seat at the window, saying: "Karasho, karasho!⁴³" by giving him the thumbs up. "The doctor says you should not worry, you will recover soon." It was only then that Farhod noticed an old Jewish man sitting at the back like a school boy, his hands in his lap. He was an interpreter. With his help, Farhod spoke with the doctor and told her about his own suffering. Her thumb came out again: "Karasho, karasho!"

In general, she had a friendly face and was a light-hearted woman. Her lips were somehow short, so her mouth was always open in a permanent smile showing her big white teeth. She was nimble with her work, too. But she did not look like a doctor; she looked like a cleaning lady. Her lab coat was black down the sides and round the pockets. Without washing her hands, she first rubbed Farhod's shoulders with her plump hands then started to crumple his earlobes for about fifteen minutes.

According to the interpreter, this method helps soften the ear, improve blood circulation and revive nerve cells. This was stated with unswerving certainty. Well, why not? Logically, he is right. It's no wonder if those numb nerve cells get more blood and recover soon, since any kind of numbness is brought on by lack of motion or lack of blood in that part of the body. Blood

---

43 Good, good in Russian.

is a life giving wonder. Therefore that article was also entitled "The Wonder of Qi Gong."

Auntie "Karasho" took the money he gave her, thrust it in her pocket and said he should come another nine times to complete the first level of his treatment.

"Is there any other level?" Farhod asked the interpreter.

"Why of course there is! Who told you that this chronic complaint of yours could be treated in a ten-day period?"

The woman stayed there with her "Karasho" and Farhod, who was not satisfied by the treatment, went out rather perplexed.

He wanted to go to the Central Union for an update on his travel permit. But since he did not run into grave-faced Sur'at, he went directly to the recreation centre instead.

Over lunch, Mr. Akobirov asked him:

"Where were you yesterday? Did you go to Gulya's house? Did you have a good meeting? Did you see her daughter? She's a real beauty, isn't she? Did Gulya give her room to you, too? Did she tell you the story of the leopard skin there?"

Farhod was dumbstruck.

"How do you know?"

"We know everything," Mr. Akobirov said cleaning his spectacles. "I've been there, too. Last time I could not find a room in a hotel and was obliged to stay with her. Actually she took me in herself. She said that the skin had once belonged to a tiger and that it was a gift from a Caucasian friend. Can you imagine? She did not let me sleep with her, though, the slut!"

"Don't say that in front of me, brother Ravshan, I don't think she's a bad woman," Farhod said, feeling uncomfortable.

"Oh, she's a very nice woman, to be sure!.. Do you know her history? She was an excellent schoolgirl and went to "Artek" Young Pioneer camp. She found someone there to make love to. When she got back to Tashkent she was passed from one person to another. So she wasn't sure she'd be able to find a husband, that's why she came here and found herself a blond guy. But they divorced after a while. Did you see her daughter? She is really beautiful. She looks like Sophie Loren!

"I didn't see her," Farhod said, thinking about something else. "Her mother said she'd gone somewhere."

"Illegitimate children are usually beautiful, aren't they Farhod-jon?

"I don't know." Farhod had never expected to hear such things from Mr. Akobirov, so this saddened him; in his mind Mr. Akobirov had become a small, petty man. "It would have been better if you hadn't told me this, brother Ravshan."

Mr. Akobirov frowned.

"Don't listen if you don't want!"

Something more interesting happened as they were strolling silently in the square after lunch.

All of a sudden their colleague Igor Semashenkov appeared before them. He was from Tashkent, too. Strange, when did he arrive?

Farhod was usually irritated by this swarthy, grimy, black-haired person who always wore a frown. Whenever they ran into each other he barely greeted him, or he just tried to escape and avoid shaking hands with him. Perhaps Igor Semashenkov sensed this, too, so whenever he saw Farhod he would fix him with a cold stare and try to glean something from his expression. He was an extreme chauvinist and a Russian nationalist, too! And his tongue had really loosened up during those days of Glasnost. He used to take the floor at meetings, all a-quiver, and deliver his belligerent speeches as a representative of the "big brother." When he found himself in Uzbek-only circles, he would insult his own fellow nationals, calling them "bloody pork-eaters;" he often singled out his own colleagues for particularly caustic attacks. In short, he was a miserable, spineless man beyond help!

However, everyone, including those masters of ceremonies and officials, was afraid of him and had to keep in his good books. Just try to disobey! He would take you to the peak of political nonsense. Someone, it seemed, was pulling his strings, using him. Someone who must have benefited from his behaviour and even coached him in it.

You see this man, a writer of scenarios for documentaries, would carry out special orders to the letter, orders that others would try their very best to avoid.

"Ravshan Usmonovich, one moment please," Semashnikov said with a grin as he blocked their way.

"What do you want?" Mr. Akobirov did not even turn his face and passed by as if he were swatting flies.

But Semashenkov followed them insolently.

"I have something to tell you, Ravshan Usmonovich."

"In Tashkent, you always gossip that I am Pro-Russian, but here you blacken my name saying: "He is an Uzbek nationalist." Is this what you are going to tell me now?"

"What are you saying, Mr. Akobirov?" Semashenkov wanted to barricade him in again, but Akobirov pushed him side making way for himself. But he softened nevertheless:

"Semashenkov, don't you see my younger brother is with me now? We have some topics to discuss."

"Is he your younger brother? So that means he's like you, right?

Mr. Akobirov stopped walking.

"What? So what if he looks like me?"

"But you are from a mountainous area!"

"So what if I am from a mountainous area?"

"You are not Uzbek!"

"Who told you that? Who are you, anyway, do you know?"

"Who? Well, if you really want to know, I'm completely Russian! I'm the son of the great Russian people!"

Mr. Akobirov, who was several steps ahead, stopped, turned back and beckoned him with his forefinger: come here! Semashenkov came right up to him: what do you want?

"Listen to me, son of the great Russian people!" Akobirov said emphatically. "Do you want me to tell who you are? You are neither Russian nor anything else! You are too untalented, stingy and an envious gossip-mongerer, understand?! Now, turn round! Go on! Turn around!" Mr. Akobirov grabbed him by his shoulders, turned him around and kneed him in the back. "Get out of my sight! Go! Quick march!"

"What?! What are you on about? You are a nationalist, Akobirov! I will not let this go!"

"So that means we are the same, we are colleagues, then, aren't we, Semashtein?"

"What?! What do you mean, you…?"

And with that they laid into each other! May Allah be praised, no one except Farhod was around to witness this disgrace.

"Hey, don't just stand there! Hit the bastard!" Akobirov shouted at Farhod.

Farhod quickly separated them and tried to hold Akobirov under his arm. But the captive pinched Farhod's arm as hard as he could. "Ee, go, go!" he said and went to his residence.

At dinner time he sat at a different table. He was quick to take offence! He had become smaller, like a child.

* *

9. Plato son of Socrates and a dog lover, Zuzi, a flowerpot, and more.

Hemmed in, Farhod caught sight of a flowerpot on the win-dowsill, the flower-occupants of which had long since withered. Barely managing to control his bladder, he sidled up to the pot, set it on the floor, and unleashed the contents of his bursting bladder. There was no other option. He hoped Allah would forgive him.

All of a sudden he felt better. The tight world became wider, brighter. Ah, where were you before, lightsome world? Where did you hide your release and delight earlier? You see, he had been in trouble for over an hour. True, he had seen the flow-erpot earlier, but how could he guess it might prove useful? Actually, he was aware that in such cases it was permissible to urinate even on a camel, without worrying about stopping or holding up the caravan. But this was not the Sahara, where any kind of moisture is gratefully soaked up. In the Sahara there is no shame for either camel or caravan. But here you can only find a pot, a flowerpot... So maybe that could be a solution, Allah knows. If he had had to wait even just a little longer, he would definitely have disgraced himself, and that would be con-sidered a gross misdemeanor, not a mere moistening of the Sahara!

Farhod has been sitting in this room alone for more than two hours. It was a gloomy room - the windows opened onto a yard fenced in by higher buildings and the light bulb was blown, too. One wall was lined with bookshelves laden with books on the history of world cinema and cinematography, various albums, advertisements, posters, and a pile of manuscripts. Family pho-tos nestled between the closets. There was no carpet on the floor; the room had nothing but a rocking chair to offer.

The two rooms beyond were also empty. In the first there was at least a folding bed, quilts, a writing-table and a chair festooned with clothes. The second room was given over entirely to three giant beasts, which think nothing of releasing what a human being cannot hold for a minute longer than an hour; they can even release something worse, which is why the rooms over there stink. Just imagine, this is a building right in the city centre!

Sitting in the rocking chair, Farhod read a book for about an hour. His eyes were tired. The sun was setting. Then he gave himself over to his troubles. He stood up several times and hovered by door, but he did not dare venture out. Three giant hounds were homing in on him from three sides! They were obviously waiting for their trophy, so if you are tired of living, well, go ahead!

It was not the first time he found himself in such a predicament. He remembered those times when he first came to Tashkent. One day he met up with someone from his home village and they both went to meet his friend's brother. Drinking vodka was the teacher's favorite job; perhaps that's why he lived alone in his two-room flat. While the teacher and the student clink their glasses time and time again, the villager wants to piss. But he does not know where to go. To interrupt them to ask would be impolite, so he simply left the room. But then he did not know where to go next; it didn't occur to him to go open a door in the flat to do what he wanted. He thought the toilet was outside. Well, suppose he went out, would he find the toilet there? What if he couldn't find his way back? Finally, he plucks up his courage, strides down the corridor, through the kitchen, and out onto the balcony. It is dark everywhere. Earlier, when the teacher insisted he drank a glass of vodka with them, he tasted it for the first time in his life, so he was a bit drunk when he reached the small balcony. Standing there, on the fourth floor, he urinated into the darkness. When he returned to the room his companions were sitting as he had left them; no one had missed him.

But that had been a totally different time. A young boy straight from the village did not know what he was doing there in the darkness or what he had watered. Today, as a mature man, he was fully aware of his actions, carried out in broad daylight. Small wonder if these neglected, dry flowers revive, turn green again, grow in a tumble over the windowsill and fall down onto the ground. Right then, while their owners roam around, hungry dogs come and gnaw those flowers. But the flowers are poisonous, watered with poison, so when the dogs eat them, they go mad and attack their owners just back from the meeting of democrats, tearing them into pieces. It serves them right! You don't want to have children, you love dogs instead, Plato the son of Socrates! "A golden man!"

As agreed over the phone, Farhod met him at the exit of the Arbat metro station. A grey beard covered his face. He wore a striped yellow shirt and a colourful tie fastened with a big knot. He behaved strangely, had an absent-minded air, and spoke as if he were rushing off somewhere. In short, he looked like our own Ruzi Choriev[44] - you've seen him, I'm sure.

As soon as he met Farhod, he enquired about his attitude towards democracy. The latter replied with confidence: "Ah, we'll win, you'll see!" Then he began to describe Zuzi. Apparently – who know if this is in fact true – he had agreed to treat his would-be patient on one condition: 'I'll only treat him if he supports democracy!' He really liked democrats. According

---

44 Famous Uzbek artist of the Soviet era renowned for painting the ordinary working Uzbek people.

to this windbag, Zuzi initially refused to see his patient, saying: "If he is a Muslim it will be difficult to establish a spiritual relationship with him." But in the end he agreed to receive Farhod; after all, he was a friend of his dear neighbour, and he could not say "no" to a democrat like Plato Sokratovich!

He called Farhod 'Farid' or 'Ramzan' by mistake, and when Farhod tried to correct him, he replied lightly, "Yes, yes, Gulya told me, I'll keep it in mind."

Plato Sokratovich's flat was located near Malaya Bronnaya Street, in front of the Vakhtangov Theatre, in an ancient building with thick walls and high ceilings. As he proudly stated, this ancient building was a legacy given to him by his grandfather, who was a Bolshevik-revolutionist, and his father, who worked as People's Commissar. By the way, his grandfather died heroically in Central Asia fighting basmachi guerilla soldiers, ah, he was so proud of him!

When they had both reached the second floor, Plato Sokratovich resolutely pressed the doorbell on the right. The door was covered with the skin of a rare animal and there was a name plate on the wall: "Zuzi." Another name plate below it read: "Zinaida Gavrilovna Niku."

An unattractive, yellow-haired woman opened the door. Farhod was surprised: could this be "Zuzi"? But everything fell into place when he glanced inside the room. A witch-like woman with dishevelled jet black hair was blocking the whole of the corridor with her body, gazing at him.

"Oh, Sokratich, Sokratich!" said the lady, who seemed to be her maid. "He was called for and taken recently. Was called for from On High!"

"Ah, and he was just telling me how he does not even want to even set eyes on those partocrats," Plato Sokratovich replied, looking at his watch. "I have to go to a meeting now. What shall we do? Do you think he will be back in an hour or two, Lena-khon?"

"I think he'll be back in about an hour and a half."

"If so, please let this man meet with Zinaida Gavrilovna, OK? I've already spoken to her about him. Do you have the key to my flat?"

"Yes, I do," the woman said, looking at Farhod with great interest. "Yes, I do, Plato Sokratich. Don't worry, I'll do just as you say."

When Plato Sokratovich put his key into the door opposite, something hit the door from inside with a rhythmical banging. Barking could be heard, too.

When they entered the flat, three huge hounds immediately encircled their master and began prancing about, standing on their hind legs. One of them barked at the unfamiliar smell. Terrified, Farhod flattened himself against the back wall.

"Cesar, stop that!" Plato shouted and took the three of them to the kitchen, stroking them as they went.

Farhod glanced around hurriedly. Spotting a door ajar, he quickly slipped behind it.

"Don't be afraid of them, Farid, they're the most wonderful creatures in the world!" said their master with glee as he entered the room behind him. "They're a thousand times better than those partocrats! Now listen to me, my friend: I'll be back in a couple of hours. The books in this room are at your disposal. Don't be shy, just help yourself, OK?" He attempted to turn on the light by flicking the switch on the wall, but there was no reaction, so he merely shrugged indifferently and left.

He again fussed over his dogs for several minutes, then, with a quick "Alright, see you later," he closed the door and locked it from outside.

More than two hours passed, but the dog-fancier still had not come home. Farhod was about to explode. Thank goodness he saw that flowerpot!

Relived at last, he went back to the bookshelf and began browsing through the photos, starting from the beginning.

So, like most others, this person has his own children, too. This lady smiling behind his shoulders must be his wife. He also has two daughters, one tall, one short, standing side by side in their school uniforms. And here are the four of them: husband and wife sitting holding hands, their grown-up daughters standing behind them. A happy family! Where are they now? Or did they get fed up with these huge hounds and leave? Who knows?

Farhod stared at an old framed photograph standing on its own. It was of a red soldier in a Budyonovka hat, his chest and shoulders covered in special belts. The blurry yellow photo had an inscription on it which read: "Fiery revolutionist S.P. Knyazov. 1894-1922." Perhaps this was Plato's grandfather, the one who had "died heroically during the war against Basmachis."

Did it say Knyazov? Isn't it our own "Father Knyaz" in Zarang? Farhod was aware that there had been many fights around his birthplace during the Basmachi period. His father had wanted Farhod to study history and become a great scholar; he didn't approve his choice to study arts. He had dreamt of seeing his son as both historian and party member, and later as chief secretary of some district. Actually, that was the dream of his life!

Reaching into his childhood memories, Farhod saw an important, sacred, influential tomb near the walls of the old mound at the exit of Zarang Central District. It was enclosed by an iron latticed fence; even the tall, angular statue in the middle was made of iron. A reddish copper starlet shone on it. Schoolchildren who wanted to become Pioneers often took their oath at that tomb, and in return they cleaned and painted it: lattice into blue, statue into silver.

The people of the district used it as a reference point: "Not far from the tomb of Father Knyaz" or "Right after you pass Father Knyaz," they would say.

Was that really our Father Knyaz[45] in this photo? If so, then it is indeed a small world! Farhod was not particularly interested in such things, so he never paid much attention to inscriptions and the like, which is why he found it difficult to be sure now. In fact, shrines like that had become neglected in recent years. Father Knyaz's tomb may well have fallen into disrepair, its iron lattice fence broken or rusty, its inscription worn or overgrown. Anyway, there have been so many lords and people called Knyazev, Lordson.

Not knowing how to amuse himself, Farhod was really feeling wretched. What was he doing here, anyway? Hadn't he tried his luck with psychics and miracle-workers before? He had seen plenty in Tashkent! Once a folk healer-cum-sieve maker tried to treat him, saying: "The back of your head got flattened because you slept on your back in the cradle, so now your blood circulation is poor. That's what all that noise comes from." And so saying, he put a sieve-like tool into his head and set about twisting and turning it every which way. However, instead of getting rid of the noise, it just gave Farhod a headache.

Later he went to see another medicine-man, a so-called "stare doctor" who sat Farhod down in front of him and just stared and stared at him. The "doctor's" eyes shone out from under those bushy eyebrows as if they could bore right through him or break him into pieces. At first you don't know what to do or where to look, then you start squirming, and finally you

---

45 Knyaz – the Russian for 'prince.'

giggle uncontrollably as if someone is tickling you mercilessly. Do you think it is easy to sit stock still when someone's staring at you like that?

Psychics and miracle workers were popping up everywhere. Almost one in four of your acquaintances turned out to have "magic hands." None of them, however, could cure Farhod. Perhaps this Zuzi whom everyone talks so much about is just another of these charlatans. True enough, he is very famous and is known as "the magic Greek prince." True enough, he can cure officials "sitting On High" and partocrats bigger than these huge hounds of Plato. True enough, Farhod got goose bumps at the mere sight of his photo in the hallway. Well. we'll see what kind of miracle this highly-acclaimed one can perform.

* *

The Studio Director's wife fell ill. From time to time, she felt as if a bird were coming out of her heart. It was clear that the bird came out but it was not clear where it perched. There was a good psychic, Abusharof, who, they say, would be able to determine the bird's exact location. So of course, he had to be found, and a film must be made about him!

I was approached by Producer Botirbek, a handsome man who always wore a large parasol cap and whose hair flopped over the back of his head like a thin waterfall. With his pomp-ous bag slung over his shoulder, he said cheerily: "Let's go, old man!" The Director had insisted on one condition: if I agreed to write the script, my long-forgotten scenario written two years earlier would finally be filmed. And that meant the return to a life of luxury for me: filming in Sijjak or Oqtosh once again; attending the annual month-long creative seminar for young scriptwriters in Yalta again (which actually was quite useless apart from the location); more workshops in Isfara for the young creative people of Central Asia – in short, a plethora of delightful and interesting trips!

I liked this request very much – it was a good chance for me to show my ear to the doctor-cum-psychic.

The "Abusharof" medical centre was situated in the basement of one of the old buildings on Navoi Street. It was a busy place, the courtyard was full of cars. Despite the long queue, Botirbek sailed right through everyone with me in tow, right into the magical doctor's room. Abusharof was a hairy person. He had hair on his ears, in his nose, in short, everywhere. He was about fifty years old. As if he sensed the smell of glory oozing from Botirbek's jaunty cap and pompous bag, he quickly dismissed the patient he was dealing with and came to greet us:

"Welcome, brothers, can I help you?"

"Our boss says you are to cure his wife and we will make a film about you," Botirbek said bluntly without any introductions. "This is the scriptwriter!"

It turned out that the doctor did not like Botirbek's barked way of communicating, so hearing the word "scriptwriter," he turned to me, assuming I was the main person here.

He wrote down the telephone number and home address of the patient whose "heart had a flying bird" and promised to pay her a visit. It was agreed that I should come here several times to familiarize myself with his methods and note down former patients' words of gratitude.

Brother Abusharof and I almost became friends. Sometimes we had lunch together, as his clients would sometimes bring kebab or samsa with meat for him. Making the most of such opportunities, I told him about my own ear problem and he at once seated me on the patient's chair and began rotating his palm over my ear. "Is it warming up? Do you feel anything?"

he asked from time to time. "Yes, yes," I replied to the famous healer and my companion of the last three days. It was obvious that if you put your hands over your ears for a moment, your temples would definitely warm up or even get hot.

Actually, I found Abusharof quite amusing. First of all, he calls himself "extra-seanse" not "extra-sense[46]" - he didn't know the exact word for "psychic." He like to boast that he had cured so many famous people. Moreover, as if we had agreed in advance he would often call me to confirm his words in front his patients: "This man saw it with his own eyes, you can ask him yourself." Or: "This man knows that my previous patient recovered quickly, am I right?"

In short, I soon knew our healer's secrets, now all he had to do was stop the bird flying from that troubled heart.

One day he invited me to his grandchild's birthday party. We agreed that he would pick me up in his car from the Palace of Arts on Sunday. I did not mind since I owed him.

By the way, why do you think these details relating to that ignominious healer are so unforgettable? It is because there was a curious story I could not forget. I have never seen such a beautiful lady. Actually, I felt I had seen her somewhere before, she seemed so familiar to me, and to my heart. But no, this was in fact the first time I had seen her. But she really was so charming, so beautiful, and if a bird (this one is different) didn't sing in your heart when you saw her for the first time, then only you are to blame!

It was this very lady in her bright atlas dress who met us at the door of a flat on the ninth floor of a multi-storey block of flats situated in the Yunusabad District.

---

46 Russian for 'psychic.'

Brother Abusharof greeted her with a kiss, then introduced her to me as "our bride."

I was a little taken aback; does a father-in-law kiss his daughter-in-law like that? Where is the son who should present his wife to his father to kiss? There was no sign of him.

Well, that's tolerable. But the bride spoke to me so sweetly, right in front of her father-in-law, that I was really rather alarmed.

Three older women and two simple-looking men wearing new skullcaps were sitting talking among themselves at one corner of the banquet table. One of the women was dandling a toddler on her lap.

They welcomed us warmly as friends of the father-in-law and invited us to take a seat in the place of honour. Naturally, more attention and respect were shown to brother Abusharof than to me. He played with the little boy for a while, put some U.S. dollars into his pocket and returned him to his grandmother.

The usual food, the usual first and second courses, accompanied by the usual modest topics of conversation ruled the banquet. For some reason, no introductions were made. It turned out that everyone except me knew each other very well. But it was clear that there were some secrets, too. The exchanges struck me as stiff and rather brief. The strange spirit of this birthday party was palpable. Nevertheless, the young mother was serving everyone. Everyone paid attention to brother Abusharof who was sitting there like a king. Everybody waited for him to speak.

"Excuse me, dear healer," one of the old men with a skullcap said. "What happened to your finger, can you tell us, please?"

Abusharof was missing the little finger on his left hand. Actually, I had noticed this earlier but it never occurred to me to ask him about it: what if there is no finger?

"It was during the war," the healer replied casually.

"War? Did you go to war?" the man asked in surprise. "You look too young."

"The war in America," the healer said, closing the conversation.

Had there been any war in America over the past few years? If so, how could this man go there? No one asked him any details. Perhaps he himself did not know the details, either. But by now I was already accustomed to hearing such outlandish statements.

Those present thought that brother Abusharof was not only a healer but also a scholar, an educated person who knew everything about everything. So when the name Navoi was heard coming from the TV-set in the corner, the curious old man piped up again:

"Sir, why do we call him Navoi, what does that mean?"

"His father was a "novvoy" – a baker, that's why his name was Navvoi."

I did not want to show off and meddle in the conversation. At any other place or time I would have raised an objection, but something was holding back both my hands and my tongue that day.

After a while I whispered into my companion's ear that I had some other work to do and needed to go. He did not mind. Actually, I seemed quite superfluous.

What surprised me more was what happened in the hallway. It's still a mystery to me! Who and what actually was that 'bride' and why did she tell me what she did?

When the healer came to see me off, the young wife was waiting for us in the hallway:

"Now you know where I live, so you can come here alone some time," she said to me.

"Our young wife is a great fan of the arts," her father-in-law said, somewhat embarrassed.

"Oh, yes, films, you mean?" I mumbled, unable to think of anything else to say.

Even though her father-in-law was present, the young wife said enthusiastically:

"Yeah, films, and the rest!"

Well, how is one to reply?

That really was a very strange family!

I did not meet with the healer again after that. I don't even know what happened to the woman with the flying bird in her heart, since, luckily, the Studio Director was removed from his post a week later. We don't need that film now. I once reminded Botirbek about it, but he didn't want to think about it, either.

Two or three years later I saw the healer at Alay bazaar, but we both pretended not to know each other. I heard from someone that he was actually sick and was being treated at a hospital for the mentally ill. Who knows, maybe it's true, maybe it's not.

And what about that beautiful, strange young wife, where is she now? Who was she really?

* *

Suddenly the lock rattled and the door opened. That creep was back at last! Shame on you, Plato, son of Socrates!

"Where are you, young man?" came a woman's voice from the hallway.

Who could she be? Farhod opened his door a crack and saw the maid. May Allah be merciful to her, she immediately understood the situation, locked those bloody dogs in their special room and came back.

"Oh, poor man, were you sitting all locked up?" she tutted. "You could have tried knocking on the wall but I suppose it's too thick. Zinaida Gavrilovna called to say that she would not be able to come to see you."

"Thanks, thank you!" said Farhod and quickly hurried out, startling the maid.

As he rushed down the stairs he noticed several brawny, bearded Caucasians carrying large boxes packed in bright papers. Were they meant for Zuzi? A present, perhaps, sent from "On High" or from senior officials?

... Some time later he heard from Sur'at that Plato Sokratovich had been detained after the democrat victory. Strangely enough, Farhod's first thought was for his "four-legged friends." What happened to them? Perhaps his good neighbour is taking care of them. Even though he had been imprisoned with those dogs, he always respected democrats.

* *

10. "The princess of Buryot." "You are free, go, go..."

When a person is very much involved in something, even though he knows that nothing will come of it, he never loses hope. Isn't it true that your temples will definitely grow warm if someone keeps pinching your ears and head? And once they've warmed up, half-dead cells will revive. Life means action. You imagine that the cursed noise in your ear and mind has stopped or lessened, that if you try just a little more you'll be rid of the disease completely. Victory!

Farhod travelled into the city every morning, his multi-pocketed leather bag hanging by his side. First he walked across some scrubland until he reached a railway station, and from there he took a suburban electrical train to the Yaroslav station. After that he took a bus or trolleybus and finally arrived at the Qi Gong Medical Centre.

He never felt bored during those journeys. He used to enjoy listening to his small radio as he watched the scenery from the train window. No one was surprised by his behaviour in the train – many people do the same. Everyone was eager to listen to "Echo Moskvi[47]" (Echo of Moscow) news; it was the time of various political intrigues.

Every time he went to the medical centre, that famous Ms. "Karasho" jabbered away in her own language, pinched his ears for about fifteen minutes and heated them up. Finally, she would pummel his shoulders a bit, and say her usual "Karasho!" giving the thumbs up. "The doctor says you are recovering gradually," the old interpreter explained, as delighted as if he himself were experiencing the improvement in Farhod's ear. "There is a positive change!"

Then Farhod rushed to a clinic. A compassionate female doctor asked him to lie down on the bed covered with a white sheet and injected the rear of his ear, asking him questions about some long-forgotten places in Tashkent. The doctor winced in sympathy because of the pain, which was enough to make even a brave man cry. But Farhod had to bear it.

Sometimes he visited the Union twice a day. He was given the same explanation, the same reasons: "You have to wait. Your scenario has to be considered by the secretariat."

Next time he went there he decided to let bygones be bygones and called in to see Sur'at, who was slouching around as usual. He told Farhod he had been to Tallinn on a business trip and bragged all about it. When Farhod started talking about

---

47 One of Russia's more independent radio stations, even in the Soviet era.

the scenario he had sent to "Cinema almanac," Sur'at openly admitted he had given it a critical write-up. Leaning down, he rummaged in his drawer asking: "Do you want to read it?"

"Don't worry," Farhod replied getting a bit angry. "I can guess what you might write about my work." Sur'at did not pay any attention to his sarcasm, just looked at him as if to say: "Yes, it's me and you can do whatever you want." Ah, why were they friends? Even if you held your tongue, this miserable bastard was ready to kill you with a blunt knife.

Farhod was going to have a rest in his room, but heard something rustling outside his door. Then came a knock, and then Valya's cheeky face appeared.

"Farid, I've brought two guests for you, wouldn't you like to let them in?"

Gulya Lagutina entered the room, a large bag over her shoulder. Her hair was untidy and a little grey. She was that black-haired woman whom Farhod had often seen before with the statesman and lover from Leninabad.

"Please call me if you need anything, Farid," Valya said and left the room.

Irritated by her words, Gulya shrugged and, turning to Farhod so he could kiss her, said: "Hi there, escapee!" and quickly approached him with her bag in her hand and put her face to Farhod to kiss. After that she began complaining about Farhod to her friend:

"When he comes to visit he always makes a quick escape, and it's the same whenever he goes to see a doctor. Look how he's hiding himself away here even though he's famous now, thanks to my newspaper!" And she pulled several copies of Sovetskaya Kultura and a bottle of Armenian cognac out of her bulging bag: "Here is your interview, and here is your fee!"

"Thank you, thank you so much," Farhod said, hurriedly taking the newspapers, even forgetting to invite his guests to sit down.

"Now I'm going to interview Bolat. I hope you know Bolat Esdauletov from Kazakhstan. By the way, he graduated from the advanced classes several years earlier than you. A very talented person! He has written six or seven films!

"Yes, yes, I've heard of him," Farhod said, leafing through the paper. He was jealous of another person's fame then. Now she would take this Bolat back to her flat, too. Why does she need to create a genius out of everyone she meets?

Gulya gently took the papers out of his hand:

"You can read it later, they are all for you," she said. "By the way, do you know Diana, Farhod?" she pointed to her friend. "Diana Ochirova, young film critic, also my student and friend. She is the princess of Buryot. She works for Film Art magazine and is a contributor to Literature Russia."

"Very nice to meet you. I've seen you a few times, I believe," said Farhod turning to "the princess of Buryot" and slightly bowing his head. "Please, take a seat, and let's celebrate our meeting and the interview!"

"Sorry, my dear Farhod, I can't. I came here with a driver who's waiting downstairs so I need to get back to the city right away. We have a section meeting this evening and I have to be there on time. I popped into Elmira's room but she wasn't there, there was just her son asleep there. She must have gone out. I just wanted to see you both. If I don't manage to catch her, please give her my regards. Do come and visit me soon – you, Elmira, and Diana, OK? We'll make a good party together!" Gulya gently kissed Farhod's cheek and quickly left them, saying "Diana-khon, have a good time with Farhod!"

Farhod remembered that he had wanted to ask Gulya something, but it slipped his mind. Well, they would meet again.

When he went out to the hallway to see them off, Diana gave him a flirty glance, as if to say she was always ready to fulfill Gulya's request.

Having seen them off, Farhod went back to his room, and leafed through the pages of the Sovetskaya Kultura again, but his mind was full of "the princess of Buryot's" playful smile.

This young woman, who had a clear, rosy complexion and arched eyebrows, stood out from other women in the resort with her long black hair, beautiful figure, her dignity and pride. Every time the statesman from Leninabad saw her he used to say "I wish I could spend a night with this black-haired beauty! Unfortunately, my own heart is sick."

It was true that in the mornings and evenings this man would stroll through the grove of trees alone. He said he had come here to recuperate after a serious heart attack. But it was not for him to talk about women admiringly. Whenever he saw "the princess of Buryot" he could barely control himself, always pointing her out lustfully: "Look, look at her, Farhod-jon!" Although Farhod did not know this lady at all, the man's attitude towards her irritated him.

This former film boss's favourite pastime was making pilaf. Whenever he saw a black-eyed person he insisted: "Let's make pilaf. I'll get ill if I keep eating the food they give me here, so let's cook pilaf and have a real meal. OK? I'll buy the ingredients."

He held Mr. Akobirov in high esteem. Whenever he saw him he fussed around: "Ravshan-jon, Ravshan-jon!" Mr. Akobirov, however, did not respect this feeble-minded old man and openly made fun of him. "Our teacher is so good. He worked at the Central Committee," he would start by praising him. "Tell us, please, how you measured a film, teacher." And the dim-wit old man, swelled by the cheap praise, would begin telling the same story again: "Well, I used to work for the Central Committee then, Shavkat-jon. You know it, I believe. One day I was called and they told me they were going to send me to be the director of a studio. "I'm no film specialist, I'm just a history teacher," I told them, but they insisted. "You are a Party member, so you should know everything, and this is on the orders of our Party!" So I agreed and went there. There was a mess everywhere! They stole money claiming they'd shot one episode several times. "Why?" I asked. "Just shoot it once. Why do you need to shoot one episode three or four times?" So I went into the store room, asked them to show me the films and started to measure them, arm-span at a time! Yes, that was a funny story, really! Later I became a professional. If they shoot three or five times, we learnt to shoot ten times. I worked there for eleven years, just imagine! Ravshan-jon also came there to do film. Am I right, Ravshan-jon? Do you remember, Ravshan-jon?"

"Yes, that was great," Mr. Akobirov approved his words. "Now, teacher, please tell us about how you were the director for the bathhouse."

"Ah, enough stories for today," the old man would say seriously. "So, when are we going to make pilaf? I'll find a pot myself, I already have all the ingredients, but the carrots are red..."

* *

When Farhod finished his dinner and was about to leave, "the princess of Buryot," Diana, appeared before him. She seemed even more beautiful and was very well dressed.

"So tell me, how can I relieve your boredom? I was asked to take care of you, remember?"

Farhod could not withstand such an open attack.

"Well, we can drink that cognac together," he said cheerfully. "Do you agree?"

"Alright, I agree, but where?"

"In my room. Let's go and drink."

"No," said Diana. "This place is dangerous, there are too many people here. Let's go to my room. It's over there, house number seven. It's quiet and carefree."

Later, when it was dark outside, he put the bottle of cognac into his bag and went out, but then all of a sudden he was attacked by doubts. "What will Lagutina think about this if she hears? Maybe she was just joking about relieving my boredom? Or did they hatch this plan together? Well, anyway, she invited me herself, not the other way round."

That wooden house nestling in the grove of trees was meant for two occupants; it had two verandas, one on each side. As Diana had mentioned earlier, this was a quiet, peaceful place.

Dressed in red shorts and a thin t-shirt, Diana met him at the door, and sidled up close to him:

"I've been waiting and waiting for you, thanks for coming."

Everything moved quickly after that. Sitting face to face in the moonlight they spoke about general, trivial things for a while.

He found out that Diana was busy with her research paper. She was not married, and her five-year-old son, Deniska, was in the city with her mother.

When the bottle of cognac was half empty, she moved to the sofa next to him and put her hand on his shoulders

"My only request is that Gulya should not know about this."

The night was well on when Farhod returned to his own room, but he did not feel pleased with his deeds of that night.

In his dreams, he was riding a horse through the Buryatian steppe. He was a Buryat, with slanted eyes and prominent cheek bones. He was wearing a special hat, a heavy coat, and high crooked boots. He was riding a horse, flying along.

The next day he tried to avoid Diana. But she sauntered past after lunch while he and the old man were speaking about cooking pilaf. She looked in their direction then went into the building.

"The man who could 'entertain' this lady would be the happiest man alive, wouldn't you say, Farhod-jon?" the old man said. "Unfortunately my own heart is sick," he went on, caressing the left side of his chest.

"Far from it," Farhod blurted out. "He'd be disgusted by her blowing into his face."

"Will she blow in your face? Why? Hey, hey, Farhod-jon, hold on a minute, have you already spent a night with her?"

"No, no, I'm joking, teacher. How do I know if she blows or spits?"

"You are not a simple person, Farhod-jon, you know how to act," the old man said, looking at him with a mix of doubt and jealousy.

Two days later, another concierge, a fat old woman, Antonina Mikhailovna entered his room breathing heavily.

"A woman is asking for you on the phone."

Farhod nipped down quickly before the old woman could get there and took the receiver. It was Diana.

"Hi, what's the matter?" asked Farhod, surprised.

"Why aren't you coming round?"

"What shall we do?"

"We have a half bottle of cognac left."

"I have a headache and I don't want to drink cognac now. Finish it yourself."

"We could talk about films?"

"What kind of films?"

"I'm bored, why don't you understand?"

"Sorry, Diana, I told you, I've got a headache now."

"Well, I'll cure your headache, please come."

Farhod did not know what to say and stood there hesitating. But he regretted what he had done that night.

"No, Diana-khon, please don't be upset with me, I can't come."

"What if I tell you, you are my first real man!"

O Merciful One, does she mean I was the first man she's slept with? Where did her five-year-old Deniska appear from, then?

"You seem a bit drunk. Who are you drinking with?"

"If I were drunk I would go to your room myself. I'm leaving tomorrow, Farhod. My time here is over, so I have to go. I just wanted to say farewell to you."

"Good bye, good luck, Diana. Please don't' be upset with me."

Silence reigned for a moment. Farhod held the receiver close to his ear, heard nothing, and hung up.

Then, for some reason he gazed at the old concierge and strode angrily to the stairs.

"If you want to go,

Go, my sweetheart, in despair,

I don't care, I don't care..."

As he was reading the latest issue of Ogonyok on his bed the next day, not intending to go to the city, Antonina Mikhailovna brought a piece of paper to him and said timidly:

"You were asked to ring this number. It's urgent. Someone in the new building said it was urgent."

"Who is it?" asked Farhod getting up heavily.

"No, no, Fidel Mirzaevich, don't worry, please! It's a man, it's a man!"

11. "Don't worry, it's a man."
Raw materials for an unwritten scenario

Although this was not the first time Mr. Akobirov had invited him to his room, Farhod still had not see it, as he had never been in the new building.

Farhod took a key from the duty officer, went to the third floor and opened the door at the end of the corridor. The whole building, with its comfortable corridors and neat rooms, was totally different from the building where he himself was staying. Here, everything was perfect, the furniture gleamed, everything was fresh and bright.

Mr. Akobirov had a large room which was divided into two sections. In the first part he could watch TV or sit with a guest and chat. The second part was a bedroom with a nice, comfortable bed set against the wall.

Farhod went straight into the bedroom and opened a drawer in the desk by the window. There were so many bits and bobs: a plane ticket, trip related papers, coins, a watch on a chain, etc. He rummaged right at the back of the drawer, found a passport and, turning the pages just in case, was struck dumb. Nevertheless, he brought it down and, before handing it to the driver of the black Volga, he again looked at the passport in disbelief: yes, it really was like that!

The man who had rung earlier asking Farhod to call him back was Mr. Akobirov.

"How are you, Farhod-jon?" he asked as if his friend had not seen anything. "It's good you were in. I was wondering who to turn to. I'm in the city now, at the Union. A driver will come soon. Please go up to my room, fetch my passport and give it to the driver for me. I've already asked the concierge, you can take the key for my room. My passport is in the bedroom, in the top left drawer of the desk. Please send it as soon as possible. I have an issue to resolve here, I'll explain later, OK?"

Having sent the passport to him, Farhod installed himself on the bench at the edge of the square, mulling over the name in the passport: "Akobirov Ravshanbek Usmonovich, born 1950 in the village of Beshchorbogh in the Zarang District of Kushdaryo region."

How odd that he hadn't known earlier! And Mr. Akobirov himself had never said a word about it. Beshchorbogh, Usmon Akobirov, the kolkhoz director whose house burnt down…

And for a while Farhod forgot about the noise in his ear, for other noises, from years long gone, surfaced in his mind.

* *

My father's attitude changed after that event. He stopped questioning me regularly and whenever he ordered me to do something, he asked politely, even sometimes addressing me with great respect. I became anxious about him being so reserved, as he was a rather rude, strict person, who held quite an influential position in the district.

I also tried to not meet my father face to face after that: I sensed it would lead to some unchangeable calamity or unhappiness if I saw him, and I felt to blame for that.

You see, the door was open and unlocked. My mother and sisters had gone to my aunt's to attend a women's get-together. I was tired of playing football on the street and hurried home to do my lessons. But when I went inside, I just froze!

I have replayed that scene over and over again in my mind, trying to find an explanation. Maybe I had somehow misunderstood, maybe nothing had actually happened back then, I would say to myself, but I still could not find a satisfactory explanation. How had that woman, who rarely came to our place, appeared there? And how about my father, who used to come home from the fields late in the evening every day?

There was an ample supa[48] set in the shade of the vines in our garden. The lady was well dressed, as always, and there she was sitting on the supa hugging her knees. My father was standing behind it, one arm round the lady's neck. When he saw me coming, he turned pale: "Hey, what are you doing here?!"

I turned around and ran away. I headed straight to the back of the graveyard. There was a single tree there which I would sit under for hours when my father insulted me or when I was upset about something.

So I sat there for some time and cried, and in the evening I went back home. The door was still open, but no one was there.

That incident, that secret, remained in my mind and in my heart. I did not tell anyone about it, not even my mother, who was always busy with her children and the housework and who deeply respected my father. What should I say? I liked my father; for me, he was the best, the most honest person in the world.

Even after so many years my father would still sometimes look at me thoughtfully and, as if asking my pardon, he would smile awkwardly.

That lady – sister Parizod –was in fact a member of our family who used to come to our house from time to time. My mother

---

48 A raised platform or cot where people could recline, take tea or simply rest.

said that sister Parizod helped bring me up when I was little. My father worked at an orphanage then, and sister Parizod was there, too. When my mother was carrying my younger sister, she came and helped round the house. Perhaps because of my mother's stories about her or maybe because I was old enough by then, but I sometimes vaguely remember a girl playing with me in the scrubland.

My mother also said that I was fond sister Parizod and used to play up when my mother wanted to take me from her. Perhaps as a small child I sensed some possible future event...

Parizod was like a sister to my mother, who always felt so sorry she was an orphan and used to tell us stories about the poor girl's past: "She was the only daughter of kolkhoz director Akobirov. Who knows who would do such a thing, but one night someone burnt down their house. Parizod and her younger brother were staying at their grandmother's but the rest of the family all died in the fire. After that she grew up in the orphanage with your father. But it wasn't a happy life. They had an aunt whose name was Barfina. She was well-educated and became a party member. I heard that she married a Russian man called Khudoyakov. She doesn't care about her niece and nephew."

Sister Parizod left Zarang for several years. She studied somewhere, and got married, but she didn't give birth. After that she divorced, came back to Zarang and now she works as the director of the district library. She lives alone in one of the white buildings called "newcomers' house" on the central street. Not having any other relatives to visit, she used to come to visit us and called my father "brother" and my mother "sister". My mother forced us to call her "Mummy," maybe because she helped raise us. "Call her 'Mummy,' will you? Oh, if only she would be happy with that," my mother said to us.

In fact, my mother was right, she was more than simply "sister Parizod;" she was like a mother, a real mother! She used to bring delicious sweets for us and sewed beautiful dresses for my younger sisters. When she came to our place, our house was filled with her wonderful fragrance. We loved sitting next to her or listening to her sweet words and stories. Actually, she was born in this mountainous area, but her name was taken from an epic poem. Her face and eyes, as well as her words, were all different. She dressed so nicely that every woman and girl in Zarang couldn't help but envy her, in the nicest possible way.

But she was never as happy as others. I sensed she harboured some constant suffering. As my simple-hearted mother put it: she was a poor woman with a broken heart.

Sometimes when she and my mother shared their sorrows, sister Parizod wept, remembering her only brother who had left Zarang a long time ago to study in the big cities.

After that time I saw her with my father, I did not see her in our house again, except once, for a funeral. If we crossed paths on the street she looked at me as if I were a stranger.

Soon afterwards, my simple-minded mother, who knew nothing but her own family, went out somewhere one night. When she came back, she was very angry, and, gathering up all of us children, she took us to her parents' house. My grandpa had a lot of land with many houses on the edge of the mountains, my uncles and their children lived there, too. It was a wonderful place for children, we used to play with our cousins all day long.

But that was not a quiet place, either. One day, our stylish uncle with unkempt dark black hair who taught at the local school brought home a Russian girl called Anya. She was a teacher, too. She had been sent from some remote place to teach Russian at this school in the mountains. She had nowhere to stay as yet, so she had to live at my uncles' house until the department of education gave her a place of her own.

My uncle came home with Anya every day and they would both go straight to the guestroom to get ready for the next day's lesson, saying something to each other in Russian. We youngsters used to wait for her to come out, then run after her, shouting: "Aniya, Aniya!"

"What? What?" she would ask, turning to us, but we did not know what to say. My drowsy grandpa who used to nap all day long under in the shade of the grape arbor would sometimes raise his head and ask: "So how are you?"

"Not bad," Anya would reply, surprised.

One day my grandpa saw her going into the outside toilet barefoot. "O Merciful One!" he cried, horrified. The next day he went to the village and bought a pair of rubber shoes. When he gave them to Anya that evening, she was so happy she kissed my grandpa's head, saying: "Thank you, babay!"

"O Merciful One!" said my grandpa again. "Now I have to shave."

That night we all heard a row coming from the house of my stylish uncle.

"Hey, you stupid woman, I'm teaching her Uzbek! That is a task put before me by the Party!" he shouted at his wife.

"And she's been teaching you Russian! I saw you both with my own eyes!" our sister-in-law Nazokat was crying.

The next day she took her two children and went to her parents.

When I came home after playing nuts[49] with my friends, my father was sitting with my grandpa on his veranda. I really missed him, and felt sorry for him, too. But when he saw me

---

49 A game similar to bowls but using nuts.

he turned away angrily. So, unable to run up to him, I just stood stock-still.

"Adol!" my grandpa called. "Adolat!" And my mother appeared on the veranda. "I gave you to this person completely. I will not take you back! Take your children and march to your own house!"

So we went back to the District Centre in the car my father had brought.

We cooked pilaf at home that day. I thought it was a pilaf of reconciliation.

I don't know when pilaf was cooked in my stylish uncle's house. I don't know what happened to Anya, either.

As I said before, I didn't see sister Parizod at our house often after that, but I did see her once at her own house. Even though her house was just off the central street, I hadn't been there before. "The newcomers' block" always seemed a magical place. So one day I went to see it with my own eyes. All the flats there were very much alike, fitted with almost the same furniture. The ceilings were high, but because the front was covered in bindweed and long dark curtains hung at the windows facing the street, the rooms in those buildings were always gloomy, so a dim ceiling light was always switched on, even during the day-time. Instead of carpets on the walls, there was a huge cheap poster all the rage at the time: two lovebirds paddling a boat on a crystalline lake. Also, there were long supa with shiny can-opies, clean pillows neatly arranged, a "Gorizont" TV-set cov-ered with an embroidered fabric, various cabinets, the smell of freshly-washed sheets, and an unfamiliar fragrance...

I think I must have been a third-year student at the time, and I remember I went to Zarang for the summer vacation and met up with my old classmates for Rafik's birthday. That was the first time I saw the "newcomers' block." Perhaps I was a bit drunk or maybe I was just lost in memories of my childhood innocence, but either way, those places seemed so strange, as if I were no longer in Zarang, but in a far-flung corner of some unknown city.

Since the majority of my classmates were elsewhere, there were only a few of us at that party: Rafik, who was celebrating his twentieth birthday, Fotih-Fatik a Tartar, who was a driver at a construction site; light-hearted Svetka, who was working as a nurse at the district hospital after graduating from medical school; Larisa, who married local hooligan Yurka-Pakhan before she even finished school; Yura, who put on a white shirt especially for the party; and Shavkat and me who were on summer vacation.

The only other outsider in that group was Zoya, who had been invited from an orphanage. Everyone kept stealing glances at her. With her black, curly hair, freckles and her thick eyebrows which met in the middle of her forehead she looked like a Gypsy or an Armenian girl. But she struck me as beautiful, plus I was a bit drunk, so I flirted with her a little. But the birthday boy was drunk, too, so he banged on the table and shouted at me: "Hey, student! When are you going to shut up?!" I stood up quickly and left the room. In my dash for the veranda, I somehow collided with Rafik's grandmother who was bringing in some Russian-style salad.

And that was when I saw sister Parizod in the corridor. She had an armful of washing she had just taken off the clothesline outside. Seeing me there with my angry face she was surprised. I greeted her slowly and she nodded her head and let me pass.

The smell of fresh sheets – is that the smell of the city?..

* *

... The beginning of the film.

Behind the subtitle – airport. Domodedovo Airport.

A young man with a rucksack on his shoulder runs along the never-ending corridor weaving in and out of the crowd. The corridor really is endless.

The noise of the airplane dies down and the echo of religious texts rings out: "Bismillahir rohmanir rohim - In the name of Allah the most gracious the most merciful..."

The noise of the plane increases and the sorrowful face of the young man is seen.

Then only his eyes are shown.

The camera will hold still for several seconds, trained on the two eyes full of tears.

Fa-ther!..

There, no matter what happened in Zarang, the mind of the frightened son is busy with that scene, with that dreadful image.

Later when he thought about that affair he understood that it was approximately then that his father was buried. He passed away the night before.

And so Mirzo Ramazon, an energetic man, a tireless worker who loved the times he lived through, died.

A good person, Mirzo Ramazon all of a sudden passed away when he was only fifty-four years old. He was a wonderful person who named his only son Fidel. But that only son was unable to attend his funeral. The son's unusual name was left behind, too: Fidel. Fidel Castro Rus, that beardy and fiery revolutionist!

What kind of revolutions will you be organizing in this noisy world, hey Fidel – Farhod...?

In fact, where were you that night at precisely that time? Were you in the bosom of a woman, O sinful son? Isn't it true that you were clasped in some embrace at that very moment, but for some reason you were thinking of sister Parizod?

Were they similar, or was it some sixth sense connecting you? Otherwise, why would you suddenly remember her when you were in bed with a woman?

Tamara – Salomonova Tarona Samed-qizi. They say her husband was an Uzbek. Her only son, Samar or Samir, was in the war in Afghanistan. She worked at the Union as a secretary. You met her before you went to the Young Film Producers Conference at Lake Balaton in Hungary. Tamara typed up an official paper for you to take and for some reason asked a favour of you as if you were close to her. She needed a packet of Hungarian tea. By the way, it was you who had asked what you could bring her from abroad. She explained in great detail what kind of tea she wanted. Her colleagues joined in, too, but it was difficult for you to understand. Perhaps they all thought you were a miser and would not want to bring them anything at all. When they saw you had in fact brought that same present for each and every one of them, they all formed a queue to kiss you. Later Tamara said she was introducing you to everyone as her brother-in-law, a nephew of her late husband. So you /took the place of "the dead uncle" then.

Tamara was an out and out devotee of the poet Fuzuli.[50] She did not know Uzbek or even her own language yet still she always asked you to read some poems to her. And you recited whatever you knew by heart. It was always the same request, and the same lines:

Such beauty as thine only fair words doth deserve
Thou art my eyes, my heart,
My mistress to preserve...

---

50 A great Azeri poet (1483-1556).

* * * * * * * * * *

Ah, the bitter pain of parting from my sweetheart,

She whose eyes all do start, yet who so deeply wounds my heart...

The day after that night of tender poetry you showed up at the hostel only to discover everyone was looking for you. Sur'at had a telegram from Zarang in his hand.

.... It took me a full two days to reach Zarang, so I arrived on the day of a small remembrance for the deceased. As if I were my father, resurrected and returned to them, everyone rushed towards me wailing loudly. They invited me into the room where my grandmother was sitting with my aunts, relatives and neighbours. They each took their turn at hugging me tightly, crying. I saw sister Parizod was there, too. She also hugged me, putting her head to my chest and smelling me. Then she moved to one side and stood there sorrowfully, in mourning. All of a sudden I realized there was something different about her. She had grown old. What a pity that her life had passed uselessly, in vain, I thought.

* *

As Farhod was absorbed in his thoughts, Antonina Mikhailovna appeared, saying there was another phone call for him.

It was Sur'at.

"Have you heard?" he asked, trying to sound pleased. "Your brother is going to China instead of you! He has just bought an plane ticket. Can you imagine?!"

"Well, that's good," Farhod said, keeping his anger inside. What else could he say? What was he to do?

Then he went out of the building and headed to the grove.

He wandered alone for a long time, "speaking" with the trees.

The trees here are more beautiful than ours. Their bodies are smooth and tall. They can grow and grow and tolerate any kind of weather. They don't choose a particular place to grow. Yet despite all this, you cannot love them with all your heart, since there is something temporary and cold about them.

He felt the din in his ear increasing.

12. Ear-mates from the same village. "I have a cool name..."

Farhod had met this raspy-voiced writer several times in Tashkent, but although he knew of him, he had never read his books. There was something about him, he was either irritable or overly arrogant. Farhod remembered attending the discussion of a film based on his own scenario. During the creative council meeting, the author was busy jotting something down and when asked his opinion at the end of the discussion, he merely passed that paper to the chairman and left the room, nodding his 'thanks' to all those present.

The paper he had passed over was a statement. It contained his objections to the film director and demanded his name be crossed off the title lists. The chairman was dumbstruck. He could not understand why the author would behave like this when he, the director, was finally attracting local authors to the film industry; after all, they had not been allowed anywhere near the film industry before! (In fact, he was appointed the director with this specific task.) Other people sitting in the discussion session came to their senses. One of them threw up his hands in surprise: "What a man!" Another insulted him in Russian. In particular, "old hands" – authors who considered scriptwriting to be their own personal domain – openly unfurled the flag of victory: "Well, just look at this writer's behaviour! We are better than them! We never raise any objections even if the film director turns what we wrote upside down, and we always hold our tongues when our names are changed. Just so long as the director doesn't cut our fees!"

Farhod did not meddle in the discussion, although actually he thought the author's claim was reasonable. He had read the scenario before and expressed his opinion in the first discussion; while it did not fit certain "generally acknowledged" rules of filmmaking, it did include many excellent scenes. Stupid Nodir Jamolov, "a graduate of a university in the capital," reworked the original scenario turning it into nothing but a shallow melodrama. It was clear that while pretending he was off to shoot a film, in fact he was just living it up in the peaceful Oqtosh resorts, revelling with gypsy girls and hanging out in night bars.

But the reason why Farhod kept quiet during the discussion was that he and Nodir had attended the same scriptwriting course and lived together in the same hostel. And, incidentally, he agreed that the author's behaviour was uncouth.

Today, he saw him near the Pekin Hotel. What was he doing here? Look how he has changed his appearance and become like someone born in the capital! A thin but strong man, he had donned a shirt with many buttons and black sunglasses with a stylish bag slung over one shoulder. He was chatting with two ladies. But there was still something about him that gave him away as a villager.

After his visit to the Qi Gong medical centre Farhod didn't feel like going to the recreation centre so he went to see Sur'at as if unaware of any important news. But Sur'at had gone to Yerevan. Oddly enough, even though Sur'at was impolite and envious, Farhod was always happy to see his strange companion.

Every time they talked, Farhod always felt some unpleasant sensation in his heart or a weight on his shoulders, and he vowed never to meet him again. But a few days later, he would want to see him again. Perhaps it was because studying and working together brought them closer. Nothing of their old friendship remained yet they both felt some responsibility or duty towards each other. They both felt it deeply and could not cut their relationship. Sur'at wished Farhod would be unlucky and look like him. But Allah gives each according to his or her character, sometimes withholding something from one and giving it to another. So now it was Sur'at who was travelling to Tallinn and Yerevan; Farhod, feeling the pressure of the last few days, envied him.

As he left the Filmmakers' House and headed to Mayakovski metro station, Farhod caught sight of a familiar writer. The writer was not alone; he had a group of lovely young ladies around him. So he's learnt a trick or two then, has he?

The writer saw Farhod and, quickly recognizing him, gave him a friendly wave. Then he introduced Farhod to his young ladies, kissed their hands tenderly (he did it right, well done!) and bade them farewell.

In Tashkent they were only acquaintances, but here they greeted each other like close friends.

Our writer and editor had come here for a training programme with Yunost magazine, and the young ladies were workers at the department of prose (unbelievable). The writer said they sat together so he had invited them to a restaurant for lunch.

"What have you got there, melons[51]?" Farhod asked him knowingly, pointing to his bulging bag.

---

51 Melons were used as bribes.

"No, no, we don't like those methods any more!" said the writer. "That was the method our teachers used. I don't want to get my own article into Yunost. If I did, I could solve the problem without melons. Actually, something more interesting happened to me recently," he said and launched into his own story, roaring with laughter.

As he was sitting in the restaurant one day with his entourage, one of the young ladies ordered a banana. Now the writer had heard about bananas but had never seen one.[52] "I thought it was something like our cucumbers." In short, when a waitress brought bananas to their table, the young ladies asked him to peel it. So he picked it up but had no idea how to peel it. After turning it around in his hands for several minutes, he finally returned the banana to the ladies, saying: "I am not making friends with this banana." To which the "well educated" ladies replied in surprise: "Don't you know it is produced in your country?"

It soon became apparent that although he was clueless as to how to peel a banana, he was already well-versed in the art of communicating with ladies, since he had come here before to attend a training course.

The two fellow countrymen who met in a foreign land did not want to part, so they walked through Pushkin Square for a long time, talking about this and that. In this foreign land they discovered they had quite a lot in common. In fact, they were surprised they had not got to know each other until now. They also discovered they had similar ear problems, so they were not only from the same village but were "ear-mates" as well!

---

52 Bananas were rare in the Soviet Union, occasionally important from Morocco, just as oranges were occasionally available from Cuba.

Whenever people with hearing issues talk to each other, their conversation will never end.

"Don't worry, my friend, our din is nothing compared with the troubles of this world!" the writer soothed me. "Really nothing at all! Just think of it as Allah's will. I must introduce you to a friend of mine from Denau. He is taking treatment for that incurable illness. Just a treatment, not a cure. Actually, he knows his own condition better than anyone. But you'd be surprised by what he says. "Don't pay any attention to it," he says. "Keep your heart as wide open as a gypsy's knickers, so the wind can blow in and take you where you need to be." It's a simple philosophy, but it is a good comfort if you're down in the dumps, isn't it? In fact, our ears are not only given us so that we might listen to the din of this transient world!"

"Are you working on a book, my friend?" Farhod asked him.

It was an unpleasant, familiar question, but the writer smiled and said:

"A book has been working on me, my dear Farhod-boy, for many years now."

Farhod caught his gist and probed further:

"What's the title? What's it about?"

"For now, it's called "I have a strange horse...""

"Well, that's a strange name. Rather long, isn't it? Is it a novel or a short story?"

"We have a riddle, you know," said the writer without paying attention to the genre of his work. "I have a strange horse..."

"A riddle? Oh, yes, I remember. My aunt used to recite it. Didn't it go something like: its braids are curly?"

"Exactly! So you know it. You'll see it when it comes here soon..."

"You'll see it when it comes here soon and you will die from laughing. That's right, isn't it?"

"Well, what is it then, can you guess? Remember The scorpion from the altar."

Passersby looked at these two "black" people talking to each other in their own language right there on the street, oblivious to the fact that they were in the big capital of the "great country."

"Brother, ours is a wonderful nation, isn't it? Our language is perfect, too! Unfortunately, I didn't study in Uzbek."

"Yes, it's wonderful, but usually we only remember that when we come here."

"Why do you think that is?"

"We are outnumbered here. When you cut a small piece from something large no one will notice, since it is so large. But a small piece is obvious because it is tiny."

"Why?" asked Farhod, but he didn't really understand why he was asking. Perhaps he thought every question should have an answer.

Then they struck up the usual banter: "Let's go to my place." "No, let's go to mine, we can cook pilaf." "Next time. Come with me, please. Look, there's the Central House of Literature, it's just around the corner." "No, look The Filmmakers' House is closer."

The Filmmakers' House was indeed just a stone's throw away so they decided to go there. But as it happened, a big party was planned at the restaurant that evening, and the entrance was blocked with two chairs, so Farhod led his writer-brother to the bar opposite.

As their eyes were adjusting to the darkness in the bar and while they were looking for an empty table, they heard someone calling, "Hey Farhod, come on over!"

Farhod looked around and tried to spot who had hailed him. Someone was calling them from the table in the end of the bar, waving. So they made their way over.

It was Gulya Lagutina, that woman who was always so compassionate!

She was in a group of bearded, good-looking companions and seemed to be the leader of the company. She approached Farhod, her rings and bangles jingling, hugged him, kissed him, and let him kiss her. Then she turned to the writer, glanced at him for a second and hugged him too, meaning that "he was her own, too.[53]" But she did not kiss him nor did she let him kiss her; his aloof, distant manner rather put her off.

Gulya quickly pulled up a couple of chairs for them and let them sit next to her. She started to introduce them to those sitting at the table. "My Uzbeks!" she said proudly.

As they chatted, Farhod told Gulya the "heroism" of his writer-brother. She immediately retold the story to the circle, and soon all the people sitting there were staring at the writer with astonishment as if they really were looking at a hero. Gulya later asked if there was a translation of that scenario because if so, she would take it upon herself to publish it in the Cinema Almanac and interview him for Sovetskiy Ekran (Soviet Screen). "We'll see, we'll see," said the writer modestly. He was feeling rather uncomfortable and alien in that circle. He caught Farhod's eye, tapped his ear and smiled: "I can't hear anything in this noisy place, what about you?" Although Farhod was in the same predicament, it was nevertheless a great pleasure for him to sit at that table, especially under the good care and attention of passionate Gulya.

---

53 I.e. from the same nation.

Pretending to go for a breath of fresh air, the writer nipped out somewhere, came back and explained to Farhod that he needed to go to see his younger brother, who, incidentally, was also called Farhod, and who was studying and working in the city.

Farhod saw him off. The writer was staying at the guesthouse of the Representative Office of Uzbekistan in Polyanka. As they said their goodbyes, they fixed a possible time to see each other again.

Well, it was clear that the writer had shown "heroism" before, but he really was very generous; it turned out that before he left he had footed the bill for all of us that evening.

Actually, everything about him was without artifice – his hot temper, his frowns, his rudeness.

But one thing in particular struck Farhod: whoever he runs into is either from his own village or has the same hearing problem. Did he have to come to this foreign place to learn about that?

What a small world this is! And so full of coincidences! Why, don't be surprised even if a mountain meets another mountain!

13. A short commentary by the "ear-mate" author

It was then that I met Farhod Ramazon. Actually, I knew this man's reputation as a good person and was eager to get to know him better. The first time I saw him was at a seminar for creative young people in Khumson. He had just graduated from an institute in the capital of the "endless country." He wore his hair long in those days, and when I spotted him, he was speaking to two or three film ladies, in Russian. When a scenario he wrote based on Abdulla Qahhor's story "Thief" was made into a short film, many people began to notice his work.

I had previously thought he was a spoiled young man and that his film's success was only thanks to the powerful people he had around him, plus he was lucky enough to have the help of a skillful director. But I was wrong. First of all, like myself, he was a man born in a remote mountainous area (actually we are from opposite sides of the same mountain). His initial success in the film industry was not just a stroke of luck. In three or four years, he had become one of the best scriptwriters in Uzbekistan; the scenario of the first film in the Uzbek language, "Swallows," was written by this young man.

That day, when I left the "Pekin" restaurant, I said good bye to the "young ladies" as Farhod jokingly described them, and we both strolled through Pushkin Square for a long time. Then he insisted we go to the bar in the basement of the Filmmakers' House, and we had a good conversation there, too. In just one day, I became as fond of him as if he were my younger brother. He was a brilliant person, and he was very kind and helpful to me.

As it turned out, we had much in common. He, too, had hearing problems; in fact, he had come to the capital for treatment. Actually, it was here in this city that the trouble started, when he took up diving. We spoke about our own problems one after the other. I started from my own "rich" experience of treatment. First of all, I told him he should use Avicenna's method whereby one drips bitter almond oil into the ear. I myself had already tried this to no avail, so I had simply yielded to fate, but since I wanted to help this younger brother of mine, I told him, hoping it might help him.

Farhod told me he had visited a healer in Tashkent, a rather cross-eyed man who tried to even out the shape of his patient's head, putting it in a wooden mould and turning it this way and that. Farhod made fun of the healer, saying: "He was cross-eyed, he should have healed himself first!" Now I listened to him. What else could I say? This is my old problem. It cannot be cured. I 've been everywhere and done everything, but I could not be treated. I think I also wrote something about it in one of my stories. Everything was useless. But I didn't want to dash the young man's hopes. Now he's seeing a Chinese doctor and is feeling a little bit better. Let him do so, maybe he will find a cure for his illness. And maybe I will go to his doctor, too.

As I have already said, we suffer from the same hearing problems. But like me, Farhod is half blind, too. To hide it, he also wears dark sunglasses. What's more, my own brother, who is on his internship in a clinic in this city, is also called Farhod! (Later when I introduced them to each other, these two young men with the same name and of the same age forgot all about me!)

In short, Farhod and I became very close friends in just one day. Let me tell you what happened the evening we met. Many people knew him in the bar we went to, so they came up and started to kiss him. I was astonished by the leader of the circle, Gulya Lagutina. She was originally from Tashkent. She was an Uzbek woman. It's true she did look like an Uzbek woman thanks to her dark complexion, and her slightly slanted eyes, but there was something different and alien in those eyes of hers. Nevertheless, she was a very communicative and honest woman. She beautifully retold the story she had just heard from Farhod. But in fact, there was no need to tell the story for that audience, since similar stories might happen in "MosFilm[54]" every month, if not every day. But in Uzbekistan it really was heroism! Very impressive!

---

54 Moscow Film Studios.

Though I did not like to leave Farhod, I had to go, even though I was very much enjoying the group's company. I understood that Farhod wanted to stay there with his colleagues, but I had promised to meet my other Farhod. Today, our brother from Denov was due visit us and I had to be there on time so as not offend him. Besides, the noise in the bar was annoying. So I apologized and left.

As agreed, Farhod came to the hotel in Polyanka on Sunday, laden with food and drink. I had stocked up on some provisions, too, so we sat, ate and chatted.

We talked about everything and decided to write a joint scenario. As they say that there is illness but there is no cure for it, we discussed this topic and the name of the work for a good hour or so. "The Din Within and Without" is a great title," said Farhod. But I disagreed, pointing out that William Faulkner had written a novel called "The Sound and the Fury." "What if he did?" said Farhod. "Let it be so!"

Finally we agreed that the Russian title would as Farhod suggested, and the Uzbek version would be called simply: "The Din".

Although we both made a lot of noise at first, we were unable to see our mutual cooperation through. Perhaps because of the increasing din within and without. (Now, have you understood how "The Din" appeared as a book, my dear readers?)

Several years later, I heard the meaning and crux of the real din which pestered us two friends, Farhod and me, but I didn't hear it from healers or doctors; no, I heard it from an ordinary person who had himself lived through many difficulties. A travelling companion on a train heading to a remote country, tired of explaining things to me again and again, told me the following comforting words: "Don't worry, my brother. Every human being needs an illness to make him or her remember the temporary nature of this transient world!! Look, our life is full of racket and din, right? The trick is not to let yourself be swallowed up by it but to remain clean, pure. If you are able to find a melody amid the world's din, a melody to suit your soul, then you will be victorious and suffer less. So you should take care of your heart, my brother. Your heart belongs to you, the rest belongs to the world. Do you think Allah gives us ears to listen to nothing but useless noises? It does not matter if you are Muslim, Christian or Jewish. A person may have countless children, relatives, clansmen, and fellow nationals, but he or she is alone, there is but one copy of each person! Your heart is also like that, it's the only one and it's unique! The rest is just a temporary racket."

Our Farhod was also tired of going to doctors. Finally, he yielded to fate. I saw him recently with a special hearing device attached to his spectacles. By the way, he had no other choice; he's an official now and must listen to all manner of rumours and whispers. But as for me, well, despite the ear doctors' insistence, I am still stubborn: it's enough for me to listen to the din of this world. I am old enough now not to listen to the rest. I hope Allah will present me with a healthy ear in the next world since I keep away from sinful talk.

As I mentioned earlier, Farhod Ramazon now holds a higher position. I don't think he either expected or hankered after it, but slowly, slowly he was seen sitting magnificently at this or that meeting and delivering key note speeches. I try to raise this whenever I meet him, but he always shrugs it off, saying: "Don't mention it, please." I don't see any hypocrisy in his action. I only feel that he has a different suffering in his heart. Yes, it is different, but he cannot leave his current position, since he has already grown accustomed to its taste. In any case, now Farhod

Ramazon is stuck in the middle. I hope this purgatory will not last long, but its aftereffects are not good.

"What about you? What have you been doing?" he asks me, trying to change the subject. "Is "The Din" ready yet? When will you bring it?"

I know he has an excuse, but what should I say to him? Should I tell him how I could not follow the instructions of my wise travelling companion on the train, how I got sidetracked once again and could not keep my heart free and pure? No, he's checking his watch: he has to start the meeting in about 15 minutes!

14. A macho promenade from the bar. Poor, unfortunate Gulya

Having seen the writer off, Farhod retraced his steps down the darkened stairs to the bar. He caught sight of Gulya hanging on the shoulder of a tall blond girl. When she saw Farhod, she led the girl forward.

"Let me introduce my daughter, Vika," said she with delight. "Victoria Andreevna Lagutina. A future actress. So far she has only played in one film, but she will have a bright future, I hope. She's beautiful, isn't she?"

Farhod gently touched the girl's long fingers. He was surprised. Vika didn't look like her mother at all, almost as if Gulya was pretending to be her mother. When Vika smiled, a dimple appeared on one of her olive cheeks and her amazing eyes shone dark green.

If you say this girl is Uzbek, something in her deep eyes will deny it, but if you say she is not an Uzbek, you will find something about her which is very much related to Uzbeks. Actually, beautiful people have a nationality of their own, though you may wish they all were Uzbeks.

"No," said Farhod unexpectedly. "She is different!"

"Yes, you are absolutely right. She is different. She is Sophie Loren! Sophie Loren!" said Gulya, and kissed her daughter. "This is Mr. Farhod Ramazonov. That film playwright I told you about. My dear fellow countryman!

"I know him," said the girl without feeling shy. "We are familiar with each other, externally. I remember he spent a night in my room and forgot his handkerchief.

Inspired by such free behaviour, Farhod started to play the role of Othello:

"Handkerchief! Where is my handkerchief?! Bring me my handkerchief, Desdemona!"

"Calm down, Othello! I have washed your handkerchief and ironed it. Next time you don't find a place to stay and come to my bedroom, I will give it to you, my honey!" said Vika, taking on a rather surprising role.

Gulya applauded, looking from one to the other in admiration.

"Bravo, bravo!" Then she confided in Farhod: "But this girl is going to forsake us for her friends over there (she pointed two girls and a boy) and go off to some summer house. They're planning to spend the weekend there. Do you think we should let them go, Farhod Mirzevich?"

Farhod did not want to let this girl go anywhere; he had only just met her! But the girl looked at them with pleading eyes and Farhod found himself saying unexpectedly:

"Youth wins over hearts! Gulya, you and I cannot become an obstacle in their path."

"OK, you can go if you want," said Gulya rather sadly, silently giving her daughter a slight push. Then she drew closer to Farhod, took him by his arm and said: "Let's go."

Their group was still abuzz with happy, inoffensive gossip, light-hearted banter, merriment and new meetings; in short, the spirit of uselessness reigned at the table.

There were seven people, including Farhod. Two very similar looking women were sitting on Gulya's left. One of them was Lyuba, a film critic, and her friend was Natasha. They both whispered incessantly to each other. Next to them was Gugushidze with his thick moustache and rather arrogant manner. From time to time he smoked a fragrant cigarette. Clumsy Anatoliy, sitting to the right of Farhod, was knocking back the wine. No one heard him speak at the table. Valerka, sitting opposite and wearing an earring, was a quiet person, too. But he had an odd look about him. When he saw Farhod smiling, it struck him as so he tried not to look in his direction. When Farhod asked the man next to him about Valerka, Anatoliy threw a quick glance at him and just shrugged his shoulders: if I only knew! Gulya overheard and hurriedly explained: "His name is Valerka, he's a pleasant enough lad."

Seeing this "pleasant lad" reminded Farhod of one unpleasant teacher he had met while studying at the institute.

His surname was either Shomtaliev or Shomatillaev. He taught artistic dance for would-be actors. Farhod, who was at the department of theatre studies, did not know him well. The only thing he knew was that this teacher always walked on tiptoe, his arms stretched out like wings and his body trembling. When he explained something to his students he made a triangle with his thumb and forefinger. He had some other strange mannerisms, too, such as flattening his hair with his palms, or gently stroking his cheeks.

One day a simple-hearted student from a village complained to the principal: "The teacher is not keeping his promise..." It became known that the student himself stopped "visiting" the teacher.

In short, their secret was revealed and the dancer-teacher was banished from the institute. However, soon afterwards he was appointed deputy to a department head at a higher educational establishment at the ministry, and he took to summoning the old principal on trivial matters. The principal's driver, sly Vitaliy, an Armenian, used to earn money as a taxi driver in his official car, so the principal used to look for a student with a car to take him to the ministry: "My son, could you please take me to the ministry, comrade Shomataliev (Shomatillaev) has summoned me."

Farhod assumed that the majority of people sitting at this table (including those who joined them for a short time) were those who dealt with arts quite seriously, but who were not so successful, though they considered themselves professionals. He wondered what Gulya was doing among them, why she had gathered them all together, or if she was expecting something from them. But, oddly enough, he did not want to leave this circle, either. He thought Gulya might be offended if he did; besides, he had the feeling something interesting might be about to happen. Anyway, he was fed up of always hanging around in the recreation centre or going to the city and back; staying here definitely beat that!

Gulya and the cigarette-smoking Gugushidze were leading the circle. Although Gulya did not drink herself, she poured mineral water into her glass, and urged the others to drink, exchanging toasts and trying to please everyone.

Gugushidze was a good performer. Pinching his nose with his thumb and forefinger and covering his mouth with his palms, he could whistle a tune through his ear! Everyone was amazed, clapping and crying: "Bravo! Bravo!"

"Please play the Polonaise for us!" asked Natasha, applauding.

Gugushidze whispered something into her ear, whereupon she turned pale, gently slapped the man's forearm, and turned her back to him.

The performer started to grant the lady her wish. His whistling was indeed reminiscent of the famous Polonaise, but sometimes his ear veered off. Well, it's not easy to perform through the ears, when others cannot even whistle through their lips.

"Bravo, bravo!"

"Could you please play 'Podmoskovniye vechera'?"

Gugushidze raised his hands in a gesture of respect to his audience, then plonked himself back in his chair.

He told us that this kind of performance runs in his family — his forefathers had also whistled with their ear. He said their clan name was derived from this specialty. In Farsi, "gush" means "ear", "gu" means "say" or "give voice", i.e. 'let your ear sing.' They have been performing ever since. By the way, you must have heard of a famous Iranian singer called Gugush, maybe he belongs to their clan, too ...

(Two days later, Farhod spotted Gugushidze in the distance. He was speaking to two girls in Vosstaniye Square. Farhod was sure he was about to perform for them, too.)

"Wow, so you have Persian blood, too?" asked Natasha, surprised. "That's perfect! Georgian, Persian, Armenian —anything else?"

"Ah, who knows, maybe yes, maybe no," said Gugushidze nonchalantly.

"Susanevich!" exclaimed Lyuba. "Susanevich knows everything! That old man is great!"

Farhod was thinking about something else. He wasn't listening to what the people at the table were talking about, he was fed up with the din. Yet, like someone who has once tasted a delicious sweetmeat and craves that sweetness again, Farhod was sitting there with them, his heart alive with joy. As if he would taste the same sweetmeats again.

All of a sudden the group began to disperse with cries of: "Let's go, let's go."

"Are you going?" Gulya asked coming over him. "Come on, let's go."

"Where? Everybody to their own place?"

"To Susanevich's. Haven't you heard? We all agreed just now."

"Susanevich? Who's that?" Farhod asked as he followed her.

"An interesting old man. An anthropologist. He could tell you your roots at first sight."

"I know my roots very well," smiled Farhod. "Who am I? Why, I'm Uzbek, of course."

"Hey, we're all Uzbeks. Do come with me. Please," said Gulya taking his arm. "You'll see when we get there."

As they were leaving, she asked Farhod if they could stop to buy something for the old man, adding: "He's partial to wine." Farhod quickly popped into the same shop he had been to several days ago and came out with a bag full of goodies. They split into two groups, took two taxis and headed to a place called Chertanovo.

Susanevich lived alone in a three-room flat which looked more like an old storage facility than a home. Chaos reigned. Susanevich himself fitted right in: he was completely bald apart from a few thin hairs dangling around his ears and over his shoulders, making him look for all the world as though he had picked up some animal pelt, made a hole in the centre and hung it over his head. Blue veins stood out on his face, his eyes seemed bruised, and he could barely shuffle along, bent double.

"Ah, Gulenka, my dear! Come in, come in! Which wind has blown you here to me this evening?" he said, opening wide his arms. "Oh, Lyubochka has come, too, and even Natashenka! Welcome, welcome, my dears! I have missed you all so much!"

And with that, much to Farhod's disgust, Susanevich kissed Gulya, spraying foam from his half toothless mouth.

"May you perish!" thought Farhod. "Why did you hug him?"

They followed the old man into a tidy little room. Gulya took the bag of shopping from Farhod and set about spreading the goodies out on the table.

"Look what we've brought you, Mark Aronovich!"

"Thank you, Gulenka, thank you so much!" said the old man eying the now laden table.

Gulya was ad hoc lady of the house here, too. She quickly popped to the kitchen to fetch spoons, forks and glasses to lay the table for the party. Then she went back for coffee and tea. And soon they were all having a jolly old time again, speaking, discussing, dreaming, and teasing each other.

Finally sated, they got down to business. Sitting in the rocking chair at the head of the table, Susanevich pushed his glasses onto his forehead and began to tell everyone's fortune, calling each one in turn.

"We all know Gulenka," he began. "Whatever we say she is – Uzbek, Ukrainian, Polish – she is as she is. Long live the most Internationalist person!"

Lyuba and Natasha responded with enthusiastic applause. It was their turn next. The two of them were almost identical. The difference between Gulya and her two friends was that they were Byelorussians not Uzbek. But Natasha had no Polish blood at all.

"Last time you were telling me that I had some French blood, Mark Aronovich," she said, disagreeing.

"Did I say that last time? Well, I can't find anything this time," said the clairvoyant nonchalantly. Then he smiled and said again:

"Well, seems to me your bloods mixed and vanished. So what of it? Don't be offended, my dear, French blood was transitory in you from the start."

Natasha scowled as if she were indeed offended.

For some reason the old man stared at Gugushidze for a long time. He even leafed through the thick book in front of him and measured something with his ruler and other devices. But apparently unable to draw any conclusions, he again gazed at the whistler.

"You look like one of us," he said, smiling.

"One of you? Who is that? Who do I look like?" asked Gugushidze, getting flustered.

The old man asked him to come closer and whispered something in his ear. Gugushidze turned pale:

"Hey, what are you saying, old man? Yes, my surname seems Georgian, but I am one hundred percent Iranian! Admittedly, my mother had some mixed Armenian blood, but my father and all my forefathers were pure Iranians. If you don't believe it, I can show you our genealogy!"

"It's not necessary, my friend, I don't need it," said Susanevich with a dismissive wave of his hand. "I would be proud of it if I were you!"

"Be proud of yourself!" said Gugushidze jumping up. "You've spoiled everything with your great pride!"

The old man shook his head. Gugushidze went out to another room, pulling Natasha after him. The others exchanged knowing looks.

"Don't be upset, please, Mark Aronovich. Our friend lost his temper. He's just a bit drunk, that's all," said Gulya trying to console the old man.

"I wouldn't have lived to this ripe old age if I got upset at every small trifle, Gulenka," said the clairvoyant and turned to the next client — Anatoliy.

302

"No, no," said the 'dumb' alcoholic, opening his mouth for the first time that evening. "You told me last time: I'm a Ukrainian Cossack."

"Everyone knows who our Valerka is," said the old man smiling.

"Mark Aronovich," said Gulya, pointing to Farhod. "I've brought him specially tonight. He is my fellow countryman."

"It's obvious he is from Turkmenistan!" said the old man, and began nodding off in his chair

Gulya winked at Farhod: "don't pay any attention."

Anatoliy signalled to Lyubochka and they left. Valerka followed them quickly.

After a while, Farhod tapped his watch, looking at Gulya: "it's late, we should go." But just then a loud crash came from the hallway. They both rushed out, only to see Valerka leaning against the wall with a bloody nose and mouth. He grinned at them weakly.

Gugushidze was standing at the door swearing. He pulled a handkerchief from his pocket and passed it to Valerka:

"Here, wipe your nose!"

"Gugush, what happened to you?" Gulya asked angrily and, grabbing the handkerchief from Valerka, she set about wiping away the traces of blood herself.

"Sorry, Gul, sorry," said Gugushidze touching his lips to her shoulder. "Tell him he should stop being so bloody protective." Then he turned to his Valerka, and patted him gently on the shoulder saying: "Don't worry, my lad, you'll be right as rain tomorrow. Come on, Natasha, let's go!" He paused in front of Farhod on his way out and said distinctly: "You should know, my friend, that you are whoever you consider yourself to be. Your nationality is like that. The rest is nothing!"

Natasha emerged from the room opposite, looked at Farhod and Gulya rather sheepishly, then glanced at herself in the mirror hanging by the door.

Anatoliy and Lyuba came out of the third room. Lyuba straightened her hair, then kissed Gulya. Gulya looked at each of them in turn before going back into the "fortune teller's parlor" to grab her bag:

"Such immodest people! Disgraceful!" she hissed.

Once they were all outside, Farhod realized they were in fact planning to go to Balashikha, to Lyuba's place, and to carry on partying until dawn. They said she had everything in her room.

Farhod's head was already spinning from everything he had seen that evening; he wanted to leave.

"Where will you go at this time of night?" Gulya asked anxiously. "The electric trains will have stopped running by the time you get to the station, you'll just be wasting your time. But if you really don't want to join us, take this key and go to my flat. There's no one there, you can have a good rest. I have to go with them... Please, come here," she said, and led Farhod a little further. "To be honest, I feel embarrassed in front of you, Farhod. Really, so embarrassed. Did you see how they carry on? Such stupidity in your presence! I don't know what to say! They are all unlucky and unfortunate. But none of them mean any harm, they're all just like children... Farhod, please kiss me."

Farhod didn't know what to do. Now he was the child, the unfortunate one, and he was the one out of place, the alien!

He approached Gulya and touched her shoulder. She put her head to his chest and cried.

They stood like that for quite a while, like a brother and sister who had not seen each other for a long time. Then Gulya turned her face away and wiped her eyes with her hands.

"Believe me, these people are not bad, they are harmless and funny. Today I thought I could cheer them up a bit, but actually I am just like them. Farhod, please forgive me..."

Farhod took a taxi to Gulya's flat in Medvedkovo. He longed to get there as soon as possible, to feel the fragrance of the room and the pillow.

... Once again, it had been impossible to ask Gulya what he was going to ask her before.

15. Vika, Vika, Victoria... Dildoriya, Dildora, Dildor

Just as he was falling asleep, he heard a commotion in the hall. Hearing a man's voice, he thought his companions had come. "What did they come here for?" Farhod muttered as he got up, grabbing his trousers from the chair and putting on his shirt. Just then the door opened and there was Vika!

"Oh! It's you? I saw a stranger's shoes in the hall and couldn't guess who it might be. I suppose you came to pick up your hand-kerchief, right?" she teased. "So you didn't go to Balashikha? Just as well! My mother's a strange woman, too; she always hangs out with those stupid people, even on her birthday!"

Farhod jumped up as if he had been caught in someone else's bed:

"Whose birthday is today? Your Mum's? Gulya's?"

"Yes, of course. Didn't she tell you? She's so odd, she never tells anyone. I bet none of the crowd she was with today had any idea it was her birthday. Crazy, isn't it?"

Farhod had already been amazed by something once that night, when he was saying goodbye to Gulya, but now he was dumbstruck. Her birthday! The only daughter is here, the mother is somewhere else! Well, it really was crazy.

"Good grief, she didn't tell me! If only I'd known..."

"Don't worry, please. She revels in it. Me and my friends didn't have a good time together today, either..."

She told him they had gone to a friend's summer cottage out in the country for a party, but the friend's father had shown up with his lady-friend so they'd had to come back to the city. And now they'd gone and woken up Farhod, she apologized

"Well, come with us now you're up," she insisted, taking her tape recorder with her.

It was true they had disturbed his sleep, but he really liked this unexpected turn of events, so he gladly joined her.

They sat in the spacious kitchen. There were two bottles of white wine, plenty of sausage and cheese. The two Farhod had seen in the bar were there – a girl and a young man. The girl was not beautiful, but the bearded young man was very handsome, and his eyes were blue like Vika's. He looked a bit like the famous film star Igor Starigin. His name was Vitalik and he was a very pleasant, chatty person. Originally he was from somewhere called Anna or Nikol in Voronezh and didn't get a place at the Institute two years in a row. Vika vowed she would burn down the Institute of Filmmakers if he wasn't accepted this year, since, according to her, he was a very talented person. But the young man was fond of his drink, emptying one bottle all by himself and getting pretty drunk. Farhod was himself a bit tipsy, so he just sat sipping from his glass.

Vika introduced him to her friends as "a playwright from Tashkent, a close friend of my Mum." It was true, what else could she say?

They pushed the table into a corner to make room for dancing. Alla Pugacheva[55] was giving her all from the tape recorder: "Ancient watches," "A Million Roses," "Maestro."

---

55 Extremely famous Soviet singer with many official titles.

Farhod was struck by how well Vika and Vitalik danced together. They moved so graciously in such perfect harmony, it was obvious they were both good dancers. Vitalka was dancing with all his heart, as if there were no one but his "beloved" in this world, as if he was Majnun[56] seeking his love in the steppes of Karbalo.

Vika was dancing marvelously, too.

Farhod was watching them with joy and jealousy; something was stirring in his heart and he was letting his anger out by smoking cigarette after cigarette.

As they danced, Vitalik maneuvered Vika into the hall. The unattractive girl, who had been sitting scowling from the moment she found out Farhod was not fond of dancing, threw him a coquettish glance: "look, we're alone now, show me what you can do."

But Farhod felt bored and continued to smoke his cigarette.

First Vika and then Vitalik appeared in the doorway and called Farhod into the hall.

Vitalka wanted to drink, they needed some money.

Taking the money, Vika quickly went out. The lift could soon be heard rumbling its way down.

Farhod did not want to go to the kitchen so he turned to go back to Vika's room for a rest. He didn't feel like sitting with them anymore.

As he looked through the window in an understandably irritated mood, he noticed the sound of music had stopped and silence reigned in the kitchen. He went out to wash his face, but when he opened the bathroom door he was greeted by a strange sight: the young man was lying in the bath with the girl sitting on his knee...

---

56 Hero of the love epic.

Farhod slowly closed the door and stood there not knowing what to do. Then he came to his senses, went back into Vika's room and jumped into bed.

As he was lying there dozing, he suddenly heard a scream, and the front door banged shut. Startled, he rushed into the hall. He saw a furious Vika in the kitchen. She was standing in the middle of the room gulping wine straight from the bottle. . . Catching sight of Farhod's silhouette, she took the bottle from her lips and whispered angrily, breathing hard:

"Bastards! I sent them both packing! Vitalik, the cheating bastard!"

And she slid the other bottle over to him, saying: "Come on, you have a drink, too!"

Obeying her automatically, Farhod took the bottle and, like Vika, began swigging wine straight from the neck.

So there they were, standing side by side satisfying their "thirst."

After a while, Vika smashed her bottle against the table, reached over to the tape recorder and pressed the button. As luck would have it, 'Maestro' was playing.

The girl stood up, took Farhod's hand and pulled him to the middle of the room. She looked at him with eyes full of tears, whispering: "He's a cheat, isn't he?"

Maestro, maestro... Ah, Farhod saw himself as a maestro then.

He felt he was repeating Vitalik's movements. Why? Was it because he wanted to please Vika? But she was busy with herself.

All of a sudden, Vika kissed his nose. Not his lips, his nose! Farhod liked it so much, he wanted her to kiss him again. The girl guessed what he wanted and kissed him again. Then she kissed a little lower. Then...

308

Well, there's no need to describe what happened then – anyone who has been in a similar situation knows well enough.

"Did you go to the pioneer camp "Artek" like your Mum?" Farhod asked her.

"Yes, some guys fooled around with me. Misspent youth...," she replied, not taking it seriously. "Is it considered a sin in your culture? I heard that if the bride misbehaves on her wedding night, the bridegroom would kill her with a knife. Is that true? That's barbarism!"

"I don't know if anyone's ever killed anyone, but what do you mean by 'in your culture'?"

"I mean Uzbeks," she said feeling a little embarrassed.

"Who are you, actually?"

"I am... Russian, Polish, Uzbek... Eh, I don't care about it. I am Vika, Victoria. Understand?"

Farhod, perhaps, was expecting it to be like that, or maybe he just thought it was like that. However, even though this girl was open and "different", she was still a virgin.

They have an interesting tradition – they never discuss anything beforehand, but whenever they face a problem, they put it before you: look, see, what we have done. "Why didn't you tell me earlier?" "Would you have done anything differently? You knew, you saw it yourself." At moments like those you want to break her into pieces, no matter how charming and attractive she is. Then you calm down: don't worry, dear, everything will be fine. It was meant to be. After that tender caressing begins. Beautiful blue eyes, thirsty lips. Always cold, the soft white fingers that warm whatever they touch... Eh, let it be so, foolish man! Don't think about anything, just think about your life today! Everything in this world is temporary, everything is transient!

When you calm down, you will feel a pain in your heart and regret for what you have done. What have you done, Farhod? You have become sinful, man! What will poor Gulya think of you? It's villainy, and it's disgraceful!

The next day he felt different somehow: sometimes his heart was full of light, at others something hurt him as though he had indeed committed a grave sin. But by the evening he couldn't help calling her. Vika was at home, she answered the phone herself. There was neither scorn nor regret in her voice. On the contrary, with her first words she dissipated the bad feelings lurking in his heart:

"Please come. I've missed you. I fell in love with you in just one night. Believe me!"

"Where is your mother? Is Gulya at home?"

Vika told him Gulya was at a hospital: it seems she got food poisoning at their get-together in Balashikha. She had to stay there for three or four days.

"How is she there?"

"Not bad, I've just come from the hospital. She sends her regards to you."

Farhod flew to Medvedkovo right away!

How he changed in those few days! He, too, fell in love with Vika! There was no one and nothing but Vika in the entire world!

As they were lying on the bed stark naked, Vika asked him:

"Are you married? Do you have children?"

"I am, and I do," he replied, but something crumpled in his heart.

"But I am alone. I only have my mother," she said pensively. Then suddenly she cried. "I have neither father nor brother nor sister!"

It's strange: she could shed tears so quickly after being so happy, or vice versa; she could laugh after sitting so sadly. Was that artistic rehearsal?

"You've become very dear to me over the past three or four days," she said, wiping her eyes with her little finger. "You are like my father."

"Do I look like him?"

"How do I know? I've never seen him!"

"What do you mean, Victoria Andreevna?"

"It's true. I've never seen him before. I only know my grandmother who lives in Seretinka. I visited her several times, but I have not seen my dad."

"I heard that he was a pilot, almost an astronaut."

"That must be my mother's fantasy! She's good at creating such myths. One time when I was in the seventh grade..."

Farhod did not hear what she was talking about. His thoughts were racing: "That means you are illegitimate, my sweetheart. But didn't she say I'm like her dad? But she's never seen him. So that means she's illegitimate... unclean... Ah, but she is so beautiful, a thousand times better than those legitimates! She is my honey! Let me kiss you, my sweetheart!"

Still lying on the bed, all of a sudden Farhod remembered Eshpay-Eshboy, a boy from his childhood. He did not even know the boy's real name, though they were the same age. Everybody just him Eshpay-Eshboy or plain Eshboy-the-illegitimate. Farhod remembered that this unfortunate boy could not join the other children playing on the street. Both young and old alike mocked him, taunting: "illegitimate, illegitimate." So of course, he did not want to go outside and would sit at home all day, like a girl. However, he was an excellent pupil. Parents would scold their children, saying: "Look at you, you can't even study better than that illegitimate!"

Eshpay-Eshboy was the youngest child of Aunt Daromad. Aunt Daromad was a woman with yellow-white skin and blue eyes, and she used to work at the district hospital as a cleaner. She had four or five children and her husband was old and sick. A new surgeon called Serapim Eshpay arrived at the hospital from somewhere and soon became known far and wide as the famous as "Doc Eshpay." People praised him, saying: "He's really professional, he can cure anything." In short, Aunt Daromad, six years after she gave birth to her youngest child, became pregnant by him and so this blond blue-eyed boy, so totally different from his swarthy brothers and sisters, came into this world. The Aunt's blue eyes saved her from the anger of her husband and the curses of the people.

Eshpay-Eshboy, who finished school with a gold medal, went to study in Russia. Since he was fluent in Russian, he became an official and even worked as the second secretary of the District Party Committee. In those days people said of him: "He may be an illegitimate, but he is capable!" Illegitimates, it would seem, are always capable.

"I was born when my mother was nineteen years old. Now I'm nineteen!" Vika said. "And I want to have a child, too. Your child!"

An unknown panic filled Farhod's heart, but he didn't let on to Vika.

"So you want to give birth to an Uzbek child, Uzbek, like your roots?"

"Why Uzbek? Why exactly Uzbek? What about myself? What about my Mum?" asked Vika. "Let's count." So she sat on the bed and started to count on her fingers. "I'm Russian on my father's side, because his surname is Russian, so he's obviously Russian. But then again, who knows if that's true? My Mum is

Uzbek, but her Mum is Polish mixed with Ukrainian. So that means I'm only 25% Uzbek, am I right?"

"What about me? Won't you count the child's father? You know I am 100% Uzbek. I don't have mixed blood. So, how much is your 25% and my 100% together?"

"One hundred and twenty-five…"

"Our child will be 125% Uzbek, right?"

"Right," Vika said relaxing. "Hey, stop, stop! A percentage can't be more than a hundred, correct?"

"But ours will be 125%! That's obvious!" teased Farhod. "Alright, let's see wait and see what comes out first."

"We'll certainly have a child! You'll see!" said Vika with great certainty.

Oh my, the girl already had a grand plan! What is she preparing for you? You are here while your own child, your copy, is somewhere far away, in a foreign land, with foreigners … Can you bear it?

"Get up!" said Farhod fearfully. "Let's go and take a bath together."

"Why? We can do it in the morning, like we always do."

"Please do as I say, honey. It's a deal."

Vika shrugged her shoulders and unwillingly got up.

As they were taking a bath together, Farhod wanted her again, right there in the bath, but…

Once out of the bathroom, Farhod insisted Vika should wear a very short black dress and put a funny scarf on her head. He dressed quickly, sat himself down on the sofa, and asked Vika to sit next to him.

He had an overwhelming certainty, a feeling deep in his heart, that he should now use this method – an interesting tradition he had once seen in a film.

He began by teaching her the only verse he knew from the Koran, repeating "La ilaha illalloh." Vika eventually mastered it, and he congratulated her: "Congratulations, Ms. Vika, you have now become a Muslim! Now we can start reciting nikoh[57]."

Vika was watching his every move with great interest.

"Nikoh? What kind of nikoh"? she asked in surprise. "What, are you a mullah?"

"Don't worry, sweetheart. Just repeat after me."

Farhod intentionally lowered his voice a few tones and 'asks himself' solemnly:

"Farhod, son of Mirzo, do you accept Ms. Viktoriya, daughter of Andrey-boy, a Muslim slave of Allah, as your wife?"

"I do, I do," said Farhod with his own voice.

"Very well," he said, again in the deeper, softer voice of the 'mullah'. "And do you, a Muslim girl, Ms. Viktoriya, daughter of Andrey-boy, do you agree that a Muslim man, a slave of Allah, Farhod son of Mirza-boy, will become your husband?"

When Vika heard the translation of the sentence, she quickly replied:

"With great pleasure! I love this man!"

Farhod explained to her that she should be patient and slowly say "yes" shaking her head, after the same question had been repeated three times.

"Whoa! What's the difference?" Vika said, puzzled. "I tell you I love you, isn't that enough? I'm ready to repeat it a hundred times, if necessary!"

"Alright, it's enough!" the 'mullah' said; he had no other choice. "Congratulations, you are now husband and wife! Now, if you have children, they will be called Muslims, inshaallah. Amen! Allah is great!"

---

57 Muslim marriage vows.

"Amen! Thanks!"

"Thanks! Amen!"

Farhod felt something stirring in his heart. Unexpectedly, he fell to his knees and started to repent with eyes full of tears, gazing into the sky through the window. Vika joined him, as if someone were looking down at them from on high.

"Bismillahir rohmanir rohim! In the name of Allah the most gracious the most merciful!" Farhod began trembling. "Please forgive your sinful slaves! You gave me this silly heart, O Merciful One, and I obeyed its wish. What can I do? Perhaps I was wrong in my actions just now, but this is all your sinful slave knows. You see we have no witness but You. You are our only support. I have committed a sin in this foreign land. As You are my witness, I had neither grudge nor ill intent. My only fault is that I followed the way of my own heart. Please accept my repentance, O Merciful One! I have one more request: please read the 'nikoh' of these sinful slaves of Yours in the heavens. Amen! Allah is great!"

As Farhod stood up he saw Vika was reciting a prayer, too, rubbing her palms over her face.

"Now, we have Allah's blessing, Dildor," he said. "From now on, according to Islamic law, you are my wife. Now you can give birth to a boy or a girl, whatever Allah gives, Dildor."

(It was their second night together and Vika had asked him what her name would be in Uzbek. Farhod replied without thinking: "Vika, Vika, Victoria... Dildoriya, Dildora, Dildor.")

Vika started at him in surprise.

"Actor!" she concluded. "A true actor! Well done!"

"Think before you speak, Dildor. I was not acting!" said Farhod frowning. Then he smiled: "I was infected by my wife who is also an actor!"

Vika came closer to him.

"Sorry, Farhod…"

They embraced in the middle of the room. Vika put her hands around his neck and kissed him, thinking this was also a continuation of the tradition. Then they tumbled onto the sofa.

The next day Gulya left hospital. The bride and groom's five days of marriage were over. Well, two or three times Farhod did take the key to Sur'at's flat in Shyolkovo and spend time there with Vika. But Sur'at insisted on knowing who he was meeting there, and since Farhod knew only too well how greedy Sur'at was about women, he did not want to tell him and so stopped asking him for his key.

At the open plenary session, Gulya came up and kissed Farhod as usual. She did not mention she had been in hospital; instead, she apologized for the unfortunate events of that night. She was completely oblivious, poor mother-in-law… Now it was impossible to ask her that old question.

16. A foreigner-chief. Archangel of women.

"You know me," Ravshan Akobirov began seriously, eyeing the conference participants. "I am the person who came from abroad. It's true that I have many friends on both sides of the discussion table. We Uzbeks have a saying that no matter which finger you bite, the pain will be the same. Am I right, Farhodjon?" he asked in Uzbek and pointed to Farhod sitting at the back on the left, waiting for his approval.

Farhod saw the audience was looking at him with interest, but he didn't know what to say, so he just shuffled a bit.

"This young man is Farhod Ramazonov, my colleague and one of Uzbekistan's well-known scriptwriters," Mr. Akobirov introduced him solemnly, returning to the official language of the conference, Russian.

Someone in the first row warmly applauded him. Farhod looked over and saw Lagutina. Actually, they had met in the foyer before the conference and greeted each other. Farhod thought Gulya seemed to have become closer, friendlier, towards him. When he entered the conference hall, Gulya called him to sit next to her, but seeing Diana on the other side, he chose to sit in a far corner with Sur'at. He was afraid Diana would tell Gulya everything. That was something he would never want. By the way, where is this merciful mother's son, Deniska? Earlier she had been trying to tie a five or six-year-old boy's shoelaces (maybe that was Deniska?). When she caught sight of Farhod looking for an ashtray for his cigarette she nodded her head like an enemy. The mere sight of him disgusted her!

The chairman of the meeting, Mr. Akobirov, was explaining to the audience:

"I think you understand my situation, so I hope you will not be upset with me. As an impartial person I can say that there is nothing to dispute between these two parties. There is nothing to quarrel over, believe me. A small disagreement left unresolved has become a serious problem today. Obviously, some tricksters want to make the most of this opportunity, but I repeat once again: our multinational cinematography will not benefit from this!"

Everyone was familiar with these more or less empty platitudes, but in the mouth of a person who "came from a foreign land" they sounded less shallow and were met with thunderous applause. The somewhat disgruntled Farhod joined in despite himself.

"Everyone knows that two opposing groups — talented and untalented, jeweler and swindler — always quarrel over arts. Isn't that right? But even the swindler thinks he is no worse than the others: he, too, is a human being and has his own hopes and dreams. He tries to reach his goals and naturally thinks he is on the right path. I am not going to repeat that all creatures in the world are created as one of a pair. I am just going to say that the arts cannot thrive without that mutual conflict and contradiction. And I believe that there are no untalented swindlers among our dear colleagues present here today..."

Actually, the participants liked the speech, especially the last phrase, since of course no one thought he or she was an untalented swindler.

The most interesting thing was that Mr. Akobirov was delivering his speech with pathos, as if he were actually creating those words at that very moment, investing them with a novel freshness.

"My thoughts remind me of Khoja Nasriddin[58]," he said, and told the story called "You are both right," at which everyone laughed and applauded. "But I'm not going to act that way..."

Farhod had seen it often enough; when they come to this great city, even very influential Uzbeks become modest or somehow smaller. Ravshan Akobirov, however, towered before his eyes. Just imagine, a film director from Uzbekistan was leading this most important Conference of Filmmakers of the 'great country'! And this wise, experienced man was doing a splendid job! He was speaking their language better than they could themselves! Bravo, bravo!

Actually, the session had begun with not a little conflict and kerfuffle.

At the request of the two opposing groups, as well as due to ever-increasing democratic values, it was decided that the session should be open for discussion, without any formality.

---

58 A famous trickster, the hero of many folktales and anecdotes throughout the Islamic world.

Since the former jury had been disbanded, there was a long discussion as to who should lead the session. Finally, a rotund film critic with yellow hair on his face and head appeared before the audience and, in a sonorous voice, nominated an old film director to be chairman of the session. The elderly gent was a director who had once-upon-a-time produced several films about a happy life and enjoyed the support of the government, but who was later forgotten. He was indeed a very old man, hard of hearing and with failing eyesight. When the session participants, tired of disputes, approved him as chairman, he barely made it up onto the stage. In keeping with the requirement of modernity, a small table and a good chair took the place of a regular podium.

The old man lowered himself onto the chair, adjusted his old tie which no longer matched his wide jacket, and then started talking about the sacredness of cinematography, rubbing his thin hair and glancing at the audience through his large, shiny spectacles. But he had barely started his speech before the audience grew restive and complaining voices were heard: "Stop!" "That's enough!" But the lecturer, oblivious, merely continued rasping out his long, long speech in a hoarse voice, soon moving onto his childhood reminiscences. By this time, the other group felt that he was a lecturer who had been commissioned especially for this session. Without warning, a chap suddenly jumped onto the stage, shook his fists at the old man to make him shut up, and started to spout his own opinion. The crowd warmed up, cries of approval and dissent were heard from all corners.

Suddenly two strong men brandishing batons appeared on stage. Everyone was dumbstruck.

"What are you doing here?!" asked the old man up on stage, terrified. "Who called you here?"

"Well, what about you? What are you doing here?" one of the armed men retorted, waving his baton menacingly. The unfortunate old speaker slowly clambered down.

"Get out of here!" someone yelled. "Off with you! Go on, get out of here, who the hell do you think you two are?!"

The two tough guys pretended not to hear and stood there for a while as if they were inspecting the stage, then slowly lumbered off.

It was the famous film director Gleb Akushin who had shouted at them. Now he stood up in front of the audience without going on stage. He was such a tall man that even anyone standing on stage would have been dwarfed by him. A leather cap with a button was perched on his big head. As small as a kettle lid, it must have been his grandson's. Maybe he had a scar on his head, which would explain why he didn't take his cap off even in that stuffy meeting room.

He glanced at the audience angrily and said:

"Dear comrades! Ladies and gentlemen! O Merciful One! I don't even know what to call you! Well, it is obvious that everyone wants to say something. If it goes on like this, the session might turn into a battlefield. I would suggest that the session is headed by a neutral colleague, someone quite far removed from the quarrels in the capital, say, our colleague from Uzbekistan, Ravshan Akobirov! You all know him, he is also a member of our council."

"An excellent suggestion, Gleb Aleksandrovich!" someone called out from the middle row. Farhod recognized him from behind: it was that hairy Plato Sokratovich. "A suggestion absolutely in keeping with present-day democratic values! Let's take a vote, colleagues!"

"Well, Ravshan Usmonovich, please come here, before the audience," Akushin said in a softer voice, calming down.

Then he joked: "As you see we don't have a worthy prophet among us."

Mr. Akobirov was sitting in the first row of activists, so he stood up, put his hands to his chest and gave a slight bow, a sign of respect to the audience.

Because of his eastern modesty and the fact that this suggestion had come from the famous filmmaker, plus the "democratic values" he cited, the conference participants calmed down and applauded the new chair of the session, a sign of their approval.

Mr. Akobirov has been chairing the session for about an hour now, using all his skills and holding everyone's attention. Whenever someone who was given the floor after being selected by the opposing group started going off track, he or she was stopped by Akobirov and quickly asked to leave the stage.

But apparently he liked this last speaker, since he praised and thanked him before he left the stage. But just then, an old bald man in a striped shirt began making his way onto the stage without asking any permission, almost as if his supporters were pushing him.

"Sorry, dear comrade, has anyone called you up on stage?"

The old man stopped at the stairs and made it clear he was about to come up.

"What, have we invited you here? Who are you? Tell us, please."

"I am... I am..." the old man murmured. "I am Surowski, Vadim Surowski. Cinematographer."

"Ah, Sur-rowski," repeated Akobirov. "We know you, we've heard about you. But now please have some rest. You can come on stage once we give you the floor, OK?"

The old man obediently returned to his seat.

People started whispering in the hall. Three or four people, allegedly supporters of Surowski, left the meeting.

Farhod was utterly amazed. Vadim Surowski was his professor, he had taught Farhod the ABCs of cinematography, and he was one of the great figures of cinematography. All textbooks and manuals on the history of cinematography carried an official photograph of him with his jet black hair neatly combed down the middle. Poor Akobirov had created a new problem for himself. It seems those fierce forces pushed him on stage. But what happened to Akobirov?

Just then, someone piped up from the back row:

"Hey, comrades! Look, why are you just keeping quiet when Akobirov's making fun of you? He's a real nationalist! You've all just seen it for yourselves..."

Everyone turned in that direction. It was Semashenkov, complaining from the corner he'd hidden himself away in. He was drunk. his face was pale, his eyes bloodshot and it was all he could do to stand up. Perhaps he wanted revenge.

Adham Delon, who, as always, was sitting near the front among the beautiful ladies of cinematography, quickly stood up.

"Hey, Igor, shut up! Have you brought your old complaints here again? Don't believe him, colleagues, he is a compulsive gossip! We are proud of Ravshanbek Usmonovich Akobirov! I know him well. We studied at the institute together. He is a real Internationalist! His wife is Russian, Margarita Il'inichna Shevtsova! She works at UzbekFilm as a designer, a designer artist. "

"Look at this man! They are all the same, always scratching each others' back," Semashenkov said angrily. "He's just said it – they studied together!"

"And so what if they did? Akobirov is a true cinematographer and a well-known film director, but who are you?"

The quarrel continued and was on the point of turning into a serious conflict when Gleb Akushin stood up again:

"Stop this backstabbing! This is a session, an official meeting. We can't achieve anything if we listen to everyone with an axe to grind. To hell with your democracy, I'm appalled by it!"

"Nothing to do with democracy here, Gleb Aleksandrovich!" said Plato Sokratovich. "It's just common hooliganism!"

Just then something rather interesting happened: the two tough guys (without their batons this time) entered the hall from the side door, grabbed Semashenkov under his arms and quickly took him away.

"Serves him right!" could be heard from many.

Adham Delon was still standing there heroically in a show of support for Akobirov.

"Take your seat, Adham," said Akobirov in Uzbek. Apparently, he was miffed at hearing his wife described as a designer.

Farhod had seen Adham Delon in the foyer earlier and they had exchanged peasantries. As always, Adham was surrounded by sumptuous cinematography ladies. Seeing Farhod, he asked him: "Did you go to Cuba? How was it?" He was always harping on about that. "How could I go by myself?" smiled Farhod.

"This is what you should do, my naive young man," he would explain. "You should write a letter to Fidel Castro…"

"And what should I write in that letter?"

"Commandant Fidel, we are namesakes, my name is also Fidel. I would like to meet you in person and see your island of liberty. That's what you should say. That's all. And you will be in Cuba! Viva Cuba!" But, seeing Farhod's unwillingness, he would go on, crestfallen: "Shame on you, Fidel! Even though you are Fidel, you are Uzbek, and it's difficult for you to be a real person!"

Adham Delon is a former kolkhoz director in the Tashkent region and the only child of Mirkomil Zarkhujaev, Hero of Socialist Labour. He had an easy, comfortable, even wealthy childhood, was handsome to boot and had a penchant for smart clothes. Most of his adult life was spent travelling, and he would return to Tashkent with some new, interesting ways. Once, for instance, he came back leaning on a flowery cane. Or another time he wound a soft silk kerchief or a butterfly-like tie around his neck. Or sometimes he would wear his hair tied up like a woman. In short, he looked like the famous Delon, Alain Delon! (They say that when he tied his hair back like a woman, his old father cut it with a blunt knife while he was sleeping.)

He was, however, a very kind, honest and generous person. He did not complain and was grateful. if you criticize his films harshly one day, the next day he will come to hug you, saying: "Don't worry, old man, I love you anyway!"

He took his work seriously and was good at it. For some reason, his less than mediocre films far removed from the ideals of Socialist Realism and built on mixed ideas always won prizes. Rumour has it that those "ladies of cinematography" travelling from one festival to another played an important role in this achievement: he may not be the famous Alain, but at least he's his double – Adham Delon! And if you listen to the gossip, you'd know those cinema ladies find him quite a good lover... But that's enough of him, otherwise we'll commit a sin!

In short, this is the job of film director Adham Zarkhujaev: his hands are there but his feet are here!

"That man is Semashenkov, Igor Semashenkov, one of our screenwriters. He is my fellow countryman. He's not a bad man," Akobirov began by way of explanation. "But he behaved strangely today. Let's just forget about it. I apologize for what he has done, dear friends."

The audience was silent for a moment then started to applaud him.

"Yes, he is a wise man," said someone sitting behind Farhod. "That's an oriental approach!"

"Your brother's so capable, isn't he?" said Sur'at giving Farhod a nudge as he sat there proudly, forgetting about his anger and thanking his fellow countryman for being so gifted.

Under that applause and approval, Akobirov continued chairing the meeting, giving the floor to someone to announce the tentative council of leadership.

One of the ladies sitting near Adham Delon jumped up and quickly went on stage, waving a sheet of paper. She was a thin woman in a sleeveless black dress.

The list, read out loudly, was corrected a little, but was generally approved.

Adham Delon also was included in the leadership council.

Thus the session concluded its work very easily.

The organizational meeting of the new board was scheduled for that afternoon, and the session was closed.

Farhod was not interested in further developments, since he was in a hurry to meet with Vika. He was sure Vika's mother would not leave this place until she had found out every last detail...

Farhod came out of the metro at Medvedkovo and was crossing the square towards the train station when he heard someone calling his name. Looking around and saw a long black car parked behind the iron railings along the main road: someone who looked familiar was waving at him from the window. Surprised, Farhod took a few steps in that direction and then suddenly pulled up short: Ravshan Akobirov! "What do you want?" he signalled to him. But since he kept calling him, Farhod looked around and went up to the car.

"Are you going to the dacha?"

"Yes."

"Take a seat." Seeing Farhod's hesitation, Akobirov beckoned him again: "Come on, get in."

It was Farhod's first time in a Mercedes with its wide and overly comfortable seats.

"Let's go," Akobirov said to Gleb Akushin who was sitting in the driver's seat. Akushin, who could barely cram himself into this car, stared at Farhod and drove away.

They both looked drunk.

It was a great pleasure for Farhod to go to the dacha in such a pompous car, especially since he usually took the electric train there. The two people sitting in front of him were chatting away to each other, and Farhod was watching the pine forest stretching away on either side of the road.

When they arrived at the recreation centre, they just kept following the concrete walls for some reason, leaving the gates behind them. Farhod quickly touched the front seat:

"Brother Ravshan!"

Mr. Akobirov just played with his finger, calming him down, "Don't worry, please."

Soon after that the Mercedes turned into a lane with similar houses, and they drove through the wide open iron gates up to a house on the left surrounded by tall, broad-trunked silver birches.

Two children – one bigger, one smaller – were playing, running around after a big dog with floppy ears. Akushin got out of the car quickly and rushed over to them. Were they his grandchildren? When the children saw him they ran up, shouting: "Daddy! Daddy!" Akushin swung them both off their feet and, looking towards the two storey house in front of them, called out:

"Dunyasha! Why don't you come out to meet us, the victors?"

A woman wearing an apron appeared at the door. Her cheeks were red like a villager's.

"Why must you roar, Glebushka?"

"Please meet my wife, my invaluable Dunyashka!" Akushin bellowed, turning to Akobirov.

A villager, an old woman in a white headscarf, peeped through the door.

"You sound like Ivan the Terrible, Gleb Aleksandrovich!" smiled the old woman.

"Really? Did you see Ivan the Terrible, Mother?"

"No, I didn't. But I guess he was like you," said she and quickly explained: "I mean your strength and your voice."

"Have you heard what your mother says about me, Dunya?" said Akushin, putting his children down and showing his great strength to her wife.

"Your dumplings are ready," said Dunya to her husband. "Remember, you ordered them this morning?"

"Dunyasha, please meet my friend Ravshan Akobirov. He is our new chairman. He is the best Uzbek!"

Dunya looked at Akobirov with great interest, and nodded her head gently, adjusting her hair.

Farhod was standing uneasily further off, not catching all that was said.

"Ravshan, your tradition allows you to have four wives, right?" asked Akushin punching Akobirov playfully in the ribs. "But I am the Archangel who carries off the souls of women, don't you know! I can be ranked as the champion in making wives older. I had four of them! Dunyasha is my fifth wife. How old are you, Dun? Are you still twenty-nine?"

"Eh, don't be silly," said Dunya, slapping her husband on the shoulder. "You know fine well! He asks me this question

on purpose in front of everyone he brings home. Show-off...
hooligan!"

In fact, Farhod had heard that some famous actresses had
been married to Gleb Akushin.

"Just joking, my dear," he said, kissing his wife on her bare
shoulder. "Well, if the dumplings are ready, please bring them
to the veranda! Let's go!" he added, addressing the guests.

They followed their host up the stairs to the high veranda. It
was open on three sides. The air was fresh and the green birch
branches waved gently in the sweet breeze. They took their
wicker seats around the round table, and Akushin fetched an
armful of clinking bottles from the small room next door. He
introduced each bottle as he plonked it on the table:

"We drank this with Anjey Vayda! This one with Emir
Kusturitsa! And this one with Woody Allen... Choose yourselves! Which one do you fancy?"

The bottles were all open, some were half empty, some were
almost full, but all of them had already been sampled. Out here,
apparently, it didn't matter whether the bottle was open, what
mattered was whom you drank it with.

"Look, Gleb," said Akobirov frankly. "Go and bring what you
usually drink with Ravshan Akobirov."

"Ah, Khuja Nasriddin, Khuja Nasriddin!" he said, wagging
his finger, and brought a new whisky from the same "storage
room".

"Ah, splendid!" said Akobirov rubbing his hands. "Pour it! If
a drop is left you can drink it with your Vayda and Kusturitsa,
OK?"

"Ah, Khuja Nasriddin! You are Khuja Nasriddin! But we don't
have any soda water left, sorry..."

"Hey, do you want to mix this with water? What do you take
me for, an idiot? Just pour it!"

Akobirov tried to behave as modestly as he could, but self-satisfied pride rang in his words and in his attitude to an influential person like Akushin. Maybe he was feeling like a hero because he had chaired the session so well that morning.

No, in fact, the reason behind his proud delight was quite different, as became apparent at the first toast:

"Dear Ravshan!" he said solemnly. "I raise my glass to you, to your wisdom and to your victory today. Let's drink to our new chairman, Ravshan Akobirov!" When he saw Farhod's surprise at this toast, he roared: "What? Didn't you know that your fellow countryman is the new chairman?! He is our chief from now on!"

"Really, brother Ravshan?" asked Farhod in Uzbek. "Well done! Congratulations!"

Akobirov, now feeling relaxed, merely said: "Here, here!"

Farhod had never tasted whisky before, so he quickly emptied his glass first. He thought it tasted like cardboard dipped in water...

"This young man looks great!" Akushin said to Akobirov with delight. "A screenwriter, you say? Have your read his work? Is it good?"

"I have filmed one of his works before. It wasn't bad at all, isn't that right, Farhod?"

"Good, good. If you filmed his work, that means he's good!" Akushin turned to Farhod: "If you have a new script I would be glad to read it. Our screenwriters here are still writing about obsolete things. I suggest you always find a new character for your work. A new person, a new character! The rest will follow by itself."

Mr. Akobirov was obviously aggravated by his host's interest in Farhod. It was nothing serious but he was jealous, as though the capital were his own and no one else could come here.

Where is the generous, tolerant person Farhod had seen that morning? Look, you already have everything! Why not let others have the leftovers?

All of a sudden Farhod was disappointed. He wanted to leave them, but he felt ashamed. Moreover, he hoped to glean some more interesting details from the day's proceedings. "After all, you are sitting in Akushin's dacha, you ungrateful wretch!" he said to himself.

"Yeah, the East really is wonderful! It's a miracle!" said the host, and invited his guests to help themselves: "Taste this cheese, it's from West Berlin, I bought it at a Jewish restaurant. It's lightly salted, most delicious!"

"They even economize on salt!" said Akobirov smiling.

Akushin laughed loudly:

"You are absolutely right! Where do you find such words, Ravshan? But first taste it and then you can judge."

Just then the hostess brought dumplings in a large saucepan. Her husband welcomed her. As she was doling out the dumplings, Akushin slapped her on the bottom, saying: "Dunyasha, Dunyasha, get ready for tonight!" Then he turned to the guests to describe her: "Ah, what a woman! I brought her from Karelia!"

According to what they said – and this was backed up by their behaviour – they had also drunk some alcohol after the election at the buffet today. Akushin was as happy as if he himself had been elected chairman, not Akobirov. It was wonderful that Akobirov had taken the chairmanship; after all, he was Akushin's close friend. Moreover, he had recommended Akobirov himself! So he had got his revenge on those quarrelsome people, and now everything would be in his hands...

After eating dumplings, the two friends began discussing how a man called Gendlin had tried to fiddle the election process.

They almost forgot the third person sitting with them, barely glancing in his direction and not letting him get a word in edgeways. Knocking back the "cardboard water" one glass after another, Farhod's head was soon spinning, and his mind wandered to his recent escapades in Medvedkovo ...

Later when he came to his senses again, he saw Gleb Akushin kneeling before Akobirov, as if thanking him.

"Dear Ravshan!" he was entreating. "Do you want me to kiss your foot now, your oriental and courageous foot? Yes, I can kiss it!"

"What are you doing? Don't do that, Gleb," Akobirov tried to make him stand up. He looked at Farhod and smiled victoriously: "See how your brother is! But you don't treasure me, you take me for a cosmopolitan far from nationalism..."

Akushin fell asleep with his head in Akobirov's lap.

Akobirov took him by the arm, leaned him against the wall, and signalled to Farhod that they should go. Seeing Farhod didn't move, he urged him again:

"Let's go!"

The yard was empty.

They went out onto the lane and kept walking through the dachas.

"If you come and live here, I will buy one of these dachas for you," said Akobirov.

Farhod, gladdened by this unrealistic but generous offer, said:

"Thanks, brother Ravshan. First you should settle down here and then we'll see."

"I know you are upset with me," said Akobirov, gently putting his hand on Farhod's shoulder. "You are still green, my young friend. Your proposal was not written well. Were you planning to go to Uyghuristan and write a scenario about an Uzbek poet from Yorkent there? Who will send you there for this project?

OK, first I will go and then we can solve your China issue. We have authority now..."

As the issue was going to be resolved, Farhod forgot his grudge; in his eyes, Akobirov had become a more powerful, influential person. In fact, he did have a certain grandeur about him, which is why the Akushins of this world were bowing to him.

As the roundabout was a little far, they took a shortcut across the middle of the recreation centre and walked through the silver birches.

"Are you originally from Zarang, brother Ravshan?"

"I don't know, do you know?"

"That's where I'm from, too. We're from the same place."

"Really? Have you only just realized that now?" smiled Akobirov.

They came across a concrete wall.

"What shall we do, Farhod-boy?"

"We need to climb over the wall."

"Isn't it too high?"

"There is no other way. Let me help you first."

"No, no, you climb over first!"

"What shall we do then? Well, I'll climb up the wall and reach down to you."

And that is what they did. In the darkness, Farhod found a small hole in the wall and clambered up with difficulty.

Once on the wall, they again began discussing who should be the first to jump down.

"Why don't you jump?"

"No, you first!"

Farhod jumped down and landed on a soft bush.

"Now it's your turn, brother Ravshan!"

Akobirov jumped down, but, alas, he landed in a muddy ditch. His legs were covered in mud and he could barely scramble out, getting more and more irate with Farhod as he struggled there.

"You asked me to jump, now see what's happened! What shall I do now?"

Actually, it was not far to their building, but the small square was crowded at this hour, it was embarrassing for him to be seen like this, especially now that he was a different Akobirov. Especially, today...!

"Do you want me to bring you some clean trousers?" asked Farhod, feeling guilty.

"What will you do with these ones?"

"Maybe you'd better take them off. We can wash them in the ditch, and then hang them on this bush. They'll dry soon, with a bit of luck."

Although Akobirov was already a boss, he was a little naïve, so he agreed to Farhod's suggestion.

Soon his trousers were hanging on the bush waving in the wind while their owner was sitting barefoot on a big stone. None other than the newly-elected chairman! The future lord over these places! Can you imagine?

"Farhod, do you have a cigarette?"

"I thought you'd given up smoking?"

"Hand me one, would you? It looks as though I'll be giving up smoking several more times..."

For some reason, Farhod suddenly felt sorry for this person who had been elected a big boss that day.

17. In a group of three. Gulya acts as matchmaker for her father

Tell me, if you would, when is knock at the door ever timely? Even someone you are waiting impatiently for will come all of a sudden and catch you off guard, right? But now there was not simply a knock at the door; someone was battering it. They would start kicking it any second… Who could it be? Is everything OK? Farhod knew some people at the recreation centre, but he had never invited anyone to his room. If the person knocking on the door was the old concierge, well, she usually knocked slowly then left. Valya wasn't so cheeky, either Anyway, she wasn't there today and Farhod wanted to make the most of her absence. Though he had no hope in his heart, for some reason he did not want to let the woman know about it. She seemed to be persecuting him as if she were after his secrets, too. I wonder if she behaves like that with everyone? Maybe she thinks all the men here are hers.

So, who could it be? They would break the door down if he simply ignored it. He should have switched the light off earlier. O Merciful One! Whoever it was, they'd picked a fine time to bother him! Alarmed, Farhod dressed quickly, glancing at Vika who was lying curled up like a ball on the bed. She was worried, too. What would they do now? He wanted to send her to hide in the toilet, but there was a chance whoever was at the door might go there, too. The wardrobe was no good, either. He looked at the dark balcony. Vika followed his gaze, understood, and, quickly wrapping herself in a sheet, went out in a huff to hide on the balcony. Getting angry, Farhod followed her, drew the curtains and went to the door.

It was Akobirov!

"Were you sleeping? So early?" he asked, entering the room without permission. "You're not sick, are you? I didn't see you at dinner, either. But I saw your light was on so I came up to see you."

"Yes, I am a little bit sick, actually," said Farhod.

"Oh-ho," exclaimed the guest as he sat down in the arm-chair, for he had noticed an open bottle of Armenian cognac and a piece of chocolate on the coffee table. For some reason there was no glasses. Allah be praised! "Oh, I see you had a nice banquet up here in your room! Did you have a guest?" said Akobirov, looking round, and fixing the wardrobe with a particularly hard stare. "You're a sly one, you are, my young friend!"

"No, no, I was drinking by myself earlier. I had a headache. Do you want some?" said Farhod picking up the bottle of cognac.

"No, thanks, I don't want to drink now," Akobirov said and picked the packet of "Rodopi" cigarette up from the table.

"You've started smoking again?"

"Yes, my little brother. I can't give up. Well, I came here to say good bye to you. We're leaving tomorrow. I'll be back in about a fortnight. We'll solve your problem as soon as I get back, OK?"

(Little did he know where he would return to; no one in the world knew it then.)

"OK, we'll see," said Farhod impatiently.

"When are you going to Tashkent? Is your treatment over? What do your doctors say?"

"I need to stay here for several more days."

Actually, he could easily return home since his treatment was over. Besides, when he rang Tashkent from Sur'at's room the other day, his friend, who was a film director, told him his script had been approved for further production and that he should return as soon as possible. It was good news for him, but he was not sure everything would be OK if he did go back.

Some days ago he' had a big disappointment with Aunt "Karasho" at the Qi Gong Centre. Since she was busy with someone, allegedly some rich man, she asked another person to deal with Farhod. That 'another person' turned out to be an ugly, dirty man, whose thin beard should have been shaved long ago. He set about massaging Farhod's ear and head. His fingers were short and grimy, as if he had not washed them for three or four days. He looked like the centre's driver ... Farhod decided not to go again, ruefully regretting the time and money he had wasted; after all, he could pinch his ear and head himself. Zuhra could do it at home!

Akobirov stayed in Farhod's room for a long time, talking about everything under the sun. Finally he stood up, saying: "See you tomorrow for breakfast."

Farhod locked the door and rushed to the balcony.

Wrapped up in the sheet, Vika was shivering outside; it was a bit nippy outside.

"Honey..."

Farhod picked her up in his arms and quickly carried her into the room.

"That man really annoys me!" said the girl through chattering teeth.

"What about me?"

"You?" Vika put two glasses on the table, tossed the sheet aside and, stark naked, hugged Farhod. "You... you... you..."

In two months, in the cool of early October, this girl would come to Tashkent with her mother Gulya Lagutina for a film festival...

* *

One evening, when their colleagues had gone with Adham Delon to a kolkhoz once led by Adham's father, supposedly to meet the public but actually to enjoy freshly-picked, sun-ripened fruit, Farhod separated mother and daughter from the group and invited them to the "Blue Domes" café (it was the best café in the city in those days.)

The three of them had a good time there together. The other customers stared at them, not at Vika, at Victoria. The regulars in particular looked at them as if they were an enemy: what is a beautiful lady with the fragrance of Paris doing here with this swarthy, gypsy-like woman and our stingy guy? Surprised, Vika was sitting there, answering the people's greedy stares and invitations to dance with a smile.

Feeling jealous and rather tipsy, Farhod invited mother and daughter to visit him at home the next day. Vika tried to avoid his gaze and merely shrugged, not wanting to reveal their mutual secret, but her mother was delighted at the invitation:

"Thank you, thank you! We'll definitely come! With pleasure! Actually, I was hoping to meet your family. We'll see how our famous screenwriter lives. We'll go, won't we, Vika?" Without waiting for her daughter's answer she turned to Farhod again: "Can I bring my father with us, too? You should meet him, he's a physics teacher, a Candidate of Sciences, broad-minded..."

"Sure, no problem," said Farhod, somewhat surprised

Well, dear reader, we don't know the father, but Gulya Lagutina herself is a good woman. As usual, although she did not drink much (her daughter, on the other hand, sipped plenty of red wine), she really enjoyed herself, delighted by every trifle and praising the food the 'waitress' brought. In fact, she completely polished off the most delicious dish – pilaf with red carrots.

When Vika went to wash her hands, her mother quickly turned to Farhod, saying:

"I know you like this girl!"

Farhod was flustered, at a loss for words. She claims he likes her daughter! Actually he had fallen in love with her! She was sitting there because of that girl!

"Everyone likes beautiful girls..." said he, feeling rather embarrassed.

"But I hear she does not take this lightly, she likes you, too..."

What can you say?

Farhod already regretted inviting them to his house the next day. But, as a man, he had to keep his promise. And anyway, Gulya Lagutina was eager to meet his family. So there was no way out.

That day Farhod did a huge shop. What's more, although he usually never lifted a finger round the house, that day he helped his wife with the cleaning. His wife, Zuhra, was surprised: "What's happened to you, I wonder? It's just a film producer who's coming, but you are going quite crazy..." But Farhod kept quiet. Vika is coming to his house, Vika! What will she say about his household? Thoughts were racing in Farhod's head ...

Fortunately, his sister-in-law, who was living with them temporarily following a quarrel with her husband, helped his wife get ready for guest's arrival, cooking delicious food and preparing cookies. She was very hospitable while the guests were present, serving them with great pleasure, whereas Zuhra just sat chatting with them.

When he met the guests at the bus stop that evening, Farhod was taken aback to see a handsome man at Gulya's side. "Ilhom Sobirovich Mansurov," Gulya introduced him, stressing each syllable. "Candidate of Science in physics and mathematics, but a poet at heart." And so finally his old question was finally answered.

Yes, a copy of that Internationalist old man Sobir-jon Mansurov was standing in front of him! His hair was not yet white and he was a little thinner, but the only real difference was that this person was a little swarthy. A chance meeting! What a small world this is!

"Welcome, welcome," said Farhod but did not let on that he knew the man's father. He brightened up at the news that Vika had a headache and had stayed behind at her grandma's. "Ah, clever girl," thought Farhod. At least, she was cleverer than her mother!

Later, as they were sitting chatting together on the veranda, Gulya's father said that they were actually descendants of Prophet Muhammad and mentioned his father.

"Is your father alive now?" asked Farhod.

Ilhom Sobirovich recited a short prayer and said in pure Uzbek:

"He passed away a long time ago. May Allah be merciful to him!"

Farhod felt ashamed and, saddened by the news, also recited a short prayer, rubbing his hands to his face: "May Allah be merciful to him!"

Then he quickly asked a question, but instantly regretted his foolishness:

"Was his funeral held according to Uzbek traditions?"

"Of course! Since he was a Muslim, everything was done according to Muslim traditions," said Ilhom Sobirovich.

An Islamic funeral, a shroud… Interesting… People convert to Islam when they enter the grave! It means that in his heart he was afraid of Allah. Yes, he trusted in Allah!

"Why are you asking about our father? Did you know him?"

Then Farhod told them everything he knew.

"Well, that's great! It turns out we are from the same place!" Ilhom Sobirovich said. "I was born in Zarang, too. We might even be relatives!"

All of them were astonished by this news.

"In the bottom of my heart I was sure this could be the case," said Gulya, rubbing Farhod's shoulder like a relative. Then she turned to Zuhra and started to praise Farhod: "Everyone envies you because of your good husband. Very talented, very generous!"

Gulya's father was a sociable, eloquent person.

"Come and join us" he said to Zebo, who was helping serve the guests. But Zebo thanked him and hastened back to the kitchen.

The "secret" of this short Q&A will be revealed later. Our scholar really was a poet...

Two days later, when the noisy banquet in honour of the closing of the festival was drawing to an end, Gulya asked Farhod to take her and Vika to her mother's house: "We're leaving tomorrow, so we should say good-bye to her."

Her mother lived on Rustaveli Street, in a basement-like floor of one of the old houses. Though he did not want to leave Vika there, he had no choice. As he was on his way out, saying: "See you tomorrow," Gulya took his arm and insisted he came in with them.

"Please, come with us, Farhod, I'll introduce you to my mother. Lyusyana Fyodorovna is a real phenomenon. You'll see how clever she is. Vika, tell him to come with us."

Farhod followed them unwillingly. This place seemed very familiar to him. There should be a small stadium nearby. He remembered that as a student he had come here several times to play volleyball with the Russian girls who worked at the textile company. He also remembered how he used to come here to find the ball when it flew over the stadium wall.

Lyusyana Fyodorovna exceeded even Gulya's description. Not only was she completely round, but also – probably in an attempt to look younger – she was wearing tracksuit bottoms and a multicoloured sleeveless T-shirt (maybe a gift from

Gulya). Her hair was done up in hair clips. She was talkative, but it was hard to understand her words.

"Markos! Look, young people have come!" she shouted all of a sudden.

An old man in a sailor's T-shirt appeared at the entrance of a room without a door. He shook his head to the guests and went back to his cubicle.

Gulya solemnly introduced Farhod to her mother:

"The best Uzbek screenwriter, Farhod Ramazonov! He is my friend, and Vika's, too. By the way, he's also our relative. Our new relative!"

Lyusyana Fyodorovna applauded and held out her plump hand again.

"Nice to meet you! Very nice to meet you! Our relative, our new relative! What a gift!"

Farhod was mildly surprised by the way mother and daughter communicated with each other; they were both equally flustered. Did they say a new relative? How? What did they mean?

Earlier, Vika had taken one look at the mess in the house and, ashamed, had slowly wandered off somewhere, winking to Farhod.

It was hard to stay here for long. There was mess everywhere. Three or four cats were chasing each other. A bad smell pervaded the room. Farhod felt sorry. How can live they here? Why does this woman behave like an aristocrat? And what has it got to do with Vika? Will she be spending the night here today? What will she do in this grimy place among these untidy people? Is she really their grand-daughter?

As Farhod was about to make his escape, the hostess stopped him:

"No, no, we won't let you go. We have to celebrate our kinship. Markos has some good homemade wine. Markos! Markos!.."

Farhod shook her off with difficulty and went out. Gulya followed him to see him off.

"Farhod, I have some important news for you. Do you want me to tell you now? You won't believe, but Ilhom Sobirovich has fallen in love with your Zebo!"

At first Farhod couldn't take it in.

"But... Wasn't he married? Doesn't he have his wife?"

"No, he is single. He didn't remarry after he divorced Lyusyana Fyodorovna. He's capricious. But he will make Zebo happy!"

"Really? But Zebo has her own husband, didn't you know?"

"She is going to get a divorce."

"Who told you that?"

"I asked your wife Zuhra myself when we were at your place."

"Gracious me! I had no idea."

"Ilhom Sobirovich is going to marry her. What do you think? We would become relatives..."

"I'm sorry, Gulya Ilhomovna, I do not own Zebo, you should ask her," said Farhod indifferently as he got in his Zhiguli and drove off.

Farhod knew Zebo would never have started this. She was a very serious, self-controlled woman, and knew her worth.

It was while he was studying at the pedagogical institute that Farhod had met these two sisters (his wife Zuhra and Zebo) in one day; one was a "boring" historian, the other interested in foreign languages. They all went together to solve their problems. They were like three girlfriends. Farhod's treated them both alike. When the time came to choose one of them, Farhod chose the younger one, Zuhra, based on the advice of one of his brothers from his own village. But today, when something in their family life was not to his liking, Farhod would annoy Zuhra, saying: "I should have married Zebo after all."

Zebo's husband was an alcoholic and even though he had such a nice wife, he was having an affair with his neighbour who was a widow. One day Zebo caught them in their bedroom. "Couldn't you have done this job at the widow's house?" Farhod thought when he found out. Farhod said as much to his brother-in-law one day, who replied with a smile: "I wanted something different!"

(Three or four days later, when Zebo heard that someone was going to marry her, she was very upset with her sister, saying: "I didn't know your guest had any such intention!" and left their house.)

18. The official from Leninabad is going to arrange a banquet! All that was a joke! History and small personalities

"Dear fellow countrymen! The country is in danger!.."

At home he got up at around seven or eight, but since his arrival here twenty days ago, he could not sleep well and woke early. Jetlagged, he could not get used to the time here. Opening his eyes, he looked at the window and turned on the radio under his pillow. "Echo of Moscow" programs are broadcast non-stop, so he listened to the radio and slept again, only opening his eyes again at about nine o'clock.

"Dear fellow countrymen! The country is in danger!.."

He was surprised by this sudden statement. He was wide awake after listening to what followed the statement, but still he could not believe his ears: were the broadcasters playing tricks, airing anything they liked? The news was repeated again several minutes later and he jumped out of bed. It didn't seem to be a joke. It really was unexpected news. Because it was obvious that soon people like Plato Sokratovich would be the victors. From the beginning Farhod was not interested in the doctrine of the genius folk with or without moustaches nor did he meddle in any of the various disputes in Tashkent. But when he heard the statement he stopped in his tracks: it was true that there was mess everywhere and it was difficult to survive, so maybe that is why... (he hesitated).

When the news was repeated over and over, he quickly pulled his clothes on and went out.

Seeing a cleaner in the corridor, he stopped and asked her:

"Have you heard?"

"What should I hear?" asked the startled cleaner.

"They say Gorbachev has been overthrown. He's been detained."

Farhod was taken aback by the cleaner's reply:

"Serves him right! You reap what you sow!"

Farhod went out. The yard was very quiet. Could it be that no one else had heard the news? Or had he misheard?

Just then a short man appeared by the flower bed. It was the man from Leninabad taking his morning stroll and breath of fresh air.

Seeing Farhod standing by the stairs not knowing what to do, he stopped:

"Morning, Farhod-jon! Is your heart sick, too? Let's walk together!"

"Aren't you aware of the news?"

"What happened? What news?" the old man asked.

When Farhod told him what he had just heard, the former official exclaimed loudly:

"Really?! Is it really true? I'll arrange a banquet for you, my little brother! Has Gorbachev been detained? That's great news! That rascal was making my heart sick…"

As he kept asking the same question again and again, Farhod became irritated and said:

"Go and listen to the radio yourself."

The old man forgot about his morning promenade and hurried over to the new building.

It was strange that all these people here were against Gorbachev.

More interesting things happened during breakfast. Those who had sat at the same table yesterday had split into groups and now sat separately. There were two opposite groups and people were talking quietly. The kitchen was in mourning – everyone was speaking in a hushed whisper.

After breakfast, when they went out, they started speaking loudly and openly. Screenwriters, a brawny bunch, some of whom had put on caps with the 5-pointed star (some of them had even found rough boots), but all of whom were true supporters of the common people and indeed belonged to them, were standing on one side. Skinny people with striped jackets and spectacles were on the other side.

Those with military shoes were standing in the middle of the square, speaking loudly and celebrating the event; those with spectacles were scattered. Most of them were queuing for the only public telephone by the entrance hall to call their relatives to ask what had happened and why.

Those with military shoes were famous for their long films about life in the kolkhoz, descriptions of evening get-togethers, and folk songs. Those with spectacles were improving their creative activity producing incomprehensible, boring and enigmatic films. They didn't acknowledge the films produced by those with military shoes and criticized their work, calling it 'primitive and shallow.'

Until now, the fight between them had been carried out in secret, but today it was out in the open …

Farhod was observing these developments when Elmira Kamolova appeared in front of him. She was wearing a head-scarf and her eyes were full of tears.

"What shall we do now, Farhod? How can we go to Uzbekistan?"

Farhod didn't know the situation was so serious.

"If I only knew," said he sorrowfully.

It was strange that this woman had put on a headscarf, and it angered Farhod: "Is it a problem for her? If not Uzbekistan, she could go to Yerevan with her Chaldranyan[59]," he said to himself.

As if Ms. Kamolova sensed his thoughts, she pulled a strange face and went away. Not knowing which group to join, she had approached Farhod thinking that at least they were from the same country.

A minibus was spotted near the old building and those keen to get to the city jumped aboard. Farhod got in, too. What could he do out here? Better to go to the city and find out what had really happened. He could visit Sur'at, and maybe even meet up with Vika; he'd not seen her for two days.

Most of the minibus passengers were people with spectacles. They rode in silence, not speaking to each other. They all were hoping for better news. Farhod felt sorry for them, though he had not come to a conclusion himself. Then he became angry: why didn't you produce films that the common people could

---

59 Vigen Chaldranyan, Armenian film director and writer.

understand? Your weird films have become a problem for you now. Those friends of yours who could promote and praise your films are far away. They can't help you now.

The minibus was taking the same road Farhod had taken with Akushin in his pompous Mercedes yesterday. Akobirov was in China now, unaware of what's happening over here. What will he do when he comes back?

The rain that had started when they were at the recreation centre turned into a thunder storm. The road shone like a mirror in the darkness. The weather was bad; fog hung over the forest on both sides of the road. The traffic was heavy.

"Look, here they are!" someone said.

Yes, there they were: tanks, armored vehicles and other military vehicles were lining up along the road with young soldiers in military uniforms standing by. Their commanders were there, too, covered in their sack-like raincoats and smoking their cigarettes.

The situation seemed serious. The poor people with spectacles peered out at the military with frightened eyes. None of them uttered a word until they reached the city.

When they finally arrived, someone sitting in one of the front rows exclaimed:

"The show is over, gentlemen!"

Though he had no special cap or shoes, it was clear who that person was.

The Filmmakers' House was empty and quiet, as if a funeral were in progress. But Sur'at was in his office. He told Farhod that a colonel who came from "that office," Bobkov or Popkov, was rounding everyone up for a meeting.

"But your brother is busy having a good time in China!" he said enviously.

"Why aren't you attending the meeting?"

"There'll be another this afternoon," said Sur'at throwing the pen he was holding down onto the table. "I need to prepare a draft resolution."

"But you don't know what they'll be talking about at the meeting, how can you draft it?"

Sur'at looked at him as if he were a child, and showed him the front page of the Pravda Vostoka newspaper:

"Everything is written here in this article. So I can write a resolution based on this."

As Sur'at continued working on his draft, Farhod had an urge to call Vika using the telephone in that office, but he changed his mind. It was better if Sur'at was not aware of their relationship, otherwise he would pester Farhod with questions about her.

A skinny old woman with her glasses on her forehead appeared in the doorway:

"Is your draft ready, Sur'at Numonovich?"

"Yes, Gertruda Vasilyevna," said Sur'at, quickly taking the paper and standing up. "I hope Mitrofanov himself will be able to finish it."

When the old woman left, he gave a stretch in the middle of his office, fastened his belt and said to Farhod:

"Let's go! The world is becoming messy, but I'm drafting something. Let's go and walk around!"

They took the metro to Barrikadnaya station to see for themselves where 'doomsday' was taking place.

Leaving The White House behind, Sur'at took Farhod to the mayor's headquarters.

There were hundreds of tanks and armored vehicles there. Chaos reigned; no sign of military discipline. Soldiers sat around on the vehicles smoking cigarettes or eating ice-creams, their guns and caps laid aside.

An old woman with unkempt hair lost control and started to bang her bag against a tank:

"Go away! Go away! Get out of here!"

But the young soldier sitting on it paid no attention to her, licking his ice-cream.

An woman from the intelligentsia asked him:

"Hey, when will you start?"

The soldier shrugged his shoulders, tossing the ice-cream wrapper down.

The two women started to quarrel with each other.

Suddenly a snowstorm of papers came floating down from the windows of the mayor's headquarters. The crowd rushed to grab them. They were the administration's resolutions, decrees, regulations, etc. There was nothing interesting, just boring, useless words.

"Now they'll take him out! He'll be handcuffed and taken out soon," people started whispering to each other.

"Who ?" asked Farhod.

"The mayor!" replied Sur'at indifferently, saying the name of the famous democrat.

"Look! Look! Over here"

Everyone was burning with curiosity. Everyone rushed in that direction. But there was nothing to be seen there except the guards standing by the entrance.

Then other rumours came flying on the wind: "He ran away! Coward! A disgrace! He was right to flee. Do you think he should stay there and be fed to the dogs? Well done! Long live democracy!"

"See what they are doing?!" said Sur'at punching his friend's shoulder. "What's the situation like in Tashkent now?"

Farhod didn't think about that. He thought this commotion was only going on here and that Tashkent was peaceful. They are trying to do something for their democracy, what's that got to do with our Tashkent?

The situation in the square in front of the White House, the cradle of democracy, was a little different. It was quiet and orderly. Tanks and armored vehicles could not enter there, they were blocked by a large crowd and the square was ringed with various other vehicles; in short, it was well defended. Several trolleybuses had even been brought there just in case.

The spirit of the demonstrators, as well as their behaviour, was quite different here. The most committed, and the muscliest, were gathering at the square. Some of them, tired by the demonstrations which had taken place that morning, were asleep, their legs stretched out of car windows. Some of them were playing cards in small groups. There were folding beds and makeshift tables with cheese, sausages, hot tea and so on. Many people were leafing through newspapers, deep in discussion.

Yet Farhod somehow had the impression they were all there for appearance's sake only. Despite everything, there was an overriding sense or spirit of normal, everyday life. It looked as though they had not just shown up at the square that morning, but as though they had been living there for days, as if their only job was to sit there, leaving everything else behind.

Actually, all eyes were fixed on that great building made of white marble, on the podium-like balconies around it: when will Yeltsin appear and announce the victory of democracy?

The front of the building was barred up until the square; there was no one on the long stairs, only guards on either side, but there was no one at all in front of the big gates.

And soon, as expected, a tall, grey-haired man flanked by of a group of officials appeared on the balcony. But he was not that legendary Yeltsin, just an official who later became the Prime Minister.

His short speech was greeted with applause by the crowd in the square.

The meeting rounded off with cries of: "Yeltsin! Yeltsin! Democracy! Democracy!"

As they were leaving the square, Farhod saw Plato Sokratovich speaking loudly near a lorry. Catching sight of Farhod, he asked, "Hey, Ramzan, who are you supporting?" But he moved off without waiting for an answer.

The two friends went to the Georgian kebab café on 1905 Street and ordered beer. All of a sudden Sur'at's scowl changed to a smirk and he began teasing his friend:

"Well, Farhod, turns out your father named you Fidel for a special purpose. You may not be a revolutionist, but here you are participating in a revolution and making history, right? You'll become a historical figure now."

"Of course! I'm a historical figure twice over now! I was at Red Square when Rust's light aircraft landed there."

"Really? When was that?" Sur'at started to ask the details. "Why I didn't know that? You never told me about it before."

"It was when we were attending the courses. You'd gone to Valday or Vologda with your Lida. I popped into the Main Department Store to get some presents for my family before going back to Tashkent, and when I came out, there were police everywhere. Red Square was so crowded I couldn't get anywhere near, so admittedly I didn't see Rust and his tiny plane for myself – they'd already taken him off. But it's true, I was there."

"Strange that you're only telling me about it now. But tonight you'll see one more historical figure like yourself!"

"Who?"

"Gorbachev!"

"Gorbachev?! Are you kidding?"

"You'll see soon enough."

Sur'at went on to say that a young man, Odil-bek from Andijan, organized a banquet every month for fellow country-men, and that's where they had to be tonight.

"Tonight? But it's chaos here! Do you think it's fitting for us to have a get-together tonight?" asked Farhod, amazed.

"Well, how could he know about the riot? He planned the banquet ages ago. He even ordered everything from Andijan! Sheep tail fat, yellow carrots, etc. Riots are for the rest. You know Uzbeks cannot live without pilaf. But he's a good person. He has eight children, two of whom are from his Russian wife here, the rest are in Andijan.

"Did you really say Gorbachev? What will he be doing there? Isn't he under house arrest in Foros now?"

"You'll see soon enough!" said Sur'at, grinning. It was impos-sible to get anything more out of him after that, as usual.

Farhod was kept guessing for quite a while. When they left the square, he took a good look at the people on the streets. They were all busy with their everyday lives, blissfully unaware that anything was going on, or so it seemed. Take the people in this café for instance. None of them seem at all worried; quite the opposite, they are all just eating and drinking without a care in the world. Yet there was a riot and "doomsday" in the square.

It means that this revolution or putsch is the work of a group of people out to get something. The rest of the population just sit back and relax, wining and dining one another.

But Farhod couldn't shake the feeling that there was some-thing fake or forced about the demonstrations he had witness that day. As if they weren't serious, just a joke or a game. But look what his companion was saying: revolution, history, his-torical figure!

The banquet was held in a room at the Uzbekistan Restaurant. It looked like a teahouse, chaikhana, complete with a traditional Uzbek supa, silk quilts and cushions. There were around eight to ten Uzbeks there, most of whom worked in the capital. But there was a Russian man among them, too, who was born and raised in Tashkent. Farhod was surprised that, even though they all looked like Russians, they all spoke to each other in Uzbek, including the Russian man. The host, Odilbek, was a man of about forty, a jolly, rotund chap. From time to time he would rub his hands together gleefully, saying: "The pilaf will be made with the fat of a black ram, you'll cut the meat with a knife and help yourselves!" The pilaf was already about to be served at their table, so the host was relaxing and drinking vodka, giving advice to his female protégée serving the guests.

Seated in the place of honour was brother Mirkamol, a man of about fifty who had come from Tashkent on a business trip. He was a strong man and looked like an official..

"Where is Mikhail Sergeevich?" he asked. "Wasn't he going to meet us here? Or did he have a long, serious meeting?"

Just then the door opened and Gorbachev appeared! Yes, the man standing there really did look like Mikhail Sergeevich! Everyone in the room applauded:

"Look, he's come from Foros! He's been released!"

Farhod was astonished. The man was Gorbachev's double! His way of speaking, his gestures, his voice – they were all identical. Oh my! He knew he looked like Gorbachev so he had imitated him over the years, finally becoming exactly like him. The only difference was that he did not have that famous red birthmark on his forehead.

Farhod didn't like the welcome this interesting person received. People made fun of him and sat him at the farthest end of the table. "Gorbachev" himself did not pay attention to anything, he just began mingling and interacting with every-one, using words such as "consensus," "confrontation," and "pluralism."

According to the young man sitting next to Farhod, this man's name was Badriddin. He was originally from Tashkent, but he had studied here in the capital, married and stayed. He was a researcher at a scientific centre. That's all.

The pilaf was brought and everyone ate it with great delight, toasting one another. Then they started chatting. They chat-ted about everything but today's demonstrations. They talked about all the usual matters one might expect to discuss in a chaikhana.

At one point Farhod and the man sitting next to him went out to get a breath of fresh air. When they returned, the "con-sensus" around the table was over, and the "confrontation" had begun: Gorbachev was debating with brother Mirkamol.

The rebellion at the square moved to the chaikhana.

"Do you know what will happen if the gold and cotton pro-duced in Uzbekistan in just one year is left in the country? If that happens, every Uzbek would be rich, brother, every Uzbek would have a golden pisspot in his house!" "Gorbachev" was saying clearly, sounding for all the world like the real Gorbachev.

"Maybe then you would go back to Uzbekistan?" brother Mirkamol asked him sarcastically.

"Did I leave something there?"

"Or do you think we should bring that golden pisspot here for you?"

"Keep that pot for yourself! You don't have an ounce of national spirit in you!"

"Well, you have more than enough for all of us! You can export it from here to us. We're used to it... Look, why are you trying to look like other people? Be it Gorbachev or someone else…"

"You are a communist! A real communist!" "Gorbachev" shouted at him, losing control.

"Allah be praised, I'm a communist! And I'm proud of it! Are you jealous? Eat your heart out! Look what happened to those loud-mouths like you?"

And "Gorbachev" made a solemn prediction:

"We' shall see what happens to you soon enough!"

Farhod didn't see brother Mirkamol strike him with his fist, but he saw poor "Gorbachev" lying on the floor. The blood on his forehead looked like Gorbachev's birthmark. Ah, if only someone had a camera, they could show it to the world!

In fact, both Gorbachevs were in real trouble. One of them was here and the other one was imprisoned somewhere. O Merciful One, save us from communists!

The "banquet" of those fellow countrymen in the strange land came to an unhappy end, like the tale of the man who started a wedding while his neighbour was in mourning.

It was already turned midnight. Farhod unwillingly went to Shyolkovo with Sur'at, but, as always, he soon regretted it. Sur'at discovered a makeup mirror in his house and interrogated Farhod about who he had brought to his house last time, hinting that he had given his key to Farhod several times… Of course, Farhod did not tell him anything. How could he?

He could not share this with anyone else…

On his way to the recreation centre the next day, he saw another demonstration there. The people with boots, now drunk were shouting loudly in the square, those with spectacles were quiet, some of them were hanging around the telephone booth, others were walking through the trees, small radios held to their ears. Many of them were not even seen at the dinner table.

Those with boots celebrated their victory till midnight.

Two days later the situation changed. Those with spectacles who seemed to have forgotten how to speak over the past days started to chat and congratulate one another. Arm in arm, they did not want to step out of the hall into the film room.

Some of those with boots disappeared. No, in fact, not the people, but their boots and caps with five-pointed stars disappeared.

Farhod saw the man from Leninabad at lunch that day and asked him when they could cook pilaf, but he just walked past, saying: "I have heart pain."

Two days later, Farhod returned to Tashkent. With Elmira Kamolova. On the same plane, sitting together. Her Bobur or Babyor slept. The two colleagues chatted throughout the flight. She was a good woman. She was, in fact, a totally different woman from the one in Farhod's mind. In particular, her Uzbek was sweet. But when they talked about her husband she just ignored him, saying: "Don't mention that alcoholic."

Several days after the film festival later that year, Farhod saw her at the Master's funeral, which was held at the Filmmakers' House. She was so beautifully dressed, except for her head-scarf. When she saw Farhod she waved to him from afar.

Even after so many years they still maintained a good, friendly relationship with one another. She wrote an article about a film related to Farhod, praising the scenario. They attended film festivals in Baku and Dushanbe together.

But every time Farhod saw her he wanted to ask her about Chaldratyan: where is he now? what has he been doing? do they exchange letters?

And each time he sees her, it brings back memories of those years of sufferings: cruel Akobirov; and his Vika, Vika, Victoria…

19. Merciless revenge. An official who cannot move without permission

… That incident was widely discussed among his colleagues in the film industry. Rumours were flying that the young screenwriter Farhod Ramazonov beat the famous film director Ravshan Akobirov. Farhod? His teacher? O Merciful One! Is that true? How could a skinny young man like that beat an ox like Akobirov? And why? What was the row about? Farhod had too much alcohol and hit him… and so it went on.

Allah is witness that you did not have any alcohol then. True, you were furious after that telephone conversation, but you had no alcohol. It would have been better if you'd gone home after work. But you couldn't. You felt you would die if you went home. A screenwriter, overjoyed because his script had been approved, insisted you stay and did not let you go.

You were at the Festival restaurant. You did not expect to see Akobirov, but there he was, sitting with a famous member of BosmachFilm, Tal'at Raf'ilullin, better known as 'Apostrophe.' Apparently, he was talking about his life in the great capital, about how he was given authority, owned it and but they did not let him leave his position. You were sure that he saw you, too, but he pretended he hadn't, turning his face away.

You stopped listening to your companion's words, just smoked your cigarette and stared straight ahead. You were afraid and too ashamed to look in their direction. You were all on fire.

Suddenly you stood up and strode purposefully over to their table.

Mr. Akobirov was busy chatting and did not see you coming. But Raf'ilullin opened his arms wide in greeting, saying: "Ah, dear Farhod, my talented young man!" Even then Akobirov merely glanced at you coldly and turned to his companion without a word.

You stood in front of them for a while wondering what to do; is there any way out of that disgraceful situation?

Yes, there is!

The strong man was felled by a single, unexpected blow. Lying there on the floor, he wiped his mouth and then grinned mockingly.

Panic-stricken, Raf'ilullin tried to stop you: "What are you doing? Have you gone mad, Farhod? Hooligan!"

Seeing several people from other tables were gathering round (after all, it was a serious matter, a young man was beating the Chairman of Filmmakers of the great country!) you just shouted "Bastard!" and left the restaurant.

But only two people knew the reason behind this row: you and the official lying on the floor.

No, there was one more person... !

It's true that you had heard from Adham Delon that he saw Akobirov with "Gulya's daughter" in a dimly-lit café. Had it been anyone else, you would not have paid any attention, but you knew only too well what kind of person Akobirov is.

"You can congratulate me, I've got a part in a film!" Vika announced solemnly over the phone in her clear, tinkling voice. "Can you believe it, it's a film by Sokurov! Yes, yes, Akobirov arranged it for me. Hey, what's up?"

"And what happened after that?" you asked her angrily.

"After that... why are you shouting at me?"

"What happened after that, tell me?!"

"What could happen, you know. He wouldn't let me go... You and I can't be together, anyway, you know. You should understand: you are there and I am here..."

"But I love you!"

"Do you think I don't love you?! But what can I do?"

"Vika, tell me the truth, did you spend a night with him?"

"Don't shout at me! Do you have to know everything?"

"Fuck you!" you cried in Uzbek, as if you were Othello. The telephone receiver was good; it didn't break after you banged it down so viciously. It was a phone belonging to the state...

Mr. Akobirov did not file any complaints. Had he wanted, he could have sent you far from Tashkent, and far from the film industry, too. But for some reason he didn't. Not long afterwards you heard he had moved to the great capital.

Now 'Apostrophe' simply ignored you whenever you met. He would have used you to play a guerilla soldier in days gone by!

You grew so skinny then. You did not want to eat. You felt you could not breathe, as if you were about to die soon. There was a constant wailing inside you. Your heart was weeping and mourning. You could not sleep well. You were so unhappy that no one in this world could comfort you. You did not care about your wife and children. Zuhra pretended she did not know anything about your sufferings. Poor woman!

Back then, whenever you heard the song "Maestro," you cried bitter tears.

You had hospital treatment. You had a disease called Vika, Vika, Victoria, Dildoriya, Dildor...You were pining away!

Do you remember how you became friends with Shaikh San'on in those crazy days? Awake or asleep, you always thought about the legend of that old man, who lived a thousand years ago and troubled the Muslim world by falling in love with a beautiful girl who was not a Muslim. You thought about Shaikh San'on's love affairs, about his sufferings, and you became like him.

You first heard his name from a writer whom you rarely met but who became very dear to you. One day the two of you went to a popular kebab café in Chighatay. You sat there longer than usual, eating and drinking. And you shared your own story with him. "Hey, you have become Shaikh San'on," said the writer, after listening to your story attentively. "It's not unusual for young people to lose their head when they hit thirty. Do you think I was any different? But please don't worry, be patient, and everything will be fine."

"I don't know," you said, feeling more hopeless than ever. You did not really want to forget about everything: "How could I go on living afterwards?" you asked yourself.

"You'll forget about it, you'll see," the writer had said, and went on to tell you the story of Shaikh San'on. You were so interested in the story that later you found everything you could about that Majnun and read it avidly.

"The Insurgency of Love" was written after that.

* *

"… A grand shrine for idols. Around it priests and idol worshippers line up proudly. There are many idlers, too.

A beautiful girl, an idol worshipper, comes down the long domed cavern. She takes her place next to an old man with a grey beard, in a white turban and a white tunic, leaning on a cane.

The crowd looks at them.

The girl takes a sip of wine and passes a full goblet to the old man:

"Take it, please, and drink every last drop, oh foreigner! Know that your wish cannot be granted if so much as a drop is left."

The old man takes the goblet and raises it to his lips... Here, the first sip...

The wine runs down the grey beard, tears run down from the dim eyes..."

"A wide courtyard in front of the shrine for idols. A fire burns, carrying the hellfire to the skies.

All around the same crowd, the same mocking faces.

The old man shivers, looking at the fire and clasping the Koran to his bosom.

"Hurry up, old man! Throw it in the flames! Throw it!"

A beautiful face appears at the high window of the shrine for idols. That same idol worshiper!

The pitiful old man looks up with his dim, dull eyes and murmurs:

"O Merciful One, please forgive your sinful slave!.."

"Hurry up! Hurry up! Throw it in now, throw it now!"

The sacred book is tossed into the fire... Then, one after another – the white turban, the white tunic, the cane made of maple...

The crowd applauds loudly, music floats through the windows of the shrine..."

"A small room like a cage. The man gazing at the ceilings in the middle of the room, begging for something, is no long recognizable. He now looks completely different. His moustache and beard are cut, a Christian hat is on his head.

'The new man,' going berserk, takes the rope from his waist and throws it into the corner.

As soon as he does so, he sees the fiery look of the girl, the beautiful idol worshiper...

Then he takes the rope and binds it around his waist four times..."

"An endless wilderness. The Shaikh, carrying the half dead idol worshiper in his arms, stumbles towards the horizon. His disciples are following him...

The Shaikh slowly puts his beloved down in the high sand dunes and raises his hands to the skies, wailing:

"Oh Allah, is it my lot to be given so many arduous trials?"

All of a sudden a voice comes down from the skies:

"My slave, you should be grateful for what you have been given; no one else in this world could have it."

The old man, the lover, falls on top of his young beloved. She is dead..."

* *

All the members of the creative council, both good and bad, praised the scenario, but the subject matter was neither modern nor topical.

Later you published it in a magazine. Who knows whether anyone read it or not.

Several years ago, Adham Delon brought good news from the old capital, namely that the ever kind and helpful Gulya Lagutina was interested in your scenario and had sent it to Hollywood via her friend Valerka. "Valerka is an effeminate guy, isn't he?" you asked him. "I don't know, but according to Gulya, he's one of the big bosses in television," he replied.

After that you didn't know what happened to "The Insurgency of Love". Now they are talking differently about it. You never know who to believe in this world.

Well, it was true that you wrote that scenario from the depths of your heart when you were fascinated by Shaikh San'on. Tell me truthfully now: if fate commanded, would you also tie the belt around your waist and feed swine?..

Forget it! Don't mention it now, my friend.

Actually, was it important to relive all those stories from the past?

Yes, it was. You are obliged to recollect them now. "I don't remember you, but you are always in my mind." Perhaps the poet who wrote these lines did not call anything to mind, or maybe he just wrote the lines for the rhyme. But sometimes you thought about what happened in the past. It's true that now you are a different person (it was your dream to be different!), but is it possible to simply rip out the pages of the past years? Is it necessary? If so, then what will be left of your short life?..

Sometimes you feel as though you are living through provisional times, a kind of draft of your life. You feel that everything in your surroundings is but a pale reflection, as though you will see everything again in your other, real, life. But the fact is that what you have now is unrepeatable, and this is all you have, and it is called your life, that's it! It is impossible to pass through your life as you wish, as you dream, clean and pure. Sometimes you face whirlpools and suddy water, and you will be forced to forge them rather than circumnavigate them. So it is important that you emerge from the mud as unsullied as possible. But it is not easy; in many cases it is impossible to rid yourself of the past.

It helps to look at fate directly and courageously. Take a long, hard look at fate. Look it in the eye. Life is good for the good, and life makes friends with the good.

Mankind's thoughts, deeds and works somehow affect his fate. For example, why did you write about Shaikh San'on, not someone else? Because there is something similar in your fate. Would you be able to write love stories or about love affairs had you not fallen in love yourself? What place is left for the old lover with his theological inspirations who lived a thousand years ago? Where is your own place? But there is a thin cord that unites you both. It is defiance in the face of the forces trying to separate two loving hearts. And it is obvious who the winner in this fight was. It is Shaikh San'on, Sahikh San'on...

Who are you? Who were you? A man of arts who today holds an influential position was as naïve as any man back then, simple-hearted and famous for his talent, but without a penny in his pocket, a little impatient and with many an axe to grind. Now, it seems your life is about to finish, your good and bad deeds will be separated. When you were young, you woke early and happy in the morning – miracles could happen. And they could happen today! you thought. But now you open your eyes in trouble: which part of my body will ache today? Does the passing of youth mean the passing of joys and hopes? From now on, it is all too obvious which direction your life is taking. Yes, every day a light will turn off in your heart and the number of lights will decrease, decrease, decrease...

Here, the world has become restless, overthrown. Coldness, losing your way, oblivion, various worldly pleasures, wailing, diseases, etc. As your writer friend said: everything will pass. So everything passed.

It's true that you wanted to see her so badly, or at least to speak over the phone. But how can you find her now, since your notebook was long since torn up? Where will you go? Whom will you ask? By the way, the messy house on Rustaveli Street, the chattering woman pretending to be young and intelligent, and the old Greek wearing a sailor's T-shirt – are they alive now? Or did they move to another place together with their relatives? Look, even our Zebo, our own Zebo, left. She refused to marry either physics or lyrics, and was upset with you for a long time, heaven knows why. Later she was hired by a foreign radio station and went to London. She married an Arab and is happy with her life now. From time to time she sends packets of foreign tea to her sister. Sometimes when you suggest to your wife: "Let's have a cup of Zebo's tea" she looks at your angrily. Ah, who can understand women. So what if I want to drink Zebo's tea? She's my sister-in-law and Zuhra's sister, isn't she?

Ravshan Akobirov did not stay in one place for long, either. In a year or so he was replaced by Gleb Akushin and he and his wife left for Canada where his daughter lived. They say that his daughter studied with a Canadian lad at the Patrice Lumumba University and married him. They are very rich people. Later, Akobirov left the artistic designer with her daughter and went to Los Angeles with a Jewish woman. Some said he was going to produce a film based on Fellini's scenario about Uzbekistan, or based on a book by an Uzbek journalist whose father was Uzbek. Who knows, Allah alone knows everything. But several years later he came back to live in the old capital

Strange, as he lay on the floor that day, why did he just grin up at me? Was he embarrassed about what he'd done, or did he mean he was victorious? The latter, as it turns out. Everything is clear now.

Remembering the last lines of Akobirov's letter, you felt sad, tears even came to your eyes: "Are you still upset with me? Forget it! Everything has passed. You know I am a poor, helpless wanderer, so why are you upset with me, my little brother?"

What a pity he lived his life for nothing.

By the way, his son now lives in Tashkent and works in tele-communications. They say he is a big boss there. But you've never seen him. Well, talk about what you have seen and what you do know. Talk about how you met that communist brother Mirkomil at a funeral. He had a big turban on his head and was wearing a long white tunic, so he turned into a good mullah after all. He was a good preacher, though. Well, he'd had plenty of experience of public speaking, using his fist. But those strong fists are still tucked up inside his long sleeves, always ready for any kind of incident or dispute. By the way, what happened to Gorbachev's double, the one who was beaten by this communist mullah? Is he alive now? Or was he beaten again and again until he passed away? Since Gorbachev is alive, his shadow must be alive somewhere in this world, too!

Now please talk about yourself. You are among the common people, but better than the common people. You have a luxurious car for official use and have many employees ready to fulfill your every command, with beard and without, with complaints and without. You have a good family and all anyone would need for a good life. Your work is going well. Your three daughters are happily married. No, don't tell lies; one of your daughters came back home, divorced. What can you do if that is her fate?

What else? Go on, please. So, where are you going now? What is your purpose? Who gave you your permit?

We know that you asked permission from the official at the higher level body. That higher level official's nickname was "Brother Khosxona," and from time to time he used to come to your office to sit on the soft sofa and enjoy a good lunch. He would annoy you by asking for a car, saying: "Your sister-in-law wants to go to the Hippodrome bazaar," or: "Our elder daughter wants to see her sister-in-law," etc. But this time he did not want to let you go, saying: "The festival is for young, professional actors, what will you do there, brother?"

"I am the head of those young actors," you said, trying to find common ground. The final answer was: "Your trip is found inexpedient, brother, please don't be upset."

"What do you mean, inexpedient?" you asked.

"What, are you a young child?"

"Actually I'm not going to a festival or any other event. I have other family matters to resolve. Will you grant me permission for that?" At the other end of the line, someone hung up.

* *

The noise of the plane changed. It flew easily. It is probably about to land.

What's this! Who is standing beside you?

It was Bakhtiyor. He was looking at you, smiling. Apparently he was going to ask you something, or maybe he was already asking something. Just a minute... You rub your ear with your hands. Now, what do you want?

"What?"

"You studied here, right, Farhod Mirzaevich? I was telling my friends, but they don't believe me..."

"I..." you start, but you cannot speak, as if something is stuck in your throat. You can only look at him smiling.

What could you tell them, my friend?..

20. The city of distant recollections. Hello, Farhod, son of Farhod!

He looked through the plane window and adjusted the device in his ear. The din in his ear turned into the moderate din of the landing plane and the passengers.

The plane left the bosom of white clouds and began to land, flying over green forests for some time.

Instead of some technical novelties, the screen at the front of the plane now shows a sky map with the plane about to land, accompanied by slow music. Some impatient passengers were already taking their luggage from the lockers above, and girls were flocking round Bakhtiyor for an autograph. Well done, my little brother!

The leader let his colleagues pass first and disembarked after them.

All of a sudden the din of the world stopped and he started hearing a mighty chant: "Bismillahir rohmanir rohim…"

As he was walking along the never-ending corridor which took them to the arrivals hall, he was surprised to find himself completely at peace. Where is the pounding heart? The rush of excitement? Oh my, everything has stopped, everything has passed. Everyone must meet their destiny. You are obliged to confess everything.

He immediately recognized the woman waiting for him, waving to him in the arrivals hall. Ah, she was even more beautiful than before!

Victoria approached him and hugged him tightly, without any reservation. She began kissing him everywhere, as if she were kissing a child, making his face and eyes red. Then she quickly took a handkerchief from her bag and tidied the "traces of her own crime."

"Oh, I forgot to kiss your nose!" said she and turned him into Father Christmas, with a red lipstick nose. "You haven't changed a bit. Your hair has gone a bit grey, but it suits you!"

"And you, you are even more beautiful! I'm amazed!"

"Well, I tried to beautify myself for you, so you won't run away like you did first time. Remember?"

Farhod felt uncomfortable.

"Where is he?" he asked.

"Who? Ravshan? He's waiting for us in his new Audi in the car park. He might be a bit shy, you know."

"No. I'm asking about the boy."

"Ah, he's over there," Victoria pointed, calling as she did so: "Farhod Farhodovich Ramazonov! One hundred and twenty-five percent Uzbek! Come here, come on!"

A teenager was standing ten paces away, leaning on an iron railing. He was looking at Farhod, frowning. His gaze was sharp.

"Hah! He doesn't even want to move! Well, he has the blood of Mirzo Ramazon, so he is like his father, very conceited!"

Farhod Ramazon strode over, handing his jacket to Victoria.

There was no way back. And anyway, he had nothing to be frightened of.

Glossary

Komsomol – a well-known abbreviation for Kommunisticheskii Soyuz Molodyozhi, or Communist Union of Youth. This was the youth division of the Communist Party of the Soviet Union (CPSU) for 14-28 year-olds. Membership was all but obligatory, and non-members often found many doors closed to them, both in terms of education and career choices. The Komsomol was also a vigorous tool for spreading the Communist teachings and preparing young people for future Communist Party membership.

Perestroika – literally 'restructuring,' the economic, social and political reforms introduced by Mikhail Gorbachev in the late 1980's. Combined with the policy of glasnost ('openness'), the introduction of these reforms exacerbated already existing political, social and economic tensions within the Soviet Union and played a major role in furthering nationalism in the constituent republics, ultimately contributing to the dissolution of the Soviet Union.

The years leading up to and following the collapse of the Soviet Union was a period of great social turmoil as old social, economic and political structures crumbled almost overnight, and people scrambled to make sense of the new world around them. Inflation was rampant, and many found their livelihoods axed, particularly those working in the fields of arts, education or indeed almost any field pertaining to the intelligentsia.

Communal flat – accommodation was a major issue in the Soviet Union, with decent housing in short supply in all the constituent republics. One solution to this was the communal flat, the conversion of a previously privately-owned residence into a series of apartments with one or more rooms, with all residents sharing a common kitchen, bathroom and hallway. Inevitable, tensions ran high.

Another solution was the provision of accommodation by the workplace. This, however, was not always readily available.

Many people sought to get around this situation by arranging marriages of convenience, as precedence was often given to newly-weds and young families when allocating accommodation.

With the new privatization laws coming into force in the early to mid-nineties, the situation changed, and, particularly in Uzbekistan, it became possible for individuals to own, build and even rent out personal property. This in turn led to new social divisions based on wealth rather than class.

Kolkhoz – collective farm. These were state-owned agricultural enterprises, initially consisting of around 75 households in the 30's to around 340 households by 1960. The kolkhoz leaders or chairmen were nominally elected by their workers, and wielded considerable power. Surplus produce was sold at official kolkhoz markets. Most collective farms were forcibly privatized in the 1990's with varying degrees of success.

The Great Land – (russ: velikaya strana). This is one of the many terms used to refer to Russia and/or the Soviet Union. Other terms used by A'zam include: the great motherland; the endless country; the big Union. All these names reflect a sense of grandeur, yet also of alienation as the Soviet Union's constituent republics sought to come to terms with being part of a wider ideological union.

Soviet Hero/The Plan – this refers to the Five-Year Plan which formed the pivot of Soviet economic policy. 'Overfulfilling the plan' was seen as a feat of great heroism, the mark of a true Soviet Hero. Thus both individuals as well as factories, kolkhozy etc all strived to at least meet but preferably go beyond the quotas set out for them in the plan.

Supa – a sitting place or low platform usually made of clay or wood and covered with cushions or mattresses. They may be placed indoors or outdoors in a shady arbor, in both private homes and teahouses. Like the chaikhana teahouses themselves, supa play a central role in Uzbek social life.

Chaikhana – teahouse. These provide a traditional place to meet, eat and discuss. They may be commercial, similar to a coffee shop or café, or private, a focal point for the local community. Traditionally, only men frequent the chaikhanas.

aksakal – an elder or respected leader of the local community.

Pilaf – traditional dish made from rice, meat and red or yellow carrots. When abroad, this is the dish Uzbeks miss most, and it is considered a sign of respect and friendship if an Uzbek makes pilaf for you. Both men and women are adept at preparing this delicious meal.

Filmmakers' Union – one of the many state-run trade unions. Virtually all workers in any profession joined their respective union, although for writers, filmmakers and the like, political correctness was a fundamental prerequisite. Union members had access to the union's facilities which could include resorts on the Black Sea, sanatoriums in the forest, and summer camps for members' children as well as guest houses and meeting places in most cities throughout the Soviet Union. The latter not only provided low-cost accommodation but also acted as an important arena for discussions, formal meetings, the exchange of ideas and so on.

Nikah – Islamic marriage contract or ceremony. Uzbeks are Muslims and practise Sunni Islam. Marriage and family are considered sacred values, with the extended family also playing an important role.

Internationalism/internationalist – very briefly, this refers to the international communist movement based on the idea of a union of the proletariat which transcends national boundaries. For internationalists, communist ideals override not only religion, but also social traditions and even language. Lenin, however, favoured a policy of national self-determination, under which republics such as Uzbekistan were encouraged to keep their national identity, and this lent support to national filmmakers and writers depicting social realism against the backdrop of their own particular republic. This in turn led to discussions on the role of national identity in art, the importance of producing films in, say, Uzbek versus Russian, and the importance of being 'a fellow countryman.'

A word on names Uzbeks, like Russians, are fond of nicknames and suffixes are often added as a sign of endearment. For example, -opa, -ochka, -khon, -boy, -jon all denote respect or endearment as in Farhod-jon, Valya-khon, Ramazon-boy, etc.

Uzbek names were often adapted by Russians, so for instance the original Uzbek Farhod Ramazon becomes Farkhad Ramazonov.

About the author

Erkin A'zam, a brilliant contemporary writer, playwright and screenwriter, is truly one of the most proficient and influential Uzbek authors of our time. Born in 1950 in the mountainous Baysun District of Uzbekistan, Erkin A'zam studied journalism at Tashkent State University before going on to work for national radio, *Guliston* and *Yoshlik* magazines, and the G'afur G'ulom Publishing House. He later joined the Uzbekistan National Information Agency as First Deputy Director. Since 1994, he has been working as Editor-in-Chief for the highly acclaimed *Tafakkur* magazine, a periodical covering social and literary issues.

Erkin A'zam has published over ten books, his plays have been widely staged at national theatres, and films based on his scripts have received awards at both local and international film festivals.

HERTFORDSHIRE PRESS

Title List

Igor Savitsky:
Artist, Collector, Museum Founder
by Marinika Babanazarova (2011)

Since the early 2000s, Igor Savitsky's life and accomplishments have earned increasing international recognition. He and the museum he founded in Nukus, the capital of Karakalpakstan in the far northwest of Uzbekistan. Marinika Babanazarova's memoir is based on her 1990 graduate dissertation at the Tashkent Theatre and Art Institute. It draws upon correspondence, official records, and other documents about the Savitsky family that have become available during the last few years, as well as the recollections of a wide range of people who knew Igor Savitsky personally.

Игорь Савитский: художник, собиратель, основатель музея

С начала 2000-х годов, жизнь и достижения Игоря Савицкого получили широкое признание во всем мире. Он и его музей, основанный в Нукусе, столице Каракалпакстана, стали предметом многочисленных статей в мировых газетах и журналах, таких как TheGuardian и NewYorkTimes, телевизионных программ в Австралии, Германии и Японии. Книга издана на русском, английском и французском языках.

Igor Savitski: Peintre, collectionneur, fondateur du Musée (French), (2012)

Le mémoire de Mme Babanazarova, basé sur sa thèse de 1990 à l'Institut de Théâtre et D'art de Tachkent, s'appuie sur la correspondance, les dossiers officiels et d'autres documents d'Igor Savitsky et de sa famille, qui sont devenus disponibles dernièrement, ainsi que sur les souvenirs de nombreuses personnes ayant connu Savistky personellement, ainsi que sur sa propre expérience de travail a ses cotés, en tant que successeur designé. son nom a titre posthume.

LANGUAGE: **ENG, RUS, FR**   ISBN: **978-0955754999**   RRP: **£10.00**
AVAILABLE ON **KINDLE**

Savitsky Collection Selected Masterpieces.
Poster set of 8 posters (2014)

Limited edition of prints from the world-renowned Museum of Igor Savitsky in Nukus, Uzbekistan. The set includs nine of the most famous works from the Savitsky collection wrapped in a colourful envelope. Selected Masterpieces of the Savitsky Collection.

[Cover] BullVasily Lysenko 1. Oriental Café Aleksei Isupov 2. Rendezvous Sergei Luppov 3. By the Sea. Marie-LouiseKliment Red'ko 4. Apocalypse Aleksei Rybnikov 5. Rain Irina Shtange 6. Purple Autumn Ural Tansykbayaev 7. To the Train Viktor Ufimtsev 8. Brigade to the fields Alexander Volkov This museum, also known as the Nukus Museum or the Savitsky

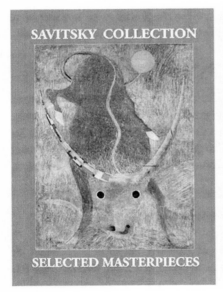

ISBN: **9780992787387**
RRP: **£25.00**

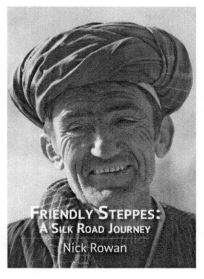

Friendly Steppes. A Silk Road Journey
by Nick Rowan

This is the chronicle of an extraordinary adventure that led Nick Rowan to some of the world's most incredible and hidden places. Intertwined with the magic of 2,000 years of Silk Road history, he recounts his experiences coupled with a remarkable realisation of just what an impact this trade route has had on our society as we know it today. Containing colourful stories, beautiful photography and vivid characters, and wrapped in the local myths and legends told by the people Nick met and who live along the route, this is both a travelogue and an education of a part of the world that has remained hidden for hundreds of years.

HARD BACK ISBN: **978-0-9927873-4-9**
PAPERBACK ISBN: **978-0-9557549-4-4**
RRP: **£14.95**
AVAILABLE ON **KINDLE**

Birds of Uzbeksitan
by Nedosekov (2012)

FIRST AND ONLY PHOTOALBUM
OF UZBEKISTAN BIRDS!

This book, which provides an introduction to the birdlife of Uzbekistan, is a welcome addition to the tools available to those working to conserve the natural heritage of the country. In addition to being the first photographic guide to the birds of Uzbekistan, the book is unique in only using photographs taken within the country. The compilers are to be congratulated on preparing an attractive and accessible work which hopefully will encourage more people to discover the rich birdlife of the country and want to protect it for future generations

HARD BACK
ISBN: **978-0-955754913**
RRP: **£25.00**

Pool of Stars
by Olesya Petrova, Askar Urmanov,
English Edition (2007)

It is the first publication of a young writer Olesya Petrova, a talented and creative person. Fairy-tale characters dwell on this book's pages. Lovely illustrations make this book even more interesting to kids, thanks to a remarkable artist Askar Urmanov. We hope that our young readers will be very happy with such a gift. It's a book that everyone will appreciate. For the young, innocent ones - it's a good source of lessons they'll need in life. For the not-so-young but young at heart, it's a great book to remind us that life is so much more than work.

ISBN: **978-0955754906** **ENGLISH** AVAILABLE ON **KINDLE**

«Звёздная лужица»

Первая книга для детей, изданная британским издательством Hertfordshire Press. Это также первая публикация молодой талантливой писательницы Олеси Петровой. Сказочные персонажи живут на страницах этой книги. Прекрасные иллюстрации делают книгу еще более интересной и красочной для детей, благодаря замечательному художнику Аскару Урманову. Вместе Аскар и Олеся составляют удивительный творческий тандем, который привнес жизнь в эту маленькую книгу

ISBN: **978-0955754906** **RUSSIAN**
RRP: **£4.95**

Buyuk Temurhon (Tamerlane)
by C. Marlowe, Uzbek Edition (2010)

Hertfordshire based publisher Silk Road Media, run by Marat Akhmedjanov, and the BBC Uzbek Service have published one of Christopher Marlowe's famous plays, Tamburlaine the Great, translated into the Uzbek language. It is the first of Christopher Marlowe's plays to be translated into Uzbek, which is Tamburlaine's native language. Translated by Hamid Ismailov, the current BBC World Service Writer-in-Residence, this new publication seeks to introduce English classics to Uzbek readers worldwide.

PAPERBACK
ISBN: **9780955754982**
RRP: **£10.00**
AVAILABLE ON **KINDLE**

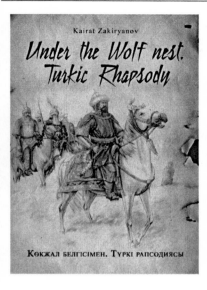

Under Wolf's Nest
by KairatZakiryanov
English –Kazakh edition

Were the origins of Islam, Christianity and the legend of King Arthur all influenced by steppe nomads from Kazakhstan? Ranging through thousands of years of history, and drawing on sources from Herodotus through to contemporary Kazakh and Russian research, the crucial role in the creation of modern civilisation played by the Turkic people is revealed in this detailed yet highly accessible work. Professor Kairat Zakiryanov, President of the Kazakh Academy of Sport and Tourism, explains how generations of steppe nomads, including Genghis Khan, have helped shape the language, culture and populations of Asia, Europe, the Middle East and America through migrations taking place over millennia.

HARD BACK
ISBN: **9780957480728**
RRP: **£17.50**
AVAILABLE ON **KINDLE**

384

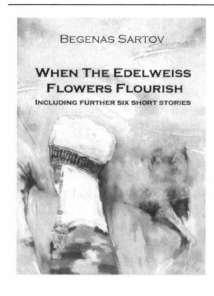

When Edelweiss flowers flourish
by Begenas Saratov
English edition (2012)

A spectacular insight into life in the Soviet Union in the late 1960's made all the more intriguing by its setting within the Sovet Republic of Kyrgyzstan. The story explores Soviet life, traditional Kyrgyz life and life on planet Earth through a Science Fiction story based around an alien nations plundering of the planet for life giving herbs. The author reveals far sighted thoughts and concerns for conservation, management of natural resources and dialogue to achieve peace yet at the same time shows extraordinary foresight with ideas for future technologies and the progress of science. The whole style of the writing gives a fascinating insight into the many facets of life in a highly civilised yet rarely known part of the world.

ISBN: **978-0955754951**   **PAPERBACK**   AVAILABLE ON **KINDLE**

Mamyry gyldogon maalda

Это фантастический рассказ, повествующий о советской жизни, жизни кыргызского народа и о жизни на планете в целом. Автор рассказывает об инопланетных народах, которые пришли на нашу планету, чтобы разграбить ее. Автор раскрывает дальновидность мысли о сохранение и рациональном использовании природных ресурсов, а также диалога для достижения мира и в то же время показывает необычайную дальновидность с идеями для будущих технологий и прогресса науки. Книга также издана на **кыргызском языке**.

ISBN: **97809555754951**
RRP: **£12.95**

Tales from Bush House
(BBC Wolrd Service)
by Hamid Ismailov
(2012)

Tales From Bush House is a collection of short narratives about working lives, mostly real and comic, sometimes poignant or apocryphal, gifted to the editors by former and current BBC World Service employees. They are tales from inside Bush House - the home of the World Service since 1941 - escaping through its marble-clad walls at a time when its staff begin their departure to new premises in Portland Place. In July 2012, the grand doors of this imposing building will close on a vibrant chapter in the history of Britain's most cosmopolitan organisation. So this is a timely book.

PAPERBACK
ISBN: **9780955754975**
RRP: **£12.95**
AVAILABLE ON **KINDLE**

Chants of Dark Fire
(Песни темного огня)
by Zhulduz Baizakova
Russian edition (2012)

This contemporary work of poetry contains the deep and inspirational rhythms of the ancient Steppe. It combines the nomad, modern, postmodern influences in Kazakhstani culture in the early 21st century, and reveals the hidden depths of contrasts, darkness, and longing for light that breathes both ice and fire to inspire a rich form of poetry worthy of reading and contemplating. It is also distinguished by the uniqueness of its style and substance. Simply sublime, it has to be read and felt for real.

ISBN: **978-0957480711**
RRP: **£10.00**

Kamila
by R. Karimov
Kyrgyz – Uzbek Edition (2013)

«Камила» - это история о сироте, растущей на юге Кыргызстана. Наряду с личной трагедией Камилы и ее родителей, Рахим Каримов описывает очень реалистично и подробно местный образ жизни. Роман выиграл конкурс "Искусство книги-2005" в Бишкеке и был признан национальным бестселлером Книжной палаты Кыргызской Республики.

PAPERBACK
ISBN: **978-0957480773**
RRP: **£10.00**

Gods of the Middle World
by Galina Dolgaya (2013)

The Gods of the Middle World tells the story of Sima, a student of archaeology for whom the old lore and ways of the Central Asian steppe peoples are as vivid as the present. When she joints a group of archaeologists in southern Kazakhstan, asking all the time whether it is really possible to 'commune with the spirits', she soon discovers the answer first hand, setting in motion events in the spirit world that have been frozen for centuries. Meanwhile three millennia earlier, on the same spot, a young woman and her companion struggle to survive and amend wrongs that have caused the neighbouring tribe to take revenge. The two narratives mirror one another, and Sima's destiny is to resolve the ancient wrongs in her own lifetime and so restore the proper balance of the forces of good and evil

PAPERBACK
ISBN: **978-0957480797**
RRP: **£14.95**
AVAILABLE ON **KINDLE**

Jazz Book, poetry
by Alma Sharipova , Russian Edition

Сборник стихов Алмы Шариповой JazzCafé, в котором предлагаются стихотворения, написанные в разное время и посвященые различным событиям из жизни автора. Стихотворения Алмы содержательные и эмоциональные одновременно, отражают философию ее отношения к происходящему. Почти каждое стихотворение представляет собой законченный рассказ в миниатюре. Сюжет разворачивается последовательно и завершается небольшим резюме в последних строках. Стихотворения раскрываются, как готовые «формулы» жизни. Читатель невольно задумывается над ними и может найти как что-то знакомое, так и новое для себя.

ISBN: 978-0-957480797
RRP: £10.00

13 steps of Erika Klaus
by Kazat Akmatov (2013)

The story involves the harrowing experiences of a young and very naïve Norwegian woman who has come to Kyrgyzstan to teach English to schoolchildren in a remote mountain outpost. Governed by the megalomaniac Colonel Bronza, the community barely survives under a cruel and unjust neo-fascist regime. Immersed in the local culture, Erika is initially both enchanted and apprehensive but soon becomes disillusioned as day after day, she is forbidden to teach. Alongside Erika's story, are the personal tragedies experienced by former soldier Sovietbek , Stalbek, the local policeman, the Principal of the school and a young man who has married a Kyrgyz refugee from Afghanistan . Each tries in vain, to challenge and change the corrupt political situation in which they are forced to live.

PAPERBACK
ISBN: **978-0957480766**
RRP: **£12.95**
AVAILABLE ON **KINDLE**

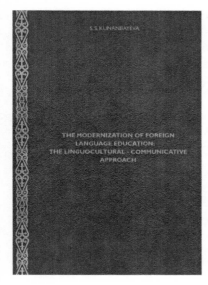

**The Modernization
of Foreign Language Education:
The Linguocultural - Communicative
Approach**
by SalimaKunanbayeva (2013)

Professor S. S. Kunanbayeva - Rector
of Ablai Khan Kazakh University
of International Relations and World
Languages This textbook is the first
of its kind in Kazakhstan to be devoted
to the theory and practice of foreign
language education. It has been written
primarily for future teachers of foreign
languages and in a wider sense for all
those who to be interested in the question
(in the problems?) of the study and use of foreign languages. This book
outlines an integrated theory of modern foreign language learning (FLL)
which has been drawn up and approved under the auspices of the school
of science and methodology of Kazakhstan's Ablai Khan University
of International Relations and World Languages.

PAPERBACK
ISBN: **978-0957480780**
RRP: **£19.95**
AVAILABLE ON **KINDLE**

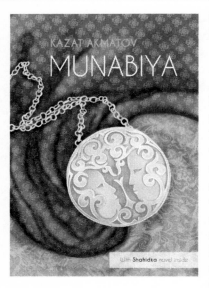

Shahidka/ Munabia
by KazatAkmatov (2013)

Munabiya and Shahidka by Kazat Akmatov National Writer of Kyrgyzstan Recently translated into English Akmatov's two love stories are set in rural Kyrgyzstan, where the natural environment, local culture, traditions and political climate all play an integral part in the dramas which unfold. Munabiya is a tale of a family's frustration, fury, sadness and eventual acceptance of a long term love affair between the widowed father and his mistress. In contrast, Shahidka is a multi-stranded story which focuses on the ties which bind a series of individuals to the tragic and ill-fated union between a local Russian girl and her Chechen lover, within a multi-cultural community where violence, corruption and propaganda are part of everyday life.

PAPERBACK
ISBN: **978-0957480759**
RRP: **£12.95**
AVAILABLE ON **KINDLE**

Howl *novel*
by Kazat Akmatov (2014)
English –Russian

The "Howl" by Kazat Akmatov is a beautifully crafted novel centred on life in rural Kyrgyzstan. Characteristic of the country's national writer, the simple plot is imbued with descriptions of the spectacular landscape, wildlife and local customs. The theme however, is universal and the contradictory emotions experienced by Kalen the shepherd must surely ring true to young men, and their parents, the world over. Here is a haunting and sensitively written story of a bitter -sweet rite of passage from boyhood to manhood.

PAPERBACK
ISBN: **978-0993044410**
RRP: **£12.50**
AVAILABLE ON **KINDLE**

The Turkic Saga
of Genghis Khan and the KZ Factor
by Dr.Kairat Zakiryanov (2014)

An in-depth study of Genghis Khan from a Kazakh perspective, The Turkic Saga of Genghis Khan presupposes that the great Mongol leader and his tribal setting had more in common with the ancestors of the Kazakhs than with the people who today identify as Mongols. This idea is growing in currency in both western and eastern scholarship and is challenging both old Western assumptions and the long-obsolete Soviet perspective. This is an academic work that draws on many Central Asian and Russian sources and often has a Eurasianist bias - while also paying attention to new accounts by Western authors such as Jack Weatherford and John Man. It bears the mark of an independent, unorthodox and passionate scholar.

HARD BACK
ISBN: **978-0992787370**
RRP: **£17.50**
AVAILABLE ON **KINDLE**

Alphabet Game
by Paul Wilson (2014)

Travelling around the world may appear as easy as ABC, but looks can be deceptive: there is no 'X' for a start. Not since Xidakistan was struck from the map. Yet post 9/11, with the War on Terror going global, could 'The Valley' be about to regain its place on the political stage? Xidakistan's fate is inextricably linked with that of Graham Ruff, founder of Ruff Guides. Setting sail where Around the World in Eighty Days and Lost Horizon weighed anchor, our not-quite-a-hero suffers all in pursuit of his golden triangle: The Game, The Guidebook, The Girl. With the future of printed Guidebooks increasingly in question, As Evelyn Waugh's Scoop did for Foreign Correspondents the world over, so this novel lifts the lid on Travel Writers for good.

PAPERBACK
ISBN: **978-0-992787325**
RRP: **£14.95**
AVAILABLE ON **KINDLE**

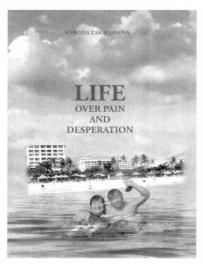

Life over pain and desperation
by Marziya Zakiryanova (2014)

This book was written by someone on the fringe of death. Her life had been split in two: before and after the first day of August 1991 when she, a mother of two small children and full of hopes and plans for the future, became disabled in a single twist of fate. Narrating her tale of self-conquest, the author speaks about how she managed to hold her family together, win the respect and recognition of people around her and above all, protect the fragile concept of 'love' from fortune's cruel turns. By the time the book was submitted to print, Marziya Zakiryanova had passed away. She died after making the last correction to her script. We bid farewell to this remarkable and powerfully creative woman.

HARD BACK
ISBN: **978-0-99278733-2**
RRP: **£14.95**
AVAILABLE ON **KINDLE**

100 experiences of Kazakhstan
by Vitaly Shuptar, Nick Rowan
and Dagmar Schreiber (2014)

The original land of the nomads, landlocked Kazakhstan and its expansive steppes present an intriguing border between Europe and Asia. Dispel the notion of oil barons and Borat and be prepared for a warm welcome into a land full of contrasts. A visit to this newly independent country will transport you to a bygone era to discover a country full of legends and wonders. Whether searching for the descendants of Genghis Khan - who left his mark on this land seven hundred years ago - or looking to discover the futuristic architecture of its capital Astana, visitors cannot fail but be impressed by what they experience. For those seeking adventure, the formidable Altai and Tien Shan mountains provide challenges for novices and experts alike

ISBN: 978-0-992787356
RRP: £19.95

Dance of Devils , Jinlar Bazmi
by AbdulhamidIsmoil
and Hamid Ismailov
(Uzbek language),
E-book (2012)

'Dance of Devils' is a novel about the life of a great Uzbek writer Abdulla Qadyri (incidentally, 'Dance of Devils' is the name of one of his earliest short stories). In 1937, Qadyri was going to write a novel, which he said was to make his readers to stop reading his iconic novels "Days Bygone" and "Scorpion from the altar," so beautiful it would have been. The novel would've told about a certain maid, who became a wife of three Khans - a kind of Uzbek Helen of Troy. He told everyone: "I will sit down this winter and finish this novel - I have done my preparatory work, it remains only to write. Then people will stop reading my previous books". He began writing this novel, but on the December 31, 1937 he was arrested.

AVAILABLE ON **KINDLE**
ASIN: B009ZBPV2M

Vanished Khans and Empty Steppes
by Robert Wight (2014)

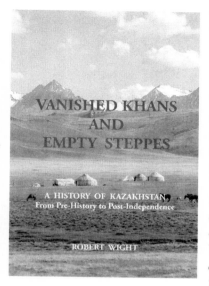

The book opens with an outline of the history of Almaty, from its nineteenth-century origins as a remote outpost of the Russian empire, up to its present status as the thriving second city of modern-day Kazakhstan. The story then goes back to the Neolithic and early Bronze Ages, and the sensational discovery of the famous Golden Man of the Scythian empire. The transition has been difficult and tumultuous for millions of people, but Vanished Khans and Empty Steppes illustrates how Kazakhstan has emerged as one of the world's most successful post-communist countries.

HARD BACK
ISBN: **978-0-9930444-0-3**
RRP: **£24.95**

PAPERBACK
ISBSN: **978-1-910886-05-2**
RRP: **£14.50**
AVAILABLE ON **KINDLE**

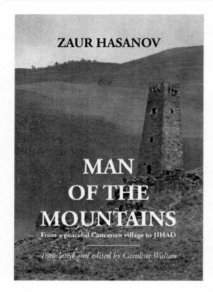

Man of the Mountains
by Abudlla Isa (2014)
(OCABF 2013 Winner)

Man of the Mountains" is a book about a young Muslim Chechen boy, Zaur who becomes a central figure representing the fight of local indigenous people against both the Russians invading the country and Islamic radicals trying to take a leverage of the situation, using it to push their narrow political agenda on the eve of collapse of the USSR. After 9/11 and the invasion of Iraq and Afghanistan by coalition forces, the subject of the Islamic jihadi movement has become an important subject for the Western readers. But few know about the resistance movement from the local intellectuals and moderates against radical Islamists taking strong hold in the area.

PAPERBACK
ISBN: **978-0-9930444-5-8**
RRP: **£14.95**
AVAILABLE ON **KINDLE**

Silk, Spice, Veils and Vodka
by Felicity Timcke (2014)

Felicity Timcke's missive publication, "Silk, Spices, Veils and Vodka" brings both a refreshing and new approach to life on the expat trail. South African by origin, Timcke has lived in some very exotic places, mostly along the more challenging countries of the Silk Road. Although the book's content, which is entirely composed of letters to the author's friends and family, is directed primarily at this group, it provides "20 years of musings" that will enthral and delight those who have either experienced a similar expatriate existence or who are nervously about to depart for one.

PAPERBACK
ISBN: **978-0992787318**
RRP: **£12.50**
AVAILABLE ON **KINDLE**

Finding the Holy Path
by Shahsanem Murray (2014)

"Murray's first book provides an enticing and novel link between her adopted home town of Edinburgh and her origins form Central Asia. Beginning with an investigation into a mysterious lamp that turns up in an antiques shop in Edinburgh, and is bought on impulse, we are quickly brought to the fertile Ferghana valley in Uzbekistan to witness the birth of Kara-Choro, and the start of an enthralling story that links past and present. Told through a vivid and passionate dialogue, this is a tale of parallel discovery and intrigue. The beautifully translated text, interspersed by regional poetry, cannot fail to impress any reader, especially those new to the region who will be affectionately drawn into its heart in this page-turning cultural thriller."

В поисках святого перевала – удивительный приключенческий роман, основанный на исторических источниках. Произведение Мюррей – это временной мостик между эпохами, который помогает нам переместиться в прошлое и уносит нас далеко в 16 век. Закрученный сюжет предоставляет нам уникальную возможность, познакомиться с историейи культурой Центральной Азии. «Первая книга Мюррей предлагает заманчивый роман, связывающий между её приемным городом Эдинбургом и Центральной Азией, откуда настоящее происхождение автора.

RUS ISBN: **978-0-9930444-8-9**
ENGL ISBN: **978-0992787394**
PAPERBACK
RRP: **£12.50**

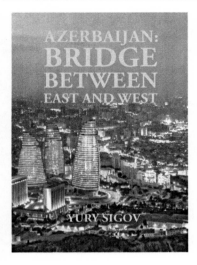

Azerbaijan:
Bridge between East and West
by Yury Sigov, 2015

Azerbaijan: Bridge between East and West, Yury Sigov narrates a comprehensive and compelling story about Azerbaijan. He balances the country's rich cultural heritage, wonderful people and vibrant environment with its modern political and economic strategies. Readers will get the chance to thoroughly explore Azerbaijan from many different perspectives and discover a plethora of innovations and idea, including the recipe for Azerbaijan's success as a nation and its strategies for the future. The book also explores the history of relationships between United Kingdom and Azerbaijan.

HARD BACK
ISBN: **978-0-9930444-9-6**
RRP: **£24.50**
AVAILABLE ON **KINDLE**

Kashmir Song
by Sharaf Rashidov
(translation by Alexey Ulko, OCABF 2014 Winner). 2015

This beautiful illustrated novella offers a sensitive reworking of an ancient and enchanting folk story which although rooted in Kashmir is, by nature of its theme, universal in its appeal.

Alternative interpretations of this tale are explored by Alexey Ulko in his introduction, with references to both politics and contemporary literature, and the author's epilogue further reiterates its philosophical dimension.

The Kashmir Song is a timeless tale, which true to the tradition of classical folklore, can be enjoyed on a number of levels by readers of all ages.

COMING SOON!!!
ISBN: 978-0-9930444-2-7
RRP: £29.50

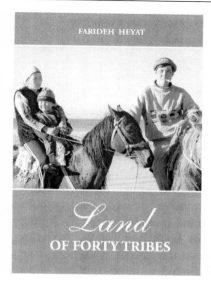

Land of forty tribes
by Farideh Heyat, 2015

Sima Omid, a British-Iranian anthropologist in search of her Turkic roots, takes on a university teaching post in Kyrgyzstan. It is the year following 9/11, when the US is asserting its influence in the region. Disillusioned with her long-standing relationship, Sima is looking for a new man in her life. But the foreign men she meets are mostly involved in relationships with local women half their age, and the Central Asian men she finds highly male chauvinist and aggressive towards women.

PAPERBACK
ISBN: **978-0-9930444-4-1**
RRP: **£14.95**

Terror: events, facts, evidence.
by Eldar Samadov, 2015

This book is based on research carried out since 1988 on territorial claims of Armenia against Azerbaijan, which led to the escalation of the conflict over Nagorno-Karabakh. This escalation included acts of terror by Armanian terrorist and other armed gangs not only in areas where intensive armed confrontations took place but also away from the fighting zones. This book, not for the first time, reflects upon the results of numerous acts of premeditated murder, robbery, armed attack and other crimes through collected material related to criminal cases which have been opened at various stages following such crimes. The book is meant for political scientists, historians, lawyers, diplomats and a broader audience.

PAPERBACK
ISBN: **978-1-910886-00-7**
RRP: **£9.99**
AVAILABLE ON **KINDLE**

THE PLIGHT OF A POSTMODERN HUNTER

Chlngiz Aitmatov □
Mukhtar Shakhanov
(2015)

"Delusion of civilization" by M. Shakhanov is an epochal poem, rich in prudence and nobility – as is his foremother steppe. It is the voice of the Earth, which raised itself in defense of the human soul. This is a new genre of spiritual ecology. As such, this book is written from the heart of a former tractor driver, who knows all the "scars and wrinkles" of the soil - its thirst for human intimacy. This book is also authored from the perspective of an outstanding intellectual whose love for national traditions has grown as universal as our common great motherland.

I dare say, this book is a spiritual instrument of patriotism for all humankind. Hence, there is something gentle, kind, and sad, about the old swan-song of Mukhtar's brave ancestors. Those who for six months fought to the death to protect Grand Otrar - famous worldwide for its philosophers and rich library, from the hordes of Genghis Khan.

LANGUAGES ENG
HARDBACK
ISBN: **978-1-910886-11-3**

The Wormwood Wind
Raushan
Burkitbayeva- Nukenova (2015)

A single unstated assertion runs throughout The Wormwood Wind, arguing, amid its lyrical nooks and crannies, we are only fully human when our imaginations are free. Possibly this is the primary glittering insight behind Nukenova's collaboration with hidden Restorative Powers above her pen. No one would doubt, for example, when she hints that the moment schoolchildren read about their surrounding environment they are acting in a healthy and developmental manner. Likewise, when she implies any adult who has the courage to think "outside the box" quickly gains a reputation for adaptability in their private affairs – hardly anyone would doubt her. General affirmations demonstrating this sublime and liberating contribution to Global Text will prove dangerous to unwary readers, while its intoxicating rhythms and rhymes will lead a grateful few to elative revolutions inside their own souls. Thus, I unreservedly recommend this ingenious work to Western readers.

HARD BACK
ISBN: **978-1-910886-12-0**
RRP: **£14.95**

My Homeland, Oh My Crimea
by Lenifer Mambetova
(2015)

Mambetova's delightful poems, exploring the hopes and fates of Crimean Tartars, are a timely and evocative reminder of how deep a people's roots can be, but also how adaptable and embracing foreigners can be of their adopted country, its people and its traditions.

LANGUAGES ENG / RUS
HARDBACK
ISBN: **978-1-910886-04-5**

GOETHE AND ABAI
by Herold Belger
2015

In this highly original extended essay, renowned author and critic Herold Belger explores an uncanny similarity between the life and career of that great genius of the Weimar Republic Johann Wolfgang von Goethe, and the legendary wordsmith from the Central Asian steppes, Abay. A resemblance previously ignored by most mainstream critics, even though a comparison that is bound to delight enlightened readers. As such, this rare and lyrical discussion examines the poetry, music, and prose of this golden period, while the author takes a number of biographical steps on a personal journey into the Germanic side of his own ethnic and cultural heritage. As such, Belger shamelessly plays with notions of shared influence, common sources, and possible pathways whereby the reading circles developed in this region are clearly revealed as mechanisms for the dispersion of high art and culture.

LANGUAGES ENG
HARDBACK
ISBN: 978-1-910886-16-8
RRP: £19.95

"Cranes in Spring"
by Tolibshohi Davlat
(2015)

This novel highlights a complex issue that millions of Tajiks face when becoming working migrants in Russia due to lack of opportunities at home. Fresh out of school, Saidakbar decides to go to Russia as he hopes to earn money to pay for his university tuition. His parents reluctantly let him go providing he is accompanied by his uncle, Mustakim, an experienced migrant. And so begins this tale of adventure and heartache that reflects the reality of life faced by many Central Asian migrants. Mistreatment, harassment and backstabbing join the Tajik migrants as they try to pull through in a foreign country. Davlat vividly narrates the brutality of the law enforcement officers but also draws attention to kindness and help of several ordinary people in Russia. How will Mustakim and Saidakbar's journey end? Intrigued by the story starting from the first page, one cannot put the book down until it's finished.

LANGUAGES ENG / RUS
HARDBACK
ISBN: **978-1-910886-06-9**
RRP: **£14.50**

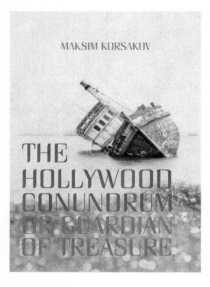

The Hollywood Conundrum or Guardian of Treasure
Maksim Korsakov
(2015)

In this groundbreaking experimental novella, Maxim Korsakov breaks all the preconceived rules of genre and literary convention to deliver a work rich in humour, style, and fantasy. Starting with a so-called "biographical" account of the horrors lurking beneath marriages of convenience and the self-delusions necessary to maintain these relationships, he then speedily moves to a screenplay, which would put most James Bond movies to shame. As if international espionage were not enough, the author teases his readers with lost treasure maps, revived Khanates, sports car jousting, ancient aliens who possess the very secrets of immortality, and the lineal descendants of legendary Genghis Khan. All in all, an ingenious book, as well as s clear critique of traditional English narrative convention.

LANGUAGES ENG / RUS
PAPERBACK
ISBN: **978-1-910886-14-4**
RRP: **£24.95**

The City Where Dreams Come True
Gulsifat Shahidi
(2016)

Viewed from the perspective of three generations, Shahidi presents a rare and poignant insight into the impact which Tajikistan'sterrible civil war had on its people and its culture during the early '90s. Informed partly by her own experiences as a journalist, these beautifully interwoven stories are imbued with both her affection for her native land and her hopes for its future. The narrators – Horosho, his granddaughter Nekbaht ,her husband Ali and his cousin Shernazar – each endure harrowing episodes of loss, injustice and violence but against all odds, remain driven by a will to survive, and restore peace, prosperity and new opportunities for themselves and fellow citizens.

LANGUAGES ENG / RUS
PAPERBACK
ISBN: 978-1-910886-20-5
RRP: £12.50

Crane
Abu-Sufyan
(2016)

In this remarkable collection of prose poems, author Abu Sufyan takes readers through a series of fairy tale scenarios, wherein are hidden a number of sour existential truths. Indeed, from the bewilderment felt by anthropomorphised cranes, to the self-sacrifice of mares galloping towards their (potential) salvation, all the way to the bittersweet biographies experienced by a girl and her frustrated mother, this book weaves darkly enchanted frame stories into highly illustrative fables. Structured, as they are, in the style of unfolding dialogues, Sufyan's haunting literary technique serves to unveil a story within a storyline. An almost Postmodern strategy, whereby an introductory, or main narrative, is presented (at least in part), for the sole purpose of sharing uncomfortable anecdotes. As such, critics have observed that emphasized secondary yarns allow readers to find themselves - so to speak - stepping from one theme into another - while simultaneously being carried into ever-smaller plots. Certainly, as adventures take place between named and memorable characters, each exchange is saturated with wit, practical jokes, and life lessons contributing to an overall Central Asian literary mosaic. All in all, this tiny volume is both a delight and a warning to its admirers.

LANGUAGES ENG
PAPERBACK
ISBN: **978-1-910886-23-6**
RRP: **£12.50**

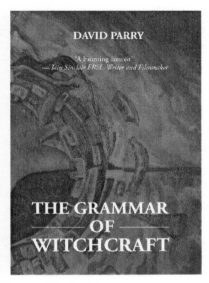

The Grammar of Witchcraft
David Parry
(2016)

In this collection of Mini-Sagas and poems, Parry narrates the final journey taken by his alter ego Caliban from the surreal delights of a lesbian wedding in Liverpool, all the way back to a non-existent city of London. In himself, the author is aiming to resolve lyrical contradictions existing between different levels of consciousness: betwixt reality and the dreaming state. And as such, unnervingly illogical scenarios emerge out of a stream of consciousness wherein bewildering theatrical landscapes actively compete with notions of Anglo-Saxon witchcraft, Radical Traditionalism, and a lack of British authenticity. Each analysis pointing towards those Jungian Spirits haunting an endlessly benevolent Archetypal world.

LANGUAGES ENG
PAPERBACK
ISBN: **978-1-910886-25-0**
RRP: **£9.95**

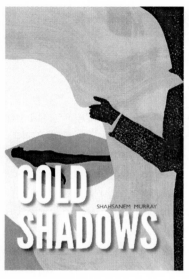

COLD SHADOWS
Shahsanem Murray
(2016)

The story, set at the end of the 1980's, revolves around a group of disparate individuals living seemingly unconnected lives in various countries.

But then a strange incident on the Moscow to Frunze train leads to the gradual exposure of complex web in which their lives, loves and profession's have long been entangled.

Bound together by an intriguing series of incidents, each struggles to survive the hardships and challenges that life throws at them, from radical changes in the political climate to the murky antics of spies and double agents. But behind everything lies love…

LANGUAGES ENG
PAPERBACK
ISBN: 978-1-910886-27-4
RRP: **£12.50**